S0-BJQ-325

From the Earth *to the* Moon

AND

Around *the* Moon

Jules Verne

From the Earth
to the Moon

AND

Around the Moon

Introduction by Jean Jules-Verne

Illustrations by Robert Shore

The Heritage Press

New York

The entire contents of this edition
are copyright © 1970 by
The George Macy Companies, Inc.

Introduction

THE value of a literary work depends, without any question, upon the author's talent and the wealth of expression of his thought, but it depends equally upon the qualities of the reader himself. The latter's intelligence is a mirror that reflects what the former's has propounded, and the harmony between the two must be as perfect as possible. The work is successful only if it awakens that fraternal resonance which allows us to assimilate what another has conceived, if only to make it the object of our own personal criticism.

Sentences committed to paper and then reflected in these innumerable mirrors, which may be of the same proportions yet are never identical, will take on different colorations according to the temperament of each reader, and an original meaning according to his dominant train of thought, even if that be only temporary.

This fine edition will give you the opportunity to reread a book written over a century ago. After exhausting the pleasure afforded by contact with paper of good quality and by exposure to painstaking printing, you will find your artistic sense coming alive as you gaze upon illustrations created by an artist whose enthusiasm has attempted to translate visually the echoes awakened in him by certain passages of the story. Some of these will cause you to smile, perhaps even to laugh, for you are sensitive to humor, while others will arouse your curiosity, and you yourself will end up by going through a text which you had somewhat forgotten.

Allow me to pose a question: How should it be reread?

In all sincerity, I confess to you that, having lived through this experience several times, I have come to the conclusion that this book, simple as it is, on each reading evoked within me quite different reactions, according to what happened to be my frame of mind at the time I undertook it.

The year 1865 was a memorable one. Though the Declaration of Independence dates back to 1776 and the Constitution to 1787, the cement which finally was to bind these united states so tightly together was supplied only by the awful Civil War that ended in Grant's victory in that year—for it is only too true that nations, like human beings, can give birth only through great pain.

At that time a young Parisian dramatist, Jules Verne, was in the process of turning away from the theatre to undertake a literary adventure which won the enthusiastic approval of Alexandre Dumas. Scientific progress appeared to him to be a human phenomenon that had furnished a new theme for any novelist with curiosity enough to explore this scholarly new world, rich in so many possibilities.

Carrying out such a project necessitated the acquisition of indispensable scientific knowledge in order to constitute the solid base from which the author's imagination might take off. While continuing simultaneously to turn out comedies, dramas, tragedies, articles, and stories; to manage the Théâtre Lyrique (better known as the Paris Opera), of which he was the devoted secretary; and to superintend the brokerage firm in which he was a partner, at dawn of each day he would plunge into his scientific studies. The Italian writer Edmondo De Amicis mentions having seen the twenty thousand file cards that Verne had worked up.

Verne's friendship with the explorer Jacques Arago at first

turned his interests toward geography. In 1862 he wrote *Five Weeks in a Balloon*; published in 1863, it met with sensational success, proving the timeliness of its appeal. The next year the prestigious *Journal des Débats* serialized his *Journey to the Center of the Earth*.

In 1865, just as the great American war drama was approaching its final curtain, the same newspaper was serializing *From the Earth to the Moon*.

It seems obvious that in the first instance it was as the caustic "theatre wit" that he took pen in hand; while rejoicing in the victory of a cause he so heartily believed in, he could not help feeling the absurdity of its having to prove its justness through the ordeal of battle.

Northerners and Southerners had applied themselves to perfecting their firearms and, what is worse, had acquired the bad habit of making use of them. Progress in artillery was so considerable that, once peace had come, the reconversion of the artillerymen, now unemployed, became a very serious problem. Quite naturally the author, accustomed as he was to making light of the most serious subjects in his *boulevard* comedies, now turned to this subject also with a satirical approach. To get rid of the dangerous artillerymen by suggesting that they devote their efforts to making a moon shot, and then, if need be, sending them off to it, was indeed a humorist's solution to the problem.

Therefore the reader with the slightest sense of humor will find a goodly share of it is in *From the Earth to the Moon* and its sequel—and, reading the book in that light, will be able to derive considerable pleasure from it.

The practical mind will be concerned about factualism, which the author did not neglect—since, being scrupulous by nature, he could not stint on conscientious studies to shore up a fable which he had at first looked upon only as a relaxation. For he had exerted overwhelming efforts to guide us in our discovery of Africa (*Five Weeks in a Balloon*) and to develop our interest in geology during that strange initial *Journey to the Center of the Earth,* and he had already set to work on his tale of *The Adventures of Captain Hatteras,* a powerful accomplishment which Dr. J. B. Charcot, the Antarctic explorer, considered "the best of all logbooks."

The reader of *From the Earth to the Moon* will applaud Barbicane's selection of Florida for the launching. Stone Hill is hardly more than a stone's throw from Cape Kennedy; and Barbicane's splashdown in the Pacific a bare two and a half miles from where the American astronaut Borman's capsule was to be recovered, led the latter to write: "There is more to this than just fantastic coincidence."

The similarities in the weight and height of the imaginary and real space ships will certainly surprise the reader. But then he will pull up short: the use of a cannon and shell could never be practical! The author was always fully aware of this, and indeed was at great pains to explain to us that the acceleration of the projectile would have been such that its passengers would be crushed. But after thus making allowance for the laws of mechanics, Verne is artful enough to get us to admit that his engineer has found a way to overcome this obstacle; the adventure then becomes plausible.

Yet I have no doubt that our exacting reader will still remain unconvinced, and will ask this question: Why, then, did he use a cannon? Verne might have answered by giving two reasons:

"The first," he would have said, "is that at the time I was merely trying to have a little fun at the expense of the artillerymen, and it was obvious that those cannon-crazy specialists would have thought of using nothing but a cannon!

"A rocket would have been much more practical, since its acceleration would have been progressive. In the state of science at that time, I could not suggest the use of any fuel other than gunpowder, of which it would have been necessary to compress quite considerable quantities; and keeping control over it would have been a serious problem. So I had to settle for the suggestion of powder-fueled retro-rockets which might cushion the fall to the moon; and that turned out to be a good idea, since it later allowed my primitive astronauts to escape from lunar gravitation, just as is actually done today.

"Nor am I unaware of the heating caused by friction against the strata of the atmosphere, both on takeoff and on return. My friend Nicholl did not fail to explain this in detail to Michel Ardan. Barbicane was the one who got him to admit that the thickness of the metal would overcome this hazard. My shell returned to earth in the guise of a meteorite turned fireball because of its velocity and the friction against the atmospheric strata. I have, indeed, heard it said that your own capsules, in spite of all the modern braking apparatuses, are subject to similar ordeals.

"After all, I am only a novelist, and I make no claim to having made any profound study of a trip to the moon; all that I had to do, was to show that it was possible to accomplish such a feat and that, if scientists seriously set their minds to this problem, they would find a solution to it. Do you think I was wrong to put my trust in them? If I succeeded in entertaining you and causing you to dream a little 'by opening a window on the wide-open spaces' as well as on outer space, I have achieved my aim."

It would really require ill will on our part for us to believe that Jules Verne was either an ignoramus or a dupe—and that he really allowed scientific heresies to creep into his tale either by inadvertence or because he had not thought them out—when he gives us such refined details on certain specific points. We must merely recognize that this is the poet at work (to borrow physicist Charles-Noël Martin's phrase).

If he had not used a storyteller's devices for overcoming the objections which he was fair enough to point out to us in their time, he would have deprived us of a narrative which still echoes so tellingly down the years. How can we admit that an author who was capable of foreseeing the building of a telescope seventeen feet in diameter on the Rocky Mountains, powerful enough to allow for the "breaking down of the Crab Nebula,"* should have been ignorant of basic principles?

One incident has been highly criticized, that of the corpse of the dog thrown out into space through a rapidly opened and shut porthole, when Verne knew very well that an intermediate pressure chamber would have been necessary. But to him this was merely a chance to give an amusing illustration of the phenomenon of satellization pointed out by Newton. It has been claimed that Verne and Verne alone was daring enough and had the extraordinary intuition to conceive of the possibility of sending an artillery shell to the moon, as well as the even more amazing fact of "satellizing" the dog's remains around the projectile, and the projectile itself around the moon. In the same way, later on, the shell in *The Begum's Fortune* (1879), the meteorite in *The Meteor Hunt* (1902), the fragment of a continent in *Hector Servadac* (1877), and our own present-day artificial satellites would orbit around the earth, and the shell of *Topsy-Turvy* (1889) would orbit around the sun.

Without question, the corpse of the dog would have exploded under the effect of its internal pressure, as Barbicane of course explained to Michel Ardan when the latter expressed a desire to try a space walk, but it is perfectly acceptable to imagine that after that it might indeed become "flattened like a deflated bagpipe" as a result of the power of intercellular cohesion.

It is not reasonable to take too much stock of such severe criticism, which is perhaps not always fair. Can it be maintained that Barbicane did not allow for the speed of the earth's rotation, since the note from the Cambridge Observatory clearly establishes the deviation due to it? (If I am not mistaken, it must end up as a curve toward the east.)

* Fantastic premonitions, which bear witness to the extent of Verne's knowledge; for giant telescopes with eight-, ten-, and now sixteen-foot diameters have actually been set up on Mount Palomar, and the detailed study of the Crab Nebula has been going on for the past twenty years or so.

Introduction

The author of these extraordinary journeys never claimed to be writing as either a scientist or an engineer. He was content merely to seize upon options which were truly daring—and it must be admitted that he did so with rare felicity.

Still a third reader will look at this book from a different viewpoint: He will scarcely be concerned with discussing it in detail; he will bow to Barbicane's superior knowledge, fume at that old spoilsport Nicholl, and share Michel Ardan's enthusiasm. "Everything happened just the way Jules Verne predicted it would over a century ago!" he will exclaim. To him, the storyteller becomes a visionary, a prophet.

And this reader will not be entirely wrong, when he thus makes room for poets' dreams and their sense of divination, as they venture into the twilight zone that scientists are patiently busy trying to clear away. The taste for questioning the unknown, a peculiarly human characteristic, is an overdevelopment of the ingenuity of *homo faber* inventing the means necessary to assure his survival, whereas *homo sapiens* is concerned not only with surviving but also with knowing and understanding the why and wherefore of things. What is the basis for pure research, if not the pursuit of a dream that is always to be found in the background of all great enterprises, made up of what Jules Verne termed "excessive expectations"? The great theoreticians of science are being poets when they enunciate hypotheses before getting down to the tedious prose of patient experiments which will lead them on to other hypotheses.

It is through imagination that science is related to poetry.

Jules Verne enjoyed the privilege of becoming an ecumenical author within the brief span of a human lifetime, a phenomenon which can be explained by the fact that he was a poet of science and space, and that poetry is a language accessible to all.

However far back in time we may go, man has always been intrigued by the faithful companion to our planet. While in English you refer to the man in the moon, in French the moon is feminine; the slightly mocking smile she seems to be about to display, her feminine withdrawals and teasing reversals, make a coquette of her.

Who among us has not dreamt his dreams beneath her pale light? Who has not imagined himself flying off among the spheres—whisked up on a ray of moonlight like Cyrano de Bergerac, or carried away in the ludicrous little balloon of Poe's Hans Pfaall? Of course, those were merely dreamings, which day-light wafted away. . . .

Jules Verne's distinction is that he was able to hang on to the dream and bring it alive within our waking state by making it possible, acceptable, albeit at the extreme limit of what we might accomplish by the means at our command, which therefore needed only to be perfected a bit more.

Consciously or unconsciously, this still-excessive expectation made its way onward within the minds of the public and of the scientific world; it became a goal which our techniques were fi-nally allowing us to attain.

"Anything that one man is able to imagine," Jules Verne said, "some other man is able to accomplish." As he kept his publisher abreast of the progress of his work, he told him that he "was living in his space ship" and that in so doing he gradually dis-covered new problems which had to be overcome. He added that if M. Bertrand, then permanent secretary of the French Academy of Sciences, had given the matter a week's thought, he would never have told Verne that all there was in his story was material for a quick little book.

Men have since arisen who put this maxim to the test, who took such risks, both intellectual and physical. Just like the writer, they had to spend long periods of time living in a simulated space vehicle to see how they could solve the problems that arose as the duration of the voyage grew; they had to learn to foresee them in their most minute details, since overlooking even one of them was likely to result in fatal consequences.

Introduction

Few will recall the experiments of the German engineer who first wanted to utilize jets in the propulsion of vehicles on rail lines; it took the onset of a war for the necessary effort to be made enabling the study of such a motor to be brought to fruition (military fruition, alas!), and for the first missiles to come into being. Beyond that, it was in preparation for the most horrible of all possible wars yet to come that this dynamic system was carried even further in ruinously expensive works, mobilizing thousands of scientific men and technicians.

Yet it would appear that purely military considerations have faded into the background and that, for the first time in history, a people has undertaken to make sacrifices for an unselfish scientific enterprise, crystallizing the energies of researchers—which can sometimes be dangerous because they are applied abstractly —by following Barbicane's example of channeling them into a peaceful direction: the moon!

The conquest of this celestial body thus opens a whole new era to us; these first footsteps on the surface of the moon are the first step on the path of man's mind toward an ideal of peace. Divided against itself, mankind may perhaps here discover the humility which will allow us—castaways in space that we are— to gain awareness of our solidarity.

As they took leave of this planet, the first men to voyage to the moon's surface inevitably felt a certain anxiety. Nevertheless, they were able to overcome it, and to face up with composure to any incident which, however minute it might be, could have had irreversible consequences and spelled their doom. They displayed a quiet courage as they took stock of all the dangers, and then proved that man can truly go beyond his own limitations. What finer justification than that can there be for the motto of the Vernian hero: "There are no unconquerable obstacles; there are only determinations that are more or less forceful, that is all."

This American accomplishment was a victory for the entire human race, for it was the capstone of all the knowledge accumulated by scientists of all periods and all nations. Sciences know no frontiers; they will certainly find none on our satellite. Is it not the same research that is going on, whether the observers are at the foot of the Urals, the Rockies, Mont Blanc, the Himalayas, or Fujiyama?

I am happy that an American was the first to have "scored a goal," for no one more than a citizen of the United States appears to me likely to become the citizen of the world of tomorrow. And, besides, wasn't Impey Barbicane American?

It is hardly likely that in the immediate future the material benefits of this prodigious accomplishment will become apparent, even though the very fact of preparing for it has by now already brought about considerable progress. But I am convinced that in the future it will favor us with enrichment in areas we still do not even suspect—first on a theoretical level, and later on a practical one.

Had it done nothing more than convince us of the inanity of our sublunar quarrels—and thereby brought about just a bit of that good will that was preached in vain two thousand years ago —the whole Moon Venture would have paid for itself.

Was the mental shock it provoked great enough to overcome human selfishness, whose fermentation threatens to entail the most awful catastrophes? Man has been shaken by so many tragedies, without growing any the wiser, that we may well doubt. But this event was truly one of world significance, and it is likely that, sooner or later, despite so many artificial barriers, it will become known to all men. Its universal character gives unusual power to this message from outer space, and allows us to hope that it will etch itself upon the subconscious of every human being, whatever his race, nationality, creed, or ideology, since in the final analysis we all have the same fatherland: Earth.

JEAN JULES-VERNE

Le Vieil Huba, Toulon

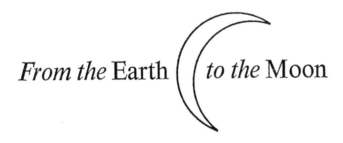

From the Earth *to the* Moon

Contents

Illustrations

CHAPTER 1

The Gun Club

URING the American Civil War, a new and influential club was established in the city of Baltimore in the State of Maryland. It is well known with what energy the taste for military matters became developed among that nation of ship-owners, shopkeepers, and mechanics. Simple tradesmen jumped their counters to become improvised captains, colonels, and generals, without ever having gone through the Military Academy at West Point; nevertheless, they quickly rivaled their compeers of the old continent, and, like them, carried off victories by dint of lavish expenditure in ammunition, money, and men.

But the point in which the Americans singularly outdistanced the Europeans was in the science of gunnery. Not that their weapons reached a considerably higher degree of perfection, but that they exhibited unusual dimensions, and consequently attained hitherto unheard-of ranges. In point of grazing, plunging, oblique, or enfilading, or point-blank firing, the English, French, and Prussians have nothing to learn; but their cannon, howitzers, and mortars are mere pocket-pistols compared with the formidable devices of American artillery.

This fact need surprise no one. The Yankees, the greatest mechanics in the world, are engineers—just as the Italians are musicians and the Germans metaphysicians—by birth. Nothing is more natural, therefore, than to perceive them applying their audacious ingenuity to the science of gunnery. Hence, these gigantic cannon, much less useful than sewing-machines, but just as amazing, and even more widely admired. The marvels of Parrott, Dahlgren, and Rodman are well known in this field. The Armstrongs, Pallisers and Treuille de Beaulieus could only bow to their rivals across the sea.

So, during that terrible struggle between the North and the South, the artillerymen were in the saddle; the newspapers of the Union sang the praises of their inventions, and there was no tradesman so hard-pressed nor booby so simple that he did not stay up nights trying to figure out fantastic trajectories.

Now, when an American has an idea, he looks for another who shares it. If there are three of them, they elect a president and two secretaries. Given four, they name a keeper of records, and the office is ready for work; five, they convene a general meeting, and the club is fully constituted. So things were managed in Baltimore. The inventor of a new cannon associated himself with the caster and the borer. Thus was formed the nucleus of the Gun Club. In a single month after its formation it numbered 1,833 active members and 30,575 corresponding members.

One condition was imposed as a *sine qua non* upon every candidate for admission into the association, and that was the condition of having designed or at least perfected a cannon; or, in default of a cannon, a firearm of some description. It may, however, be mentioned that mere inventions of fifteen-shot revolvers, pivoting carbines, and similar small arms, met with but little consideration. Artillerymen always commanded the chief place of favor.

"The esteem in which they are held," one day said one of the most learned speakers of the Gun Club, "is proportionate to the 'calibers' of their cannon, and 'in direct ratio to the square of the distance' reached by their projectiles!"

This was all but Newton's law of universal gravitation transferred to a moral plane.

The Gun Club once founded, it is easy to conceive the result of the inventive genius of the Americans. Their military weapons attained colossal proportions, and their projectiles, exceeding the prescribed limits, unfortunately occasionally cut some innocent bystanders in two. These inventions left far in the rear the timid instruments of European artillery, as can be judged from the following figures.

In the "good old days," a 36-pound cannon ball, fired at a distance of three hundred feet, would go through 36 horses standing sideways and 68 men. That was only the first step. After that, the projectiles had really gone their way. The Rodman cannon, delivering a half-ton cannon ball seven miles away, would easily have knocked over 150 horses and 300 men. It was even suggested that the Gun Club make a formal test of this. But, while the horses were willing to try it, men were unfortunately hard to find.

Be that as it may, the effect of these cannon was very deadly, and at each shot men fell like grain before the scythe. Beside such projectiles, what was the famous cannon ball which at Coutras in 1587 put 25 men out of action, or the other one which, at Zorndorff in 1758, killed forty foot soldiers, and, in 1742, the Kesselsdorf Austrian cannon, which brought down seventy enemy at every shot? What

3

the amazing fire power at Jena or Austerlitz that determined the outcome of the battle? They were far surpassed during the Civil War! At Gettysburg, a pointed shell from a rifled cannon accounted for 173 Confederates; and, at the crossing of the Potomac, one Rodman cannon ball sent 215 Southerners to an obviously better world. Mention must also be made of the formidable mortar invented by J. T. Maston, a distinguished member and permanent secretary of the Gun Club; it had an even more lethal effect, since, at its trial run, it killed no less than 337 persons—by blowing up, it is true!

What can be added to these numbers which speak for themselves? Nothing. So there is no need to contest the following computation, worked out by the statistician Pitcairn: dividing the number of victims felled by the cannon balls by the number of members in the Gun Club, he found that each one of the latter had personally accounted for an "average" of 2,375 men plus a fraction.

Considering such a figure, it becomes evident that the sole concern of this learned society was the destruction of humanity in a philanthropic aim, and the perfecting of weapons of war, held to be instruments of civilization.

This was a meeting of Exterminating Angels, who were at the same time the most devoted of mothers' sons.

It is only fair to add that these Yankees, courageous enough to stand up to any test, did not restrict themselves to theory but personally participated in all this. Among them were to be counted officers of all ranks, from lieutenants to generals; military men of every age, from those who were just making their début in the profession of arms up to those who had grown old on the gun-carriage. Many had succumbed on the field of battle and their names figured in the Book of Honor of the Gun Club; and of those who had returned the greater proportion bore the marks of their indisputable valor. Crutches, wooden legs, artificial arms, steel hooks, rubber jaws, silver craniums, platinum noses, were all to be found in the collection; and it was calculated by the above-mentioned statistician Pitcairn that throughout the Gun Club there was not quite one arm for four persons, and barely two legs for six.

Nevertheless, these valiant artillerists took no particular account of these little facts, and felt justly proud when the despatches of a battle returned the number of victims at tenfold the quantity of the projectiles expended.

One day, however—sad and melancholy day!—peace was signed between the survivors of the war; the thunder of the guns gradually ceased, the mortars were silent, the howitzers were muzzled for an indefinite period, the cannon bowed their heads and returned to the arsenals, the shot were piled, all bloody reminiscences were effaced; the cotton-plants grew luxuriantly in the fields thus abundantly fertilized, all mourning garments were laid aside, together with grief; and the Gun Club was relegated to profound inactivity.

Some few of the more dogged and inveterate theorists continued to work upon calculations regarding the laws of projectiles. They dreamt unceasingly of gigantic shells and howitzers of unparalleled caliber. Still, without practical experience, what was the value of mere theories? Consequently, the clubrooms became deserted, the servants dozed in the antechambers, the newspapers grew mouldy on the tables, sounds of snoring came from dark corners, and the members of the Gun Club, once so noisy, were reduced to silence by this disastrous peace and dozed over their dreams of Platonic artillery.

"This is horrible!" said good old Tom Hunter one evening, while charring his wooden legs in the fireplace of the smoking-room. "Nothing to do! Nothing to look forward to! What a loathsome existence! When again shall the guns arouse us in the morning with their delightful reports?"

"Those days are gone," said jolly Bilsby, trying to stretch his missing arms. "It was delightful then. You invented a gun, and, hardly was it cast, when you could hasten to try it out on the enemy! Then you returned to camp with a word of encouragement from Sherman or a friendly shake of the hand from McClellan! But now the generals are gone back to their counters; and in place of projectiles, they despatch harmless bales of cotton. By Jove, the future of gunnery in America is lost!"

"Yes, Bilsby," exclaimed Colonel Blomsberry, "these are cruel disappointments indeed! One day, we give up our peaceful habits, practice the manual of arms, leave Baltimore for the battlefields, where we behave like heroes, and two, three years later, we have to lose the fruit of so much effort, to go back to sleep in deplorable idleness and keep our hands in our pockets."

Whatever he might say about it, the brave colonel would have been hard put to give such evidence of his own idleness, though not for lack of pockets.

"And no war in sight!" continued the famous James T. Maston, scratching with his steel hook his gutta-percha cranium. "Not a cloud in the horizon! and that too at such a critical period in the progress of the science of artillery! I who address you have myself this very morning perfected a model (plan, section, elevation, etc.) of a mortar destined to change all the conditions of warfare!"

"Really?" asked Tom Hunter, his thoughts reverting involuntarily to the last invention of the Hon. J. T. Maston.

"Fact!" he replied. "Still, what is the use of so many studies worked out, so many difficulties vanquished? Aren't they all a pure waste of time? The peoples of the New World seem to have passed the word to live in peace; and our bellicose *Tribune* predicts some approaching catastrophes due to the scandalous increase of population."

"Nevertheless," replied Colonel Blomsberry, "they are still struggling in Europe to maintain the principle of nationalities."

"Well?"

"Well, there might be some field for enterprise over there; and if they accept our services——"

"What are you dreaming of?" screamed Bilsby; "work at gunnery for the benefit of foreigners?"

"That would be better than doing nothing at all," returned the colonel.

"Quite so," said J. T. Maston; "it would be better, but still we should not even dream of that expedient."

"And why not?" demanded the colonel.

"Because their ideas of progress in the Old World are contrary to our American habits of thought. Those fellows believe that one can't become a general without having served first as a second lieutenant; which is as much as to say that one can't aim a gun without having first cast it oneself! Now, that is just——"

"Ridiculous!" replied Tom Hunter, whittling with his bowie-knife the arms of his easy-chair; "but since that is the case, all that is left for us is to plant tobacco or distill whale-oil."

"What!" roared J. T. Maston. "Shall we not employ these remaining years of our lives in perfecting firearms? Shall there never be a fresh opportunity of trying the ranges of projectiles? Shall the air never again be lighted with the flash of our guns? Shall no international difficulty ever arise to enable us to declare war against some transatlantic power? Shall not the French sink one of our steamers, or the English, in defiance of the rights of nations, hang a few of our countrymen?"

"No such luck," replied Colonel Blomsberry; "nothing of the kind is likely to happen; and even if it did, we should not benefit from it! America is becoming less touchy each day, and little by little we are becoming effeminate!"

"Yes, we are becoming humble!" Bilsby shot back.

"And being humiliated!" added Tom Hunter.

"That is only too true," replied J. T. Maston, with fresh vehemence; "there are a thousand grounds for fighting, and yet we don't fight. We save our arms and legs—for people who don't know what to do with them! But stop—without going out of one's way to find a cause for war—did not North America once belong to the English?"

"Of course," replied Tom Hunter, stoking the fire furiously with the tip of his crutch.

"Well, then," replied J. T. Maston, "why should not England in her turn belong to the Americans?"

"It would be but just and fair," said Colonel Blomsberry.

"Go and propose it to the President of the United States," cried J. T. Maston, "and see how he will receive you."

"He will receive us badly," murmured Bilsby through the four teeth the war had left him.

"Egad!" cried J. T. Maston, "he'd better not count on my vote at the next election!"

"Nor on ours," unanimously replied all the bellicose invalids.

"Meanwhile," replied J. T. Maston, "allow me to say that, if I cannot get an opportunity to try my new mortars on a real battlefield, I shall resign from the Gun Club, and go bury myself in the prairies of Arkansas!"

"And we with you!" replied all the others.

Matters were at such a pass; tempers were growing shorter and shorter and the club was threatened with approaching dissolution, when an unexpected circumstance occurred to prevent so deplorable a catastrophe.

The very day after this conversation every member of the association received a circular couched in the following terms:

BALTIMORE, October 3

The president of the Gun Club has the honor to inform his colleagues that, at the meeting of the 5th instant, he will bring before them a communication of an extremely interesting nature. He requests, therefore, that they make it convenient to attend in accordance with the present invitation.

Very cordially

IMPEY BARBICANE

President

CHAPTER 2

President Barbicane's Communication

ON the 5th of October, at eight P.M., a dense crowd pressed toward the saloons of the Gun Club at 21 Union Square. All the members of the association resident in Baltimore responded to the invitation of their president. As for the corresponding members, express trains brought them by the hundreds to the city, and, large as was the great hall, it was quite inadequate to accommodate the crowd of *savants*. They overflowed into the adjoining rooms, down the narrow passages, into the outer courtyards. There they ran against the vulgar herd who pressed up to the doors, each struggling to reach the front ranks, all eager to learn the nature of the important communication of President Barbicane; all pushing, squeezing, crushing with that perfect freedom of action which is peculiar to the masses when educated in ideas of "self-government."

On that evening a stranger who might have chanced to be in Baltimore could not have gained admission for love or money into the great hall. That was reserved exclusively for resident or corresponding members; no one else could possibly have obtained a place; and the city magnates, no-tables, and selectmen were compelled to mingle with the mere townspeople in order to catch stray bits of news from inside.

Meantime, the vast hall presented a curious spectacle. Its immense area was singularly adapted to the purpose. Lofty pillars formed of cannon, superposed upon huge mortars as a base, supported the fine ironwork of the arches, a perfect piece of cast-iron lacework. Trophies of blunder-busses, matchlocks, arquebuses, carbines, all kinds of fire-arms, ancient and modern, were picturesquely interlaced against the walls. Illuminating gas came in full glare from myriads of revolvers grouped in the form of chandeliers, while groups of pistols, and candelabra formed of muskets bound together, completed this magnificent display of bril-liance. Models of cannon, bronze castings, sights covered with dents, plates battered by the shots of the Gun Club, assortments of rammers and sponges, chaplets of bombs, wreaths of projectiles, garlands of shells—in short, all the apparatus of the artilleryman—enchanted the eye by their wonderful arrangement and induced a kind of belief that their real purpose was more ornamental than deadly.

In the place of honor, sheltered in a magnificent display case, was a piece of a breech, broken and twisted by the ex-plosion of powder, a precious relic of J. T. Maston's cannon.

At the further end of the saloon the president, assisted by four secretaries, occupied a large platform. His chair, supported by a carved gun-carriage, was modeled upon the ponderous proportions of a 32-inch mortar. It was pointed at an angle of ninety degrees, and suspended upon trun-nions, so that the president could rock himself in it as in a rocking-chair, a very agreeable thing to do in the very hot weather. Upon the table (a huge iron plate supported upon six carronades) stood an inkstand of exquisite elegance, made of a beautifully chased Spanish piece, and a hand bell, which, when rung, went off like a revolver. During violent debates this novel kind of bell was hardly enough to drown out the clamor of these excitable artillerymen.

In front of the table benches arranged in zigzag form, like the circumvallations of a retrenchment, formed a succession of bastions and curtains set apart for the use of the members of the club; and on this special evening one might truly say, "It was crowded on the ramparts." The president was sufficiently well known, however, for all to be assured that he would not have put his colleagues out without a most important motive.

Impey Barbicane was a man of forty years of age, calm, cold, austere; of a singularly serious and determined mind, punctual as a chronometer, of imperturbable temper and immovable character; by no means chivalrous, yet adventurous withal, and always bringing practical ideas to bear upon the very rashest enterprises; a New Englander *par excellence,* a Northern colonist, a descendant of the old anti-Stuart Roundheads, and the implacable enemy of the Southern gentlemen, those old Cavaliers of the mother country. In a word, he was all Yankee and a yard wide.

Barbicane had made a large fortune in the lumber business. Appointed director of artillery during the war, he proved himself fertile in invention. Bold in his conceptions, he contributed powerfully to the progress of that arm and gave an immense impetus to experimental researches.

He was a man of middle height, and a rare exception in the Gun Club, having all his limbs intact. His strongly marked features seemed drawn by square and rule; and if it be true that, in order to judge of a man's character one must look at his profile, Barbicane, so examined, exhibited the most certain indications of energy, daring, and *sang-froid*.

At this moment he was sitting motionlessly in his arm-chair, silent, absorbed, lost in reflection, sheltered under his high-crowned hat—a kind of black silk cylinder which seems to be screwed on to all American heads.

His colleagues were talking noisily all about him without disturbing him; they questioned each other, advanced speculative theories, scanned the face of their president, but it was in vain to seek the answer to the mystery there.

Just when the deep-toned clock in the great hall struck eight, Barbicane, as if he had been set in motion by a spring, raised himself up. A profound silence ensued, and the speaker, in a somewhat emphatic tone of voice, commenced as follows:

"Worthy colleagues, too long already a paralyzing peace has plunged the members of the Gun Club into deplorable inactivity. After a period of a few years full of incidents we have been compelled to abandon our labors, and to stop short on the road of progress. I do not hesitate to state, boldly, that any war which should recall us to arms would be welcome!"

"Yes, war!" cried the impetuous J. T. Maston.

"Hear, hear!" came the shout from all sides.

"But war," said Barbicane, "is impossible under existing circumstances; and, however we may desire it, many years may elapse before our cannon shall again thunder in the field of battle. We must make up our minds, then, to seek in another order of ideas some field for the activity which we all pine for."

The meeting felt that the president was now approaching the critical point, and redoubled their attention accordingly.

"For some months past, my worthy colleagues," continued Barbicane, "I have been asking myself whether, while sticking to our own particular specialty, we could not enter upon some great experiment worthy of the nineteenth century; and whether the progress of artillery science would not enable us to carry it to a successful conclusion. I have been considering, working, calculating; and the result of my studies is the conviction that we can now succeed in an enterprise which to any other country would appear wholly impracticable. This project, the result of long elaboration, is the object of my present communication. It is worthy of yourselves, worthy of the antecedents of the Gun Club; and it cannot fail to make some noise in the world."

"A great deal of noise?" asked an excited artilleryman.

"A great deal of noise in the truest sense of the word," Barbicane answered.

"Let him go on!" several voices cried out.

"Now, then, good colleagues," the president resumed, "I would ask you to give me your closest attention."

A thrill of excitement ran through the meeting. Barbicane, having by a rapid movement firmly fixed his hat upon his head, calmly continued his harangue:

"There is no one among you, my friends, who has not seen the moon, or, at least, heard speak of it. Don't be surprised if I am about to discourse to you regarding this Queen of the Night. It is perhaps reserved for us to become the Columbuses of this unknown world. Only enter into my plans, and support me with all your strength, and I will lead you to its conquest, and its name shall be added to those

14

The valorous members of the Gun Club

of the thirty-six States which compose this Great Union."

"Three cheers for the moon!" roared the Gun Club, with one voice.

"The moon, gentlemen, has been carefully studied," continued Barbicane; "her mass, density, and weight; her constitution, motions, distance, as well as her place in the solar system, have all been exactly determined. Selenographic maps[1] have been constructed with a perfection which equals, if it does not even surpass, that of our terrestrial maps. Photography has given us proofs of the incomparable beauty of our satellite;[2] in short, we know about the moon all that mathematical science, astronomy, geology, and optics can learn about her. But up to the present moment no direct communication has been established with her."

A violent movement of interest and surprise here greeted these words.

"Permit me," he continued, "to remind you briefly of how certain ardent spirits, starting on imaginary journeys, claimed to have penetrated the secrets of our satellite. In the seventeenth century a certain David Fabricius boasted of having seen with his own eyes the inhabitants of the moon. In 1649 a Frenchman, one Jean Baudoin, published a *Journey Made from the Earth to the Moon by Domingo Gonzalez, Spanish Adventurer*. At the same period, Cyrano de Bergerac published that celebrated expedition which met with such success in France. Somewhat later, another Frenchman—the French are really quite concerned with the Moon—this one named Fontenelle, wrote his *Plurality of the Worlds,* a masterpiece in its time; but science, in its progress, brushes aside even masterpieces! About 1835, a

---

[1] From *selene,* Greek for *moon.*
[2] For instance, the magnificent views taken by Mr. Waren de la Rue.

15

small treatise, translated from *The New York American,* was published in France. It related how Sir John Herschel, having been despatched to the Cape of Good Hope for the purpose of making there some astronomical calculations, had, by means of a telescope brought to perfection through internal lighting, reduced the apparent distance of the moon to eighty yards! He then distinctly was said to have perceived caverns frequented by hippopotami, green mountains bordered by golden lace-work, sheep with horns of ivory, a white species of deer and inhabitants with membranous wings, like bats. This brochure, the work of an American named Locke, had a great sale. But it was soon discovered to be a scientific hoax, and the French were the first to laugh at it."

"Laughing at an American!" cried J. T. Maston. "Why, there is our reason for declaring war! . . ."

"Do not be alarmed, my worthy friend. Before laughing at it, the French were completely taken in by our countryman. So to bring this rapid sketch to a close, I will only add that a certain Hans Pfaal, of Rotterdam, launching himself in a balloon filled with a gas extracted from nitrogen, thirty-seven times lighter than hydrogen, reached the moon after a passage of nineteen days. This journey, like all previous ones, was purely imaginary; still, it was the work of a popular American author endowed with strange contemplative genius—I mean Edgar Allan Poe!"

"Hurrah for Edgar Allan Poe!" roared the assemblage, electrified by their president's words.

"I have now enumerated," said Barbicane, "the experiments which I call purely paper ones, and wholly insufficient to establish serious relations with the Queen of Night. Nevertheless, I am bound to add that some practical geniuses have attempted to establish actual communication with her. Thus, a few days ago, a German geometrician proposed to send a scientific expedition to the steppes of Siberia. There, on those vast plains, they were to describe enormous geometric figures, formed by the use of reflectors, among which was the proposition regarding the 'square of the hypotenuse,' commonly called the 'Ass's Bridge' by the French. 'Every intelligent being,' said the geometrician, 'must understand the scientific meaning of that figure. The Selenites,[3] if they exist, will respond by a similar figure; and, communication being thus once established, it will be easy to form an alphabet which shall enable us to converse with the inhabitants of the moon.' So spoke the German geometrician; but his project was never put into practice, and up to the present day there is no bond in existence between the earth and her satellite. It is reserved for the practical genius of Americans to establish communication with the sidereal world. The means of achieving this is simple, easy, certain, infallible—and that is the subject of my present proposal."

A veritable hubbub, a storm of acclamations greeted these words. There was not a single person in the whole audience who was not overcome, carried away, lifted out of himself by the speaker's words.

"Listen, listen! Silence!" came the shouts from all sides.

When the excitement had partially subsided, Barbicane resumed his speech in a somewhat graver voice.

"You know," said he, "what progress artillery science has made during the last few years, and what a degree of perfection firearms of every kind would have reached, had the war gone on. Moreover, you are well aware that, in general, the resisting power of cannon and the expansive force of

[3] Moon-people.

gunpowder are practically unlimited. Well! starting from this principle, I ask myself whether, supposing adequate apparatus, constructed upon the conditions of ascertained resistance, it might not be possible to project a shot up to the moon?"

At these words a murmur of amazement escaped from a thousand panting chests; then succeeded a moment of perfect silence, resembling that profound stillness which precedes the bursting of a thunderstorm. In point of fact, a thunderstorm did peal forth, but it was the thunder of applause, of cries, and of uproar which made the very hall quake. The president attempted to speak, but could not. It was fully ten minutes before he could make himself heard.

"Allow me to finish," he calmly continued. "I have looked at the question in all its bearings, I have resolutely attacked it, and by incontrovertible calculations I find that a projectile endowed with an initial velocity of 12,000 yards per second, and aimed at the moon, must necessarily reach it. I therefore have the honor, my worthy colleagues, to propose to you that we attempt this little experiment!"

CHAPTER 3

Effect of the President's Communication

I T is impossible to describe the effect produced by the last words of the honorable president—the cries, the shouts, the succession of roars, hurrahs, and all the varied vociferations which the American language is capable of supplying. It was a scene of indescribable confusion and uproar. They shouted, they clapped, they stamped on the floor of the hall. All the weapons in the museum discharged at once could not have more violently set in motion the waves of sound. One need not be surprised at this. There are some cannoneers nearly as noisy as their own guns.

Barbicane remained calm in the midst of this enthusiastic clamor; perhaps he was desirous of addressing a few more words to his colleagues, for by his gestures he demanded silence, and his loud desk-bell rang out in desperate appeals. No attention, however, was paid to his request. He was presently torn from his seat, carried off in triumph, and passed from the hands of his faithful colleagues into the arms of a no less excited crowd.

Nothing can astound an American. It has often been asserted that the word "impossible" is not French. People have evidently been using the wrong dictionary. In America, all is easy, all is simple; and as for mechanical difficulties, they are overcome before they arise. Between Barbicane's proposition and its realization no true Yankee would have allowed even the semblance of a difficulty to be possible. A thing with them is no sooner said than done.

The triumphal progress of the president continued throughout the evening. It was a regular torchlight procession. Irish, Germans, French, Scotch, all the heterogeneous individuals who make up the population of Maryland shouted in their respective vernaculars; and the "vivas," "hurrahs," and "bravos" intermingled in inexpressible enthusiasm.

Just at this crisis, as though she comprehended that all this agitation concerned her, the moon shone forth with serene splendor, eclipsing by her intense illumination all the surrounding lights. The Yankees all turned their eyes toward her resplendent orb, some waving to her, others calling her endearing names; still others peered carefully at her, while some shook their fists at her. Between eight o'clock and midnight, one Jones'-Fall Street optician made his fortune selling opera-glasses. The star of the night was gawked at like some high-born lady. The Americans gave her the once-over as familiarly as if she belonged to them. It seemed that blonde Phoebe was already the property of these daring conquerors and a part of the territory of the Union. And yet all that was proposed was to aim a projectile at her, which is a rather brutal way to establish contact, even with a satellite, albeit a quite customary one among civilized nations.

Midnight arrived, and the enthusiasm showed no signs of

diminution. It prevailed equally among all classes of citizens —men of law, scientists, shopkeepers, merchants, porters, the educated as well as the "greenhorns," were stirred in their innermost fibres. A national enterprise was at stake. The whole city, high and low, the quays bordering the Patapsco, the ships lying in the basins, were filled with a crowd drunk with joy, gin, and whisky. Every one chattered, argued, discussed, disputed, applauded, from the gentleman lounging upon the barroom settee with his tumbler of sherry-cobbler before him down to the waterman who got drunk on his "thorough knock-me-down" in the dingy taverns of Fell's Point.

About two A.M., however, the excitement began to subside. President Barbicane reached his house, bruised, crushed, and bone-weary. Hercules could not have resisted a similar outbreak of enthusiasm. The crowd gradually deserted the squares and streets. The four railways from Philadelphia and Washington, Harrisburg and Wheeling, which converge at Baltimore, carried the multitude away to the four corners of the United States, and the city subsided into comparative tranquillity.

It would, incidentally, be a mistake to imagine that, during this memorable evening, Baltimore was the only city in the throes of the excitement. All the other great centers of the Union, New York, Boston, Albany, Washington, Richmond, the Crescent City of New Orleans, Charleston, Mobile—from Texas to Massachusetts, from Michigan to Florida—joined in the madness. For, the thirty thousand corresponding members of the Gun Club were all familiar with the President's letter, and they were just as eagerly awaiting his famous communication of October 5th. So, that same evening, as the words came off the lips of the speaker, they were transmitted by the telegraph wires throughout the United States, at a rate of 248,487 miles a second (the speed of electricity). It can therefore be asserted with absolute conviction that at the very same instant the whole of the country, ten times the size of France, joined in one single hurrah, and that 25,000,000 hearts, swollen with pride, beat with one same pulsation.

On the following day, fifteen hundred newspapers and journals, daily, weekly, fortnightly, or monthly, all took up the question. They examined it under all its different aspects, physical, meteorological, economic, or moral, up to its bearing on politics or civilization. They debated whether the moon was a finished world, or whether it was still destined to undergo any further transformation. Did it resemble the earth at the period when the latter was destitute as yet of an atmosphere? What kind of spectacle would its hidden hemisphere present to our terrestrial spheroid? Granting that the question at present was simply that of sending a projectile up to the moon, every one must see that that involved the commencement of a series of experiments. All must hope that some day America would penetrate the deepest secrets of that mysterious orb; and some even seemed to fear that its conquest might significantly upset the equilibrium of Europe.

Not one publication questioned the feasibility of the project under discussion; reports, pamphlets, bulletins, official journals of scientific, literary, or religious organizations all underlined its advantages; and the Society of Natural History of Boston, the Society of Science and Art of Albany, the Geographical and Statistical Society of New York, the Philosophical Society of Philadelphia, and the Smithsonian Institution of Washington sent innumerable letters of congratulation to the Gun Club, together with offers of immediate assistance and money.

So it can be said that no proposal was ever supported by so many; hesitations, doubts, worries were voiced by none. As for the jokes, the cartoons, the songs that in Europe, and especially in France, would have greeted the idea of sending a projectile to the moon, here they would have backfired on their authors; and all the "life-preservers"[1] in the world would not have been enough to protect them from the universal indignation. There are some things which are not laughing matters in the New World. From that day forward Impey Barbicane became one of the greatest citizens of the United States, a kind of Washington of science. A single trait of feeling, taken from many others, will serve to show the point which this homage of a whole people to a single individual attained.

Some few days after this memorable meeting of the Gun Club, the manager of an English company announced, at the Baltimore Theatre, the production of *Much Ado About Nothing*. But the populace, seeing in that title an allusion that was disrespectful to Barbicane's project, broke into the auditorium, smashed the benches, and compelled the ill-advised manager to alter his play-bill. Being a sensible man, he bowed to the public will and replaced the offending comedy by *As You Like It* and for many weeks did fabulous business at the box-office.

[1] A pocket weapon made of flexible whalebone and a metal ball.

CHAPTER 4

Reply from the
Observatory of Cambridge

B ARBICANE, however, lost not one moment amid all the enthusiasm of which he had become the object. His first move was to reassemble his colleagues in the boardroom of the Gun Club. There, after some discussion, it was agreed to consult the astronomers regarding the astronomical part of the enterprise. Their reply once ascertained, they could then discuss the mechanical means, and nothing would be neglected to assure the success of this great experiment.

A note couched in precise terms, containing special interrogatories, was therefore drawn up and addressed to the Observatory of Cambridge in Massachusetts. This city, where the first university of the United States was founded, is justly celebrated for its astronomical staff. There are to be found assembled all the most eminent men of science. Here is to be seen at work that powerful telescope which enabled Bond to resolve the nebula of Andromeda, and Clarke to discover the satellite of Sirius. This celebrated institution fully justified on all points the confidence reposed in it by the Gun Club.

So, after two days, the reply so impatiently awaited was placed in the hands of President Barbicane.

Reply from the Observatory

It was couched in the following terms:

The Director of the Cambridge Observatory
to the President of the Gun Club at Baltimore

CAMBRIDGE, October 7

On receipt of your favor of the 6th instant, addressed to the Observatory of Cambridge in the name of the members of the Baltimore Gun Club, our staff was immediately called together, and it was judged expedient to reply as follows:

The questions which have been put to it are these:

1. Is it possible to transmit a projectile up to the moon?

2. What is the exact distance which separates the earth from its satellite?

3. What will be the period of transit of the projectile when endowed with sufficient initial velocity? and, consequently, at what moment ought it to be discharged in order that it may touch the moon at a particular point?

4. At what precise moment will the moon present herself in the most favorable position to be reached by the projectile?

5. What point in the heavens ought the cannon to be aimed at which it is intended to discharge the projectile?

6. What place will the moon occupy in the heavens at the moment of the projectile's departure?

Regarding the *first* question, "Is it possible to transmit a projectile up to the moon?"

Yes; provided it possesses an initial velocity of 12,000 yards per second; calculations prove that to be sufficient. In proportion as we recede from the earth the action of gravitation diminishes in inverse ratio to the square of the distance; that is to say, *at three times a given distance the action is nine times less.* Consequently, the weight of a shot will rapidly decrease, and will become reduced to *zero* at the instant that the attraction of the moon exactly counterpoises that of the earth; that is to say, at $^{47}\!/_{52}$ of its passage. At that instant the projectile will have no weight whatever; and, if it passes that point, it will fall into the moon by the sole effect of lunar attraction. The *theoretical pos-*

25

sibility of the experiment is therefore absolutely demonstrated; its *success* must depend upon the power of the weapon employed.

As to the *second* question, "What is the exact distance which separates the earth from its satellite?"

The moon does not describe a *circle* round the earth, but rather an *ellipse,* of which our earth occupies one of the *foci;* the consequence, therefore, is, that at certain times it approaches nearer to, and at others it recedes farther from, the earth; in astronomical language, it is at one time in *apogee,* at another in *perigee.* Now the difference between its greatest and its least distance is too considerable to be left out of consideration. In point of fact, in its apogee the moon is 247,552 miles away, and in its perigee, only 218,657; a fact which makes a difference of 28,895 miles, or more than one-ninth of the entire distance. The perigee distance, therefore, is that which ought to serve as the basis of all calculations.

To the *third* question, "What will be the period of transit of the projectile when endowed with sufficient initial velocity? and, consequently, at what moment ought it to be discharged in order that it may touch the moon at a particular point?"

If the shot should preserve continuously its initial velocity of 12,000 yards per second, it would require little more than nine hours to reach its destination; but, inasmuch as that initial velocity will be continually decreasing, it results that, taking everything into consideration, it will require 300,000 seconds, that is 83hrs. 20m. to reach the point where the attraction of the earth and moon will be *in equilibrio.* From this point it will fall into the moon in 50,000 seconds, or 13hrs. 53m. 20sec. It will be desirable, therefore, to discharge it 97hrs. 13m. 20sec. before the arrival of the moon at the point aimed at.

Regarding question *four,* "At what precise moment will the moon present herself in the most favorable position to be reached by the projectile?"

After what has been said above, it will be necessary, first of all, to choose the period when the moon is at its perigee, and *also* the moment when it is crossing the zenith, which latter event will further diminish the entire distance by a length equal to the radius of the earth, *i. e.* 3,919 miles; the result of which will be that the final passage remaining to be accomplished will be 214,976 miles. But although the moon passes her perigee every month, she does not reach the zenith always at *exactly the same moment*. She does not appear under these two conditions simultaneously, except at long intervals of time. It will be necessary, therefore, to wait for the moment when her passage in perigee coincides with that in the zenith. Now, by a fortunate circumstance, on the 4th of December in the ensuing year the moon *will* present these two conditions. At midnight she will be in perigee, that is, at her shortest distance from the earth, and at the same moment she will be crossing the zenith.

On the *fifth* question, "At what point in the heavens ought the cannon to be aimed?"

The preceding remarks being admitted, the cannon ought to be pointed to the zenith[1] of the place. The shot, therefore, will be perpendicular to the plane of the horizon; and the projectile will more rapidly pass beyond the range of terrestrial attraction. But, in order for the moon to reach the zenith of a given place, it is necessary that the place situated not exceed in latitude the declination of the luminary; in other words, it must be situated between 0° and 28° of lat. N. or S.[2] In every other spot the shot would necessarily have to be oblique, which would seriously militate against the success of the experiment.

As to the *sixth* question, "What place will the moon occupy in the heavens at the moment of the projectile's departure?"

At the moment when the projectile is discharged into space, the moon, which travels forward daily 13° 10′ 35″, will be distant from the zenith point by four times that quantity, *i. e.* by 52° 42′ 20″, a space which corresponds to the path which she will describe during the entire journey of the projectile. But, inas-

---

[1] The zenith is the point in the sky vertically directly above the observer's head.

[2] Only in regions of the globe between the equator and the 28th parallel does the moon reach the zenith; beyond the 28th parallel, the moon gets less close to the zenith as one comes closer to the poles.

much as it is equally necessary to take into account the deviation which the rotary motion of the earth will impart to the shot, and as the shot cannot reach the moon until after a deviation equal to 16 radii of the earth, which, calculated upon the moon's orbit, are equal to about eleven degrees, it becomes necessary to add these eleven degrees to those which express the retardation of the moon just mentioned: that is to say, in round numbers, about sixty-four degrees. Consequently, at the moment of firing the visual radius applied to the moon will describe, with the vertical line of the place, an angle of sixty-four degrees.

These are our answers to the questions put to the Observatory of Cambridge by the members of the Gun Club.

To sum up—

1st. The cannon must be set up in a country situated between 0° and 28° of N. or S. latitude.

2d. It must be pointed directly toward the zenith of the place.

3d. The projectile must be propelled with an initial velocity of 12,000 yards per second.

4th. It must be discharged at 10hrs. 46m. 40sec. of the 1st of December of the ensuing year.

5th. It will meet the moon four days after its discharge, precisely at midnight on the 4th of December, at the moment of its transit across the zenith.

The members of the Gun Club ought, therefore, without delay, to commence the works necessary for such an experiment, and to be prepared to set to work at the moment determined upon; for, if they should suffer this 4th of December to go by, they will not find the moon again under the same conditions of perigee and of zenith until eighteen years and eleven days afterward.

The staff of the Cambridge Observatory place themselves entirely at their disposal in respect to all questions of theoretical astronomy; and herewith add their congratulations to those of all the rest of America.

For the Astronomical Staff

J. M. BELFAST, *Director*

CHAPTER 5

The Romance of the Moon

AN observer endowed with an infinite range of vision, and placed in that unknown center around which the entire world revolves, might have beheld myriads of atoms filling all space during the chaotic epoch of the universe. Little by little, as ages went on, a change took place; a general law of attraction manifested itself, to which the hitherto errant atoms became obedient: these atoms combined together chemically according to their affinities, formed themselves into molecules, and composed those nebulous masses with which the depths of the heavens are strewn.

These masses became immediately endowed with a rotary motion around their own central point. This center, formed of indefinite molecules, began to revolve round its own axis during its gradual condensation; then, following the immutable laws of mechanics, in proportion as its bulk diminished by condensation, its rotary motion became accelerated, and these two effects continuing, the result was the formation of one principal star, the center of the nebulous mass.

By attentively watching, the observer would then have perceived the other molecules of the mass, following the example of this central star, become likewise condensed by gradually accelerated rotation, and gravitating round it in the shape of innumerable stars. Thus was formed the *Nebula,* which astronomers today consider to be one of nearly 5,000.

Among these 5,000 nebulae there is one which has received the name of the Milky Way, and which contains eighteen millions of stars, each of which has become the center of a solar world.

If the observer had then specially directed his attention to one of the more humble and less brilliant of these stellar bodies,[1] a star of the fourth class, that which is arrogantly called the Sun, all the phenomena to which the formation of the Universe is to be ascribed would have been successively fulfilled before his eyes.

In fact, he would have perceived this sun, as yet in the gaseous state, and composed of moving molecules, revolving round its axis in order to complete its work of concentration. This motion, faithful to the laws of mechanics, would have been accelerated with the diminution of its volume; and a moment would have arrived when the centrifugal force would have overpowered the centripetal, which causes the molecules all to tend toward the center.

Another phenomenon would then have passed before the observer's eye, and the molecules situated at the level of the equator, escaping like a stone from a sling of which the cord had suddenly snapped, would have formed around the sun various concentric rings resembling that of Saturn. In their turn, again, these rings of cosmic matter, excited by a rotary motion round the central mass, would have been broken up and decomposed into secondary nebulosities, that is to say, into planets.

[1] According to Wallaston, the diameter of Sirius must be twelve times as great as that of the Sun, or almost eleven million miles.

Moon seekers and dreamers: Cyrano, Copernicus, Galileo, Herschel, Verne

Similarly he could have observed these planets throw off one or more rings each, which became the origin of the secondary bodies which we call satellites.

Thus, then, advancing from atom to molecule, from molecule to nebulous mass, from nebulous mass to nebula, from that to a principal star, from star to sun, from sun to planet, and hence to satellite, we have the whole series of transformations undergone by the heavenly bodies since the earliest days of the world.

The sun appears to be lost in the immensity of the stellar world, and yet it is connected, according to present-day theories of science, to the nebula of the Milky Way. It is the center of a world and, however small it may appear to be up there in the ethereal regions, it is nevertheless enormous, for its size is fourteen hundred thousand times that of the Earth. Around it gravitate eight planets, which were issued from its very entrails in the earliest times of Creation. They are, starting with the closest of these and going toward the farthest, Mercury, Venus, Earth, Mars, Jupiter, Saturn, Uranus, and Neptune. Moreover, between Mars and Jupiter, there is a constant circulation of less sizable bodies, which are perhaps the wandering débris of a larger one that broke into several thousands of pieces. As of now, the telescope has identified ninety-seven of them.[2]

Several of these attendant bodies which the sun maintains in their elliptical orbits by the great law of gravitation in turn have their own satellites. Uranus has eight, Saturn eight, Jupiter four, Neptune possibly three, and the Earth one. The latter, one of the smallest of the entire solar system, we call the Moon; and this was what the daring genius of the Americans proposed to set about conquering.

The moon, by her comparative proximity, and the con-

[2] Some so small one could get around them in a day at double time.

stantly varying appearances produced by her several phases, in the beginning vied with the sun for the attention of the Earth's inhabitants; but the sun tires the eyes, and the brilliance of its light forces those who contemplate it to look away. Blonde Phoebe, being more human on the other hand, allows one to observe her at one's leisure in her modest graciousness; she is kind to the eye, without ambition, and yet, at times presumes to eclipse her brother, radiant Apollo, while never being eclipsed by him. The Mohammedans understood the debt of gratitude they owed to this faithful friend of Earth's, and they established their month in terms of her revolution.[3]

The earliest peoples were all given to special worship of this chaste goddess. The Egyptians called her Isis; the Phoenicians gave her the name of Astarte; the Greeks worshiped her under the name of Phoebe, daughter of Latona and Jupiter, and they explained her eclipses by the mysterious visits of Diana to the handsome Endymion. If the mythological legends can be believed, the Nemean lion roamed the lunar countryside before making its appearance on Earth. The poet Agesianax, quoted by Plutarch, sang in his verses of the soft eyes, the charming nose and the lovely mouth, made up by the luminous parts of adorable Selene.

Yet, while the ancients well understood the character and nature, in a word, the moral qualities of the Moon from the mythological standpoint, even the most learned among them remained quite ignorant in matters of selenography.

Nevertheless, several astronomers of those early periods made certain discoveries which have been borne out by the science of today. The Arcadians claimed to have lived on Earth at a time when the Moon was not yet in existence;

[3] About 29½ days.

Tatius regarded it as a fragment detached from the solar disc; Clearchus, Aristotle's disciple, held it to be a polished mirror reflecting the images of the ocean; others, finally, saw in it only an accumulation of vapors exhaled by the Earth, or a globe that was half fire, half ice, revolving upon itself—yet a few scientists, through their shrewd observations, even without optical instruments, suspected most of the laws which actually do govern the star of the night.

Thus, Thales of Miletus, in 460 B.C., expressed the opinion that the moon was illuminated by the sun. Aristarchus of Samos gave a correct explanation of its phases. Cleomedes taught that it shone because of reflected light. The Chaldean Berossus discovered that the duration of its rotation was equal to that of its revolution, and in that way he explained how it was that the moon always showed the same face to us. Finally Hipparchus, two centuries before the Christian Era, detected some irregularities in the visible movements of Earth's satellite.

These various observations were later confirmed and were most useful to the astronomers who followed. Ptolemy, in the second century, and the Arab Abul-Wefa, in the tenth, filled in Hipparchus' remarks about the irregularities the moon undergoes as it follows the undulating line of its orbit under the influence of the sun. Then, Copernicus, in the fifteenth[4] century, and Tycho Brahe, in the sixteenth, made a complete exposition of the system of the world and the part played by the moon in the assemblage of heavenly bodies.

At that time, its movements had been more or less completely determined; but of its physical constitution, man still knew very little. That was when Galileo explained the phe-

4 [Actually the sixteenth—one of Verne's inaccuracies.—*Ed.*]

nomena of light produced in certain phases through the existence of mountains to which he ascribed an average height of some 27,000 feet.

After him, Hevelius, an astronomer in Danzig, reduced the highest of these altitudes to something over 15,000 feet; but the calculations of Riccioli raised them again to 21,000.

At the close of the eighteenth century Herschel, armed with a powerful telescope, considerably reduced the preceding measurements. He assigned a height of 11,400 feet to the maximum elevations, and reduced the mean of the different altitudes to a scant 2,400 feet. But Herschel's calculations were in their turn corrected by the observations of Schroeter, Louville, Halley, Nasmyth, Bianchini, Pastorf, Lohrmann, and Gruithuysen; but it was reserved for the labors of Beer and Maedler finally to resolve the question. Thanks to them, the altitudes of the mountains of the moon are all known today, for they succeeded in measuring 1,905 different elevations, of which six exceed 15,000 feet, and twenty-two exceed 14,400 feet. The highest summit of all towers to a height of 22,806 feet above the surface of the lunar disc.[5]

At the same period the examination of the moon was being completed. She appeared completely riddled with craters, and her essentially volcanic character was apparent at each observation. By the absence of refraction in the rays of the planets occulted by her we conclude that she is almost absolutely devoid of an atmosphere. The absence of air entails the absence of water. It became, therefore, manifest that the Selenites, to support life under such conditions, must possess a special organization of their own and differ remarkably from the inhabitants of the earth.

[5] The altitude of Mont Blanc is 15,787 ft. above sea level.

The Romance of the Moon

At length, thanks to modern methods, instruments of still higher perfection searched the moon without intermission, not leaving a single point of her surface unexplored; and notwithstanding that her diameter measures 2,150 miles, her surface equals one-thirteenth that of our globe, and her bulk one-forty-ninth that of the terrestrial spheroid —not one of her secrets was able to escape the eyes of the astronomers; and these skillful men of science carried to an even greater degree their prodigious observations.

Thus they remarked that, during full moon, the disc appeared scored in certain parts with white lines; and, during the phases, with black. On prosecuting the study of these with still greater precision, they succeeded in obtaining an exact account of the nature of these lines. They were long and narrow furrows sunk between parallel ridges, bordering generally upon the edges of the craters. Their length varied between ten and 100 miles, and their width was about 1,600 yards. Astronomers called them chasms, but they could not get any further. Whether these chasms were the dried-up beds of ancient rivers or not, they were unable thoroughly to ascertain. The Americans, among others, hoped one day or other to determine this geological question. They also undertook to examine the true nature of that system of parallel ramparts discovered on the moon's surface by Gruithuysen, a learned professor of Munich, who considered them to be a system of fortifications thrown up by Selenite engineers. These two points, yet obscure, as well as others, no doubt, could not be definitively settled by direct communication with the moon.

Regarding the degree of intensity of its light, there was nothing more to learn on this point. It was known that it is 300,000 times weaker than that of the sun, and that its heat has no appreciable effect upon the thermometer. As to the phenomenon known as "ashy light," it is explained naturally by the effect of the transmission of the solar rays from the earth to the moon, which give the appearance of completeness to the lunar disc, as it presents itself in its crescent form during the first and last phases.

Such was the state of established knowledge regarding the earth's satellite, which the Gun Club was now undertaking to perfect in all its aspects, cosmographic, geological, political, and moral.

CHAPTER 6

The Permissible Limits of Ignorance and Belief in the United States

The immediate result of Barbicane's proposition was to call back into question all the astronomical facts relative to the Queen of Night. Everybody set to work to study assiduously. One would have thought that the moon had just appeared for the first time, and that no one had ever before caught a glimpse of her in the heavens. She became fashionable; she lost none of her modesty for being lionized, and though now a "star" did not let it go to her head. The papers revived all the old anecdotes in which this "sun of the wolves" played a part; they recalled the influences which the ignorance of past ages ascribed to her; they pulled out all the stops; they all but quoted her witty sayings; all America was seized with selenomania, or moon-madness.

The scientific journals, for their part, dealt more especially with the questions which touched upon the enterprise of the Gun Club. The letter of the Observatory of Cambridge was published by them, and commented upon and approved without reservation.

In short, it was no longer permissible, even for the most illiterate of Yankees, to be in the dark about any one of the facts concerning his satellite, nor for the most narrow-minded of old wives to admit to superstitious errors about it. Science came at them in every possible shape; it assailed their eyes and their ears; one could no longer be an ass—in astronomy.

Until that time many people had been ignorant of the mode in which the distance which separates the moon from the earth is calculated. They took advantage of this fact to explain to them that this distance was obtained by measuring the parallax of the moon. The term parallax proving "caviare to the general," they further explained that it meant the angle formed by two straight lines drawn from either extremity of the earth's radius to the moon. On doubts being expressed as to the correctness of this method, they immediately proved that not only was the mean distance 234,347 miles, but that astronomers could not possibly be in error in their estimate by more than seventy miles either way.

To those who were not familiar with the motions of the moon, they demonstrated that she possesses two distinct motions, the first being that of rotation upon her axis, the second that of revolution round the earth, accomplishing both together in an equal period of time, that is to say, in twenty-seven and one-third days.[1]

The motion of rotation is that which produces day and night on the surface of the moon; save that there is only one day and one night in the lunar month, each lasting three hundred and fifty-four and one-third hours. But, happily for her, the face turned toward the terrestrial globe is illuminated by it with an intensity equal to the light of fourteen moons. As to the other face, always invisible to us, it has of

[1] The time of one sidereal revolution, that is, the time it takes the moon to come back to the same star.

necessity three hundred and fifty-four hours of absolute night, tempered only by that "pale glimmer which falls upon it from the stars." This phenomenon is due exclusively to the peculiar fact that the movements of rotation and revolution take exactly the same length of time, a phenomenon shared, according to Cassini and Herschel, by the satellites of Jupiter, and very probably also by all the other satellites.

Some well-intentioned but rather obstinate persons could not at first comprehend how, if the moon invariably displays the same face to the earth during her revolution, she can describe one turn round herself. To such they answered, "Go into your dining-room, and walk round the table in such a way as always to keep your face turned toward the center; by the time you have achieved one complete circle you will have completed one turn round yourself, since your eye will have traversed successively every point of the room. Well, then, the room is the heavens, the table is the earth, and the moon is yourself." And they would go away delighted with the comparison.

So, then, the moon invariably displays the same face to the earth; nevertheless, to be quite exact, it is necessary to add that, in consequence of certain fluctuations from north to south, and from west to east, termed her libration, she permits slightly more than half, or 57/100 of her, to be seen.

As soon as the ignoramuses came to understand as much as the director of the observatory himself knew, they began to worry themselves regarding her revolution round the earth, whereupon twenty scientific reviews immediately came to the rescue. They pointed out to them then that the firmament, with its infinitude of stars, may be considered as one vast dial-plate, upon which the moon travels, indicating the true time to all the inhabitants of the earth; that it is during this movement that the Queen of Night exhibits her different phases; that the moon is *full* when she is in *opposition* with the sun, that is, when the three bodies are on the same straight line, the earth occupying the center; that she is *new* when she is in *conjunction* with the sun, that is, when she is between it and the earth; and lastly, that she is in her *first* or *last* quarter, when she makes with the sun and the earth a right angle of which she herself occupies the apex.

A few observant Yankees then drew a conclusion from this, namely, that eclipses could occur only at times of conjunction or opposition, and they were correct. In conjunction, the moon can eclipse the sun, whereas in opposition, the earth in turn may eclipse it, and if such eclipses do not occur twice within each lunar month, it is because the plane on which the moon moves is inclined toward the ecliptic, in other words, toward the plane on which the earth itself moves.

Regarding the altitude which the moon attains above the horizon, the letter of the Cambridge Observatory had said all that was to be said in that respect. Every one knew that this altitude varies according to the latitude of the observer. But the only zones of the globe in which the moon passes the zenith, that is, the point directly over the head of the spectator, are of necessity located between the twenty-eighth parallels and the equator. Hence the importance of the advice to try the experiment upon some point of that part of the globe, in order that the projectile might be discharged perpendicularly, and so the sooner escape the action of gravitation. This was an essential condition to the success of the enterprise, and continued actively to engage the public attention.

Regarding the path described by the moon in her revolution round the earth, the Cambridge Observatory had demonstrated that this path is a re-entering curve, not a perfect circle, but an ellipse, of which the earth occupies one of the *foci.* Such elliptical orbits are common to all planets, as well as satellites, and rational mechanics proves conclusively that it could not be otherwise. It was of course understood that it is farthest removed from the earth during its *apogee,* and approaches most nearly to it at its *perigee.*

Such then was the extent of knowledge possessed willynilly by every American on the subject, and of which no one could decently profess ignorance. Still, while these true principles were being rapidly disseminated many errors and illusory fears proved less easy to eradicate.

For instance, some worthy persons maintained that the moon was an ancient comet which, in describing its elongated orbit round the sun, happened to pass near the earth, and became confined within her circle of attraction. These drawing-room astronomers professed so to explain the charred aspect of the moon—a disaster which they attributed to the intensity of the solar heat; only, on being reminded that comets have an atmosphere, and that the moon has little or none, they were fairly at a loss for a reply.

Others again, belonging to the timorous class, expressed certain fears concerning the moon. They had heard it said that, according to observations made in the time of the Caliphs, her revolution was becoming accelerated to a certain degree. Hence they concluded, logically enough, that an acceleration of motion must be accompanied by a corresponding diminution in the distance separating the two bodies; and that, supposing the double effect to be continued indefinitely, the moon would end by one day falling into the earth. However, they became reassured as to the fate of

41

future generations on being apprised that, according to the calculations of Laplace, this acceleration of motion is confined within very restricted limits, and that a proportional diminution of speed will be certain to succeed it. So, then, the stability of the solar system would not be upset in ages to come.

And lastly there was the superstitious class of ignoramuses; they are not content merely not to know what is true, but they also believe what is not true, and on the score of the moon that was a great deal. Some of them considered her disc a polished mirror, by means of which people could see each other from different points of the earth and interchange their thoughts. Others claimed that out of one thousand new moons that had been observed, nine hundred and fifty had brought about remarkable disturbances, such as cataclysms, revolutions, earthquakes, deluges, etc. They therefore believed that she exercised some mysterious influence over human destinies, that she was the "true counterpart" of our existence—with every Selenite attached to some inhabitant of the earth by a tie of sympathy. Along with Dr. Mead, they maintained that our entire vital systems were governed by her, claiming doggedly that boys are born mostly during the new moon, girls during the last quarter, and so on and on. But in the end it was necessary to give up these vulgar misconceptions, come back to the truth alone, and while the moon, shorn of her influence, lost out in the minds of some partisans of the all-powerful, while a few backs were turned on her, yet the vast majority did adopt the truth. As for the Yankees, they no longer had any other ambition than to take possession of this new continent of the sky, and to plant upon the summit of its highest point the star-spangled banner of the United States of America.

CHAPTER 7

The Hymn to the Cannon-Ball

THE Observatory of Cambridge in its memorable letter had treated the question from a purely astronomical point of view. The mechanical part still remained. At that point the practical problems would have seemed insurmountable in any country other than America. Here they were child's play.

President Barbicane had, without loss of time, appointed a working committee of the Gun Club. The duty of this committee was to resolve the three great questions of the cannon, the projectile, and the powder. It was composed of four members of great technical knowledge, Barbicane (with the prevailing vote in case of a tie), General Morgan, Major Elphinstone, and J. T. Maston, who was made secretary.

On the 8th of October the committee met at the house of President Barbicane, 3 Republican Street. Since it was important that stomachs not start to growl and interrupt the meeting, the four committee members sat down around a table covered with sandwiches and sizable teapots. J. T. Maston immediately screwed his pen into his iron hook, and the meeting began.

Barbicane was the first to speak:

"My dear colleagues," he said, "we have to solve one of the most important problems in all of gunnery, that noblest of sciences, which deals with the movement of projectiles, that is, objects projected into space by any given propelling power, and then left to themselves."

"Ah, gunnery, sweet gunnery!" cried J. T. Maston with deep emotion.

"It might perhaps have appeared more logical," Barbicane went on, "to devote this first session to a discussion of the propelling device."

"Quite so," replied General Morgan.

"Nevertheless," Barbicane continued, "after mature consideration, it has appeared to me that the question of the projectile must take precedence over that of the cannon, and that the dimensions of the latter must necessarily be determined by those of the former."

"I would like to have the floor," J. T. Maston broke in.

His request was granted with the alacrity warranted by his magnificent past record.

"My good friends," he said in an inspired accent, "our president is right in placing the question of the projectile ahead of all others! The cannon-ball that we are about to launch toward the moon is our messenger, our ambassador to her, and I ask your permission here to consider it from a strictly moral point of view."

This new way of considering a projectile singularly aroused the curiosity of the members of the committee; and they therefore paid the keenest attention to the words of J. T. Maston.

"My worthy colleagues," he went on, "I will be brief; I will skip the physical cannon-ball, the missile that can kill, to consider only the mathematical cannon-ball, the philosophical projectile. The cannon-ball to my mind is the most magnificent manifestation of human power; it is indeed the sum total of that power; it was when he created it that man came closest to his own Creator!"

"Well said!" exclaimed Major Elphinstone.

"Yes, indeed," the speaker went on, "if God made the stars and the planets, man made the cannon-ball, that criterion of speed on earth, that smaller version of the heavenly bodies, which are nothing, in the final analysis, but projectiles themselves! Let God have the speed of electricity, the speed of light, the speed of the stars and comets, of planets and satellites, the speed of sound, even of the wind! We have the speed of the cannon-ball, a hundred times greater than that of trains or of the fastest horses!"

J. T. Maston was transported with emotion; his voice assumed lyrical accents as he sang this sacred hymn to the cannon-ball.

"Do you want figures?" he challenged. "Well, here are some persuasive ones! Take as an example the simple 24-pound shot. While it goes eight hundred thousand times less fast than electricity, six hundred and forty thousand times less fast than light, seventy-six times less fast than the earth in its orbit around the sun, nevertheless, when it leaves the cannon, it is traveling faster than sound,[1] going four hundred yards a second, four thousand yards in ten seconds, fourteen miles a minute, 840 miles an hour, 20,100 miles a day—which is to say, at the same speed as points on the equator in the earth's rotation, 7,336,500 miles per year. It would therefore require eleven days to reach the moon,

---

[1] So that, once one has heard the shot, he can no longer be struck by the projectile.

twelve years to get to the sun, 360 years to get to Neptune at the outer limits of the solar system. That is what that modest cannon-ball, the work of our own hands, could do! What then will it be like when, increasing its speed twentyfold, we send it out at a rate of seven miles a second! Ah, superb cannon-ball, magnificent projectile, I like to believe that up there you will be received with all the honors due an ambassador from earth!"

Cheers greeted this soaring conclusion, and J. T. Maston, overcome with emotion, sat down amidst the congratulations of his colleagues.

"And now," said Barbicane, "having given poetry its due, let us get down to the question at hand."

"By all means," replied the members of the committee, as each consumed a half-dozen sandwiches.

"You know the problem before us," the president resumed. "It is how to impart to a projectile a speed of 12,000 yards per second. I have every reason to believe we will succeed. But let us at present examine the velocities hitherto attained. General Morgan will be able to enlighten us on this point."

"And the more easily," replied the general, "that during the war I was a member of the committee of experiments. I may say, then, that the Dahlgren 100-pounders, which carried a distance of 5,000 yards, imparted to their projectile an initial velocity of 500 yards a second."

"Fine. What about the Rodman Columbiad?" the president asked.

"The Rodman Columbiad, tested at Fort Hamilton, near New York, sent a shot weighing half a ton a distance of six miles, with a velocity of 800 yards per second—a result which Armstrong and Palliser never obtained in England."

"Oh, the English!" said J. T. Maston, waving his formidable hook toward the eastern horizon.

"This," replied Barbicane, "is, I believe, the maximum velocity ever attained?"

"It is so," replied the general.

"Ah!" groaned J. T. Maston, "if my mortar had not burst——"

"Yes," quietly replied Barbicane, "but it did burst. We must take, then, for our starting point, this velocity of 800 yards. We must increase it twentyfold. Now, reserving for another discussion the means of producing this velocity, I will call your attention to the dimensions which it will be proper to assign to the shot. You understand that we have nothing to do here with projectiles weighing at most but half a ton."

"Why not?" asked the major.

"Because the shot," quickly replied J. T. Maston, "must be big enough to attract the attention of the inhabitants of the moon, if there are any."

"Yes," replied Barbicane, "and for another reason more important still."

"What do you mean?" the major inquired.

"I mean that it is not enough to discharge a projectile, and then take no further notice of it; we must follow it throughout its course, up to the moment when it reaches its goal."

"What?" shouted the general and the major in great surprise.

"Undoubtedly," replied Barbicane composedly, "or else our experiment would produce no result."

"But then," replied the major, "you will have to give this projectile enormous dimensions."

"No! Be so good as to listen. You know that optical instruments have acquired great perfection; with certain telescopes we have succeeded in obtaining enlargements of 6,000 times and reducing the moon to within forty miles' distance. Now, at this distance, any objects sixty feet wide would be perfectly visible.

"If, then, the penetrative power of telescopes has not been further increased, it is because that power detracts from their light; and the moon, which is but a reflecting mirror, does not give back sufficient light to enable us to perceive objects of lesser magnitude."

"Well, then, what do you propose to do?" asked the general. "Would you give your projectile a diameter of sixty feet?"

"Not at all."

"Do you intend, then, to increase the luminous power of the moon?"

"Exactly."

"Very nice!" cried J. T. Maston, sarcastically.

"Yes, nice and simple," Barbicane went on. "The point is, if I can succeed in diminishing the density of the atmosphere through which the moon's light has to travel, will I not have rendered her light more intense?"

"Yes, indeed."

"Well, to obtain that result, it will be enough to establish a telescope on some elevated mountain. Which is what we will do."

"I give up, I give up," answered the major. "You have such a way of simplifying things. And what enlargement do you expect to obtain in this way?"

"One of 48,000 times, which should bring the moon within an apparent distance of five miles; and, in order to be visible, objects need not have a diameter of more than nine feet."

"So then," cried J. T. Maston, "our projectile will be nine feet in diameter?"

"Precisely."

"Let me observe, however," interrupted Major Elphinstone, "this will involve such a weight that—"

"My dear major," replied Barbicane, "before discussing its weight permit me to enumerate some of the marvels which our ancestors have achieved in this respect. I don't mean to pretend that the science of gunnery has not advanced, but it is as well to bear in mind that during the middle ages they obtained results more surprising, I will venture to say, than ours."

"For instance?" Morgan challenged.

"Prove your point!" J. T. Maston demanded.

"Nothing could be easier," Barbicane replied. "I have all the examples I need. Thus, during the siege of Constantinople by Mahomet II, stone shot of 1,900 pounds were used, and they must have been a good size!"

"Oh, oh!" the major exclaimed, "1,900 pounds is quite a figure!"

"At Malta, in the time of the knights, there was a certain gun at the fortress of Saint Elmo that fired 2,500-pound projectiles."

"Unbelievable!"

"Finally, according to a French historian, under Louis XI, there was a mortar that fired a bomb weighing only 500 pounds, but that bomb could carry from the Bastille, a place where the insane locked up the sane, all the way to Charenton, a place where the sane confined the insane."

"Very well!" said J. T. Maston.

"And, now, what is the extent of what we have seen ourselves? Armstrong guns discharging shot of 500 pounds, and the Rodman projectiles of half a ton! It seems, then, that if projectiles have gained in range, they have lost in weight. Now, if we turn our efforts in that direction, we ought to arrive, with the progress of science, at ten times the weight of the shot of Mahomet II and the Knights of Malta."

"Clearly," replied the major; "but what metal do you calculate upon employing?"

"Simply cast iron," said General Morgan.

"Bah! Cast iron!" exclaimed J. T. Maston with profound disdain. "That is very ordinary material for a cannon-ball that is going to the moon."

"Let us not overdo it, my honorable friend," Morgan replied. "Cast iron will do very well."

"But," interrupted the major, "since the weight of a shot is proportionate to its volume, an iron ball of nine feet in diameter would be of tremendous weight."

"Yes, if it were solid, not if it were hollow."

"Hollow? then it would be a shell?"

"In which we could enclose messages," said J. T. Maston, "and samples of our earthly products!"

"Yes, a shell," replied Barbicane; "decidedly it must be. A solid shot of 108 inches would weigh more than 200,000 pounds, a weight obviously far too great. Still, as we must reserve a certain stability for our projectile, I propose to give it a weight of 20,000 pounds."

"What, then, will be the thickness of the sides?" asked the major.

"If we follow the usual proportion," replied Morgan, "a diameter of 108 inches would require sides of two feet thickness, at least."

"That would be too much," replied Barbicane; "for you will observe that what we want is not a shot intended to pierce an iron plate: it will suffice, therefore, to give it sides strong enough to resist the pressure of the gas. The problem, therefore, is this—What thickness ought a cast-iron shell to have in order not to weigh more than 20,000 pounds? Our lightning calculator, good old Maston, will soon enlighten us upon this point."

"Nothing easier," replied the worthy secretary of the committee. And he rapidly traced a few algebraical formulæ upon paper, among which π and x^2 frequently appeared. Then, after apparently extracting a cube root without any great effort, he presently said:

"The sides will require a thickness of less than two inches."

"Will that be enough?" asked the major doubtfully.

"Clearly not!" replied the president.

"What is to be done, then?" said Elphinstone, with a puzzled air.

"Employ another metal instead of iron."

"Copper?" said Morgan.

"No; that would still be too heavy. I have better than that to suggest."

"What is that?" asked the major.

"Aluminum!" replied Barbicane.

"Aluminum?" cried his three colleagues in chorus.

"Unquestionably, my friends. As you know, a famous French chemist, Henri Sainte-Claire Deville, in 1854, succeeded in producing aluminum in a compact mass. Now, this valuable metal possesses the whiteness of silver, the indestructibility of gold, the tenacity of iron, the fusibility of copper, and the lightness of glass. It is easily wrought, is very

51

widely distributed, forming the base of most rocks, is three times lighter than iron, and seems to have been created for the express purpose of furnishing us with the material for our projectile."

"Hurrah for aluminum!" shouted the secretary of the committee, who always became very loud when he was enthusiastic.

"But, my dear president," said the major, "is not the cost price of aluminum extremely high?"

"It was so at its first discovery, when it cost $260 to $280 a pound; then it came down to $27 and today it costs only $9 a pound."

"But still, $9 a pound!" replied the major, who was not willing readily to give in; "even that is an enormous price."

"Undoubtedly, my dear major; but not beyond our reach."

"What will the projectile weigh then?" asked Morgan.

"Here is the result of my calculations," replied Barbicane. "A shot of 108 inches in diameter, and twelve inches in thickness, would weigh, in cast-iron, 67,440 pounds; cast in aluminum, its weight will be reduced to 19,250 pounds."

"Fine!" Maston approved. "That fits right into our program."

"Capital!" cried the major; "but do you know that, at $9 a pound, this projectile will cost——"

"$173,250. I know it quite well. But fear not, my friends; the money will not be wanting for our enterprise, I will answer for it."

"It will come raining into our coffers," said J. T. Maston.

"Well, what do you think of aluminum now?" asked the president.

"Adopted," replied the three committee members.

"As to the shape of the shot," Barbicane continued, "it is

not of great importance. For, once outside the atmosphere, the projectile will be in a vacuum. I therefore suggest that it be a round ball, which can rotate as it pleases, and act as it sees fit."

Thus ended the first meeting of the committee. The question of the projectile had been definitely settled, and J. T. Maston was delighted to be sending an aluminum shot up to the Selenites—"as it would give them some fine idea of what Earth people are like!"

CHAPTER 8

The Story of the Cannon

THE resolutions passed at the last meeting produced a great effect in the outside world. A few timorous people took fright at the idea of a shot weighing 20,000 pounds being launched into space; they wondered what cannon could ever transmit a sufficient velocity to such a mighty mass. The minutes of the second meeting were destined triumphantly to answer such questions.

The following evening, the four members of the Gun Club again sat down before mountains of sandwiches, beside a veritable sea of tea. This time, the discussion was immediately resumed, without any preamble.

"My dear colleagues," said Barbicane, "the subject now before us is the construction of the cannon, its length, its shape, its composition, and its weight. It is probable that we shall end by giving it gigantic dimensions; but however great may be the difficulties in the way, our mechanical genius will readily surmount them. Be good enough, then, to give me your attention, and do not hesitate to make objections point-blank. I am not afraid of them."

A grunt of approval greeted this statement.

"Let us not forget," Barbicane went on, "where we had gotten in our discussion yesterday. The problem now before us is how to impart an initial speed of 12,000 yards per second to a 108-inch shell weighing 20,000 pounds."

"Yes, indeed, that is the problem," chorused Major Elphinstone.

"I go on from there," said Barbicane. "When a projectile is propelled into space, what happens? It is affected by three independent forces: the resistance of the air, the attraction of the earth, and the power of the impulsion that has been imparted to it. Let us examine these three forces. The resistance of the air will not be great, for the atmosphere of earth extends only forty miles. Now, at the proposed rate of 12,000 yards, the projectile will have traversed this in five seconds, and that time is brief enough so that the air resistance can be dismissed as trivial. Let us proceed, then, to the attraction of the earth, which is to say, the weight of the shell. We know that this weight will diminish in inverse ratio to the square of the distance. When a body left to itself falls to the surface of the earth, it falls five feet in the first second; and if the same body were removed 247,552 miles farther off, in other words, to the distance of the moon, its fall would be reduced to about 1/24 of an inch in the first second. That is almost equivalent to a state of perfect rest. Our business, then, is to overcome progressively this action of gravitation. The mode of accomplishing that is by the force of impulsion."

"There's the difficulty," broke in the major.

"True," replied the president; "but we will overcome that, for this force of impulsion that we need will depend upon the length of the cannon and the quantity of powder employed, the latter being limited only by the resisting power of the former. Our business, then, today is with the dimensions of the cannon. It is of course understood that we can set it up in conditions of almost unlimited resistance, since it does not have to be moved."

"All of that is obvious," answered the general.

"Up to now," Barbicane said, "our longest guns, the enormous Columbiads, have not exceeded twenty-five feet in length. We shall therefore astonish a great many people by the dimensions we shall be obliged to adopt."

"We certainly shall," exclaimed J. T. Maston. "I, for one, think it would be a cannon at least half a mile long!"

"Half a mile long!" protested the major and the general.

"Yes, half a mile, and it will still only be half long enough!"

"Come on, Maston," Morgan answered. "You're exaggerating."

"Not at all!" replied the ebullient secretary. "And I really don't know why you should accuse me of exaggeration."

"Because you're going too far!"

"Be informed, gentlemen," replied J. T. Maston, getting up on his high horse, "that an artilleryman is like a cannonball: he can never go too far!"

The argument was obviously getting personal, so the president intervened.

"Let us be calm, my friends, and reason this out. It must obviously be a gun of great range, since the length of the piece will increase the explosiveness of the gases accumulated beneath the projectile, but there is no advantage in going beyond certain limits."

"Quite so," said the major.

"What are the usual rules in such a case? Ordinarily the length of the barrel is 20 to 25 times the diameter of the cannon-ball, and the gun is 235 to 240 times its weight."

"That is not enough," cried J. T. Maston impetuously.

"I agree with you, my good friend; and, in fact, following this proportion for a projectile nine feet in diameter, weighing 20,000 pounds, the gun would only have a length of two hundred and twenty-five feet, and a weight of 4,800,000 pounds."

"Ridiculous!" rejoined Maston. "As well take a pistol."

"I think so too," replied Barbicane; "that is why I propose to quadruple that length, and to construct a gun nine hundred feet long."

The general and the major offered some objections; nevertheless, the proposition, actively supported by the secretary of the Gun Club, was finally adopted.

"But," said Elphinstone, "what thickness must its sides have?"

"A thickness of six feet," replied Barbicane.

"You surely don't think of mounting a mass like that upon a carriage?" asked the major.

"It would be a superb idea, though," said Maston.

"But impracticable," replied Barbicane. "No; I am thinking of casting this cannon right in the earth, binding it with hoops of wrought iron, and finally surrounding it with a thick mass of masonry of stone and cement, so that the ground around it will lend it resistance. The piece once cast, it must be bored with great precision, so as to preclude any possible windage.[1] In this way, there will be no loss whatever of gas, and all the expansive force of the powder will be employed in the propulsion."

"Hurrah! Hurrah!" shouted J. T. Maston. "Now we have our cannon."

"Not quite yet!" replied Barbicane, quieting his impatient friend with his hand.

---

[1] The space sometimes existing between the projectile and the bore.

"And why not?"

"Because we have not discussed its shape. Will it be a cannon, a howitzer, or a mortar?"

"A cannon," Morgan replied.

"A howitzer," countered the major.

"A mortar!" shouted J. T. Maston.

Another lively discussion was about to get started, with each of the three arguing for his favorite weapon, but the president stopped it cold.

"My friends," he said, "I am going to bring you all into agreement: our Columbiad will be in part all three of those arms at once. It will be a cannon, since the powder chamber will be of the same diameter as the bore. It will be a howitzer, since it will be firing a shell. Finally, it will be a mortar, since it will be pointed to an elevation of ninety degrees and, allowing for no recoil, being immovably set in the ground, it will transmit to the projectile all of the propulsive power accumulated within it."

"Adopted! Adopted!" answered the committee members.

"One simple question," said Elphinstone. "Will this can-howitzo-mortar be rifled?"

"No, certainly not," replied Barbicane; "we require enormous initial velocity, and you are well aware that the shot leaves a rifled gun much less rapidly than it does a smooth-bore."

"That's true."

"Well, anyway, we've got it, this time!" J. T. Maston repeated.

"Not quite yet," replied the president.

"And why not?"

"Because we still don't know what metal it will be made of."

"Let's decide that right now."

"That was just what I was about to suggest."

The four committee members each gulped down a dozen sandwiches followed by a bowl of tea, and the discussion resumed.

"Gentlemen," said Barbicane, "our cannon must be possessed of great tenacity, great hardness, be infusible by heat, indissoluble, and inoxydable by the corrosive action of acids."

"There is no doubt about that," replied the major; "and as we shall have to employ an immense quantity of metal, we shall not have too many to choose from."

"Well, then," said Morgan, "I propose that this Columbiad be made of the best alloy thus far known, which consists of one hundred parts of copper, twelve of tin, and six of brass."

"I admit," replied the president, "that this composition has yielded excellent results, but in the present case it would be too expensive, and very difficult to work. I think, then, that we ought to adopt an excellent but low-priced material, such as cast iron. What is your opinion, major?"

"I quite agree with you," replied Elphinstone.

"In fact," continued Barbicane, "cast iron costs ten times less than bronze; it is easy to cast, can be run readily into moulds of sand, is easy of manipulation, and is thus at once economical of money and of time. In addition, it is excellent as a material, and I well remember that during the war, at the siege of Atlanta, some iron guns fired a thousand rounds at intervals of twenty minutes without harm to them."

"Cast iron is very brittle, though," replied Morgan.

"Yes, but it possesses great resistance. Anyway, we are not going to blow it up. I promise you that."

59

"Blowing up is not necessarily a disgrace," said J. T. Maston sententiously.

"Of course not," Barbicane answered. "I will now ask our worthy secretary to calculate the weight of a cast-iron cannon 900 feet long, with a nine-foot bore, and six-foot-thick walls."

"In a trice," replied Maston.

Then, as he had done the day before, he wrote his formulae down with wondrous agility, and after a minute said:

"The cannon will weigh 68,040 tons."

"And, at two cents a pound, it will cost—?"

"$2,721,600."

Maston, the major, and the general turned worried eyes toward Barbicane.

"Well, gentlemen," said the president, "I repeat what I said yesterday. Do not be concerned. The millions will not be lacking!"

With this assurance from their president, the committee separated, after having fixed their third meeting for the following evening.

CHAPTER 9

The Question of the Powders

THERE remained for consideration merely the question of powders. The public awaited with interest its final decision. The size of the projectile, the length of the cannon being settled, what would be the quantity of powder necessary to produce impulsion? This awesome agent, whose effects man has nevertheless mastered, was going to be called upon to play a part of unusual proportions.

It is generally asserted that gunpowder was invented in the fourteenth century by the monk Schwartz, who paid for his grand discovery with his life. It is, however, pretty well proved that this story ought to be ranked among the legends of the middle ages. Gunpowder was not invented by any one; it was the lineal successor of the Greek fire, which, like itself, was composed of sulphur and saltpeter. However, since that time, these mixtures, which had been only fusing mixtures, had been turned into explosive ones.

But, while scientists are well aware of the false history of gunpower, few persons are acquainted with its mechanical power. Now this is precisely what is necessary to be understood in order to comprehend the importance of the question submitted to the committee.

A litre of gunpowder weighs two pounds; during combustion it produces 400 litres of gas. This gas, on being liberated and acted upon by temperature raised to 2,400 degrees, occupies a space of 4,000 litres: consequently the volume of powder is to the volume of gas produced by its combustion as 1 to 4,000. One may judge, therefore, of the tremendous pressure on this gas when compressed within a space 4,000 times too confined.

All this was, of course, well known to the members of the committee when they met on the following evening. Barbicane gave the floor to Major Elphinstone, who had been the director of the gunpowder factories during the war.

"Gentlemen," said this distinguished chemist, "I begin with some irrefutable figures which will serve as the basis of our calculation. The old 24-pound shot which J. T. Maston so poetically described for us required for its discharge only sixteen pounds of powder."

"You are certain of the amount?" broke in Barbicane.

"Quite certain," replied the major. "The Armstrong cannon employs only seventy-five pounds of powder for a projectile of eight hundred pounds, and the Rodman Columbiad uses only one hundred and sixty pounds of powder to send its half-ton shot a distance of six miles. These facts cannot be called into question, for I myself raised the point during the hearings of the artillery committee."

"Quite true," said the general.

"Well," continued the major, "these figures go to prove that the quantity of powder is not increased with the weight of the shot; that is to say, if a 24-pound shot requires sixteen pounds of powder;—in other words, if in ordinary guns we employ a quantity of powder equal to two-thirds of the weight of the projectile, this proportion is not constant. Calculate, and you will see that for a half-ton shot in place of three hundred and thirty-three pounds of powder, the quantity is reduced to no more than one hundred and sixty pounds."

"What are you aiming at?" asked the president.

"If you push your theory to extremes, my dear major," said J. T. Maston, "you will get to this, that as soon as your shot becomes sufficiently heavy you will not require any powder at all."

"Our friend Maston is always at his jokes, even in serious matters," cried the major; "but let him rest assured. I am going presently to propose gunpowder enough to satisfy his pride as an artilleryman. I only keep to statistical facts when I say that, during the war, and for the very largest guns, the weight of powder was reduced, as the result of experience, to a tenth of the weight of the shot."

"Perfectly correct," said Morgan; "but before deciding the quantity of powder necessary to give the impulse, I think it would be well to decide what kind it should be."

"We shall have to employ a large-grained powder," continued the major; "its combustion is more rapid than that of the small."

"No doubt about that," replied Morgan; "but it is very destructive, and ends by enlarging the bore of the pieces."

"Granted; but that which is injurious to a gun destined to perform long service is not so to our Columbiad. We shall run no danger of an explosion; and it is necessary that our powder should take fire instantaneously in order that its mechanical effect may be complete."

"We must have," said Maston, "several touch-holes, so as to fire it at different points at the same time."

"No doubt," replied Elphinstone; "but that would render

the working of the piece more difficult. I return then to my large-grained powder, which removes those difficulties."

"Right," said the general.

"For his Columbiad charges Rodman employed a powder as large as chestnuts, made of willow charcoal, simply dried in cast-iron pans. This powder was hard and glittering, left no trace upon the hand, contained hydrogen and oxygen in large proportion, took fire instantaneously, and, though very destructive, did not sensibly injure the mouth-piece."

"Well, it seems to me," replied J. T. Maston, "that there is no reason to hesitate. Our choice has been made for us."

"Unless, of course, you prefer gold powder," said the major in jest, to which his touchy friend answered by a threatening wave of his hook.

Up to this point Barbicane had kept aloof from the discussion; he let the others speak while he himself listened; he evidently had an idea. He now simply said, "Well, my friends, what quantity of powder do you propose?"

The three members looked at one another.

"Two hundred thousand pounds," at last said Morgan.

"Five hundred thousand," added the major.

"Eight hundred thousand," shouted Maston.

This time, Elphinstone did not dare accuse his friend of exaggeration. The fact was, they were planning to send a 20,000-pound projectile to the moon and to give it an initial speed of twelve thousand yards per second. A moment of silence followed the triple proposal made by the three colleagues.

It was at last broken by President Barbicane.

"Gentlemen," he said quietly, "I start from the principle that the resistance of a gun constructed under given conditions is unlimited. I shall surprise our friend Maston, then, by stigmatizing his calculations as timid; and I propose to double his 800,000 pounds of powder."

"Sixteen hundred thousand pounds?" shouted Maston, leaping up on his seat.

"Just so."

"We shall have to come then to my ideal of a cannon half a mile long."

"Of course," said the major.

"1,600,000 pounds," the secretary went on, "will occupy a space of about 22,000 cubic feet; and since the contents of your cannon do not exceed 54,000 cubic feet, it would be half full; and the bore will no longer be long enough for the gas to communicate to the projectile sufficient impulse."

There was no gainsaying this. J. T. Maston was right. They all looked at Barbicane.

"Nevertheless," said the president, "I hold to that quantity of powder. Now, 1,600,000 pounds of powder will create 6,000,000,000 litres of gas. Six thousand millions! You quite understand?"

"What is to be done then?" said the general.

"The thing is very simple; we must reduce this enormous quantity of powder, while preserving to it its mechanical power."

"Good; but by what means?"

"I am going to tell you," replied Barbicane quietly.

They all stared at him.

"Nothing is easier than to reduce this mass to one quarter of its bulk. You all know that curious matter which constitutes the elementary tissues of vegetables, known as cellulose?"

"Ah," said the major, "I am beginning to understand, Barbicane."

65

"This substance," the president went on, "is found quite pure in many bodies, especially in cotton, which is nothing more than the down of the seeds of the cotton plant. Now cotton, combined with cold nitric acid, becomes transformed into a substance eminently insoluble, combustible, and explosive. It was first discovered in 1832, by Braconnot, a French chemist, who called it xyloidine. In 1838 another Frenchman, Pelouze, investigated its different properties, and finally, in 1846, Schoenbein, professor of chemistry at Basel, proposed its employment for purposes of war. This powder is now known as nitric cotton—"

"Or pyroxylin," cut in Elphinstone.

"Or gun cotton," added Morgan.

"Is there no American name that can be signed to this discovery?" exclaimed J. T. Maston, animated by a strong feeling of national pride.

"Not a single one, unfortunately," replied the major.

"However, to keep friend Maston happy," the president went on, "it can be stated that the work of one of our countrymen is related to cellulose; for collodion, which is one of the principal agents used in photography, is simply pyroxylin dissolved in a solution of ether and alcohol, and it was discovered by Maynard, then a medical student at Boston."

"Well, hooray for Maynard and for gun cotton!" shouted the noisy secretary of the Gun Club.

"Let us get back to pyroxylin," said Barbicane. "You know of its properties, which are going to make it so useful to us. It can be prepared with the greatest facility, simply by soaking cotton for fifteen minutes in fulminating[1] nitric acid,

---

[1] So called because, upon contact with moist air, it evaporates into thick whitish fumes.

66

then washing it well with water, drying it, and that is all."

"Nothing could be more simple," said Morgan.

"Moreover, pyroxylin is unaltered by moisture—a valuable property to us, inasmuch as it would take several days to charge the cannon. It ignites at 170 degrees in place of 240, and its combustion is so rapid that one may set light to it on the top of ordinary powder, without the latter having time to ignite."

"Perfect!" exclaimed the major.

"Only it is more expensive."

"What matter?" cried J. T. Maston.

"Finally, it imparts to projectiles a velocity four times superior to that of gunpowder. I will even add that, if we mix with it one-eighth of its own weight of nitrate of potassium, its expansive force is again considerably augmented."

"Will that be necessary?" asked the major.

"I think not," replied Barbicane. "So, then, in place of 1,600,000 pounds of powder, we shall have but 400,000 pounds of cotton; and since we can, without danger, compress 500 pounds of cotton into twenty-seven cubic feet, the whole quantity will not occupy a height of more than 180 feet within the bore of the Columbiad. In this way the shot will have more than 700 feet of bore to traverse under a force of 6,000,000,000 litres of gas before taking its flight toward the moon."

At this juncture J. T. Maston could not repress his emotion; he flung himself into the arms of his friend with the violence of a projectile, and Barbicane would have been stove in if he had not been bombproof.

This incident terminated the third meeting of the committee.

Barbicane and his bold colleagues, to whom nothing

seemed impossible, had succeeded in solving the complex problems of projectile, cannon, and powder. Their plan was drawn up, and it only remained to put it in execution.

"A mere matter of detail, a bagatelle," said J. T. Maston.

N. B.—In the course of this discussion, President Barbicane attributed the invention of collodion to one of his compatriots. This is an error, however unpleasant to the worthy J. T. Maston, growing out of the similarity of two names.

In 1847, Maynard, a Boston medical student, did get the idea of using collodion as "new skin" in the treatment of wounds, but collodion had been known since 1846. It was a Frenchman, a most distinguished mind, a scholar who was at once painter, poet, philosopher, Hellenist, and chemist, M. Louis Ménard, who had the honor of being credited with its discovery.

CHAPTER 10

One Enemy out of
Twenty-five Million Friends

THE American public took a lively interest in the
smallest details of the enterprise of the Gun Club. It followed day by day the discussions of the committee. The most
simple preparation for the great experiment, the questions
of figures which it involved, the mechanical difficulties to
be resolved—in one word, the entire plan of work—roused
the popular excitement to the highest pitch.

More than a year was to go by between the beginning
of the work and its completion; but this period of time was
not to be without excitement. The site to be selected for
the emplacement, the construction of the mold, the casting
of the Columbiad, its highly dangerous loading, all of these
were more than enough to arouse public curiosity. The projectile, once fired, would be out of sight in a few tenths of a
second. After that, what would happen to it, how it would
act in outer space, the way it would get to the moon would
be seen only by a small number of privileged individuals
with their own eyes. Therefore, it was the preparation of
the experiment, the precise details of its being brought off
that constituted the real elements of public interest.

Nevertheless, the purely scientific attraction of the enterprise was suddenly heightened by the following incident:

We have seen what legions of admirers and friends Barbicane's project had rallied round its author. There was, however, one single individual alone in all the States of the Union who protested against the attempt of the Gun Club. He attacked it furiously at every opportunity, and human nature is such that Barbicane felt more keenly the opposition of that one man than he did the applause of all the others.

He was well aware of the motive of this antipathy, the origin of this solitary enmity, the cause of its personality and old standing, and in what rivalry of self-love it had its rise.

This persevering enemy the president of the Gun Club had never seen. Fortunate that it was so, for a meeting between the two men would certainly have been attended with serious consequences. This rival was a man of science, like Barbicane himself, of a fiery, daring, determined and violent disposition; a pure Yankee. His name was Captain Nicholl; he lived in Philadelphia.

Everyone is aware of the curious struggle which arose during the Civil War between the guns and the armor of iron-plated ships. The result was the entire reconstruction of the navies of the states on both continents; as the one grew heavier, the other became thicker in proportion. The *Merrimac,* the *Monitor,* the *Tennessee,* the *Weehawken* discharged enormous projectiles, after having been armor-clad against the projectiles of others. In fact they did to others that which they would not they should do to them—that grand principle of immorality upon which rests the whole art of war.

Now if Barbicane was a great caster of shot, Nicholl

was a great forger of plates; the one cast night and day at Baltimore, the other forged day and night at Philadelphia. Each followed a basically different line of thought.

As soon as Barbicane invented a new shot, Nicholl invented a new plate.

The president of the Gun Club devoted his life to making holes, the captain to keeping him from doing so. Whence a rivalry in all things, which extended to personalities. Nicholl appeared in Barbicane's dreams as a plate of impenetrable armor against which he struck in vain, and Barbicane, in Nicholl's imaginings, was a shot that ran him through.

Nevertheless, although they followed two such diverging lines, these scientists would eventually have met each other, despite all the axioms of geometry; but then, of course, it would have been on the dueling-ground. Happily for these citizens, so useful to their country, a distance of from fifty to sixty miles separated them from one another, and their friends had made sure that they had never yet met.

Which of these two inventors had the advantage over the other it was difficult to decide from the results obtained. By last accounts, however, it would seem that the armor-plate would in the end have to give way to the shot.

Nevertheless, there were competent judges who had their doubts on the point. At the last experiment the cylindro-conical projectiles of Barbicane struck like so many pins in the Nicholl plates. On that day the Philadelphia iron-forger then believed himself victorious, and could not evince contempt enough for his rival; but when the other afterward substituted for conical shot simple 600-pound shells, at very moderate velocity,[1] the captain was obliged to give in. In

---

[1] The powder used being only one-twelfth the weight of the shell.

fact, these projectiles knocked his best metal-plate to shivers.

Matters were at this stage, and victory seemed to rest with the shot, when the war came to an end on the very day when Nicholl had completed a new armor-plate of wrought steel. It was a masterpiece of its kind, and defiance to all the projectiles in the world. The captain had it conveyed to the Polygon at Washington, challenging the president of the Gun Club to break it. Barbicane, peace having been declared, declined to try the experiment.

Nicholl, now furious, offered to expose his plate to the shock of any shot, solid, hollow, round, or conical. Refused by the president, who did not choose to compromise his last success.

Nicholl, disgusted by this obstinacy, tried to tempt Barbicane by offering him every chance. He proposed to fix the plate within two hundred yards of the gun. Barbicane still obstinate in refusal. A hundred yards? Not even seventy-five!

"At fifty then!" roared the captain through the newspapers. "At twenty-five yards! and I'll stand behind it myself!"

Barbicane returned for answer that, even if Captain Nicholl were so good as to stand in front, he still would not fire.

Nicholl could not contain himself at this reply; he threw out hints of cowardice; insinuated that a man who refused to fire a cannon-shot was pretty near being afraid of it; that artillerists who fight at six miles' distance are substituting mathematical formulae for individual courage, and moreover that it took no more courage to stand behind a plate when a shot was fired than it did to do the firing.

To these insinuations Barbicane returned no answer;

72

perhaps he never heard of them, so absorbed was he in the calculations for his great enterprise.

When his famous communication was made to the Gun Club, the captain's wrath passed all bounds; with his intense jealousy was mingled a feeling of absolute impotence. How was he to invent anything to beat this 900-foot Columbiad? What armor-plate could ever resist a projectile of 20,000 pounds weight? Overwhelmed at first under this violent shock, he by and by recovered himself, and resolved to crush the proposal by the weight of his arguments.

He then violently attacked the labors of the Gun Club, published a number of letters which the newspapers carried, endeavored to undermine the scientific validity of Barbicane's works. Once the war was on, he used every type of argument, often specious and of doubtful relevance.

First of all, Barbicane's figures were attacked; Nicholl tried to prove by $A + B$ that his formulae were wrong, and accused him of being ignorant of the most rudimentary principles of gunnery. Among other things, on the basis of his own figures, Nicholl maintained that it was absolutely impossible to impress upon any body whatever a velocity of 12,000 yards per second; that algebra proved that even with such a velocity a projectile of such a weight could not transcend the limits of the earth's atmosphere. It would never rise to 25 miles. What was more, even regarding the velocity to be acquired, and granting it to be sufficient, the shell could not resist the pressure of the gas developed by the ignition of 1,600,000 pounds of powder; and supposing it to resist that pressure, it would be the less able to support that temperature; it would melt on quitting the Columbiad, and fall back in a red-hot shower upon the heads of the imprudent spectators.

Barbicane continued his work without regarding these attacks.

Nicholl then took up the question in its other aspects. Without touching upon its uselessness in all points of view, he regarded the experiment as fraught with extreme danger, both to the citizens, who might sanction by their presence so reprehensible a spectacle, and to the towns in the neighborhood of this deplorable cannon. He also observed that if the projectile did not succeed in reaching its destination (a result absolutely impossible), it must inevitably fall back upon the earth, and that the shock of such a mass, multiplied by the square of its velocity, would seriously endanger some point of the globe. Under the circumstances, therefore, and without interfering with the rights of free citizens, it was a case for the intervention of Government, which ought not to endanger the safety of all for the pleasure of one individual.

Despite these excessive claims, however, Captain Nicholl remained alone in his opinion. Nobody listened to his dire predictions. He was allowed to cry his lungs out, since that was what he wanted. But he was pleading a case that was lost in advance; he was heard, but not listened to, and he did not succeed in alienating a single admirer from the president of the Gun Club. The latter did not even take the pains to refute the arguments of his rival.

Nicholl, falling back on his final positions, and unable to do anything personally for his cause, decided to fight with money. He published, therefore, in the *Richmond Enquirer* a series of wagers, conceived in these terms, and on an increasing scale:

No. 1 ($1,000)—That the necessary funds for the experiment of the Gun Club will not be forthcoming.

No. 2 ($2,000)—That the operation of casting a cannon of 900 feet is impracticable, and cannot possibly succeed.

No. 3 ($3,000)—That it is impossible to load the Columbiad, and that the pyroxylin will take fire spontaneously under the pressure of the projectile.

No. 4 ($4,000)—That the Columbiad will burst at the first shot.

No. 5 ($5,000)—That the shot will not travel farther than six miles, and that it will fall back again a few seconds after its discharge.

It was an important sum, therefore, which the captain risked in his invincible obstinacy. He had no less than $15,000 at stake.

Notwithstanding the importance of the challenge, on the 19th of October he received a sealed envelope containing the following superbly laconic reply:

BALTIMORE, October 18

DONE

BARBICANE

CHAPTER 11

Florida and Texas

ONE question yet remained to be decided; it was necessary to choose a favorable spot for the experiment. According to the advice of the Observatory of Cambridge, the gun must be fired perpendicularly to the plane of the horizon, that is to say, toward the zenith. Now the moon does not traverse the zenith, except in places situated between 0° and 28° of latitude, in other words, its declination was only 28°. It became, then, necessary to determine exactly that spot on the globe where the immense Columbiad should be cast.

On the 20th of October, at a general meeting of the Gun Club, Barbicane produced a magnificent map of the United States by Z. Belltropp. But, before he had time to unfold it, J. T. Maston had asked for the floor with his habitual vehemence and begun to speak as follows:

"Worthy colleagues, the question before us today is one of true national importance, and it will allow us a chance for great proof of our patriotism."

The members of the Gun Club looked at each other, not knowing what the speaker was driving at.

"None of you," he went on, "would dream of compromising the glory of our country, and if there is one thing the Union is entitled to, it is to contain within its borders the formidable cannon of the Gun Club. Now, under present circumstances—"

"Good old Maston," said the president.

"Allow me to pursue my thought," the speaker continued. "In the present circumstances, we are forced to select a site rather close to the Equator, so that the experiment can be carried out in the best conditions—"

"If you will allow me—," said Barbicane.

"I insist on a full and free airing of ideas," replied the fiery Maston, "and I insist that the territory from which our glorious projectile is launched must belong to the Union."

"Without question!" a few members replied.

"Well then, since our frontiers are not extensive enough, since on the south the ocean presents an impassable barrier to us, since we must seek outside the United States but within a bordering country for the twenty-eighth parallel, that is a legitimate *casus belli,* and I propose that we forthwith declare war on Mexico!"

"No! No!" came the reply from all sides.

"No, indeed!" retorted J. T. Maston. "That is a word that I am surprised to hear within these precincts!"

"Hear us out!"

"Never! Never!" the impassioned orator went on. "Sooner or later this war will have to be fought, and I demand that it be declared this very day!"

"Maston," Barbicane said, noisily pounding his bell, "you no longer have the floor!"

Maston wanted to make an answer, but several of his colleagues succeeded in holding him back.

"I agree," said Barbicane, "that this experiment cannot

and ought not to be tried anywhere but within the limits of the soil of the Union, and if my impatient friend had allowed me to speak, if he had cast his eyes upon a map, he would have known that there is no reason to declare war on our neighbors, for certain frontiers of the United States extend beyond the twenty-eighth parallel. You see, we have at our disposal the whole of the southern portion of Texas and Florida."

The incident was closed; yet, it was not without regret that J. T. Maston gave in. And it was agreed, therefore, that the Columbiad must be cast on the soil of either Texas or Florida. The result, however, of this decision was to create a rivalry entirely without precedent between the different towns of these two States.

The 28th parallel, on reaching the American coast, traverses the peninsula of Florida, dividing it into two nearly equal portions. Then, plunging into the Gulf of Mexico, it subtends the arc formed by the coast of Alabama, Mississippi, and Louisiana; then skirting Texas, off which it cuts an angle, it continues its course over Mexico, crosses Sonora and Lower California, and loses itself in the Pacific Ocean. It was, therefore, only those portions of Texas and Florida which were situated below this parallel which came within the conditions of latitude prescribed by the Cambridge Observatory.

Florida, in its southern part, reckons no cities of importance; it is simply studded with forts raised against the roving Indians. One solitary town, Tampa Town, was able to put in a claim in favor of its situation.

In Texas, on the contrary, the towns are much more numerous and important. Corpus Christi, in the county of Nueces, and all the cities situated on the Rio Bravo, Laredo,

Captain Nicholl proves the impossibility o
firing a projectile to the moo

...STRONAUTS SWING INTO MOON ORBIT
N PREPARATIO... ...DAY'S LANDING

...alk the Moon

...s exposed himself to a variety of hostile
...nts. He has scaled the loftiest peaks, where
...o thin it can barely sustain life. He has de-
...o the ocean floor where, under great pres-
...must breathe a special mixture of gases.
...ver, has anyone set foot on such alien ter-
...at which Astronauts Armstrong and Aldrin
...ence early tomorrow.

...ere is no air, they will be unable to hear
...'s voices except by radio. Even at close
...out could not travel from one man to the
...a meteorite crashes nearby the astronauts
...nothing, even though the ground trembles
...feet.

...ence of air makes for harsh contrasts.
...grour
...nlight

CITIES AND STATES AGREE WITH U.S. ON FUND SHARING

Informal Compromise Gives
Each Entity a Portion
of Federal Revenues

By EDWIN L. DALE JR.

Evolution Into Space

In a world long given to marking off its historical
progress in periods—the Age of Faith, the Renaissance,
the Age of Reason, the Industrial Revolution—language seems too impoverished to encompass so neatly
the era that begins with man's first walk on the
moon. As a term, the Space Age is grossly inadequate
failing completely to convey the nature of the change
that this event portends. For the lunar landing of the
astronauts is more than a step in history; it is a step
in evolution.

The journey of Neil Armstrong and his companions
cannot be viewed... ...perspective as the
voyage of Col... ...traveler in re-
...th, Coumbus's
...ze than Arm-

CREWMEN EAGER

NASA Aides See No
Obstacles in the Way
of Touchdown

By JO...
HOU...

Man on th...

A Fate...

HOUSTON—If the
...u'e carrying two Am...
...nauts lands safely o...
...this afternoon, it w...
...ably be a land...
...h-stor...
...cept proved, we m...
...portior...
...witness...

...ASTING HOMEWARD
...EARTH'S GRAVITY
...AMMOTH... ...LCOM...
...na... Trips...

Queen of the Night

No matter what they bring back from t...
men who arrive here today will not alte...
light that has fascinated man and warme...
since he first took sh...

...ow that the moon is res...
...ean's tides but for an ea...
...flows.

October moon, January n...
...of visions and poems.

IN THE U...

Ast...
A...

rn 5: 'M...str...

Most Po...al
...rgest in

...M A. MRAZEK

...vide the then unprec...
...1.5 million pounds.
" This jerry-built rig...
...to the side of a m...
...crete test stand, it...
...and thunder from a...
...the first time on Apr...
...cept proved, we...
...it fly.

Since the Satu...
...purely as a resear...
...fort, there was no...
...there were no plans...
...Our cost-consciousness caused us to rec-
...ognize the value of re-using such an ex-
...pensive piece of equipment, rather than
...discarding it in the ocean after depletion
...of its fuel and separation from the sec-
...ond stage. So we drew up plans for...
...parachute recovery of this rather larg...
...first stage. All these diverse requir...
...ments kept the design engineers on th...
...toes.

At the Pad, E...
Is a 5-Month...

By ROCCO A...

THE liftoff of an Apollo space vehicle with three men aboard is an
awesome "moment of truth," but it h...

of France, who
...wrote ...dest and most
...astronomics.

(1880-1944),
...made theoretical
...required for the
...the moon and
...course, is indi-
...ssion plan
...lunar fli...
...landing

...of what had lon...
...gravity ...had ta...
...rote ...an had...
...and Goddard an equal...
...eikovsky was an obscure Rus...
...and Friedrich A...Tsander...

...MOON
...nnedLunar... ...nding

...moon ...been studied in vacuum chambers at the...

...42, a 46-
...d liquid o...
...ered into
...ic shore.
...master pi...
...who h...
...their c...
...ovsky, th...
...age of m...
...1944 th...
...h called
...lled "bu...
...ction o...
...nce-Wea...
...V-2 app...
...War II.
...ances
...arheads.
...st men
...s after t...
...ed the V...
...nt prog...
...les
...ne Amer...
...express...
...A-I an...
...s were
...manne...
...or Pro...
...A-I fo...
...th had
...alized
...al and
...nned

MERCURY-   MERCURY-   GEMINI-   POSEIDON
REDSTONE   ATLAS   TITAN 2

to...

...the Apo...
...ically "flew
...r in an ov...
...gs In." Th...
...the groun...
...During th...
...tion in flight—every valve...
...d sensor—is activated t...
...it it operates the way it...
...to and on the proper tim...
...we have the space vehicle...

Best Wishes
To
APOLLO 11

Comalites, San Ignacio in Webb County, Roma and Rio Grande City in Starr County, Edinburgh in Hidalgo, Santa Rita, El Panda, Brownsville in Cameron, formed an imposing league against the pretensions of Florida.

So, scarcely was the decision known, when the Texas and Florida delegates arrived at Baltimore in an incredibly short space of time. From that moment on President Barbicane and the influential members of the Gun Club were besieged day and night by formidable claims. If seven cities of Greece contended for the honor of having given birth to Homer, here were two entire States threatening to come to blows over a cannon.

The rival parties promenaded the streets with arms in their hands; and at every occasion of their meeting a collision was to be apprehended which might have been attended with disastrous results. Happily the prudence and skill of President Barbicane averted the danger. These personal demonstrations found a division in the newspapers of the different States. The *New York Herald* and the *Tribune* supported Texas, while the *Times* and the *American Review* espoused the cause of the Florida delegates. The members of the Gun Club could not decide to which to give the preference.

Texas produced its array of twenty-six counties; Florida replied that twelve counties were better than twenty-six in a State only one-sixth the size.

Texas plumed itself upon its 330,000 natives; Florida, with a far smaller territory, boasted of being much more densely populated with 56,000. Moreover, it accused Texas of being a hotbed of malarial fevers which, year in and year out, cost the lives of several thousands of inhabitants. Which was true.

79

Texas, in turn, replied that when it came to fevers Florida could easily hold its own, and that at the very least it was ill-becoming to call other areas unwholesome when one had the honor of being afflicted with *vomito negro* in a chronic state. Which was equally true.

"Besides," claimed the Texans through the columns of the *New York Herald,* "some regard should be given a state which grew the best cotton in all America, produced the best green oak for the service of the navy, and contained the finest oil besides iron mines in which the yield was fifty per cent pure metal."

To this the *American Review* replied that the soil of Florida, although not equally rich, afforded the best conditions for the molding and casting of the Columbiad, consisting as it did of sand and clay soil.

"That may be all very well," replied the Texans; "but you must first get to this country. Now the communications with Florida are difficult, while the coast of Texas offers the bay of Galveston, which possesses a circumference of fourteen leagues, and is capable of containing the navies of the entire world!"

"A pretty notion truly," replied the papers in the interest of Florida, "that of Galveston Bay *below the 29th parallel!* Have we not got the bay of Espiritu Santo, opening precisely upon *the 28th degree,* and by which ships can reach Tampa Town by direct route?"

"A fine bay! half choked with sand!"

"Choked yourselves!" returned the others. "Next you'll be saying we're a country of savages."

"Well, the Seminoles still infest your prairies!"

"And your Apaches and Comanches are civilized, eh?"

Thus the war went on for several days, when Florida endeavored to draw her adversary away on to fresh ground; and one morning the *Times* hinted that, the enterprise being "essentially American," it ought not to be attempted upon other than "purely American territory."

To these words Texas retorted, "American! are we not as much so as you? Were not Texas and Florida both incorporated into the Union in 1845?"

"Undoubtedly," replied the *Times;* "but we have belonged to the Americans ever since 1820."

"Yes!" returned the *Tribune;* "after having been Spaniards or English for two hundred years, you were sold to the United States for five million dollars!"

"Well! and why need we blush for that? Was not Louisiana bought from Napoleon in 1803 at the price of sixteen million dollars?"

"Scandalous!" roared the Texas delegates. "A wretched little strip of country like Florida to dare to compare itself to Texas, who, in place of selling herself, asserted her own independence, drove out the Mexicans on March 2, 1836, and declared herself a federal republic after the victory gained by Samuel Houston, on the banks of the San Jacinto, over the troops of Santa Anna!—a country, in fine, which voluntarily annexed itself to the United States of America!"

"Because it was afraid of the Mexicans!" said Florida.

"Afraid!" From the moment this word was used the state of things became intolerable. A sanguinary encounter seemed daily imminent between the two parties in the streets of Baltimore. It became necessary to keep an eye upon the delegates.

President Barbicane knew not which way to look. Notes, documents, letters full of menaces showered down upon his house. Which side ought he to take? As regarded the appropriation of the soil, the facility of communication, the rapidity of transport, the claims of both States were evenly balanced. As for political prepossessions, they had nothing to do with the question.

This dead block had existed for some little time, when Barbicane resolved to get rid of it at once. He called a meeting of his colleagues, and laid before them a proposition which, it will be seen, was profoundly sagacious.

"On carefully considering," he said, "what is going on now between Florida and Texas, it is clear that the same difficulties will recur with all the towns of the favored State. The rivalry will descend from State to city, and so on downward. Now Texas possesses eleven towns within the prescribed conditions which will further fight over the honor and create more troubles for us, while Florida has only one. So, let us go for Florida and Tampa Town."

This decision, on being made known, utterly crushed the Texas delegates. Seized with an indescribable fury, they addressed threatening letters to the different members of the Gun Club by name. The Baltimore authorities had but one course to take, and they took it. They chartered a special train, forced the Texans into it whether they would or no; and they were sent from the city at a speed of thirty miles an hour.

Quickly, however, as they were despatched, they found time to hurl one last and bitter sarcasm at their adversaries.

Alluding to the narrowness of Florida, a mere peninsula confined between two seas, they claimed that it could never sustain the shock of the discharge, and that it would "blow up" at the very first shot.

"Very well, let it blow up!" replied the Floridians, with a brevity worthy of the days of ancient Sparta.

CHAPTER 12

Urbi et Orbi

THE astronomical, mechanical, and topographical difficulties resolved, finally came the question of finance. The sum required was far too great for any individual, or even any single State, to provide the requisite millions.

President Barbicane undertook, in spite of the matter being a purely American affair, to render it one of universal interest, and to request the financial co-operation of all peoples. It was, he maintained, the right and duty of the whole earth to interfere in the affairs of its satellite. The subscription opened at Baltimore extended properly to the whole world—*Urbi et orbi*.

This subscription was successful beyond all expectation; notwithstanding that it was a question not of lending but of giving the money. It was a purely disinterested operation in the strictest sense of the term, and offered not the slightest chance of profit.

The effect, however, of Barbicane's communication was not confined to the frontiers of the United States; it crossed the Atlantic and Pacific, invading simultaneously Asia and Europe, Africa and Oceania. The observatories of the Union placed themselves in immediate communication with those of foreign countries. Some, such as those of Paris, Petersburg, Capetown, Berlin, Altona, Stockholm, Hamburg, Buda, Bologna, Malta, Lisbon, Benares, Madras, Peking and others, transmitted their good wishes; the rest maintained a prudent silence, quietly awaiting the result.

As for the observatory at Greenwich, seconded as it was by the twenty-two astronomical establishments of Great Britain, it spoke plainly enough. It boldly denied the possibility of success, and pronounced in favor of the theories of Captain Nicholl. So that, while various learned societies promised to send delegates to Tampa Town, the Greenwich staff, in meeting assembled, brutally dismissed the Barbicane proposal. But this was nothing more than British jealousy.

On the whole, the effect was excellent in the scientific world, and from there went on to the masses who, in general, took a passionate interest in the question; which was of the highest importance, since the masses were going to be called upon to subscribe a considerable capital.

On the 8th of October President Barbicane published a manifesto full of enthusiasm, in which he made an appeal to "all men of good will upon the face of the earth." This document, translated into all languages, met with immense success.

Subscription lists were opened in all the principal cities of the Union, with a central office at the Baltimore Bank, 9 Baltimore Street.

In addition, subscriptions were received at the following banks in the different states of the two continents:

At Vienna, S. M. de Rothschild
At Petersburg, Stieglitz and Co.

At Paris, The Crédit Mobilier
At Stockholm, Tottie and Arfuredson
At London, N. M. Rothschild and Son
At Turin, Ardouin and Co.
At Berlin, Mendelssohn
At Geneva, Lombard, Odier and Co.
At Constantinople, The Ottoman Bank
At Brussels, S. Lambert
At Madrid, Daniel Weisweller
At Amsterdam, Netherlands Credit Co.
At Rome, Torlonia and Co.
At Lisbon, Lecesne
At Copenhagen, Private Bank
At Buenos Aires, Maua Bank
At Rio de Janeiro, Maua Bank
At Montevideo, Maua Bank
At Valparaiso and Lima, Thos. La Chambre and Co.
At Mexico, Martin Daran and Co.

Three days after President Barbicane's manifesto $4,000,-000 had been paid into the different towns of the Union. With such a balance the Gun Club might begin operations at once.

But some days later advices were received to the effect that the foreign subscriptions were being eagerly taken up. Certain countries distinguished themselves by their liberality; others untied their pursestrings with less facility—matter of temperament.

Figures are, however, more eloquent than words, and here is the official statement of the sums which were paid in to the credit of the Gun Club at the close of the subscription.

Russia paid in as her contingent the enormous sum of 368,733 rubles. No one need be surprised at this, who bears in mind the scientific taste of the Russians, and the impetus which they have given to astronomical studies—thanks to their numerous observatories, the greatest of which cost two million rubles.

France began by deriding the pretensions of the Americans. The moon served as a pretext for a thousand stale puns and a score of ballads, in which bad taste contested the palm with ignorance. But just as formerly the French had paid after singing, so now they paid after having had their laugh, and they subscribed for a sum of 1,253,930 francs. At that price they had a right to enjoy themselves a little.

Austria showed herself quite generous in the midst of her financial crisis. Her public contributions amounted to the sum of 216,000 florins—a perfect godsend.

Fifty-two thousand rix-dollars were the remittance of Sweden and Norway; the amount is large for the country, but it would undoubtedly have been considerably increased had the subscription been opened in Christiania simultaneously with that at Stockholm. For some reason or other the Norwegians do not like to send their money to Sweden.

Prussia, by a remittance of 250,000 thalers, testified her high approval of the enterprise. Her various observatories enthusiastically subscribed money and were among the foremost to encourage President Barbicane.

Turkey behaved generously; but she had a personal interest in the matter. The moon, in fact, regulates the cycle of her years and her fast of Ramadan. She could not do less than give 1,372,640 piastres; and she gave them with an eagerness which denoted, however, some pressure on the part of the government.

Belgium distinguished herself among the second-rate

states by a grant of 513,000 francs—about twelve centimes (or two cents) per head of her population.

Holland and her colonies interested themselves to the extent of 110,000 florins, only asking an allowance of five per cent discount for cash.

Denmark, a little contracted in territory, gave nevertheless 9,000 ducats, proving her love for scientific experiments.

The Germanic Confederation pledged itself to 34,285 florins. It was impossible to ask for more; besides, they would not have given it.

Though very much crippled, Italy found 200,000 lire in the pockets of her people, by turning them inside out. If she had had Venetia she would have done better; but she did not have Venetia.

The States of the Church thought that they could not send less than 7,040 Roman crowns; and Portugal carried her devotion to science as far as 30,000 cruzados.

As for Mexico, it was the widow's mite—eighty-six piastres; but empires in the making are always rather short of money.

Two hundred and fifty-seven francs, this was the modest contribution of Switzerland to the American work. One must freely admit that Switzerland did not see any practical side to the matter. It did not seem to her that the mere despatch of a shot to the moon could possibly establish business relations with her; and it did not seem prudent to her to embark her capital in so hazardous an enterprise. After all, perhaps she was right.

As to Spain, she could not scrape together more than 110 reals. She gave as an excuse that she had her railways to finish. The truth is, that science is not very favorably regarded in that country. It is still a backward state; and, moreover, certain Spaniards, not by any means the least educated, did not form a correct estimate of the bulk of the projectile compared with that of the moon. They feared that it would disturb the established order of things and bring it crashing into Earth. In that case it were better to keep aloof; which they did, except for a few reals.

There remained but England; and we know the contemptuous antipathy with which she received Barbicane's proposition. The English have but one soul for the whole twenty-five million inhabitants which Great Britain contains. They hinted that the enterprise of the Gun Club was contrary to the "principle of non-intervention." And they did not subscribe a single farthing.

At this intimation the Gun Club merely shrugged its shoulders and returned to its great work. When South America, that is to say, Peru, Chile, Brazil, the provinces of La Plata and Colombia, had poured their quota into its hands, the sum of $300,000, it found itself in possession of a considerable capital, of which the following is a statement:

United States subscriptions. . . . $4,000,000
Foreign subscriptions. 1,446,675

Total. $5,446,675

Such was the sum which the public poured into the treasury of the Gun Club.

Let no one be surprised at the vastness of the amount. The work of casting, boring, masonry, the transport of workmen, their establishment in an almost uninhabited country, the construction of furnaces and workshops, the plant, the powder, the projectile, and incidental expenses, would, according to the estimates, absorb nearly the whole. Certain cannon-shots in the Civil War cost one thousand dollars apiece. This one of President Barbicane's, unique in the annals of gunnery, might well cost five thousand times more.

On the 20th of October a contract was entered into with the manufactory at Cold Spring, near New York, which during the war had furnished Parrott with his largest cast-iron guns.

It was stipulated between the contracting parties that the manufactory of Cold Spring should transport to Tampa Town, in southern Florida, the necessary materials for casting the Columbiad. The work was bound to be completed at latest by the 15th of October following, and the cannon delivered in good condition under penalty of a forfeit of one hundred dollars a day to the moment when the moon should again present herself under the same conditions—that is to say, in eighteen years and eleven days. The engagement of the workmen, their pay, and all the necessary details of the work, devolved upon the Cold Spring Company.

This contract, executed in duplicate, was signed by I. Barbicane, president of the Gun Club, and T. Murchison, director of the Cold Spring manufactory, who thus executed the deed on behalf of their respective principals.

CHAPTER 13

Stone Hill

WHEN the decision was arrived at by the Gun Club, to the disparagement of Texas, every one in America, where reading is a universal acquirement, set to work to study the geography of Florida. Never before had there been such a sale for works like Bertram's *Travels in Florida*, Roman's *Natural History of East and West Florida*, Williams' *Territory of Florida*, and *Cleland on the Cultivation of the Sugar-Cane in Florida*. It became necessary to issue fresh editions of these works. They sold madly.

Barbicane had something better to do than to read. He desired to see things with his own eyes, and to mark the exact position of the proposed gun. So, without a moment's loss of time, he placed at the disposal of the Cambridge Observatory the funds necessary for the construction of a telescope, and entered into negotiations with the house of Breadwill and Co., of Albany, for the construction of an aluminum projectile of the required size. He then left Baltimore, accompanied by J. T. Maston, Major Elphinstone, and the manager of the Cold Spring factory.

On the following day, the four fellow-travelers arrived at New Orleans. There they immediately embarked on board the *Tampico,* a despatch-boat belonging to the Federal navy, which the government had placed at their disposal; and, getting up steam, the Louisiana coast speedily disappeared from sight.

The passage was not long. Two days after starting, the *Tampico,* having made four hundred and eighty miles, came in sight of the coast of Florida. On a nearer approach Barbicane found himself in view of a low, flat country of somewhat barren aspect. After coasting along a series of coves abounding in lobsters and oysters, the *Tampico* entered the bay of Espiritu Santo.

This bay is divided into two elongated harbors, Tampa and Hillsborough, and the steamer was soon through its neck. A short time later, the commanding batteries of Fort Brooke could be seen above the water, and the town of Tampa appeared, lying lazily at the end of the small natural port formed by the mouth of the Hillsborough River.

This was where she finally anchored, at seven P.M. on the 22nd of October. Our four passengers disembarked at once.

Barbicane could feel his heart beat violently as he stepped down on Florida soil; he appeared to be testing it with his foot, as an architect does to measure the solidity of a house. J. T. Maston scratched the earth with the end of his hook.

"Gentlemen," Barbicane then said, "we have no time to lose; tomorrow we must obtain horses, and proceed to reconnoiter the country."

Barbicane had scarcely set his foot on shore when the three thousand inhabitants of Tampa Town came forth to meet him, an honor due to the president who had favored them by his choice. They received him with impressive acclaim; but declining every kind of ovation, Barbicane ensconced himself in a room of the Franklin Hotel. He was not suited to the role of famous man.

The next day, October 23rd, some of those small horses of the Spanish breed, full of vigor and of fire, stood snorting under his windows; but instead of four steeds, here were fifty, together with their riders. Barbicane descended with his three fellow-travelers; and much astonished were they all to find themselves in the midst of such a cavalcade. He remarked that every horseman carried a carbine slung across his shoulders and pistols in his holsters. On expressing his surprise at these preparations, he was speedily enlightened by a young Floridian, who quietly said:

"Sir, there are Seminoles there."

"What do you mean by Seminoles?"

"Savages who roam the prairies. We thought it best, therefore, to escort you on your road."

"Pooh!" cried J. T. Maston, mounting his steed.

"All right," said the Floridian; "but it is safer this way."

"Gentlemen," answered Barbicane, "I thank you for your kind attention; but it is time to be off."

The small troop left immediately and disappeared in a cloud of dust. It was five A.M.; the sun was up already and the temperature was 84 degrees; but cool sea breezes kept this excessive heat down.

Barbicane, on leaving Tampa Town, made his way south along the coast in the direction of Alifia Creek. This little river falls into Hillsborough Bay twelve miles below Tampa Town. Barbicane and his escort skirted its right bank to the eastward. Soon the waves of the bay disappeared behind a bend of rising ground, and the Florida countryside alone offered itself to view.

Florida is made up of two parts: the northern one, more

populated, less wild, has Tallahassee as its capital and boasts Pensacola, one of the main naval arsenals of the United States; the other, caught between the Atlantic and the Gulf of Mexico whose waters press it on either side, is but a narrow peninsula gnawed at by the Gulf Stream, a point of land lost out in the middle of a small archipelago, with the numerous craft in the Bahama Channel constantly going back and forth along it. It is the forward sentinel of the gulf for tropical storms. The area of the State is 38,033,267 acres, among which the aim was to select one located this side of the twenty-eighth parallel and suitable to the undertaking at hand. Therefore, Barbicane, as he rode along, attentively examined the configuration of the soil and its special qualities.

Florida, discovered on Palm Sunday, in 1512, by Juan Ponce de Leon, was originally named *Pascha Florida* (or Flowering Easter). It little deserved that designation, with its dry and parched coasts. But a few miles in from the coast the nature of the soil gradually changes and the country shows itself worthy of the name. The earth is dotted with a network of creeks, rios, waterways, ponds, and little lakes; one might take it for Holland or Guiana. But the countryside rises gently and cultivated plains soon appear, where are united all the productions of the northern and tropical floras, terminating in prairies abounding with pineapples and yams, tobacco, rice, cotton-plants, and sugar-canes, which extend beyond reach of sight, flinging their riches broadcast with careless prodigality.

Barbicane appeared highly pleased on observing the progressive elevation of the land; and in answer to a question of J. T. Maston, replied:

"My worthy friend, we cannot do better than sink our Columbiad in these high grounds."

"To get nearer to the moon, perhaps?" said the secretary of the Gun Club.

"Not exactly," replied Barbicane, smiling. "A few yards make little difference. But do you not see that among these elevated plateaus we shall have a much easier work of it? No struggles with the watersprings, which will save us long and expensive tubings; and that is a consideration, for we will have to sink a well some nine hundred feet deep."

"You are right," said the engineer Murchison. "As much as possible, we must avoid waterways during the digging; but if we do come across some springs, that will be no obstacle; we will pump them out with our machines, or go around them. What we have here is not an Artesian well,[1] narrow and dark, in which drill, casing, probe, and all the other digger's tools work in the dark. No. We will be working beneath an open sky, out in the daylight, pick and shovel in hand, and, with blasting to help us, we will move forward quickly."

"Nevertheless," Barbicane countered, "if the elevation or character of the ground allows us to avoid a struggle with underground waters, the work will be faster and more perfect; so let us try to cut our trench somewhere that is a few hundred yards above sea level."

"You are right, Mr. Barbicane, and, if I mistake not, we shall ere long find a suitable spot for our purpose."

"I wish we were at the first stroke of the pickaxe," said the president.

"And I wish we were at the *last!*" cried J. T. Maston.

"We will get there, gentlemen," answered the engineer. "And, believe me, Cold Spring will not have to pay you any delay indemnity."

---

[1] It took nine years to dig the 1,794-foot-deep well at Grenelle.

Barbicane and his associates expl(
the launching s

"By heaven! You have to be right!" replied J. T. Maston. "A hundred dollars a day until the moon returns under the same conditions, in other words for eighteen years and eleven days: do you realize that comes to $658,100?"

"No, sir," said the engineer. "We do not realize it, and will never have occasion to find out."

About ten A.M. the little band had crossed a dozen miles. Fertile plains were succeeded by a region of forests. There perfumes of the most varied kinds mingled together in tropical profusion. These almost impenetrable forests were composed of pomegranate, orange, lemon, fig, olive, apricot and banana trees, and huge vines, whose blossoms and fruits rivaled each other in color and perfume. Beneath the odorous shade of these magnificent trees fluttered and warbled a little world of brilliantly plumaged birds, among which one especially noticed the crab-eaters, whose nests should be jewel-boxes to be worthy of these feathered gems.

J. T. Maston and the major could not repress their admiration on finding themselves in the presence of the glorious beauties of this wealth of nature. President Barbicane, however, less sensitive to these wonders, was in haste to press forward; the very luxuriance of the country was displeasing to him. Although scarcely hydroscopic, he could sense the water beneath his feet, and kept looking in vain for signs of absolute aridity. Yet they pressed onward, and were compelled to ford several rivers, not without danger, for they were infested with huge alligators from fifteen to eighteen feet long. Maston courageously menaced them with his steel hook, but he only succeeded in frightening some of the pelicans, teal, and tropic birds, the wild inhabitants of these waters, while tall red flamingos stared stupidly at the party.

At length these denizens of the swamps disappeared in their turn; smaller trees became thinly scattered among less dense thickets—a few isolated groups detached in the midst of endless plains over which ranged herds of startled deer.

"At last," cried Barbicane, rising in his stirrups, "here we are at the region of pines!"

"Yes! and of savages, too," replied the major.

In fact, some Seminoles had just come in sight upon the horizon; they rode violently backward and forward on their fleet horses, brandishing their spears or discharging their guns with a dull report. These hostile demonstrations, however, had no effect upon Barbicane and his companions.

They were then occupying the center of a rocky plain, a huge open space of several acres, which the sun scorched with its parching rays. This was formed by a considerable elevation of the soil, which seemed to offer to the members of the Gun Club all the conditions requisite for the construction of their Columbiad.

"Halt!" said Barbicane, reining up. "Does this place have a local name?"

"It is called Stone Hill," replied one of the Floridians.

Barbicane, without saying a word, dismounted, seized his instruments, and began to note his position with extreme exactness. The little band, drawn up in rear, watched his proceedings in profound silence.

At this moment the sun passed the meridian. Barbicane, after a few moments, rapidly wrote down the result of his observations, and said:

"This spot is situated eighteen hundred feet above the level of the sea, in 2° 7′ N. lat. and 5° 7′ W. long. of the meridian of Washington. It appears to me by its rocky and barren character to offer all the conditions requisite for our experiment. On that plain will be raised our magazines, workshops, furnaces, and workmen's huts; and here, from this very spot," said he, stamping his foot on the summit of Stone Hill, "hence shall our projectile take its flight into the regions of the Solar World."

CHAPTER 14

Pickaxe and Trowel

THE same evening Barbicane and his companions returned to Tampa Town; and Murchison, the engineer, re-embarked on board the *Tampico* for New Orleans. His object was to enlist an army of workmen, and to bring back the greater part of the materials. The members of the Gun Club remained at Tampa Town, for the purpose of setting on foot the preliminary works by the aid of the people of the country.

Eight days after its departure, the *Tampico* returned into the bay of Espiritu Santo, with a whole flotilla of steamboats. Murchison had succeeded in assembling together fifteen hundred artisans. In the old bad days of slavery, he would have been wasting his time and efforts. But since America, land of liberty, had only free men among its people, the latter hastened anywhere that well-retributed employment called. And the Gun Club was not short on money; it offered its men high pay, with considerable proportionate bonuses. The workman hired for Florida could anticipate, after the end of the job, an account in his name in a Baltimore bank. Murchison had only to choose among them, and could be demanding on the score of intelligence and skill. It can be believed that he enlisted a choice legion of stokers, iron-founders, lime-burners, miners, brickmakers, and artisans of every trade, without distinction of color. As many of these people brought their families with them, it was a veritable emigration.

On the 31st of October, at ten o'clock in the morning, the troop disembarked on the quays of Tampa Town; and one may imagine the activity which pervaded that little town, whose population was thus doubled in a single day. Indeed, Tampa Town was to benefit enormously from the initiative of the Gun Club, not because of the number of the workmen, who were sent directly to Stone Hill, but thanks to the influx of the curious who gradually converged on to the Florida peninsula from every point of the globe.

During the first few days they were busy discharging the cargo brought by the flotilla, the machines, and the rations, as well as a large number of huts constructed of iron plates, separately pieced and numbered. At the same time Barbicane laid the first ties for a fifteen-mile-long railway, intended to link Stone Hill and Tampa Town.

The way in which American railways are built is well known. Twisting whimsically, climbing any grade, scornful of guard-rails and engineering works as it goes up hill and down dale, the railroad runs blindly along without concern for the straight line. It is not costly, it does not get in the way. However, it has derailments and accidents to the heart's content. The road from Tampa Town to Stone Hill was a mere bagatelle, and cost neither much money nor much time to set up.

Besides, Barbicane was the very soul of all these people assembled at his call. He animated them, imparted his breath, his enthusiasm, his conviction to them. He was everywhere at once, as if gifted with ubiquity, and always flanked by J. T. Maston, his buzzing fly. His practical mind suggested a thousand inventions. To him, there were no obstacles, no difficulties, never an embarrassment; he was miner, mason, mechanic as much as artilleryman, with an answer for every question and a solution to every problem. He kept up an active correspondence with the Gun Club and Cold Spring, and day and night, its lights on, its boilers stoked up, the *Tampico* lay at anchor in the harbor of Hillsborough awaiting his orders.

On the first of November Barbicane left Tampa Town with a detachment of workmen and on the following day a whole town of huts was erected round Stone Hill. This they enclosed with palisades; and in respect of energy and activity, it might have shortly been mistaken for one of the great cities of the Union. Everything was placed under a complete system of discipline, and the works were commenced in most perfect order.

The nature of the soil having been carefully examined, by means of repeated borings, the work of excavation was fixed for the 4th of November.

On that day Barbicane called together his foremen and addressed them as follows: "You are well aware, my friends, of the object with which I have assembled you together in this wild part of Florida. Our business is to construct a cannon measuring nine feet in its interior diameter, six feet thick, and with a stone revetment of nineteen and a half feet in thickness. We have, therefore, a well of sixty feet in diameter to dig down to a depth of nine hundred feet. This great work must be completed within eight months, so that you have 2,543,400 cubic feet of earth to excavate in 255 days; that is to say, in round numbers, 10,000 cubic feet per day.

What would present no difficulty to a thousand workmen laboring in open country will be of course more troublesome in a comparatively confined space. However, the thing must be done, and I reckon for its accomplishment upon your courage as much as upon your skill."

At eight o'clock in the morning the first stroke of the pickaxe was struck upon the soil of Florida; and from that moment that prince of tools was never inactive for one moment in the hands of the excavators. The gangs relieved each other in four shifts per day.

In truth, colossal though the operation was, it was not beyond the limit of human strength. Far from it. How many more truly difficult enterprises, in which the elements had to be struggled with directly, have been successfully brought off! To mention only comparable works, there is "Father Joseph's Well," built near Cairo by Sultan Saladin, at a time when machines had not yet multiplied man's strength a hundredfold: it goes down to the very level of the Nile, three hundred feet deep! Or the well dug at Coblentz by Margrave Johann of Baden, six hundred feet down into the ground! Well, what was needed here? Three times the depth, but on a width ten times greater, which made the digging that much easier! And there was not one foreman nor workman who doubted that the operation would be brought off successfully.

One important decision, made by engineer Murchison in agreement with President Barbicane, further accelerated the work. A clause in the contract had specified that the Columbiad would be reinforced with wrought-iron rings put on while white-hot. This was a useless precaution, for the cannon could easily dispense with such compressor rings. So the clause was dropped.

Whence, great saving of time, for they were able thereafter to employ the new digging system now universally adopted in making wells, in which the masonry is built in as the hole is dug. Thanks to this simple procedure, it is no longer necessary to shore up the earth with braces; the wall holds it in with unshakable strength and goes down under its own weight.

This maneuver was to start only when the pickaxe had reached the solid part of the ground.

On the 4th of November fifty workmen commenced digging, in the very center of the enclosed space on the summit of Stone Hill, a circular hole sixty feet in diameter.

The pickaxe first struck upon a kind of black earth, six inches in thickness, which was speedily disposed of. To this earth succeeded two feet of fine sand, which was carefully laid aside as being valuable for serving for the casting of the inner mold.

After the sand appeared some compact white clay, resembling the chalk of Great Britain, which extended down to a depth of four feet.

Then the iron of the picks struck upon the hard bed of the soil; a kind of rock formed of petrified shells, very dry, very solid, and which the picks would encounter from here on. At this point the excavation exhibited a depth of six and a half feet and the work of masonry was begun.

At the bottom of this excavation they constructed a wheel of oak, a kind of circle strongly bolted together, and of immense strength. The center of this wooden disc was hollowed out to a diameter equal to the exterior diameter of the Columbiad. Upon this wheel rested the first layers of the masonry, the stones of which were bound together by hydraulic cement, with irresistible tenacity. The workmen, after laying the stones from the circumference to the center, were thus enclosed within a kind of well twenty-one feet in diameter.

When this work was accomplished, the miners resumed their picks and cut away the rock from underneath the wheel itself, taking care to support it as they advanced upon blocks of great thickness. At every two feet which the hole gained in depth they successively withdrew the blocks. The wheel then sank little by little, and with it the massive ring of masonry, on the upper bed of which the masons labored incessantly, always reserving some vent holes to permit the escape of gas during the operation of casting.

This kind of work required on the part of the workmen extreme nicety and minute attention. More than one, in digging underneath the wheel, was dangerously injured by the splinters of stone, some even killed. But their ardor never relaxed, night or day. By day they worked under the rays of the scorching sun which, a few months later, would reach 99° in these parched plains; by night, under the gleam of the electric light. The sounds of the picks against the rock, the blasting of mines, the grinding of the machines, the wreaths of smoke scattered through the air, traced around Stone Hill a circle of terror which the herds of buffaloes and the war parties of the Seminoles never ventured to pass.

Nevertheless, the work advanced regularly, as the steam-cranes speeded removal of the rubble. Of unexpected obstacles there was little account; and with regard to foreseen difficulties, they were speedily disposed of.

At the expiration of the first month the well had attained the depth assigned for that lapse of time, namely, 112 feet. This depth was doubled in December, and trebled in January. During the month of February the workmen had to contend with a sheet of water which made its way right across the outer soil. It became necessary to employ very powerful pumps and compressed-air engines to drain it off, so as to close up the orifice from whence it issued; just as one stops a leak on board ship. They at last succeeded in getting the upper hand of these untoward streams; only, in consequence of the loosening of the soil, the wheel partly gave way, and a partial collapse ensued. One may judge the awful weight of this ring of masonry 450 feet high! The accident cost the lives of several workmen.

It took three weeks to shore up the stone revetment, build a support beneath it and restore the wheel to its previous stable condition. But, thanks to the skill of the engineer and the power of the machines at hand, the structure, compromised for a time, was put back on a level, and the digging could be resumed.

No fresh accident thenceforward arrested the progress of the operation; and on the 10th of June, twenty days before the expiration of the period fixed by Barbicane, the well, lined throughout with its facing of stone, had attained the depth of 900 feet. At the bottom the masonry rested upon a massive block measuring thirty feet in thickness, while on the upper portion it was level with the surrounding soil.

President Barbicane and the members of the Gun Club warmly congratulated their engineer Murchison: his cyclopean work had been accomplished with extraordinary rapidity.

During these eight months Barbicane never left Stone Hill for a single instant. Keeping ever close by the work of excavation, he busied himself incessantly with the welfare and health of his workpeople, and was singularly fortunate in warding off the epidemics common to large communities of men, and so disastrous in those regions of the globe which are exposed to the influences of tropical climates.

Several workmen, it is true, paid with their lives for the rashness inherent in these dangerous labors; but these deplorable mishaps are impossible to avoid, and they are details with which the Americans trouble themselves but little. They have in fact more regard for humanity in general than for the individual in particular. Nevertheless, Barbicane professed principles opposite to these, and put them in force at every opportunity. So, thanks to his care, his intelligence, his useful intervention in all difficulties, his prodigious and humane sagacity, the average of accidents did not exceed that of countries overseas noted for their excessive precautions—France, for instance, among others, where they reckon about one accident for every two hundred thousand francs of work.

CHAPTER 15

The Fete of the Casting

DURING the eight months which were employed in the work of excavation the preparatory works of the casting had been carried on simultaneously with extreme rapidity. A stranger arriving at Stone Hill would have been surprised at the spectacle offered to his view.

At 600 yards from the well, and circularly arranged around it as a central point, rose 1,200 reverberatories, each six feet in diameter, and separated from each other by an interval of a yard. The circumference occupied by these 1,200 furnaces presented a length of two miles. Being all constructed on the same plan, each with its high rectangular chimney, they produced a most singular effect. J. T. Maston considered this a superb architectural design. It reminded him of the Washington monuments. He was sure there was nothing finer in the world, not even in Greece, "where," as he was quick to point out, "he had never been anyway."

It will be remembered that on their third meeting the committee had decided to use cast iron for the Columbiad, and in particular the white variety. This metal, in fact, is the most durable, ductile, flexible, and malleable, and consequently suitable for all molding operations; and when smelted with pit coal, is of superior quality for all engineering works requiring great resisting power, such as cannon, steam boilers, hydraulic presses, and the like.

Cast iron, however, if subjected to only one single fusion, is rarely sufficiently homogeneous; and it requires a second fusion completely to refine it by dispossessing it of its last earthen impurities.

So before being forwarded to Tampa Town, the iron ore, molten in the great furnaces of Cold Spring, and brought into contact with coal and silicium heated to a high temperature, was carburized and transformed into cast iron.[1] After this first operation, the metal was sent on to Stone Hill. They had, however, to deal with 136,000,000 pounds of iron, a quantity far too costly to send by railway. The cost of transport would have been as much again as that of material. It appeared preferable to charter vessels at New York, and to load them with the iron in bars. This, however, required no less than sixty-eight vessels of 1,000 tons, a veritable fleet, which, quitting New York on the 3d of May, went by way of the ocean, along the American coastline, through the Bahama Channel around the tip of Florida, and on the 10th of the same month ascended the Bay of Espiritu Santo, and discharged their cargoes, without damage, in the port at Tampa Town.

Thence the iron was transported by rail to Stone Hill, and about the middle of January this enormous mass of metal was delivered at its destination.

It will be easily understood that 1,200 furnaces were not too many to melt simultaneously these 68,000 tons of iron. Each of these furnaces could hold nearly 114,000 pounds of

---

[1] The removal of this carbon and silicium in the refining operation of the puddling furnace is what turns cast iron into ductile iron.

metal. They were all built after the model of those which served for the casting of the Rodman gun; they were trapezoidal in shape, and very low-slung. The hearth and chimney were at opposite ends of the furnace, which was thus heated evenly throughout. These furnaces, constructed of fireproof brick, were exclusively made for burning pit coal, with a flat bottom upon which the iron bars were laid. This bottom, inclined at an angle of 25 degrees, allowed the metal to flow into the receiving troughs; and the 1,200 converging trenches carried the molten metal down to the central well.

The day following that on which the works of the masonry and boring had been completed, Barbicane set to work upon the central mold. His object now was to raise within the center of the well, and with a coincident axis, a cylinder 900 feet high, and nine feet in diameter, which should exactly fill up the space reserved for the bore of the Columbiad. This cylinder was composed of a mixture of clay and sand, with the addition of a little hay and straw. The space left between the mold and the masonry was intended to be filled up by the molten metal, which would thus form the walls six feet in thickness.

This cylinder, in order to maintain its equilibrium, had to be bound by iron bands, and firmly fixed at certain intervals by cross-clamps fastened into the stone lining; after the casting these would be buried in the block of metal, without damaging it.

This operation was completed on the 8th of July, and the run of the metal was fixed for the following day.

"This fete of the casting will be a grand ceremony," said J. T. Maston to his friend Barbicane.

"Undoubtedly," said Barbicane "but it will not be a public fete."

The Fete of the Casting

"What! will you not open the gates of the enclosure to all comers?"

"I would not dream of it, Maston. The casting of the Columbiad is an extremely delicate, not to say a dangerous operation, and I should prefer its being done privately. At the discharge of the projectile, a fete if you like—till then, no!"

Barbicane was right. The operation involved unforeseeable dangers, which a great influx of spectators would have hindered him from averting. It was necessary to preserve complete freedom of movement. No one was admitted within the enclosure except a delegation of members of the Gun Club, who had made the voyage to Tampa Town. Among these were the brisk Bilsby, Tom Hunter, Colonel Blomsberry, Major Elphinstone, General Morgan, and the rest of the lot to whom the casting of the Columbiad was a matter of personal interest. J. T. Maston appointed himself their guide. He omitted no point of detail; he conducted them throughout the magazines, the workshops, through the midst of the engines, and compelled them to visit all of the 1,200 furnaces one after the other. At the end of the twelve-hundredth visit they were pretty well knocked out.

The casting was to take place at twelve o'clock precisely. The previous day each furnace had been charged with 114,-000 pounds of metal in bars disposed crossways to each other, so as to allow the hot air to circulate freely between them. At daybreak the 1,200 chimneys vomited their torrents of flame into the air, and the ground was agitated with dull tremblings. As many pounds of metal as there were to cast, so many pounds of coal were there to burn. Thus there were 68,000 tons of coal which projected in the face of the sun a thick curtain of smoke.

The heat soon became unbearable within the circle of furnaces, the rumbling of which resembled the rolling of thunder. The powerful ventilators added their continuous blasts and saturated with oxygen the glowing hearths.

The operation, to be successful, had to be conducted with great rapidity. On a signal given by a cannon shot each furnace was to give vent to the molten iron and completely empty itself.

These arrangements made, foremen and workmen awaited the preconcerted moment with impatience mingled with a certain amount of emotion. Not a soul remained within the enclosure. Each superintendent took his post by the aperture of the run.

Barbicane and his colleagues, perched on a neighboring eminence, watched the operation. In front of them was a piece of artillery ready to fire at a signal from the engineer.

Some minutes before midday the first driblets of metal began to flow; the reservoirs filled little by little and, by the time the whole melting was completely accomplished, it was kept in abeyance for a few minutes in order to facilitate the separation of foreign substances.

Twelve o'clock struck. A gunshot suddenly pealed forth and shot its flame into the air. Twelve hundred melting-troughs were simultaneously opened and twelve hundred fiery serpents crept toward the central well, unrolling their incandescent curves. There, down they plunged with a terrific noise to a depth of 900 feet. It was an exciting and magnificent spectacle. The ground trembled, while these molten waves, sending into the sky their wreaths of smoke, evaporated the moisture of the mold and hurled it upward through the vent-holes of the stone lining in the form of dense vapor-clouds. These artificial clouds unrolled their thick spirals to a height of 1,000 yards into the air. A savage, wandering somewhere beyond the limits of the horizon, might have believed that some new crater was forming in the bosom of Florida, although there was neither eruption, nor typhoon, nor storm, nor struggle of the elements, nor any of those terrible phenomena which nature is capable of producing. No, it was man alone who had produced these reddish vapors, these gigantic flames worthy of a volcano itself, these tremendous vibrations resembling the shock of an earthquake, these reverberations rivaling those of hurricanes and storms; and it was his hand which precipitated into an abyss, dug by himself, a whole Niagara of molten metal!

CHAPTER 16

The Columbiad

HAD the casting succeeded? They were reduced to mere conjecture. There was indeed every reason to expect success, since the mold had absorbed the entire mass of the molten metal; still some considerable time must elapse before they could arrive at any certainty upon the matter.

In fact, when Major Rodman had cast his 160,000-pound cannon, it had taken no less than a fortnight for it to cool. How long then would this monstrous Columbiad, crowned with its clouds of vapor and protected by its intense heat, keep itself hidden from the eyes of its admirers? That was hard to reckon.

The patience of the members of the Gun Club was sorely tried during this period of time. But they could no nothing. J. T. Maston escaped roasting by a miracle. Fifteen days after the casting an immense column of smoke was still rising in the open sky and the ground burned the soles of the feet within a radius of two hundred feet around the summit of Stone Hill.

The days went by; weeks followed one another. There was no way to cool the immense cylinder. It was impossible to approach nearer. All they could do was to wait with what patience they might.

"Here we are at the 10th of August," exclaimed J. T. Maston one morning, "only four months to the 1st of December! We still have to remove the inside mold, calibrate the bore, and load the Columbiad! We shall never be ready in time! We cannot even get near the cannon! Will it never cool off? That would be a cruel joke, indeed!"

They tried in vain to calm the impatient secretary. Barbicane said nothing, but his silence covered a seething irritation. To be completely stopped by an obstacle which only time could overcome—time, a formidable enemy under the circumstances—and to be at the mercy of an enemy, this was a hard thing for warriors.

Meanwhile, daily observations revealed a certain change going on in the state of the ground. About the 15th of August the vapors ejected had sensibly diminished in intensity and thickness. Some days afterward the earth exhaled only a slight puff of smoke, the last breath of the monster enclosed within its coffin of stone. Little by little, the shaking of the earth subsided, the belt of heat contracted, the more impatient spectators came closer; four yards one day, eight yards the next; until on the 22d of August, Barbicane, his colleagues, and the engineer were able to set foot on the iron sheet which lay level upon the summit of Stone Hill, a place where, to be sure, one could not have cold feet.

"At last!" exclaimed the president of the Gun Club, with an immense sigh of relief.

The work was resumed the same day. They proceeded at once to extract the interior mold, for the purpose of clearing out the bore of the piece. Pickaxes and boring irons were set to work without intermission. The clayey and sandy soils had acquired extreme hardness under the action of the heat; but, with the aid of the machines, they were able to remove the still scorching mixture from the cast-iron walls, and the rubbish on being dug out was rapidly carted away on railway wagons; and such was the ardor of the work, so persuasive the arguments of Barbicane's dollars, that by the 3d of September all traces of the mold had entirely disappeared.

Immediately the operation of boring was commenced; and the powerful machines bored away all roughness from the barrel. A few weeks later, the inner surface of the immense tube had been rendered perfectly cylindrical, and the bore of the piece had acquired a thorough polish.

At length, on the 22d of September, less than a twelvemonth after Barbicane's original proposition, the enormous weapon, accurately bored, and exactly vertically pointed, was ready to work. There was only the moon now to wait for; and they were sure that she would not fail in the rendezvous.

The ecstasy of J. T. Maston knew no bounds, and he narrowly escaped a frightful fall while staring down the 900-foot tube. But for the strong right arm of Colonel Blomsberry, the worthy secretary, like a modern Erostratus, would have found his death in the depths of the Columbiad.

The cannon was thus finished; there was no possible doubt as to its perfect completion. So, on the 6th of October, Captain Nicholl opened an account between himself and President Barbicane, in which he debited himself to the latter in the sum of two thousand dollars. One may believe that the captain's wrath was increased to its highest point, and made him seriously ill. However, he had still three bets of three, four, and five thousand dollars, respectively; and if he won two of these, his position, if not excellent, would not be very bad. But the money question did not enter into his calculations; it was the success of his rival in casting a cannon against which iron plates sixty feet thick would have been ineffectual, that dealt him a terrible blow.

After the 23d of September the enclosure of Stone Hill was thrown open to the public; and it will be easily imagined what was the concourse of visitors to this spot!

Indeed, innumerable curiosity-seekers, coming from every part of the United States, converged on Florida. The city of Tampa had grown prodigiously during the past year, entirely devoted to the work of the Gun Club, and it now numbered a population of 150,000 souls. After having swallowed Fort Brooke into its spreading network of streets, it now extended along the spit of land which separated the two harbors of the bay of Espiritu Santo; new neighborhoods, new squares, a whole forest of houses had grown up on these recently deserted shores, under the warm American sun. Companies had been founded for the building of churches, schools, private homes, and in less than a year the area of the city had increased tenfold.

It is well known that Yankees are born traders; wherever fate sends them, from the arctic zone to the tropical, their business sense has to find a useful outlet. That is why mere curiosity-seekers, people who came to Florida only to watch what the Gun Club was doing, allowed themselves to become involved in commercial transactions as soon as they had settled in Tampa. The ships chartered for the transportation of materials and workmen had given the port an unprecedented activity. Soon other ships, of all shapes and sizes, carrying food, supplies, merchandise, plied the bay and its two harbors; huge shippers' and chandlers' offices opened in the city, and each day the *Shipping Gazette* recorded new arrivals at the port of Tampa.

While the roads were proliferating about the city, the latter, in view of the prodigious increase in its population and trade, had finally been linked by a railroad to the Southern states of the Union. One line ran from Mobile to Pensacola, the great Southern naval arsenal; then, from that important point, it went on to Tallahassee. There, there was already a short twenty-one-mile-long spur, through which Tallahassee was connected to Saint Marks, on the coast. This line was what was extended on to Tampa Town, reawakening and reviving along its route the dead or dormant portions of central Florida. So that Tampa, thanks to these wonders of industry born of the idea that started one fine day in the brain of one man, was able justifiably to begin acting like a great city. It had been given the nickname of "Moon City," and it was subjecting the capital of Florida to a total eclipse, visible from every point on earth.

Now anyone can understand why there had been so great a rivalry between Texas and Florida, and why the Texans were so irritated when they found their claims thrown out by the decision of the Gun Club. With the wisdom of foresight, they had understood what a region might gain from the experiment being undertaken by Barbicane and all the good that such a cannon-shot might bring. Texas was thus losing a great trading center, railroads, and a considerable increase in population. All these advantages were accruing to that wretched Florida peninsula, thrown out like a jetty between the waters of the Gulf and the depths of the Atlantic. And now Barbicane was almost as unpopular in Texas as General Santa Anna.

Yet with all this, despite its business boom and its industrial impetus, the new population of Tampa Town was far from forgetting the interesting operations of the Gun Club. Quite the contrary. The slightest details of the undertaking, its least spadework, were hot news. There was an incessant flow of people between the city and Stone Hill, a procession or, better yet, a pilgrimage.

It was already clear to be seen that, on the day of the experiment itself, the aggregate of spectators would be counted by millions; for they were already arriving from all parts of the earth upon this narrow strip of promontory. Europe was emigrating to America.

Up to that time, however, it must be confessed, the curiosity of the numerous comers was but scantily gratified. Most had counted upon witnessing the spectacle of the casting, and they were treated to nothing but smoke. This was sorry food for hungry eyes; but Barbicane would admit no one to the operation. Then ensued grumbling, discontent, murmurs; they blamed the president, taxed him with dictatorial conduct. His proceedings were declared "un-American." There was very nearly a riot around Stone Hill; but Barbicane remained inflexible.

When, however, the Columbiad was entirely finished, this state of closed doors could no longer be maintained; besides it would have been bad taste, and even imprudence, to affront the public feeling. Barbicane, therefore, opened the enclosure to all comers; but, true to his practical disposition, he determined to coin money out of the public curiosity.

It was something, indeed, to be able to contemplate this immense Columbiad; but to descend into its depths, this seemed to the Americans the *ne plus ultra* of earthly felicity. Consequently, there was not one curious spectator who was not willing to give himself the treat of visiting the interior of this metallic abyss. Baskets suspended from steam-cranes permitted them to satisfy their curiosity. They went wild. Women, children, old men, all made it a point of duty to penetrate the mysteries of the colossal gun. The fare for the descent was fixed at five dollars per head; and, despite this high charge, during the two months which preceded the experiment, the influx of visitors enabled the Gun Club to pocket nearly five hundred thousand dollars!

It is needless to say that the first visitors of the Columbiad were the members of the Gun Club. This privilege was justly reserved for that illustrious body. The ceremony took place on the 25th of September. A basket of honor took down the president, J. T. Maston, Major Elphinstone, General Morgan, Colonel Blomsberry, and other members of the club, numbering ten in all. How hot it was at the bottom of that long tube of metal! They were half suffocated. But what delight! What ecstasy! A table had been laid with ten covers on the massive stone which formed the bottom of the Columbiad, and lighted by a ray of electric light resembling that of day itself. Numerous exquisite dishes, which seemed to descend from heaven, were placed successively before the guests, and the richest wines of France flowed in profusion during this splendid repast, served nine hundred feet beneath the surface of the earth!

The feast was animated, not to say somewhat noisy. Toasts flew backward and forward. They drank to the earth and to her satellite, to the Gun Club, the Union, the Moon, Diana, Phoebe, Selene, the "peaceful courier of the night!" All the hurrahs, carried upward upon the sonorous waves of the immense acoustic tube, arrived with the sound of thunder at its mouth; and the multitude ranged round Stone Hill heartily united their shouts with those of the ten revelers hidden from view at the bottom of the gigantic Columbiad.

J. T. Maston was no longer master of himself. Whether he shouted or gesticulated, ate or drank most, would be a difficult matter to determine. At all events, he would not have given his place up for an empire, "not even if the cannon—loaded, primed, and fired at that very moment—were to blow him in pieces out into planetary space."

CHAPTER 17

A Telegram

THE great works undertaken by the Gun Club had now virtually come to an end; and two months still remained before the day for the discharge of the shot to the moon. To the general impatience these two months appeared as long as years! Hitherto the smallest details of the operation had been daily chronicled by the journals, which the public devoured with eager eyes; but it was to be feared that henceforth this "dividend of interest" distributed to the public would be greatly diminished, and everyone was afraid that he would no longer receive his daily share of excitement.

Not at all. Just then, the most unexpected, extraordinary, unbelievable, improbable event occurred, to excite flagging minds and whet the whole world's sense of dramatic adventure.

One day, the 30th of September, at 3:47 P.M., a telegram, transmitted by cable from Valentia (Ireland) to Newfoundland and the American mainland, arrived addressed to President Barbicane.

The president tore open the envelope, read the message, and, despite his remarkable powers of self-control, his lips turned pale and his eyes grew dim, on reading the twenty words of this telegram.

Here is the text of the dispatch, which figures now in the archives of the Gun Club:

FRANCE, PARIS, 30 September, 4 A.M.

Barbicane
Tampa Town, Florida, United States

Substitute for your spherical shell a cylindro-conical projectile. I shall go inside. Shall arrive by steamer Atlanta.

MICHEL ARDAN

CHAPTER 18

The Passenger of the *Atlanta*

I<small>F</small> this astounding news, instead of flying on electric wires, had simply arrived by post in an ordinary sealed envelope—if, therefore, French, Irish, Newfoundland and American employees had not already been let in on the secret of the message—Barbicane would not have hesitated a moment. He would have held his tongue about it, both as a measure of prudence, and in order not to discredit his project. This telegram might be a cover for some jest, especially as it came from a Frenchman. What human being would ever have conceived the idea of such a journey? And, if such a person really existed, he must be an idiot, whom one would shut up in a lunatic ward, rather than within the walls of the projectile.

The contents of the dispatch, however, speedily became known; for the telegraphic officials possessed but little discretion, and Michel Ardan's proposition ran at once throughout the several States of the Union. Barbicane had, therefore, no further motive for keeping silence. Consequently, he called together such of his colleagues as were at the moment in Tampa Town, and without any expression of his own opinions simply read to them the laconic text itself.

"Impossible!" "That's incredible!" "It's a joke!" "Someone is making fun of us!" "Ridiculous!" "Absurd!"

It was thus greeted for several minutes with every conceivable expression conveying doubt, incredulity, foolishness, madness, and all the usual accompanying gestures. Each one smiled, laughed, shrugged, or roared, according to his own nature, except J. T. Maston, who exclaimed,

"Say, that *is* a grand idea!"

"Yes," replied the major. "But while a person may sometimes be allowed an idea like that, it is only on condition that he not even try to carry it out."

"And why not?" sharply retorted the secretary of the Gun Club, all ready for an argument. But no one pursued the matter.

Meantime, the name of Michel Ardan was already circulating around Tampa. Strangers and natives exchanged knowing glances, questioned each other, and joked, not about this European—obviously a figment, a mythical character—but about J. T. Maston who had actually believed in the imaginary individual's existence. When Barbicane originally proposed to send a shot to the moon everyone looked upon the enterprise as simple and practicable enough—a mere matter of gunnery! But for a reasonable being to offer to take passage within the projectile, to undertake this impossible trip, then it became a laughing matter, a joke, a farce or, in simpler language, a humbug!

The joking went on until evening without interruption, and it can be asserted that the entire Union was engulfed in the wild laughter, which is hardly usual in a country where the most unlikely undertakings easily find supporters, adherents, and partisans.

Nevertheless, Michel Ardan's proposition, like all new ideas, would not leave off running through certain minds. It upset their usual patterns of thinking. "How does it happen that no one thought of that before?" This incident soon turned into an obsession because of its very strangeness itself. People kept thinking about it. How many things there were that had been denied one day, and yet the next day had turned into realities! Why should such a voyage not in fact be carried out some day or other? But, at any rate, the man who was ready thus to risk his life would have to be crazy, and besides, since obviously no one would take his proposal seriously, he would have done better to keep quiet, instead of upsetting an entire population with such ridiculous notions.

But, in the first place, did such a person really exist? What a question! The name, Michel Ardan, was not completely unknown in America! It belonged to a European who had very often been mentioned for his daring undertakings. And now, this telegram flashed across the depths of the Atlantic, the designation of the vessel on which the Frenchman said he had taken his passage, the date assigned for his speedy arrival, all combined to impart a certain character of reality to the proposal. They must get some clearer notion of the matter. Scattered groups of individuals condensed under the effect of curiosity like atoms under molecular attraction, and finally formed into a compact crowd which made straight for the residence of President Barbicane.

The latter, since the arrival of the telegram, had not made any statement; he had allowed the opinion of J. T. Maston to be spread around, without expressing either approval or disapproval; he remained quiet, and intended to watch events as they developed. But he was counting without public impatience; and it was with no pleasant countenance that he watched the population of Tampa Town gathering under his windows. The murmurs and vociferations below presently obliged him to appear. It can be seen that he now had all the duties and, consequently, all the troubles of celebrity.

He came forward, therefore, and on silence being procured, a citizen put point-blank to him the following question: "Is the person mentioned in the telegram, under the name of Michel Ardan, on his way here? Yes or no?"

"Gentlemen," replied Barbicane, "I know no more about it than you do."

"We must know," roared the impatient voices.

"Time will show," calmly replied the president.

"Time has no business to keep a whole country in suspense," replied the orator. "Have you altered the plans of the projectile according to the request of the telegram?"

"Not yet, gentlemen; but you are right! We must have better information to go by. The telegraph started this, and it must complete its information."

"To the telegraph!" roared the crowd.

Barbicane descended; and heading the immense assemblage, led the way to the telegraph office.

A few minutes later a telegram was dispatched to the secretary of the underwriters at Liverpool, requesting answers to the following queries:

"What is the ship *Atlanta*? When did she leave Europe? Did she have on board a Frenchman named Michel Ardan?"

Two hours afterward Barbicane received information too exact to leave room for the smallest remaining doubt.

"The steamer *Atlanta* from Liverpool put to sea on the 2d of October, bound for Tampa Town, having on board a

Frenchman borne on the list of passengers by the name of Michel Ardan."

At this confirmation of the first telegram, the eyes of the president lit up with a sudden flame, his fists clenched violently, and he was heard to mutter:

"So, it's true! It is possible! This Frenchman does exist! And in a fortnight he will be here! But he must be crazy, a hot head! I will never allow—"

And yet, that very evening, he wrote to Breadwill & Co., requesting them to suspend the casting of the projectile until further notice.

Now, to try to describe the excitement that gripped all of America; to tell how the impression created by Barbicane's communication was ten times surpassed; what the newspapers of the Union said, the manner in which they greeted the news and the tone in which they heralded the arrival of this hero from the Old World; to paint the feverish activity in which everyone lived, counting the hours, the minutes, the seconds; to give even a faint idea of the exhausting obsession of all the minds possessed of a single thought; to show the occupations being replaced by a single concern, the works stopped, the trade interrupted, the ships ready to sail remaining berthed in port so as not to miss the arrival of the *Atlanta,* the convoys arriving loaded and deadheading back, the Bay of Espiritu Santo constantly crisscrossed by steamers, packet-boats, pleasure yachts, fly-boats of all sizes; to count the myriads of the curious who in two weeks quadrupled the population of Tampa Town and were forced to camp out under tents like an army on the march— all of this would be a task beyond human strength, that would be presumptuous to attempt.

On the 20th of October, at nine A.M., the semaphores of

Michel Ardan arrives with "l'esprit de la Franc

PARIS
MATCH
/ 26 JUILLET 1969 / 2 F

0:02
0:01
0:00

the Bahama Channel signaled a thick smoke on the horizon. Two hours later a large steamer exchanged identifying signals with them. The name of the *Atlanta* flew at once over Tampa Town. At four o'clock the English vessel entered the Bay of Espiritu Santo. At five she crossed the passage of Hillsborough Harbor at full steam. At six she cast anchor at Tampa.

The anchor had scarcely caught the sandy bottom when five hundred boats surrounded the *Atlanta,* and the steamer was taken by assault. Barbicane was the first to set foot on deck, and in a voice of which he vainly tried to conceal the emotion, called "Michel Ardan."

"Here!" replied an individual perched on the poop.

Barbicane, with arms crossed, looked fixedly at the passenger of the *Atlanta.*

He was a man of about forty-two years of age, of large build, but slightly round-shouldered, somewhat like those caryatids that carry balconies on their shoulders. His massive head momentarily shook a shock of reddish hair, which resembled a lion's mane. His face was short with a broad forehead, and furnished with a mustache as bristly as a cat's and little patches of yellowish whiskers on the cheeks. Round, wildish eyes, slightly near-sighted, completed a physiognomy essentially feline. His nose was firmly shaped, his mouth particularly sweet in expression, high forehead, intelligent and furrowed with wrinkles like a constantly-plowed field. The body, finally, was powerfully developed and firmly fixed upon long legs. Muscular arms, that were powerful and well attached, and a determined look showed that this European was a solidly built fellow, "forged rather than cast," to borrow one of its expressions from the art of metallurgy.

Disciples of Lavater or Gratiolet might readily have detected on the skull and physiognomy of the man indubitable signs of aggressiveness, that is to say, courage in the face of danger and a tendency to overcome all obstacles, as well as the marks of benevolence and the sense of wonderment, the instinct that leads certain human temperaments to devote themselves to what seems superhuman; but, on the other hand, the bumps of acquisitiveness, the greed for having and holding, were totally absent.

To complete the physical description of the passenger of the *Atlanta,* we must remark upon his broadly cut clothing, sweeping in its folds, his trousers and coat made of such ample materials that Michel Ardan himself nicknamed himself "death on fabric," his loose cravat, his freely opened shirt collar, from which a robust neck extended, and his invariably unbuttoned cuffs, through which his active hands escaped. One could feel that, even in the harshest of winters or facing the gravest dangers, such a man could never get cold—not even cold feet.

Moreover, on the deck of the steamer, in the midst of the crowd, he bustled to and fro, never still for a moment, "dragging at anchor," as the sailors say, gesticulating, hailfellow-well-met with everyone, and biting his nails with nervous avidity. He was one of those originals whom the Creator invents during a moment's whim, and then immediately breaks the mold.

Indeed, Michel Ardan's personality offered a broad scope for the observations of an analyst. This amazing man lived in a perpetual state of hyperbole and had not yet outgrown the age of superlatives: objects impressed themselves on his retina in outsized dimensions; whence gigantic associations of ideas; so that he saw everything magnified—except for obstacles and men.

He had, in addition, a luxuriant nature. An artist by instinct, he was a wit, not one who kept up a running fire of striking remarks, but rather got off each one like a sniper's shot. In argument, disdainful of logic, not given to syllogisms, which he would never have thought of on his own, he had his own special ways. A real iconoclast, he would hurl unfailing *ad hominem* arguments at point-blank range, and he loved to fight tooth and nail in defense of lost causes.

Among other idiosyncrasies, he gave himself out as "sublimely ignorant," like Shakespeare, and professed supreme contempt for scientists, "people," as he described them, "fit only to keep score while we play the game." He was, in short, a Bohemian from the Land of Many Marvels, adventurous, but not an adventurer, a daredevil, a Phaëthon driving the chariot of the sun at top speed, an Icarus with extra sets of wings. Beyond that, he was always getting himself into the thick of things, rushing headlong into the maddest undertakings, burning his ships behind him with more enthusiasm than Agathocles, and, though ready to risk his neck at any hour, he invariably ended up by landing on his feet, like those untippable little pith figures that are sold for children's toys.

In two words, his motto was "Despite everything!" And the love of the impossible was his ruling passion, to quote Pope's fine phrase.

But this enterprising worthy also had the faults that went with his qualities! Nothing ventured, nothing gained, it is said. Ardan ventured often, but had not gained much! He was a spendthrift, a bottomless pit. Absolutely without regard for personal profit, he acted as often from the dictates of his heart as from those of his head; ever helpful, chivalrous, he would not have signed a death warrant for his cruelest enemy, and he would have sold himself into slavery to buy the freedom of one Black.

All over France and Europe, everyone knew this noisy, brilliant character. Were not the hundred voices of Fame continuously growing hoarse talking about him? Did he not live in a glass house, making the entire world the confidant of his most intimate secrets? But he also had a perfectly admirable collection of enemies, among those he had more or less offended, hurt, knocked over without pity, as he elbowed his way through the crowd.

However, he was generally liked, and treated like a spoiled child. He was, as the popular expression went, a "take it or leave it" man, and most people took it. Everyone was interested in his daring undertakings and watched him with concern. They knew him to be so imprudently audacious! When some friend tried to stop him by predicting impending catastrophe, he would answer with a charming smile, "The forest can be burned only by its own trees," without ever realizing he was quoting the most attractive of all Arab proverbs.

Such was the passenger of the *Atlanta,* always excitable, as if boiling under the action of some internal fire, always excited, not by what he planned to do in America—he never even thought about that—but by the character of his own physical organization.[1] If ever two individuals offered a striking contrast to each other, these were certainly Michel Ardan and the Yankee Barbicane; both, moreover, being equally enterprising and daring, each in his own way.

The scrutiny which the president of the Gun Club had

---

[1] An observant reader may note that Ardan is an anagram for Nadar, the name of Verne's friend, the adventurous aeronaut and pioneer photographer, after whom he is reputed to have modeled this character.—ED.

instituted regarding this new rival who threatened to push him into the background was quickly interrupted by the shouts and hurrahs of the crowd. The cries became at last so uproarious, and the popular enthusiasm assumed so personal a form, that Michel Ardan, after having shaken hands some thousands of times, at the imminent risk of leaving his ten fingers behind him, at last had to make a bolt for his cabin.

Barbicane followed him without utttering a word.

"You are Barbicane, I suppose?" said Michel Ardan, in a tone of voice in which he would have addressed a friend of twenty years' standing.

"Yes," replied the president of the Gun Club.

"All right! how d'ye do, Barbicane? How are you getting on? Pretty well? Good!"

"So," said Barbicane without further preliminary, "you are quite determined to go."

"Quite decided."

"Nothing will stop you?"

"Nothing. Have you modified your projectile according to my telegram?"

"I waited for your arrival. But," asked Barbicane again, "have you carefully thought this over?"

"Thought it over? Have I any time to waste? I find an opportunity of making a tour on the moon, and I mean to do it. Why think about it?"

Barbicane looked hard at this man who spoke so lightly of his project with such complete absence of anxiety.

"But, at least," said he, "you have some plans, some means of carrying your project into execution?"

"Excellent, my dear Barbicane; only permit me to offer one remark: My wish is to tell my story once for all, to everybody, and then to have done with it; then there will be no need for recapitulation. So, if you have no objection, assemble your friends, colleagues, the whole town, all Florida, all America if you like, and tomorrow I shall be ready to explain my plans and answer any objections whatever that may be advanced. You may rest assured I shall be fully prepared. Will that suit you?"

"All right," replied Barbicane.

So saying, the president left the cabin and informed the crowd of the proposal of Michel Ardan. His words were received with clappings of hands and shouts of joy. They had removed all difficulties. Tomorrow everyone would contemplate at his ease this European hero. However, some of the more stubborn spectators would not leave the deck of the *Atlanta*. They passed the night on board. Among others J. T. Maston got his hook fixed in the combing of the poop, and it would have required a capstan to get it out again.

"He is a hero! a hero!" he cried, a theme of which he was never tired of ringing the changes; "and we are only like weak, silly women, compared with this European!"

As to the president, after having suggested to the visitors it was time to retire, he re-entered the passenger's cabin, and remained there till the bell of the steamer made it midnight.

But by then the two rivals in popularity were shaking hands heartily and parting on terms of intimate friendship.

CHAPTER 19

A Monster Meeting

O N the following day the sun rose too late to suit the public impatience. People felt it was indeed a lazy sun, for one that was to light up such an occasion. Barbicane, fearing that indiscreet questions might be put to Michel Ardan, was desirous of reducing the number of the audience to a few of the initiated, his own colleagues for instance. He might as well have tried to hold back Niagara Falls! He was compelled, therefore, to give up the idea, and to let his new friend run the chances of a public gathering. The main room of Tampa's new Stock Exchange, despite its colossal size, was considered too small for the ceremony, which now was taking on the proportions of a monster mass meeting.

The place chosen for it was a vast plain situated outside the town. In a few hours, thanks to the help of the shipping in port, an immense roofing of canvas was stretched over the parched prairie, and protected it from the burning rays of the sun. There three hundred thousand people braved for many hours the stifling heat while awaiting the arrival of the Frenchman. Of this crowd of spectators a first third could both see and hear; a second third saw badly and heard nothing at all; and as for the third, it could neither see nor hear anything at all. Yet it was not the least loud in its applause.

At three o'clock Michel Ardan made his appearance, accompanied by the principal members of the Gun Club. He was supported on his right by President Barbicane, and on his left by J. T. Maston, more radiant than the midday sun, and nearly as ruddy. Ardan mounted a platform, from the top of which his view extended over a sea of black hats. He exhibited not the slightest embarrassment; he was just as gay, familiar, and pleasant as if he were at home. To the hurrahs which greeted him he replied by a graceful bow; then, waving his hand to request silence, he spoke in perfectly correct English as follows:

"Gentlemen, despite the very hot weather I request your patience for a short time while I offer some explanations regarding the projects which seem to have so interested you. I am neither an orator nor a man of science, and I had no idea of addressing you in public; but my friend Barbicane has told me that you would like to hear me, and I am quite at your service. Listen to me, therefore, with your six hundred thousand ears, and please to excuse the faults of the speaker."

This informal beginning was deeply appreciated by the listeners, who expressed their delight by a roar of satisfaction.

"Gentlemen," he went on, "no sign of approval or disapproval is forbidden. That being understood, I will begin. But, pray do not forget that you see before you a perfect ignoramus whose ignorance goes so far that he cannot even understand the difficulties! It seemed to him that it was a matter quite simple, natural, and easy to take one's place in a projectile and start for the moon! That journey must be undertaken sooner or later; and, as for the mode of locomotion adopted, it follows simply the law of progress. Man began by walking on all-fours; then, one fine day, on two feet; then in a wagon, a cart, a carriage; then in a stagecoach; and lastly by railway. Well, the projectile is the vehicle of the future, and the planets themselves are nothing but cannon-balls fired by the Creator! But, back to our own vehicle. Some of you, gentlemen, may imagine that the velocity we propose to impart to it is extravagant. It is nothing of the kind. All the stars exceed it in rapidity, and the earth herself is at this moment carrying us round the sun at three times as rapid a rate.

"Here, gentlemen, is the speed of the different planets. I must confess that, despite my ignorance, I know this small astronomical detail very precisely; but in two minutes you will know as much about it as I. Neptune travels at 12,500 miles an hour; Uranus at 17,500; Saturn, 22,145; Jupiter, 29,190; Mars, 55,030; Earth, 68,750; Venus, 80,080; Mercury, 131,300; and some comets at 3,500,000 miles an hour at their perihelion! As for us, we will be mere loungers by comparison, stick-in-the-muds whose speed will not exceed 24,200 miles at the start, with our velocity continually decreasing! Is it not evident, then, I ask you, that there will some day appear velocities far greater than these, of which light or electricity will probably be the mechanical agent?"

No one appeared to question this assertion of his.

"Yes, gentlemen," continued the orator, "in spite of the opinions of certain narrow-minded people, who would shut up the human race upon this globe, as within some magic circle which it must never outstep, we shall one day travel to the moon, the planets, and the stars, with the same facility, rapidity, and certainty as we now make the voyage from Liverpool to New York! The ocean of space will be crossed, as will be those of the moon. Distance is but a relative expression, and must end by being reduced to zero."

The assembly, strongly predisposed as they were in favor of the French hero, were slightly staggered at this bold theory. Michel Ardan perceived the fact.

"Gentlemen," he continued with a pleasant smile, "you do not seem quite convinced. Very good! Let us reason the matter out. Do you know how long it would take for an express train to reach the moon? Three hundred days; no more! And what is that? The distance is only 214,000 miles, or no more than nine times the circumference of the earth; and there are no sailors or travelers, of even moderate activity, who have not traveled farther than that in their lifetime. And now consider that I shall be only ninety-seven hours on my journey. Ah! I see you are reckoning that the moon is a long way off from the earth, and that one must think twice before making the experiment. What would you say, then, if we were talking of going to Neptune, which revolves at a distance of more than 2,867,500,000 miles from the sun! That is a trip that very few people could afford, even if it cost only ten cents a mile! Baron Rothschild himself, for all his $200,000,000, could not pay for it, and would be left behind for want of $86,750,000."

This line of reasoning seemed to appeal greatly to the audience; and Michel Ardan, imbued with his subject, threw himself headlong into it with superb enthusiasm. He felt he was being avidly listened to, and went on with admirable assurance:

"Well, my friends, the distance from Neptune to the sun is as nothing, when compared to that of the stars; indeed, to evaluate the distances to these bodies, one must enter into that dazzling sphere of mathematics in which the smallest number is followed by nine ciphers, and the billion is the basic unit. I beg your pardon for not being better versed in this matter, but it is fascinating. Listen and judge for yourselves! Alpha Centauri is 20,000 billion miles away; Vega and Sirius at 125,000 billion miles each; Arcturus, 130,000 billion; Polaris, 292,000 billion; Capella, 425,000 billion; and there are other stars that are thousands and millions and billions of billions of miles away! And then you talk of the distance which separates the planets from the sun! And there are people who affirm that such a thing as distance exists. Absurdity, folly, idiotic nonsense! Would you know what I think of our own solar universe? Shall I tell you my theory? It is very simple! In my opinion the solar system is a solid homogeneous body; the planets which compose it are in actual contact with each other; and whatever space exists between them is nothing more than the space which separates the molecules of the densest metal, such as silver, iron, or platinum! I have the right, therefore, to affirm, and I repeat, with the conviction which must penetrate all your minds, 'Distance is but an empty word; distance does not exist!' "

"Right you are! Bravo! Hurrah!" shouted the whole crowd in one voice, as it was electrified by the gestures and tones of the speaker, and the daring of his conceptions.

"No," echoed J. T. Maston even more energetically than the others. "Distance does not exist!"

And, overcome by the energy of his movements, he nearly fell from the platform to the ground. But he regained his equilibrium, and just escaped a severe fall, which would have proved to him that distance was by no means an empty word. Then the engaging speaker resumed his talk.

137

"My friends," said Michel Ardan, "I believe this question has now been resolved. If I did not convince all of you, it is because I was backward in my demonstrations, weak in my arguments, and you will have to blame my inadequate theoretical preparation. But, however that may be, I repeat, the distance between the earth and her satellite is a mere trifle, and unworthy of serious consideration. I do not believe I am exaggerating when I say that soon there will be trains of projectiles, in which the trip from the earth to the moon will be made comfortably. There will be neither shock nor bump, nor any derailment to fear, and the goal will be reached quickly, without exhaustion, straight away, 'in a bee line,' to use the language of your trappers. Within twenty years, half the people on earth will have visited the moon!"

"Hurrah! Hurrah for Michel Ardan!" shouted the audience, even the least convinced among them.

"Hurrah for Barbicane!" the orator modestly replied.

This act of recognition for the promoter of the enterprise was greeted with universal applause.

"Now, my friends," Michel Ardan went on, "if you have any question to put to me, you will, I fear, sadly embarrass a poor man like myself; still I will do my best to answer you."

Up to this point the president of the Gun Club had been satisfied with the turn which the discussion had assumed, as it dealt with the speculative theories in which Michel Ardan, with his vivid imagination, was so brilliant. It became now, however, desirable to divert Ardan from questions of a practical nature, with which he was doubtless far less conversant. Barbicane, therefore, hastened to get in a word, and began by asking his new friend whether he thought that the moon and the planets were inhabited.

"You put before me a great problem, my worthy president," replied the orator, smiling. "Still, men of great intelligence, such as Plutarch, Swedenborg, Bernardin de St. Pierre, and others, if I mistake not, pronounced in the affirmative. Looking at the question from the natural philosopher's point of view, I should agree with them and say that nothing useless existed in the world; and, replying to your question by another, I should venture to assert, that if these worlds are habitable, they either are, have been, or will be inhabited."

"Well put!" cried the first rows of spectators, who set the tone for the others.

"No one could answer more logically or fairly," replied the president. "The question then reverts to this: Are these worlds habitable? For my own part I believe they are."

"And I feel certain of it," said Michel Ardan.

"Nevertheless," retorted one of the audience, "there are many arguments against the habitability of the worlds. The conditions of life must evidently be greatly modified upon the majority of them. To mention only the planets, we should be either broiled alive in some, or frozen to death in others, according as they are more or less removed from the sun."

"I regret," replied Michel Ardan, "that I have not the honor of personally knowing my contradictor, for I would have attempted to answer him. His objection has its merits, I admit; but I think we may successfully combat it, as well as all others which affect the habitability of the other worlds. If I were a natural philosopher, I would tell him that if less of caloric were set in motion upon the planets which are nearest to the sun, and more, on the contrary, upon those which are farthest removed from it, this simple fact would alone suffice to equalize the heat, and to render the temperature of those worlds supportable by being organized like ourselves. If I were a naturalist, I would tell him that, according to many illustrious men of science, nature has furnished us with instances upon the earth of animals existing under very varying conditions of life; that fish breathe in a medium fatal to other animals; that amphibious creatures possess a double existence very difficult of explanation; that certain denizens of the seas maintain life at enormous depths, and there support a pressure equal to that of fifty or sixty atmospheres without being crushed; that several aquatic insects, insensible to temperature, are met with equally among boiling springs and in the frozen plains of the Polar Sea; in fine, that he cannot help recognizing in nature a diversity of means of operation oftentimes incomprehensible, but none the less real, up to and including omnipotence. If I were a chemist, I would tell him that the aerolites, bodies evidently formed outside of our terrestrial globe, have, upon analysis, revealed indisputable traces of carbon, a substance which owes its origin solely to organized beings, and which, according to the experiments of Reichenbach, must necessarily itself have been endued with animation. And lastly, were I a theologian, I would tell him that the scheme of the Divine Redemption, according to St. Paul, seems to be applicable, not merely to the earth, but to all the celestial worlds. But, unfortunately, I am neither theologian, nor chemist, nor naturalist, nor philosopher; therefore, in my absolute ignorance of the great laws which govern the universe, I confine myself to saying in reply, 'I do not know whether the worlds are inhabited or not: and since I do not know, I am going to see!' "

Whether Michel Ardan's antagonist hazarded any further arguments or not it is impossible to say, for the uproarious shouts of the crowd would not allow any expression of opinion to gain a hearing. On silence being restored throughout the assembly, the triumphant orator contented himself with adding the following remarks:

"My good Yankee friends, you will observe that I have but slightly touched upon this great question. I am not lecturing nor supporting any thesis on this score. There is another altogether different line of argument in favor of the habitability of the stars, which I omit for the present. I only desire to call attention to one point. To those who maintain that the planets are *not* inhabited one may reply: You might be perfectly right, if you could only show that the earth is the best possible world, which is not so, in spite of what Voltaire has said. She has but *one* satellite, while Jupiter, Uranus, Saturn, Neptune have each several, an advantage by no means to be despised. But that which renders our own globe so uncomfortable is the inclination of its axis to the plane of its orbit. Hence the inequality of days and nights; hence the disagreeable diversity of the seasons. On the surface of our unhappy spheroid we are always either too hot or too cold; we are frozen in winter, broiled in summer; it is the planet of colds, coughs, bronchitis; while on the surface of Jupiter, for example, where the axis is but slightly inclined,[1] the inhabitants may enjoy uniform temperatures. It possesses zones of perpetual springs, summers, autumns, and winters; every Jovian may choose for himself what climate he likes, and there spend the whole of his life in security from all variations of temperature. You will, I am sure, readily admit this superiority of Jupiter over our own planet, to say nothing of its years, which each equal twelve of ours!

[1] Only 3° 5′.

Under such auspices and such marvelous conditions of existence, it appears to me that the inhabitants of so fortunate a world must be in every respect superior to ourselves, its scholars more scholarly, its artists more artistic, its villains less bad and its good people better. All we require, in order to attain to such perfection, is the mere trifle of having an axis of rotation less inclined to the plane of its orbit!"

"Well!" roared an energetic voice, "let us unite our efforts, invent the necessary machines, and rectify the earth's axis!"

A thunder of applause followed this proposal, the author of which was, of course, none other than J. T. Maston. And, in all probability the fiery secretary had been prompted by his engineer's instincts to make so daring a suggestion. Yet, it must be said—since it is true—that many supported him with their shouts, and no doubt, had they had the fulcrum propounded by Archimedes, the Americans would have constructed a lever capable of raising the world and straightening its axis. The point of support was all that these daring mechanics were lacking.

Nevertheless, this "highly practical" idea caught on tremendously; all argument ceased for a good quarter of an hour and for a long, long time throughout the United States there was talk of the proposal so energetically brought forward by the permanent secretary of the Gun Club.

CHAPTER 20

Attack and Riposte

THIS appeared to end the argument. As a closing remark, it could not be improved upon. Yet, as soon as the excitement had subsided, the following words were heard uttered in a strong and determined voice:

"Now that the speaker has favored us with so much imagination, would he be so good as to return to his subject, and give us a little practical view of the question?"

All eyes were directed toward the person who spoke. He was a little dried-up man, with a determined face, adorned by a long goatee. Profiting by the different movements in the crowd, he had managed by degrees to gain the front row of spectators. There, with arms crossed and stern gaze, he watched the hero of the meeting. After having put his question he remained silent, and appeared to take no notice of the thousands of looks directed toward himself, nor of the murmur of disapproval excited by his words. Meeting at first with no reply, he repeated his question with marked emphasis, adding,

"We are here to talk about the *moon* and not about the *earth*."

"You are right, sir," replied Michel Ardan; "the discussion has gone afield. We will return to the moon."

"Sir," said the unknown, "you pretend that our satellite is inhabited. Very good; but if Selenites do exist, that race of beings assuredly must live without breathing, for—I warn you for your own sake—there is not the smallest particle of air on the surface of the moon."

At this remark Ardan pushed up his shock of red hair; he saw that he was on the point of being involved in a struggle with this person upon the very gist of the whole question. He looked sternly at him in his turn and said:

"Oh! so there is no air on the moon? And pray, if you are so good, who ventures to affirm that?"

"The men of science."

"Really?"

"Really."

"Sir," replied Michel, "joking aside, I have a profound respect for men of science who do possess science, but a profound contempt for men of science who do not."

"Do you know of any who belong to the latter category?"

"Decidedly. In France there are some who maintain that, 'mathematically,' a bird cannot possibly fly; and others who demonstrate theoretically that fishes were never made to live in water."

"I have nothing to do with persons of that description, and I can quote, in support of my statement, names which you cannot refuse deference to."

"Then, sir, you will sadly embarrass a poor ignoramus who, indeed, asks nothing better than to learn."

"Why, then, do you tackle scientific questions if you have never studied them?" asked the unknown somewhat rudely.

"For the reason that 'he is always brave who does not suspect the danger.' I know nothing, it is true; but it is precisely my weakness which constitutes my strength."

"Your weakness amounts to folly," retorted the unknown with passion.

"All the better," replied our Frenchman, "if it carries me up to the moon."

Barbicane and his colleagues devoured with their eyes the intruder who had so boldly placed himself in antagonism to their enterprise. Nobody knew him, and the president, uneasy as to the result of so free a discussion, watched his new friend with some anxiety. The audience began to be somewhat concerned also, for the contest directed their attention to the dangers, if not the actual impossibilities, of the proposed expedition.

"Sir," replied Ardan's antagonist, "there are many and incontrovertible reasons which prove the absence of an atmosphere in the moon. I might say that, *a priori,* if one ever did exist, it must have been absorbed by the earth; but I prefer to bring forward indisputable facts."

"Bring them forward then, sir, as many as you please."

"You know," said the stranger, "that when any luminous rays cross a medium such as the ear, they are deflected out of the straight line; in other words, they undergo refraction. Well! When stars are occulted by the moon, their rays, on grazing the edge of her disc, exhibit not the least deviation, nor offer the slightest indication of refraction. It follows, therefore, that the moon cannot be surrounded by an atmosphere."

All eyes were on the Frenchman. For, if this were admitted, the consequences would be serious.

"In point of fact," replied Ardan, "this is your chief, if not your *only* argument; and a really scientific man might be puzzled to answer it. For myself, I will simply say that it is defective, because it assumes that the angular diameter of the moon has been completely determined, which is not the case. But let us proceed. Tell me, my dear sir, do you admit the existence of volcanoes on the moon's surface?"

"Extinct, yes! In activity, no!"

"These volcanoes, however, were by all logic at one time in a state of activity?"

"True! but, as they could furnish themselves the oxygen necessary for combustion, the mere fact of their eruption does not prove the presence of an atmosphere."

"Proceed again, then; and let us set aside this class of arguments in order to come to direct observations. But I warn you that I shall be bringing forward some names."

"Bring them on."

"Here they are. In 1715, the astronomers Louville and Halley, watching the eclipse of the 3rd of May, noted some very extraordinary scintillations. These jets of light, rapid in nature, and of frequent recurrence, they attributed to thunderstorms generated in the lunar atmosphere."

"In 1715," replied the unknown, "the astronomers Louville and Halley mistook for lunar phenomena some which were purely terrestrial, such as meteoric or other bodies which are generated in our own atmosphere. This was the scientific explanation at the time of the facts; and that is my answer now."

"On again, then," replied Ardan, untroubled by the reply. "Herschel, in 1787, observed a great number of luminous points on the moon's surface, did he not?"

"Yes! but without offering any solution of them. Herschel himself never inferred from them the necessity of a lunar atmosphere."

"Well countered," said Michel Ardan with a bow to his opponent. "I can see that you are well versed in moon lore."

146

"Very well indeed, sir, and I might add that Beer and Maedler, the two great authorities upon the moon, are quite agreed as to the entire absence of air on its surface."

A movement was here manifest among the assemblage, who appeared to be growing excited by the arguments of this singular personage.

"Let us proceed," replied Ardan, with perfect coolness, "and come to one important fact. A skillful French astronomer, M. Laussedat, in watching the eclipse of July 18, 1860, noted that the horns of the solar crescent were rounded and truncated. Now, this appearance could only have been produced by a deviation of the solar rays in traversing the atmosphere of the moon. There is no other possible explanation of the fact."

"But is this established as a fact?"

"Absolutely certain!"

A counter-movement here took place in favor of the hero of the meeting, whose opponent was now reduced to silence. Ardan resumed the conversation; and, without exhibiting any exultation at the advantage he had gained, simply said:

"You see, then, my dear sir, we must not pronounce with absolute positiveness against the existence of an atmosphere in the moon. That atmosphere is, probably, of extreme rarity; nevertheless at the present day science generally admits that it exists."

"Not in the mountains, at all events," returned the unknown, unwilling to give in.

"No! but at the bottom of the valleys, and not exceeding a few hundred feet in height."

"In any case you will do well to take every precaution, for the air will be terribly rarefied."

"My good sir, there will always be enough for a solitary

individual; besides, once arrived up there, I shall do my best to economize, and not to breathe except on grand occasions!"

A tremendous roar of laughter rang in the ears of the mysterious interlocutor, who glared fiercely round upon the assembly.

"Then," continued Ardan, with a careless air, "since we are in accord regarding the presence of a certain atmosphere, we are forced to admit the presence of a certain quantity of water. This is a happy consequence for me. Moreover, my amiable contradictor, permit me to submit to you one further observation. We only know *one* side of the moon's disc; and if there is but little air on the face presented to us, it is possible that there is plenty on the one turned away from us."

"And for what reason?"

"Because the moon, under the action of the earth's attraction, has assumed the form of an egg, which we look at from the smaller end. Hence it follows, by Hansen's calculations, that its center of gravity is situated in the other hemisphere. Hence it results that the great mass of air and water must have been drawn away to the other face of our satellite during the first days of its creation."

"Pure fancies!" cried the unknown.

"No! Pure theories! which are based upon the laws of mechanics, and it seems difficult to me to refute them. I appeal then to this meeting, and I put it to them whether life, such as exists upon the earth, is possible on the surface of the moon?"

Three hundred thousand auditors at once applauded the proposition. Ardan's opponent tried to get in another word, but he could not obtain a hearing. Cries and menaces fell upon him like hail.

"Enough! enough!" cried some.

"Drive the intruder off!" shouted others.

"Turn him out!" roared the exasperated crowd.

But he, holding firmly on to the platform, did not budge an inch, and let the storm pass on, which would soon have assumed formidable proportions, if Michel Ardan had not quieted it by a gesture. He was too chivalrous to abandon his opponent in such an extremity.

"You wished to say a few more words?" he asked, in a pleasant voice.

"Yes, a hundred, a thousand; or rather, no, only one! If you persevere in your enterprise, you must be a——"

"Very rash person! How can you treat me as such when I have asked Barbicane for a cylindro-conical projectile, in order to prevent turning round and round on my way like a squirrel?"

"But, unhappy man, the dreadful recoil will smash you to pieces at your starting."

"My dear contradictor, you have just put your finger upon the true and the only difficulty; nevertheless, I have too good an opinion of the industrial genius of the Americans not to believe that they will succeed in overcoming it."

"But the heat developed by the rapidity of the projectile in crossing the strata of air?"

"Oh! the walls are thick, and I shall soon have crossed the atmosphere."

"But victuals and water?"

"I have calculated for a twelvemonth's supply, and I shall be only four days on the journey."

"But for air to breathe on the road?"

"I shall make it by chemical process."

"But your fall on the moon, supposing you ever reach it?"

"It will be six times less dangerous than a sudden fall

149

upon the earth, because the weight will be only one-sixth as great on the surface of the moon."

"Still it will be enough to smash you like glass!"

"What is to prevent my retarding the shock by means of rockets conveniently placed, and fired at the right times?"

"But after all, supposing all difficulties surmounted, all obstacles removed, supposing everything combined to favor you, and granting that you may arrive safe and sound in the moon, how will you come back?"

"I am not coming back!"

At this reply, almost sublime in its very simplicity, the assembly became silent. But its silence was more eloquent than could have been its cries of enthusiasm. The unknown profited by the opportunity and once more protested:

"You will inevitably kill yourself!" he cried; "and your death will be that of a madman, useless even to science!"

"Go on, my dear stranger, for truly your prophecies are most agreeable!"

"This is really too much!" cried Michel Ardan's adversary. "I do not know why I should continue so frivolous a discussion! Do as you please about this insane expedition! We need not blame you for this!"

"Pray don't stand on ceremony!"

"No! another person is responsible for your act."

"Who, may I ask?" demanded Michel Ardan in an imperious tone.

"The ignoramus who organized this equally absurd and impossible experiment!"

The attack was direct. Barbicane, ever since the interference of the stranger, had been making fearful efforts of self-control, trying to "burn his smoke" as certain blast-furnaces do; now, however, seeing himself directly attacked, he rose suddenly, and was rushing upon the enemy who thus braved him to the face, when all at once he found himself separated from him.

The platform was lifted by a hundred strong arms, and the president of the Gun Club shared with Michel Ardan triumphal honors. The shield was heavy, but the bearers came in continuous relays, disputing, struggling, even fighting among themselves in their eagerness to lend their shoulders to this demonstration.

However, the stranger had not profited by the tumult to run away. Besides he could not have done it in the midst of that compact crowd. There he held on in the front row with crossed arms, glaring at President Barbicane.

The latter did not take his eyes off him, and the two men's looks crossed like impatient swords.

The shouts of the immense crowd continued at their highest pitch throughout this triumphal march. Michel Ardan took it all with evident pleasure. His face beamed with delight. Several times the platform seemed seized with pitching and rolling like a weather-beaten ship. But the two heroes of the meeting had good sea-legs. They never stumbled; and their vessel arrived without damage at the port of Tampa Town. Michel Ardan managed fortunately to escape from the last embraces of his vigorous admirers. He made for the Hotel Franklin, quickly gained his chamber, and slid under the bedclothes, while an army of a hundred thousand men kept watch under his windows.

During this time a scene, short, grave, and decisive, took place between the mysterious personage and the president of the Gun Club.

Barbicane, free at last, had gone straight at his adversary.

"Come!" he said shortly.

The other followed him on to the quay; and the two presently found themselves alone at the entrance of an open wharf on Jones' Fall.

The two enemies, still mutually unknown, gazed at each other.

"Who are you?" asked Barbicane.

"Captain Nicholl!"

"So I suspected. Hitherto chance has never thrown you in my way."

"I am come for that purpose."

"You have insulted me."

"Publicly!"

"And you will answer to me for this insult?"

"At this very moment."

"No! I desire that all that passes between us shall be secret. There is a wood situated three miles from Tampa, the wood of Skersnaw. Do you know it?"

"I know it."

"Will you be so good as to enter it tomorrow morning at five o'clock, on one side?"

"Yes! if you will enter at the other side at the same hour."

"And you will not forget your rifle?" said Barbicane.

"No more than you will forget yours," replied Nicholl.

These words having been coldly spoken, the president of the Gun Club and the captain parted. Barbicane returned to his lodging; but, instead of snatching a few hours of repose, he passed the night in endeavoring to discover a means of evading the recoil of the projectile, and resolving the difficult problem proposed by Michel Ardan during the discussion at the meeting.

CHAPTER 21

How a Frenchman
Settles an Argument

WHILE the contract of this duel was being discussed by the president and the captain—this dreadful, savage duel, in which each adversary became a man-hunter —Michel Ardan was resting from the fatigues of his triumph. Resting is hardly an appropriate expression, for American beds rival marble or granite tables for hardness.

Ardan was sleeping, then, quite poorly, tossing about between the towels which served him for sheets, and he was dreaming of making a more comfortable couch in his projectile when a frightful noise disturbed his dreams. Thundering blows shook his door. They seemed to be caused by some iron instrument. A great deal of loud talking was distinguishable in this racket, which was rather too early in the morning.

"Open the door," some one shrieked, "for heaven's sake!"

Ardan saw no reason for complying with a demand so roughly expressed. However, he got up and opened the door just as it was giving way before the blows of this determined visitor. The secretary of the Gun Club burst into the room. A bomb could not have entered the room with less ceremony.

"Last night," cried J. T. Maston, *ex abrupto,* "our president was publicly insulted during the meeting. He has challenged his adversary, who is none other than Captain Nicholl! They are fighting this morning in the wood of Skersnaw. I heard all the particulars from the mouth of Barbicane himself. If he is killed, our scheme is at an end. We must prevent this duel! One man alone has enough influence over Barbicane to stop him, and that man is Michel Ardan."

While J. T. Maston was speaking, Michel Ardan, without interrupting him, had hastily put on his clothes; and, in less than two minutes, the two friends were making for the suburbs of Tampa Town with rapid strides.

It was during this walk that Maston told Ardan the state of the case. He told him the real causes of the hostility between Barbicane and Nicholl; how it was of old date, and why, thanks to mutual friends, the president and the captain had, as yet, never met face to face. He added that it arose simply from a rivalry between iron plates and shot, and, finally, that the scene at the meeting was only the long-sought opportunity for Nicholl to pay off an old grudge.

Nothing is more dreadful than these private duels in America. The two adversaries stalk each other through the brush like wild beasts. Then it is that they might well covet those wonderful properties of the Indians of the prairies—their quick intelligence, their ingenious cunning, their tracking ability, their scent of the enemy. A single mistake, a moment's hesitation, a single false step may cause death. On these occasions Yankees are often accompanied by their dogs, and as both hunter and hunted keep up the struggle for hours on end.

"What demons you are!" cried Michel Ardan, when his companion had depicted this scene to him with much energy.

"Yes, we are," replied J. T. modestly; "but we had better make haste."

Though Michel Ardan and he had raced across the plains still wet with dew, and had taken the shortest route over creeks and ricefields, they could not reach Skersnaw before half past five. Barbicane must have gone in half an hour earlier.

There was an old bushman working there, occupied in making firewood from the trees that he had chopped down.

Maston ran toward him, saying, "Have you seen a man go into the wood, armed with a rifle? Barbicane, the president, my best friend?"

The worthy secretary of the Gun Club thought that his president must be known by all the world. But the bushman did not seem to understand him.

"A hunter?" said Ardan.

"A hunter? Yes," replied the bushman.

"Long ago?"

"About an hour."

"Too late!" cried Maston.

"Have you heard any gunshots?" asked Ardan.

"No!"

"Not one?"

"Not one! That hunter does not seem to be having much luck!"

"What is to be done?" said Maston.

"We must go into the wood, at the risk of being hit by a bullet which is not intended for us."

155

"Ah!" cried Maston, in a tone which could not be mistaken, "I would rather have twenty bullets in my own head than one in Barbicane's."

"Forward, then," said Ardan, pressing his companion's hand.

A few moments later the two friends had disappeared in the copse. It was a dense thicket, in which rose huge cypresses, sycamores, tulip-trees, olives, tamarinds, live oaks, and magnolias. These different trees had interwoven their branches into an inextricable maze, through which the eye could not penetrate. Michel Ardan and Maston walked side by side in silence through the tall grass, cutting themselves a path through the strong creepers, casting curious glances at the bushes and the branches buried in foliage, and momentarily expecting to hear the sound of rifles. As for the traces which Barbicane must have left of his passage through the wood, there was not a vestige of them visible: so they blindly followed these barely marked paths along which an Indian would have followed his enemy step by step.

After an hour spent in vain pursuit the two stopped, in intensified anxiety.

"It must be all over," said Maston, discouraged. "A man like Barbicane would not dodge his enemy, or ensnare him, nor even maneuver! He is too open, too brave. He went straight ahead, right into the danger, and doubtless far enough from the bushman for the wind to prevent his hearing the report of the rifles."

"But surely," replied Michel Ardan, "since we entered the wood we should have heard!"

"And what if we came too late?" cried Maston in tones of despair.

For once Ardan had no reply to make; he and Maston

resumed their walk in silence. From time to time, indeed, they raised great shouts, calling alternately Barbicane and Nicholl, neither of whom, however, answered their cries. Only the birds, awakened by the sound, flew past them and disappeared among the branches, while some frightened deer fled precipitately before them.

For another hour their search was continued. The greater part of the wood had been explored. There was nothing to reveal the presence of the combatants. The information of the bushman was beginning to seem questionable, and Ardan was about to propose their abandoning this useless pursuit, when all at once Maston stopped.

"Hush!" said he. "There is someone down there!"

"Someone?" repeated Michel Ardan.

"Yes; a man! He seems motionless. His rifle is not in his hands. What can he be doing?"

"But can you recognize him?" asked Ardan, whose short sight was of little use to him in such circumstances.

"Yes! yes! He is turning toward us," answered Maston.

"And it is?"

"Captain Nicholl!"

"Nicholl?" cried Michel Ardan, feeling a terrible pang of grief.

Nicholl unarmed! He had, then, no longer anything to fear from his adversary!

"Let us go to him," said Michel Ardan, "and find out what happened."

But he and his companion had barely taken fifty steps, when they paused to examine the captain more attentively. They expected to find a bloodthirsty man, concentrating on his revenge. When they saw him, they remained stupefied.

A net, composed of very fine meshes, hung between two

157

enormous tulip-trees, and in the midst of this snare, with its wings entangled, was a poor little bird, uttering pitiful cries, while it vainly struggled to escape. The bird-catcher who had laid this snare was no human being, but a venomous spider, peculiar to that country, as large as a pigeon's egg, and armed with enormous claws. The hideous creature, instead of rushing on its prey, had seemingly beaten a sudden retreat and taken refuge in the upper branches of the tulip-tree, for a formidable enemy now menaced its stronghold.

Here, then, was Nicholl, his gun on the ground, forgetful of danger, trying if possible to save the victim from its cobweb prison. At last it was accomplished, and the little bird flew joyfully away and disappeared.

Nicholl lovingly watched its flight, when he heard these words pronounced by a voice full of emotion:

"You are indeed a most worthy man!"

He turned. Michel Ardan was before him, repeating in a different tone:

"And a kindhearted one!"

"Michel Ardan!" cried the captain. "What are you doing here, sir?"

"I came to shake your hand, Nicholl, and prevent you from either killing Barbicane or being killed by him."

"Barbicane!" returned the captain. "I have been looking for him for the last two hours in vain. Where is he hiding?"

"Nicholl," said Michel Ardan, "this is not courteous! We ought always to treat an adversary with respect; rest assured if Barbicane is still alive we shall find him; all the more easily because, if he has not, like you, been amusing himself with freeing oppressed birds, he must be looking for *you*. When we have found him, Michel Ardan's word of honor, there will be no duel between you."

"You have insulted me

"Between President Barbicane and myself," gravely replied Nicholl, "there is a rivalry which the death of one of us——"

"Pooh, pooh!" said Ardan. "Good men like you may hate each other, but you still respect each other. You shall not fight!"

"I will fight, sir!"

"No!"

"Captain," said J. T. Maston, with much feeling, "I am a friend of the president's, his *alter ego,* his second self; if you really must kill someone, *shoot me!* It will do just as well!"

"Sir," Nicholl replied, seizing his rifle convulsively, "these jokes——"

"Our friend Maston is not joking," replied Ardan. "I fully understand his idea of being killed himself in order to save his friend. But neither he nor Barbicane will fall before the shots of Captain Nicholl. Indeed I have so attractive a proposal to make to both you rivals, that you will both be eager to accept it."

"What is it?" asked Nicholl with manifest incredulity.

"Patience!" exclaimed Ardan. "I can reveal it only in the presence of Barbicane."

"Let us go in search of him!" cried the captain.

The three men started off at once; the captain, having unloaded his rifle, threw it over his shoulder, and advanced in silence.

Another half-hour passed, and the pursuit was still fruitless. Maston was oppressed by sinister forebodings. He looked fiercely at Nicholl, asking himself whether the captain's vengeance had been already satisfied, and the unfortunate Barbicane, shot, was perhaps lying dead beneath some bloody bush. The same thought seemed to occur to

Ardan; and both were casting inquiring glances at Nicholl, when suddenly Maston paused.

The motionless figure of a man leaning against a gigantic catalpa twenty feet off appeared, half-veiled by the foliage.

"It is he!" said Maston.

Barbicane never moved. Ardan looked at the captain, but he did not wince. Ardan went forward crying:

"Barbicane! Barbicane!"

No answer! Ardan rushed toward his friend; but in the act of seizing his arms, he stopped short and uttered a cry of surprise.

Barbicane, pencil in hand, was tracing formulae and geometrical figures in a memorandum book, while his unloaded rifle lay beside him on the ground.

Absorbed in his studies, Barbicane, in his turn forgetful of the rivalry and the duel, had seen and heard nothing.

When Ardan took his hand, he looked up and stared at his visitor in astonishment.

"Ah, it is you!" he cried at last. "I have found it, my friend, I have found it!"

"What?"

"My plan!"

"What plan?"

"The plan for counteracting the effect of the shock at the departure of the projectile!"

"Indeed?" said Michel Ardan, looking at the captain out of the corner of his eye.

"Yes! water! simply water, which will act as a spring! Ah, Maston," cried Barbicane, "you here also?"

"In person," replied Ardan; "and permit me to introduce to you at the same time the worthy Captain Nicholl!"

"Nicholl!" cried Barbicane, who jumped up at once.

"Pardon me, captain, I had quite forgotten—I am ready!"

Michel Ardan interfered, without giving the two enemies time to say anything more.

"Thank heaven!" said he. "It is fortunate that good men like you two did not meet sooner! We should now have been mourning for one or the other of you. But, thanks to Providence, which interfered, there is now no further cause for alarm. When one can forget his hatred, to solve problems in mechanics, or play tricks on spiders, that hatred is not dangerous to anyone."

Michel Ardan then told the president how the captain had been found occupied.

"I put it to you now," said he in conclusion, "were two such good fellows as you created to shoot each other's heads off?"

This whole situation had something so ridiculous, so unexpected, about it, that Barbicane and Nicholl no longer knew what face to put on for each other. Michel Ardan could feel this, and decided to force the reconciliation.

"My good friends," said he, with his most bewitching smile, "this is nothing but a misunderstanding. Nothing more! Well, to prove that it is all over between you, since you are both men of courage, accept frankly the proposal I am going to make to you."

"Make it," said Nicholl.

"Our friend Barbicane believes that his projectile will go straight to the moon?"

"Yes, certainly," replied the president.

"And our friend Nicholl is persuaded it will fall back upon the earth?"

"I am certain of it," cried the captain.

"Good!" said Ardan. "I cannot hope to make you agree;

but I suggest this: Come with me, and see whether we are stopped on our journey."

"What?" exclaimed J. T. Maston, stupefied.

The two rivals, on this sudden proposal, looked steadily at each other. Barbicane waited for the captain's answer. Nicholl watched for the decision of the president.

"Well?" said Michel. "There is now no fear of the shock!"

"Done!" cried Barbicane.

But quickly as he pronounced the word, he was not before Nicholl.

"Hurrah! bravo! hip! hip! hurrah!" cried Michel, giving a hand to each of the late adversaries. "Now that it is all settled, my friends, allow me to treat you in the French manner. Let us be off to breakfast!"

CHAPTER 22

The New Citizen
of the United States

THAT very day all of America learned at the same time about the duel between Captain Nicholl and President Barbicane, as well as its strange outcome. The part played in the affray by the chivalrous European, his unexpected proposal that resolved the matter, the simultaneous acceptance by the two rivals, the conquest of the lunar continent upon which France and the United States were now to set off together, all contributed to increasing even further Michel Ardan's popularity.

The frenzy with which Yankees can become enthusiastic over an individual is well known. In a country where staid public officials harness themselves to a dancing star's carriage and pull it in triumphal procession, one can picture the excitement unleashed by the audacious Frenchman. If his horses were not unhitched, it was probably only because he did not have any, but all the other signs of popularity were accorded him. There was not a citizen who did not identify with him body and soul. *E pluribus unum,* as the motto of the United States put it.

From that day forth, Michel Ardan had not one moment's rest. Deputations from all corners of the Union harassed him without cessation or intermission. He was compelled to receive them all, whether he would or no. How many hands he shook, how many people he was "hail-fellow-well-met" with, it is impossible to guess! His teeth were soon on edge; his voice became hoarse from the innumerable speeches he had to make, and now came out only in unintelligible sounds, and he came close to contracting gastro-enteritis from all the toasts he had to drink to every county in the Union. Such a triumphal result would have intoxicated any other man; but he managed to keep himself in a state of delightful *semi*-tipsiness.

Among the deputations of all kinds which assailed him, the "lunatics" were careful not to forget what they owed to the future conqueror of the moon. One day, some of these poor people, rather numerous in America, came to call upon him, and requested permission to return with him to their native country. Some of them claimed they could speak "moon language" and offered to teach it to Michel Ardan. He went along with their harmless manias and undertook to deliver messages from them to their friends "back home."

"Singular madness!" said he to Barbicane, after having dismissed the deputation. "And one that often afflicts truly intelligent people. One of our most illustrious scientists, Arago, was telling me that many very wise people, and very conservative in their opinions, were subject to great exaltations, unbelievably strange behavior, whenever the moon possessed them. Do you believe in the influence of the moon on people's health?"

"Scarcely!"

"Nor do I, despite some remarkable recorded facts of

history. For instance, during an epidemic in 1693, a large number of persons died on January 21, at the very moment of an eclipse. The celebrated Bacon always fainted during an eclipse of the moon, to revive only when the moon came out again. Charles VI relapsed six times into madness during the year 1399, all during either the new or the full moon. Some doctors have classified epilepsy among the illnesses affected by the phases of the moon. Nervous diseases often seem to reflect its influence. Mead tells of a child who went into convulsions whenever the moon was in opposition. Gall observed that insane persons underwent an accession of their disorder twice in every month, at the epochs of new and full moon. In fact, numerous observations about vertigos, fevers, somnambulisms, and other human maladies, seem to prove that the moon does exercise some mysterious influence upon man."

"But the how and the wherefore?" asked Barbicane.

"Well, I can only give you the answer which Arago borrowed from Plutarch, which is nineteen centuries old. 'Perhaps the stories are not true!'"

At the height of his triumph, Michel Ardan had to put up with all the annoyances incidental to being a celebrity. Managers of entertainments wanted to exhibit him. Barnum offered him a million to make the tour of the United States in his sideshow, on display like a freak. Michel Ardan called him an elephant-tender and told him *he* was the freak.

Yet, if he refused to lend himself thus to satisfying public curiosity, his pictures, at least, went around the world and were put in the place of honor in everyone's albums. Prints of them were made in all sizes, from life-size down to microscopic postage-stamp thumbnails. Everyone could have pictures of his hero in all imaginable poses, portraits, bust photos, full-length, full face, in profile, in three-quarters, or from behind. More than a million and a half copies were made of them, and this was a fine opportunity for him to piece himself out in relics, but he did not take advantage of it. If he had only sold his hairs at a dollar apiece, he had enough left to make a fortune!

All in all, this popularity did not displease him. On the contrary. He was always at the disposal of the public and corresponded with the whole world. His witticisms were picked up, repeated everywhere, especially those he had not said. They were all attributed to him, as is customary, for on this score he had become rich.

But it was not only the men who were for him, but the women also. He might have married well a hundred times over, if he had been willing to settle in life. The old maids, in particular, of forty and upward, who were drying on the vine, dreamt before his photographs day and night.

They would have married him by hundreds, even if he had made them accompany him into space. He had, however, no intention of transplanting a race of Franco-Americans upon the surface of the moon. He therefore declined all offers.

"Go up there and play Adam with some daughter of Eve?" he exclaimed. "No, thanks, I might meet the serpent."

As soon as he could withdraw from these somewhat embarrassing demonstrations, he went, accompanied by his friends, to pay a visit to the Columbiad. It was the least he could do. Moreover, he had become quite an expert in gunnery, what with associating with Barbicane, J. T. Maston, and all the others. His greatest amusement consisted of telling these fine artillerymen that they were nothing but kindly, scholarly murderers. He never ran out of jokes on this score. On the day he visited the Columbiad, he was most impressed with it, and made the descent to the bottom of the tube of this gigantic machine which was presently to launch him to the regions of the moon.

"At least," he said, "this cannon is not going to do anyone any harm, which is rather unusual for a cannon. But as for your destroying, burning, breaking, killing machines, don't mention them to me—for, even though, in French, their bore is called their *soul,* I know they don't have any!"

It is necessary here to mention a proposal of J. T. Maston's. When the secretary of the Gun Club found that Barbicane and Nicholl accepted the proposal of Michel Ardan, he determined to join them, and make it "a foursome." So one day he requested to be accepted as one of the travelers. Barbicane, pained at having to refuse him, gave him clearly to understand that the projectile could not possibly contain so many passengers. Maston, in despair, went in search of Michel Ardan, who counseled him to resign himself to the situation, adding one or two arguments *ad hominem.*

"You see, old fellow," he said, "you must not take amiss what I say; but really, between ourselves, you are in too incomplete a condition to appear in the moon!"

"Incomplete?" shrieked the valiant invalid.

"Yes, my dear fellow! Imagine our meeting some of the inhabitants up there! Would you like to give them such a melancholy notion of what goes on down here? To teach them what war is, to inform them that we employ our time chiefly in devouring each other, in smashing arms and legs, and that too on a globe which is capable of supporting a hundred billion inhabitants, and which actually does contain barely two hundred million? Why, my worthy friend, they would feel they had to turn us away!"

"But still, if you arrive there in pieces, you will be as incomplete as I am."

"Unquestionably," replied Michel Ardan; "but we shall not."

In fact, a preparatory experiment, tried on the 18th of October, had yielded the best results and caused the most well-grounded hopes of success. Barbicane, desirous of obtaining some notion of the effect of the shock at the moment of the projectile's departure, had procured a 32-inch mortar from the arsenal of Pensacola. He had this placed on the bank of Hillsborough Roads, in order that the shell might fall back into the sea, and the shock be thereby cushioned. His object was to ascertain the extent of the shock of departure, and not that of the arrival. A hollow projectile had been prepared for this curious experiment. A thick padding fastened upon a kind of elastic network, made of the best steel springs, lined the inside of the walls. It was a veritable nest most carefully wadded.

"What a pity I can't find room in there," said J. T. Maston, regretting that his height did not allow him to make the daring attempt.

Within this shell were shut up a large cat, and a squirrel belonging to J. T. Maston, and of which he was particularly fond. They were desirous, however, of ascertaining how this little animal, least of all others subject to dizziness, would endure this experimental voyage.

The mortar was charged with 160 pounds of powder, and the shell placed in the chamber. On being fired, the projectile rose with great velocity, described a majestic parabola, attained a height of about a thousand feet, and with a graceful curve came sinking down into the water.

Without a moment's loss of time a small boat put off in

the direction of its fall; skillful divers plunged into the water and attached ropes to the handles of the shell, which was quickly dragged on board. Five minutes did not elapse between the moment of enclosing the animals and that of unscrewing the coverlid of their prison.

Ardan, Barbicane, Maston, and Nicholl were present on board the boat, and assisted at the operation with an interest which may readily be comprehended. Hardly had the shell been opened when the cat leaped out, slightly bruised, but full of life, and exhibiting no signs whatever of having made an aerial expedition. No trace, however, of the squirrel could be discovered. The truth at last became apparent—the cat had eaten its fellow-traveler!

J. T. Maston grieved much for the loss of his poor squirrel, and proposed to add its name to that of the other martyrs of science.

After this experiment all hesitation, all fear disappeared. Besides, Barbicane's plans would ensure greater perfection for his projectile, and go far to cancel altogether the effects of the shock. Nothing now remained but to go!

Two days later Michel Ardan received a message from the President of the United States, an honor of which he showed himself especially sensible.

After the example of his illustrious fellow-countryman, the Marquis de La Fayette, the government had awarded him the title of "Citizen of the United States of America."

CHAPTER 23

The Projectile-Vehicle

O N the completion of the Columbiad the public interest centered on the projectile itself, the vehicle which was destined to carry the three hardy adventurers into space. No one had forgotten that, by his telegram of September 30th, Michel Ardan had requested an alteration in the plans drawn by the committee members.

President Barbicane at that time had thought that the shape of the projectile did not much matter, since, after having traversed the atmosphere in a few seconds, it would complete the rest of its journey in a total vacuum. Therefore the committee had opted for a round shape, so that the cannon-ball might revolve upon itself and assume whatever position it pleased. But, from the moment that it was to be turned into a vehicle, it was an entirely different matter. Michel Ardan had no desire to travel like a squirrel; he wished to take off with his head up, and feet down, as dignifiedly as in the basket of a balloon, at a much greater speed no doubt, but without being subjected to a succession of untoward somersaults.

The new plans had been sent to Breadwill and Co., of Albany, with the request for their speedy execution. The projectile thus altered was consequently cast on the 2d of November, and immediately forwarded by the Eastern Railway to Stone Hill, which it reached without accident on the tenth of that month, where Michel Ardan, Barbicane, and Nicholl were impatiently waiting for the "projectile-vehicle" in which they were to take flight toward the discovery of a new world.

It must be granted that it was a magnificent piece of metal, a metallurgical product to do the greatest honor to American industrial genius. For the first time, aluminum had been obtained in a rather huge quantity, which in itself could be considered a prodigious accomplishment. The precious projectile glinted in the sunlight. On seeing its impressive shape topped by its conical cap, one might easily have mistaken it for one of those thick turrets shaped like pepper-pots, which architects of the Middle Ages liked to append to the corners of château strongholds. All it lacked was gun-slots and a weathervane.

"I keep expecting," cried Michel Ardan, "to see a man-at-arms come out of it, with arquebuse and coat of steel. Inside that, we will be like feudal lords, and, with a bit of artillery, we could stand off any moon armies that might exist!"

"You like it?" Barbicane asked his friend.

"Oh, yes, no question about that," answered Michel Ardan, who was examining it with an artist's eye. "I am only sorry that its shape is not more elongated, its cone not more graceful; it should have been topped off by a tuft of ornaments made of turned metal, a chimera for instance, or a gargoyle, or a salamander arising out of the flames, with wings spread and maw open. . . ."

"What for?" asked Barbicane, whose practical mind was not too sensible to the beauties of art.

"What for, friend? Well, if you have to ask, I am afraid you would never be able to understand!"

"Tell me anyway."

"Well, as I see it, there should always be something artistic in everything one does; it is better that way. Do you know an Indian play called *The Child's Cart?*"

"I never even heard of it," answered Barbicane.

"I am not surprised," Ardan went on. "Let me tell you, then, that in that play there is a robber who, as he is about to break in to the wall of a house, wonders whether the hole he makes should be in the shape of a lyre, a flower, a bird, or an amphora. Now, tell me, friend Barbicane, if at that time you had been on the jury, would you have found that robber guilty?"

"Without hesitation," answered the president of the Gun Club, "guilty of aggravated breaking and entering."

"And I would have acquitted him, friend Barbicane! That is why you will never be able to understand me!"

"I won't even try, my fine artist."

"But, at least," said Ardan, "since the exterior of our projectile-vehicle is somewhat deficient, I trust I will be allowed to furnish it to my taste on the inside, with all the luxury that behooves ambassadors from Earth!"

"On that score, Michel," answered Barbicane, "you can do as you please, and we will not interfere with you."

But, before going on to attractiveness, the president of the Gun Club had paid close attention to the practical, and the methods he had devised to reduce the effects of the blast had been applied with consummate intelligence.

Barbicane had reasoned, correctly, that no spring would be powerful enough to cushion the shock and, during his walk through the wood of Skersnaw, he had finally resolved this great problem in an ingenious fashion. Water was what he intended to use for this outstanding service. Here is how:

The projectile was now to be filled to the depth of three feet with a bed of water, intended to support a water-tight wooden disc, which worked easily within the walls of the projectile. It was on this raft that the travelers were to take their place. This body of water was divided by horizontal partitions, which the shock of the departure would have to break in succession. Then each sheet of water, from the lowest to the highest, running off into escape tubes toward the top of the projectile, constituted a kind of spring and the wooden disc, supplied with extremely powerful plugs, could not strike the lowest plate except after the successive breaking of the different partitions. Undoubtedly the travelers would still have to undergo a violent recoil after the complete escapement of the water; but the first shock would be almost entirely canceled by this powerful spring.

It is true that three feet of water on a surface of fifty-four square feet would weigh in the neighborhood of 11,500 pounds; but the pressure of the gases accumulated within the Columbiad, according to Barbicane, would be enough to overcome this increased weight. Moreover, the shock would drive out all of this water in less than one second, and the projectile would rapidly resume its normal weight.

This was what the president of the Gun Club had devised and how he thought he had succeeded in solving the serious question of the initial shock. And what is more, this scheme, which had been intelligently understood by the Breadwill engineers, had been marvelously executed. Once the effect had been produced and the water had been driven out, the travelers could easily get rid of the broken partitions and take down the moving disc upon which they had been stationed at the moment of departure.

The upper parts of the walls were lined with a thick

padding of leather, fastened upon springs of the best steel, as flexible as watch-springs, behind which the escape tubes were completely concealed.

Thus all imaginable precautions had been taken for averting the first shock; and if they did get crushed, they must, as Michel Ardan said, be "made of very bad materials."

The projectile was nine feet in diameter on the outside and twelve feet high. In order not to exceed the predetermined weight, the thickness of its walls had been slightly reduced and its bottom part reinforced, since the latter would receive the full thrust of the gases caused by the explosion of the pyroxylin. This is how it is always done with cylindro-conical bombs and shells, the bottom being always the thickest part.

The entrance to this metallic tower was through a narrow aperture contrived in the wall, looking like the manholes of steam boilers. This was hermetically closed by a plate of aluminum, fastened internally by the pressure of powerful screws. The travelers would therefore be able to leave their flying prison at will, as soon as they reached the moon.

But getting there was not enough; they also had to see along the way. Nothing could be easier. Light and view were afforded by four portholes of thick optical glass, two cut into the circular wall itself, a third in the bottom, and the fourth in the conical top. The travelers, along their route, would thus be able to observe the earth which they were leaving, the moon which they were approaching, and the starry spaces of the sky. The portholes in turn were protected against the shock of departure by plates set solidly in grooves, which could be swung out easily by unscrewing them from the inside. In this way, the air within the projectile could not escape, but observation was made possible in all directions.

All of these mechanisms, admirably set up, functioned most easily, and the engineers had displayed no less intelligence in the internal fittings of the projectile-vehicle.

Firmly fixed reservoirs held the water and provisions necessary for the three travelers; fire and light were readily available by means of gas, contained in a special reservoir under a pressure of several atmospheres. They had only to turn a tap, and for six days the gas would light and warm this comfortable vehicle. As can be seen, they were lacking in nothing essential for life or even for comfort. Beyond this, through the efforts of Michel Ardan, attractiveness was added to usefulness in the shape of objects of art; he would have turned his projectile into a veritable artist's studio, if space had permitted. And yet, it would be wrong to imagine that three persons would find themselves cramped within this metal tower. It had an area of about fifty-four square feet by ten feet in height, which allowed its guests quite a bit of freedom of movement. They would not have been any more comfortable in the most luxurious railway car in the United States.

With food and light taken care of, there remained the question of air. It was obvious that the air contained in the projectile would not be enough to allow the travelers to breathe for four days. Each man in an hour consumes the amount of oxygen contained in about twenty-five gallons of air. Barbicane, his two companions, and the two dogs he planned to take along, would use up in twenty-four hours about six hundred gallons of oxygen, weighing about seven pounds. The air in the projectile had to be renewed. How?

By a very simple process, that of Reiset and Regnault, which Michel Ardan had outlined during the discussion at the meeting.

Now, we know that air consists of twenty-one parts of oxygen and seventy-nine parts of nitrogen. What happens when we breathe? A very simple phenomenon. The lungs absorb the oxygen in the air, admirably suited to the support of life, and reject the nitrogen intact. The air exhaled loses nearly five per cent of its oxygen and now contains nearly an equal volume of carbonic acid, produced by the combustion of the elements of the blood with the oxygen inhaled. In an air-tight enclosure, then, after a certain time, all the oxygen of the air will be replaced by the carbonic acid—a gas fatal to life.

There were two things to be done then, since the nitrogen has remained intact—first, to replace the absorbed oxygen; second, to destroy the expelled carbonic acid; both easy enough to do, by means of chlorate of potassium and caustic potash.

The former is a salt which appears under the form of white crystals; when raised to a temperature above 400 degrees centigrade, it is transformed into chloride of potassium, and the oxygen which it contains is entirely liberated. Now eighteen pounds of chlorate of potassium produce seven pounds of oxygen—the quantity necessary for the travelers during twenty-four hours. So, the oxygen is restored.

Caustic potash has a great affinity for carbonic acid; and it is sufficient to shake it in order for it to seize upon the acid and form bicarbonate of potassium. So, the carbonic acid is absorbed.

By these two means they would be enabled to restore

to the vitiated air its life-supporting properties. This was what the chemists Reiset and Regnault had proved, but it is necessary to add that the experiments had hitherto been made *in anima vili*. Whatever its scientific accuracy was, they were at present ignorant how it would affect human beings.

This was what was pointed out at the session at which this serious problem was discussed. Michel Ardan did not want to question the possibility of living on this artificial air, and he offered to try the experiment before their departure. But the honor of putting it to the test was energetically demanded by J. T. Maston.

"Since I am not to go," said the brave artilleryman, "I may at least live for a week in the projectile."

It would have been unkind to refuse him; so they consented to his wish. A sufficient quantity of chlorate of potassium and of caustic potash was placed at his disposal, together with provisions for eight days. And having shaken hands with his friends, on the 12th of November, at six A.M., after strictly informing them not to open his prison before the 20th, at six P.M., he slipped into the projectile, the plate of which was at once hermetically sealed.

What happened during that week? They could get no information. The thickness of the walls of the projectile prevented any inside sound from reaching to the outside.

On the 20th of November, at six P.M. exactly, the plate was opened. The friends of J. T. Maston had all along been in a state of much anxiety; but they were promptly reassured on hearing a jolly voice shouting a boisterous hurrah.

The secretary of the Gun Club shortly thereafter appeared at the top of the cone in a triumphant attitude. He had put on weight!

CHAPTER 24

The Telescope
of the Rocky Mountains

On the 20th of October in the preceding year, after the close of the subscription, the president of the Gun Club had credited the Observatory of Cambridge with the necessary sums for the construction of a gigantic optical instrument. This instrument, to be either a refracting or reflecting telescope, was designed for the purpose of rendering visible on the surface of the moon any object at least nine feet in diameter.

There is a significant difference between refracting and reflecting telescopes; it will be well to recall it here. The refracting telescope is made up of a tube equipped at its upper end with a convex lens known as the objective, and at its lower end with a second lens called the ocular, to which the observer applies his eye. The rays emanating from the luminous object go through the first lens and then, by refraction, go on to form an inverted image at the focus.[1] This image is seen through the ocular, which enlarges it exactly as would a magnifying glass. The tube of the refracting

[1] The point at which the light rays meet after having been refracted.

178

telescope is thus closed at either end by the objective and the ocular lenses.

On the other hand, the tube of a reflecting telescope is open at its upper end. The rays coming from the object under observation enter freely into it and go on to strike a concave, that is to say converging, metallic mirror (or object-glass). From there, the reflected rays meet a small mirror which relays them to the ocular, set up in such a way as to magnify the image produced.

Thus, in refracting telescopes, refraction is the principal mechanical operation, while in reflecting telescopes, it is reflection. Whence the fact that the former are known as refractors, and the latter reflectors. The entire difficulty in creating such optical instruments lies in the production of the objectives, whether they be lenses or metallic mirrors.

At the period when the Gun Club was trying its great experiment, such instruments had reached a high degree of perfection, and produced some magnificent results. It was a long time since the period when Galileo observed the heavenly bodies through his poor refractor that magnified them only seven times at the most. Since the sixteenth century, optical instruments had grown in breadth and length in considerable proportions, and they allowed the measuring of stellar spaces to depths previously unheard of. Among the main refractors in use at the time, there were the one at the Observatory of Pulkovo in Russia, with its 15-inch objective,[2] the one of the French optician Lerebours with an objective of the same size, and finally the refractor of the Cambridge Observatory, equipped with an objective nineteen inches in diameter.

Two telescopes in particular, at this time, were possessed

---

[2] At a cost of 80,000 rubles (somewhat over $40,000).

of remarkable power and of gigantic dimensions. The first, constructed by Herschel, was thirty-six feet in length, and had an object-glass of four feet six inches; it possessed a magnifying power of 6,000. The second was raised in Birr, Ireland, in Parsonstown Park, and belongs to Lord Rosse. The length of this tube was forty-eight feet, and the diameter of its object-glass six feet;[3] it magnified 6,400 times, and required an immense erection of brickwork and masonry for the purpose of working it, its weight being 28,000 pounds.

Still, despite these colossal dimensions, the actual enlargements did not exceed 6,000 times in round numbers; consequently, the moon was brought within no nearer an apparent distance than thirty-nine miles; and objects of less than sixty feet in diameter, unless they were of very considerable length, were still imperceptible.

In the present case, dealing with a projectile nine feet in diameter and fifteen feet long, it became necessary to bring the moon within an apparent distance of five miles at most; and, for that purpose, to establish a magnifying power of 48,000 times.

Such was the question proposed to the Observatory of Cambridge. There was no lack of funds; the difficulty was purely one of construction.

There was, first, the question of choosing between a reflecting and a refracting telescope. Refractors had advantages over reflectors. With the same size of objectives, they allowed much greater enlargements, because the rays of

---

[3] One often hears talk of refractors of much greater length; one, in particular, 300 feet long, was set up by Dominique Cassini at the Paris Observatory; but one must understand that these refractors did not have tubes. The objective was hung from a mast, and the observer, his eyepiece in hand, tried to place himself as close to the focus of the objective as possible. It is easy to see how difficult such instruments were to use and how hard it was exactly to center two lenses placed under such conditions.

light going through the lenses lose less by absorption than by the reflection of the metallic mirrors. But the thickness one can give to a lens is limited, for, if it is too thick, it no longer allows the rays to go through. Besides, the construction of these huge lenses is exceedingly difficult, and requires considerable time, often measured in years.

Therefore, even though the image is lighted better in a refractor—an inestimable advantage when one is looking at the moon, whose light is simply reflected—it was decided to use a reflector, which can be more quickly made and permits greater enlargements. However, since the light rays lose a great deal of their intensity as they go through earth's atmosphere, the Gun Club decided to set up the instrument on one of the highest mountains in the United States, which would reduce the depth of air to be traversed.

In such reflecting telescopes, as we have seen, the ocular, or eyepiece, is the magnifying glass, and the objective that will allow for the greatest magnifications is the one with the greatest diameter and the deepest length of focus. In order to magnify over 48,000 times, it was necessary to use a size significantly greater than those of the objectives of Herschel or Lord Rosse. Therein lay the difficulty, for the casting of these mirrors is a very delicate operation.

Fortunately, a few years earlier, Léon Foucault, a scientist of the Institut de France, had just perfected a process which allowed for very easy and very rapid polishing of the objectives, replacing the metallic mirrors by silver-plated ones. All that was necessary was to cast a piece of glass of the desired dimensions and then metal-plate it with silver salts. This process, which gives excellent results, was the one followed for the fabrication of the objective.

Moreover, it was set up in the manner invented by

Herschel for his telescopes. In the great instrument of the astronomer of Slough, the image of the objects, reflected by the slanted mirror at the bottom of the tube, took form for observation at the other end where the eyepiece was located. Thus, the observer, instead of being at the lower end of the tube, climbed up to its upper part, and there, with his magnifying-glass, looked down into the enormous cylinder. This disposition had the advantage that it did away with the small mirror used to send the image back to the eyepiece. The image was therefore reflected only once rather than twice. So, a smaller number of rays of light were lost to absorption; the image was that much less diluted; and finally, it was that much clearer, which was a precious advantage for the observation that had to be made.[4]

After these decisions were made, the work was finally commenced. According to the calculations of the Observatory of Cambridge, the tube of the new reflector would require to be 280 feet in length, and the object-glass sixteen feet in diameter. Colossal as these dimensions may appear, they were diminutive in comparison with the 10,000-foot telescope proposed by the astronomer Hooke only a few years ago! Yet, setting up such an instrument presented great difficulties.

Regarding the choice of locality, that matter was promptly determined. The object was to select some lofty mountain, and there are not many of these in the United States.

In fact there are but two chains of moderate elevation, between which runs the magnificent Mississippi, the "king of rivers," as these Republican Yankees would delight in calling it, if they admitted the existence of kings.

4 These reflectors are known as front-view telescopes.

The gigantic reflector is installed desp
innumerable obstac

Eastwards rise the Appalachians, the very highest point of which, in New Hampshire, does not exceed the very moderate altitude of 5,600 feet.

On the west, however, rise the Rocky Mountains, that immense range which, commencing at the Straits of Magellan, follows the western coast of South America under the name of the Andes or Cordilleras, until it crosses the Isthmus of Panama, and runs up the whole of North America to the very borders of the Polar Sea.

These mountains are not very elevated, and the Alps or Himalayas would look down on them with supreme disdain from the heights of their grandeur. Indeed, their tallest peak is but 10,701 feet, while Mont Blanc is 14,439, and Kinchinjunga is 27,776 feet above sea level.

With such an elevation, nevertheless, the Gun Club were compelled to be content, inasmuch as they had determined that both telescope and Columbiad should be erected within the limits of the Union. All the necessary apparatus was consequently sent on to the summit of Longs Peak, in the territory of Missouri.

Neither pen nor language can describe the difficulties of all kinds which the American engineers had to surmount, or the prodigies of daring and skill which they accomplished. It was truly a *tour de force.* They had to raise enormous stones, massive pieces of wrought iron, heavy corner-clamps and huge portions of cylinder, with an object-glass weighing nearly 30,000 pounds, above the line of perpetual snow at more than 10,000 feet in height, after crossing desert prairies, impenetrable forests, fearful rapids, far from all centers of population, and in the midst of savage regions, in which every detail of life become an almost insoluble problem. And yet, notwithstanding these innumerable obstacles,

American genius triumphed. In less than a year after the commencement of the works, toward the close of September, the gigantic reflector rose into the air to a height of 280 feet. It was raised by means of an enormous iron crane; an ingenious mechanism allowed it to be easily worked toward all the points of the heavens, and to follow the stars from the one horizon to the other during their journey through the heavens.

It had cost over $400,000. The first time it was directed toward the moon the observers evinced both curiosity and anxiety. What were they about to discover in the field of this telescope which magnified objects 48,000 times? Would they perceive peoples, herds of lunar animals, towns, lakes, seas? No! There was nothing which science had not already discovered! And on all the points of its disc the volcanic nature of the moon became determinable with the utmost precision.

But the telescope of the Rocky Moutains, before doing its duty to the Gun Club, rendered immense services to astronomy. Thanks to its penetrative power, the depths of the heavens were sounded to the utmost extent; the apparent diameter of a great number of stars was accurately measured; and Mr. Clark, of the Cambridge staff, resolved the Crab nebula in Taurus, which the reflector of Lord Rosse had never been able to decompose.

CHAPTER 25

Final Details

I T was the 22d of November; the departure was to take place in ten days. One operation alone remained to be accomplished to bring all to a happy termination; an operation delicate and perilous, requiring infinite precautions, and against the success of which Captain Nicholl had laid his third bet. It was, in fact, nothing less than the loading of the Columbiad, and the introduction into it of 400,000 pounds of gun-cotton. Nicholl had thought, perhaps not without reason, that the handling of such formidable quantities of pyroxylin would involve a grave catastrophe; and, at any rate, that this immense mass of eminently inflammable matter would inevitably ignite when submitted to the pressure of the projectile.

These were serious dangers, further complicated by the carefreeness and nonchalance of the Americans who, during the Civil War, had never hesitated to smoke cigars while loading their cannons. But Barbicane was determined to succeed and not to be left at the start; so he selected his best workmen, had them carry out the job before his very eyes, never once looking away from them, and, by dint of prudence and precautions, he was able to marshal all chances of success on his side.

In the first place, he was very careful not to have all of the load transported at once to the Stone Hill enclosure. He had it brought in little by little in perfectly sealed caissons. The 400,000 pounds of pyroxylin had been split up into 500-pound packages, which worked out to eight hundred solid cartridge-containers carefully made by the most skillful ordnance-men at Pensacola. Each caisson could hold ten of them, and one by one they arrived at Tampa Town by railroad; in that way there was never more than five thousand pounds of pyroxylin in the yard at any one time. On arrival, each caisson was unloaded by barefooted workmen, and each cartridge-container transported to the opening of the Columbiad, into which it was lowered by the use of hand-controlled cranes. No steam-engine was permitted to operate, and even the slightest fires were extinguished within a radius of two miles. Even in November, they feared to work by day, lest the sun's rays acting on the gun-cotton lead to unhappy results. This meant working at night, by light produced in a vacuum by means of Rühmkorff's apparatus, which threw an artificial brightness into the depths of the Columbiad. There the cartridges were arranged with the utmost regularity, connected by a metal wire, which would simultaneously send the electric spark to the heart of each of them.

A battery was to flash the fire to this mass of gun-cotton. All the wires, wrapped in an insulating material, joined into one at a small opening cut at the height at which the projectile was to be maintained, where they went through the thick cast-iron wall and on up to ground level through one of the vents in the stone revetment that had been provided toward this end. Once at the top of Stone Hill, the wire, strung on poles for a distance of two miles, led to a powerful Bunsen battery, after going through a switch. All that was needed was for the switch-button to be pressed, and contact was immediately re-established and the spark shot to all 400,000 pounds of gun-cotton. It is of course obvious that this battery was to be used only at the last moment.

By the 28th of November the eight hundred cartridges had been placed in the bottom of the Columbiad. So far the operation had been successful. But what confusion, what anxieties, what struggles were undergone by President Barbicane! In vain had he refused admission to Stone Hill; every day inquisitive neighbors scaled the palisades, some even carrying their imprudence to the point of smoking while surrounded by bales of gun-cotton. Barbicane was in a perpetual state of alarm. J. T. Maston seconded him to the best of his ability, by giving vigorous chase to the intruders, and carefully picking up the still lighted cigar ends which the Yankees threw about. A somewhat difficult task, seeing that more than 300,000 persons were gathered round the enclosure. Michel Ardan had volunteered to superintend the transport of the caissons to the mouth of the Columbiad; but the president, having caught him with an enormous cigar in his mouth, while he was hunting out the rash spectators to whom he himself offered so dangerous an example, saw that he could not trust this fearless smoker, and was therefore obliged to mount a special guard over him.

At last, since there is a god of artillerymen, nothing exploded, and the loading came to a happy termination, Captain Nicholl's third bet being thus nearly lost. It remained now to introduce the projectile into the Columbiad, and to place it on its deep layer of gun-cotton.

But before doing this, all those things necessary for the

journey had to be carefully arranged in the projectile-vehicle. These necessaries were numerous; and had Ardan been allowed to follow his own wishes, there would have been no space remaining for the travelers. It is impossible to conceive of half the things this charming Frenchman wished to convey to the moon. A veritable stock of useless trifles! But Barbicane interfered and refused admission to anything not absolutely needed.

Several thermometers, barometers, and telescopes were packed in the instrument case.

The travelers being desirous of examining the moon carefully during their voyage, in order to facilitate their studies, they took with them Beer and Maedler's excellent *Mappa Selenographica,* a masterpiece of patience and observation in four plates. This map reproduced with scrupulous fidelity the smallest details of the lunar surface which faces the earth; the mountains, valleys, amphitheatres, craters, peaks, and ridges were all represented, with their exact dimensions, relative positions, and names, from Doerfel and Leibnitz mountains, high points on the eastern side of the disc, to the *Mare frigoris* around the North Pole.

This was most useful, as they could thus study the moon even before setting foot there.

They took also three rifles and three fowling-pieces, and a large quantity of shot and powder.

"We cannot tell whom we shall have to deal with," said Michel Ardan. "Men or beasts may possibly object to our visit. It is only wise to take all precautions."

These defensive weapons were accompanied by pick-axes, crowbars, saws, and other useful implements, not to mention clothing adapted to every temperature, from the cold of the polar regions to the heat of the torrid zone.

Final Details

Ardan wished to convey a number of animals of different sorts, though not a pair of every known species, since he could not see the necessity of acclimatizing serpents, tigers, alligators, or any other noxious beasts in the moon.

"Nevertheless," he said to Barbicane, "some valuable and useful beasts, bullocks, cows, horses, and donkeys would bear the journey very well, and would also be very useful to us."

"I dare say, my dear Ardan," replied the president, "but our projectile-vehicle is not Noah's ark, from which it differs both in dimensions and object. Let us confine ourselves to possibilities."

After prolonged discussion, it was finally agreed that the travelers should restrict themselves to a sporting-dog belonging to Nicholl, and to a large and unusually powerful Newfoundland. Several cases of the most useful seeds were also included among the necessaries. Michel Ardan, indeed, was anxious to add some sacks full of earth to sow them in; as it was, he took a dozen shrubs carefully wrapped up in straw to plant in the moon.

The important question of provisions still remained; it being necessary to provide against the possibility of their landing on a portion of the moon that was absolutely barren. Barbicane managed so successfully, that he supplied them with rations sufficient for a year. These consisted of preserved meats and vegetables, reduced by strong hydraulic pressure to the smallest possible dimensions. They were highly nutritive, if not very varied, but under such circumstances, one could not be difficult. Their supply consisted of fifty gallons of brandy, but water enough for only two months, as they were confident, from astronomical observations, that there was no lack of water on the moon's surface. As to provisions, doubtless, inhabitants of the earth could find nourishment somewhere on the moon. Ardan never questioned this; indeed, had he done so, he would never have undertaken the journey.

"Besides," he said one day to his friends, "we shall not be completely abandoned by our terrestrial friends; they will take care not to forget us."

"No, indeed!" replied J. T. Maston.

"What do you mean?" asked Nicholl.

"Nothing could be simpler," replied Ardan; "the Columbiad will be always there. Well! whenever the moon is in a favorable condition as to the zenith, if not to the perigee, that is to say about once a year, could they not send us a shell packed with provisions, which we might expect on an appointed day?"

"Hurrah! hurrah!" cried J. T. Maston; "what an ingenious fellow! what a splendid idea! Indeed, my good friends, we shall not forget you!"

"I shall depend on you! Then, you see, we shall receive news regularly from the earth, and we shall indeed be stupid if we hit upon no plan for communicating with our good friends here!"

These words bespoke such confidence that Michel Ardan could have carried all of the Gun Club with him in his enthusiasm. What he said seemed so simple and so easy, so sure of success, that none could be so sordidly attached to this earth as to hesitate to follow the three travelers on their lunar expedition.

When the various objects had been installed within the projectile, the water to be used for cushioning was pumped inside its partitions, and the illuminating gas compressed into its reservoir. As for the chlorate of potassium and the caustic potash, Barbicane, guarding against unexpected delays en route, loaded aboard enough to renew the oxygen and absorb the carbonic acid for two months. An extremely ingenious and fully automatic device was to restore its life-giving properties to the air and purify it completely. The projectile was thus ready and all that remained was to place it in the Columbiad, an operation abundantly accompanied by dangers and difficulties.

The enormous shell was conveyed to the summit of Stone Hill. There, powerful cranes raised it, and held it suspended over the mouth of the cylinder.

It was a fearful moment! What if the chains should break under its enormous weight? The sudden fall of such a body would inevitably cause the gun-cotton to explode!

Fortunately this did not happen; and some hours later the projectile-vehicle descended gently into the bore of the cannon and rested on its couch of pyroxylin, a veritable bed of explosive eider-down. Its pressure had no result other than the more effectual ramming-down of the charge of the Columbiad.

"I have lost," said the captain, who forthwith paid President Barbicane the sum of three thousand dollars.

Barbicane did not wish to accept the money from one of his fellow-travelers, but gave way at last before the determination of Nicholl, who wished before leaving the earth to discharge all his obligations.

"Now," said Michel Ardan, "I have only one thing more to wish for you, my brave captain."

"What is that?" asked Nicholl.

"It is that you may lose your other two bets! Then we shall be sure to complete our journey!"

CHAPTER 26

Fire!

THE first of December had arrived, the fatal day, for, if the projectile were not discharged that very night at 10h. 46m. 40s. P.M., more than eighteen years must roll by before the moon would again present herself under the same simultaneous conditions of zenith and perigee.

The weather was magnificent. Despite the approach of winter, the sun shone brightly, and bathed in its radiant light that earth which three of its denizens were about to abandon for a new world.

How many persons lost their rest on the night which preceded this long-expected day! How many chests were constricted with apprehension! All hearts beat with disquiet, save only the heart of Michel Ardan. That imperturbable personage came and went with his habitual business-like air, while nothing whatever denoted that any unusual matter preoccupied his mind. His sleep was peaceful, like Turenne's on his gun-carriage on the eve of battle.

Since dawn, an innumerable multitude covered the prairie which extends, as far as the eye can reach, around Stone Hill. Every quarter of an hour the railway brought fresh accessions of sightseers in fantastic numbers and, according to the statement of the *Tampa Town Observer,* no less than five millions of spectators thronged the soil of Florida on that memorable day.

For a whole month previously, the mass of these persons had bivouacked around the enclosure, and laid the foundations for a town which was afterward called Ardan Town. The whole plain was covered with huts, cabins, cottages, and tents and the population of these makeshift abodes was enough to make Europe's greatest cities jealous.

Every nation under the sun was represented there; and every language might be heard spoken at the same time. It was a perfect Babel reenacted. All the various classes of American society were mingled together in terms of absolute equality. Bankers, farmers, sailors, cotton-planters, brokers, agents, merchants, watermen, magistrates, elbowed each other in the most free-and-easy way. Louisiana Creoles fraternized with farmers from Indiana; Kentucky and Tennessee gentlemen and haughty Virginians conversed with half-savage trappers from the lakes and butchers from Cincinnati. Broad-brimmed beaver hats and Panamas, blue cotton trousers from the mills at Opelousas, light-colored stockings, cambric frills, were all here displayed; while upon shirt-fronts, wristbands, and neckties, upon every finger, even upon the very ears, they wore an assortment of rings, shirt-pins, diamonds, brooches, and trinkets, of which the value equaled the execrable taste. Women, children, and servants, in equally expensive dress, surrounded their husbands, fathers, or masters, who looked like tribal chieftains in the midst of their immense households.

At meal-times all fell to work upon the dishes peculiar to the Southern States, and, with an appetite that threatened speedy exhaustion of the victualing powers of Florida, consumed dishes which would turn a European stomach, such as fricasseed frogs, stuffed monkey, fish chowder, rare roast possum, and raccoon steaks.

And as for the liquors which accompanied this indigestible repast! The shouts, the vociferations that resounded through the bars and taverns decorated with glasses, tankards, flasks, carafes, and bottles of marvelous shape, mortars for pounding sugar, and bundles of straw!

"Mint-julep!" roars one of the barmen.

"Claret sangaree!" shouts another.

"Cocktail!" "Brandy-smash!"

"Real mint-julep in the latest style!" cried out these adroit manipulators, as—like prestidigitators handling their accessories—they kept switching from glass to glass the sugar, lemon, green mint, crushed ice, water, cognac, and fresh pineapple that compose this refreshing drink.

Usually, such cries—addressed to throats parched by the fiery effects of spices—intermingled in the air to produce a bewildering deafening hubbub. But that day, the first of December, they were rare. The peddlers would have cried out in vain. No one was thinking of eating or drinking, and at four P.M. there were vast numbers of spectators who had not even taken their customary lunch! And, a still more significant fact, even the national passion for gaming seemed quelled for the time under the general excitement of the hour. On seeing the tenpins lying idle, the dice of the crap games remaining in their shakers, the roulette wheels unturning, the forgotten cribbage boards, the decks of cards for the whist, blackjack, red-and-black, monte and faro games still unopened in their original packs, it was obvious that the event of the day absorbed all interests and left room for no diversion.

Until nightfall, a dull, simmering agitation, such as precedes great catastrophes, ran through the anxious multitude. An indescribable uneasiness pervaded all minds, a painful torpor, an indefinable sensation which oppressed the heart. Every one wished it was over.

However, about seven o'clock, the heavy silence was suddenly dissipated. The moon rose above the horizon. Millions of hurrahs hailed her appearance. She was punctual to the rendezvous, and shouts of welcome greeted her on all sides, as Phoebe's pale beams shone gracefully in the clear heavens and her most affectionate rays caressed the intoxicated crowd.

At this moment the three intrepid travelers appeared. This was the signal for renewed cries of still greater intensity. Instantly the vast assemblage, as with one accord, struck up the national anthem of the United States, and *Yankee Doodle,* sung by five million hearty throats, rose like a roaring tempest to the farthest limits of the atmosphere.

Then a profound silence gradually took hold throughout the crowd. The Frenchman and the two Americans had by this time entered the reserved enclosure at the center of the multitude. They were accompanied by the members of the Gun Club, and by deputations sent from all the European observatories. Barbicane, cool and collected, was quietly giving his final directions. Nicholl, with compressed lips, his hands clasped behind his back, walked with a firm and measured step. Michel Ardan, always easy, dressed in thorough traveler's costume, leathern gaiters on his legs, pouch by his side, in loose brown velvet suit, cigar in mouth, shook hands with everyone. He was full of inexhaustible gayety, laughing, joking, playing tricks on the dignified J. T. Maston. In one word, he was the thorough "Frenchman" (and worse, a "Parisian") to the very last moment.

Ten o'clock struck. The moment had arrived for taking their places in the projectile! The necessary operations for the descent, the screwing down of the hatches, and the subsequent removal of the cranes and scaffolding that inclined over the mouth of the Columbiad, required a certain period of time.

Barbicane had regulated his chronometer to a tenth of a second on that of Murchison the engineer, who was charged with the duty of firing the gun by means of the electric spark. Thus the travelers enclosed within the projectile were enabled to follow with their eyes the impassive watch-hand which marked the precise moment of their departure.

The moment had arrived for saying "good-bye!" The scene was a touching one. Despite his feverish gayety, even Michel Ardan was touched. J. T. Maston had found in his own dry eyes one ancient tear, which he had doubtless saved for the occasion. He dropped it on the forehead of his dear president.

"Can I not go?" he said. "There is still time!"

"Impossible, old fellow!" replied Barbicane.

A few moments later, the three fellow-travelers had ensconced themselves in the projectile, and screwed down the plate which covered the entrance-aperture. The mouth of the Columbiad, now completely disencumbered, was open entirely to the sky.

Nicholl, Barbicane, and Michel Ardan were definitively enclosed within their metal coach.

What words can describe the universal emotion, now at its very highest pitch?

The moon was advancing upward in a heaven of the purest clearness, outshining in her passage the twinkling light of the stars. She was passing over the constellation

Gemini and was now nearing the halfway point between the horizon and the zenith.

A terrible silence weighed upon the entire scene. Everyone could thus see that their aim had a "lead" on the target, just as the hunter fires ahead of the hare he hopes to hit. Not a breath of wind upon the earth! Not a sound of breathing from the countless chests of the spectators! Their hearts seemed afraid to beat! All the terrified eyes were fixed upon the yawning mouth of the Columbiad.

Murchison followed with his eye the hand of his chronometer. It was scarcely forty seconds to the moment of departure, but each second seemed to last an age!

At the twentieth there was a general shudder, as it occurred to the minds of that vast assemblage that the bold travelers shut up within the projectile were also counting those terrible seconds. Some few cries here and there could be heard from the crowd.

"Thirty-five! — thirty-six! — thirty-seven! — thirty-eight! — thirty-nine! — forty! FIRE!!!"

Instantly Murchison's finger pressed the key of the electric battery, restored the contact, and discharged the spark into the breech of the Columbiad.

An appalling, unprecedented, unearthly report followed instantly, such as can be compared to nothing whatever known, not even to the roar of thunder, or the blast of volcanic explosions! An immense spout of fire shot up from the bowels of the earth as from a crater. The earth heaved up, and only a very few of the spectators were able to obtain a momentary glimpse of the projectile victoriously cleaving the air in the midst of the fiery vapors!

CHAPTER 27

Foul Weather

At the moment when that spray of fire rose to such a prodigious height in the air, the glare of the flame lit up the whole of Florida; and for the briefest moment day superseded night over a considerable extent of the country. This immense canopy of fire was visible at a distance of one hundred miles out at sea, and more than one ship's captain entered in his log the appearance of this gigantic meteor.

The discharge of the Columbiad was accompanied by a veritable earthquake. Florida was shaken to its very depths. The gases of the powder, expanded by heat, forced back the atmospheric strata with tremendous violence, and this artificial hurricane, a hundred times stronger than any natural one, rushed like a waterspout through the air.

Not a single spectator remained on his feet! Men, women, children, all lay prostrate like ears of corn under a tempest. There ensued a terrible tumult; a large number of persons were seriously injured. J. T. Maston, who, despite all dictates of prudence, had stayed too close, was pitched back 120 feet, shooting like a projectile over the heads of his fellow-citizens. Three hundred thousand persons remained deaf for a brief time, and as though struck dumb.

The blast of air, after knocking down hutments, shattering cabins, uprooting trees over a radius of twenty miles, driving railroad cars off their tracks all the way to Tampa, now struck that city like an avalanche, and destroyed some one hundred-odd buildings, including St. Mary's Church, and the brand new Stock Exchange, which split along its entire length. Some of the ships tied up in port, being dashed against each other, sank forthwith, and a dozen of the larger ones, lying at anchor in the harbor, washed ashore after having snapped their chains as if they were cotton threads.

But the circle of these devastations stretched even further, and beyond the limits of the United States. The effect of the impact, helped along by west winds, was felt out on the Atlantic as far as three hundred miles from the American shores. An artificial storm, an unexpected one, that Admiral FitzRoy's meteorology had been unable to predict, struck the ships with unheard-of violence; a number of them, caught in these terrible whirlwinds before they had a chance to strike canvas, sank with all sails aloft, among them the *Childe Harold,* out of Liverpool, in a regrettable catastrophe which brought about the sharpest protests from Great Britain.

Finally, and to cap it all, even though the fact is verified by nothing more than the word of a few natives, a half-hour after the launching of the projectile, inhabitants of Gorée and Sierra Leone claimed to have heard a dull rumble, the very last displacement of sound waves which, having crossed the Atlantic, were expiring on the coast of Africa.

But, to get back to Florida. As soon as the first effects were over, the injured, the deaf, and finally the whole crowd came to life, and the skies were rent with frenzied cries of "Hurrah for Ardan! Hurrah for Barbicane! Hurrah for Nicholl!" Several million people, their noses in the air, armed with telescopes and race-glasses, were questioning space, forgetting all contusions and emotions in the one idea of watching for the projectile. They looked in vain! It was no longer to be seen, and they were obliged to wait for telegrams from Longs Peak. The director of the Cambridge Observatory[1] was at his post on the Rocky Mountains; and to him, as a skillful and persevering astronomer, all observations had been confided.

But a phenomenon that was not foreseen, although it might have been—yet one against which nothing could be done—came in to subject the public impatience to a severe trial.

The weather, hitherto so fine, suddenly changed; the sky became heavy with clouds. It could not have been otherwise after the terrible derangement of the atmospheric strata, and the dispersion of the enormous quantity of vapor arising from the combustions of 200,000 pounds of pyroxylin! All of nature had been upset. This could not come as a surprise, since, during sea battles, the weather has often been seen to be noticeably affected by massive firing of artillery.

On the morrow the horizon was covered with clouds—a thick and impenetrable curtain between earth and sky, which unhappily extended as far as the Rocky Mountains. It was a fatality! Complaints about it arrived from every part of the globe. But nothing could be done about it, and since man had chosen so to disturb the atmosphere, he was bound to accept the consequences of his experiment.

During that first day, everyone tried to break through the dense veil of clouds, but no one succeeded, and of course they were all wrong to be looking toward the sky at

[1] Mr. Belfast.

any rate, for, as a result of the diurnal movement of the globe, the projectile was necessarily at the time on a line with the antipodes.

However that may be, when the deep, dark, impenetrable night returned to envelop the earth, and the moon had again risen above the horizon, it was impossible to see her; one might have believed she was deliberately keeping herself hidden from the eyes of the audacious earthlings who had dared fire at her. So, no observation was possible, and the telegrams from Longs Peak confirmed this sad fact.

Supposing, now that the experiment had succeeded, the travelers having started out on the first of December at 10h., 46m., 40s. P.M., were due to arrive on the 4th at exactly midnight. So, until that time, since it would have been very difficult after all to have observed, under such conditions, a body so small as the shell, they waited with what patience they could muster.

On the 4th of December, from 8 P.M. to midnight, it would have been possible to track the projectile, which would have appeared as a black speck against the bright disc of the moon. But the skies remained unremittingly overcast, which brought public exasperation to a paroxysm. People began hurling insults at the moon for not showing her face. A sorry turn of events down on earth!

In desperation, J. T. Maston left for Longs Peak. He wanted to do his observing first-hand. He never doubted that his friends would arrive safely at the goal of their journey. Besides, there had been no report that the projectile had fallen back to earth anywhere on the terrestrial islands or continents, and J. T. Maston did not for an instant admit the possibility of a fall into the oceans which cover three-quarters of the globe.

On the 5th, same weather. The great telescopes of the Old World, Herschel's, Rosse's, Foucault's, remained immovably focussed on the moon, for it so happened that the weather was magnificent in Europe; but the relative weakness of these instruments made all their observations futile.

On the 6th, same weather. Three-quarters of the globe was devoured with impatience. People started to make the most insane suggestions of ways to dispel the accumulation of clouds in the air.

On the 7th, the sky seemed to change a little. This raised some hope, but it did not last long, and in the evening the thickened clouds still closed off the heavenly vault from all eyes.

Then things started getting serious. Indeed, on the 11th, at 9h. 11m. A.M., the moon was due to enter its last quarter. After that, it would be increasingly on the wane and, even if the skies were to clear, the possibilities of observation would be singularly lessened. This meant that the moon would offer an ever smaller portion of its disc to the view and would end by becoming new, in other words, setting and then rising with the sun, whose rays would make it totally invisible. It would then be necessary to await the 3rd of January, at forty-four minutes after noon, for the moon to be full again so that observations could be resumed.

The newspapers published these facts along with a thousand commentaries, and made no bones of the fact that the public would be forced to display angelic patience.

On the 8th, nothing. On the 9th, the sun reappeared for a moment, as if to mock the Americans. It was received with hisses; and, wounded, no doubt, by such a reception, showed itself very sparing of its rays.

On the 10th, no change! J. T. Maston went nearly mad,

and great fears were entertained regarding the brain of this worthy individual, which had hitherto been so well preserved within his gutta-percha cranium.

But on the 11th one of those inexplicable tempests peculiar to those intertropical regions was let loose in the atmosphere. A terrific east wind swept away the groups of clouds which had been so long gathering, and at night the semi-disc of the orb of night rode majestically amid the soft constellations of the sky.

CHAPTER 28

A New Star

THAT very night, the startling news so impatiently awaited burst like a thunderbolt over the States of the Union, and thence, darting across the ocean, ran through all the telegraphic wires of the globe. The projectile had been detected, thanks to the gigantic reflector of Longs Peak!

Here is the note written by the director of the Observatory of Cambridge. It contains the scientific conclusion regarding this great experiment of the Gun Club.

LONGS PEAK, December 12

To the Officers of the
Observatory of Cambridge

The projectile discharged by the Columbiad at Stone Hill has been detected by Messrs. Belfast and J. T. Maston, 12th of December, at 8:47 P.M., the moon having entered her last quarter.

This projectile has not arrived at its destination. It has passed by the side; but sufficiently near to be retained by the lunar attraction.

The rectilinear movement has thus become changed into a circular motion of extreme velocity, and it is now pursuing an elliptical orbit round the moon, of which it has become a true satellite.

The elements of this new star we have as yet been unable to

determine; we do not yet know the velocity of its revolution or rotation. The distance which separates it from the surface of the moon may be estimated at about 2,833 miles.

However, two hypotheses come here into our consideration.

1. Either the attraction of the moon will end by drawing them into itself, and the travelers will attain their destination; or,

2. The projectile, following an immutable law, will continue to gravitate round the moon till the end of time.

At some future time, our observations will be able to determine this point, but until now the experiment of the Gun Club has had no other result than to provide our solar system with a new star.

J. M. BELFAST

To how many questions did this unexpected denouement give rise? What mysterious results was the future reserving for the investigations of science? Thanks to the courage and devotion of three men, this undertaking, so futile on the surface, of trying to send a shot to the moon, had just had an immense result, the consequences of which are incalculable. The travelers, imprisoned in a new satellite, if they had not attained their goal, had at least become part of the lunar world; they were in orbit around the star of the night and, for the first time, the naked human eye was in a position to penetrate its mysteries. The names of Nicholl, Barbicane, and Michel Ardan were certain to be immortalized in the annals of astronomy, for these daring explorers, in the interest of enlarging the field of human knowledge, had audaciously launched themselves out into space and gambled their lives in the strangest attempt of modern times.

However that might be, when the dispatch from Longs Peak had once become known, there was a universal feeling of surprise and alarm. Was it possible to go to the aid of these bold travelers? No! for they had placed themselves beyond the pale of humanity, by crossing the limits imposed by the Creator on his earthly creatures. They had air enough for *two* months; they had victuals enough for *twelve;—but after that?* The most insensitive hearts quailed at the thought.

There was only one man who would not admit that the situation was desperate—he alone had confidence; and that was their devoted friend, a man as daring and determined as they, J. T. Maston.

Besides, he never let them get out of sight. His home was henceforth the post at Longs Peak; his horizon, the mirror of that immense reflector. As soon as the moon rose above the horizon, he immediately caught her in the field of the telescope; he never let her go for an instant out of his sight, and followed her assiduously in her course through the stellar spaces. He watched with untiring patience the passage of the projectile across her silvery disc, and really the worthy man remained in perpetual communication with his three friends, whom he did not despair of seeing again some day.

"We will correspond with them," he told anyone who would listen, "as soon as circumstances permit. We will get news from them and send them news of us! For I know them; they are ingenious men. Those three men have carried into space all the resources of art, science, and industry. With that, one can do anything; and you will see that, in the end, they will come out all right."

Around *the* Moon | A SEQUEL TO
From the Earth *to the* Moon

Contents

Illustrations

PRELIMINARY

Recapitulating the First Part of this Work
and Serving as a Preface to the Second

During the year 186—, the whole world was greatly excited by a scientific experiment unprecedented in the annals of science. The members of the Gun Club, a circle of artillerymen formed at Baltimore after the American war, conceived the idea of putting themselves in communication with the moon—yes, with the moon—by sending a projectile to her. Their president, Barbicane, the promoter of the enterprise, having consulted the astronomers of the Cambridge Observatory upon the subject, took all necessary means to insure the success of this extraordinary enterprise, which had been declared practicable by the majority of competent judges. After setting on foot a public subscription, which netted close to $6,000,000, they began the gigantic work.

According to the advice forwarded from the members of the Observatory, the gun destined to launch the projectile had to be set up in a country situated between the o and 28th degrees of North or South latitude, in order to aim at the moon when at the zenith; and its initial velocity was fixed at twelve thousand yards to the second. Launched on the first of December, at 10hrs. 46m. 40s. P.M., it was to reach the moon four days after its departure, that is on the 5th of December, at midnight precisely, at the moment of her attaining her perigee, or her nearest distance from the earth, which is 238,833 miles mean distance.

The principal members of the Gun Club, President Barbicane, Major Elphinstone, the secretary J. T. Maston, and other learned men, held several meetings, at which the shape and composition of the projectile were discussed, as well as the position and nature of the gun, and the quality and quantity of the powder to be used. It was decided: First, that the projectile should be a shell made of aluminum with a diameter of 108 inches and a thickness of twelve inches to its walls; and should weigh 19,250 pounds. Second, that the gun should be a Columbiad cast in iron, 900 feet long, and run perpendicularly into the earth. Third, that the charge should contain 400,000 pounds of gun-cotton, which, creating six billion liters of gas behind the projectile, would easily carry it toward the orb of night.

These questions prompted President Barbicane, assisted by Murchison the engineer, to choose a spot situated in Florida, at latitude 27° 7′ north, and longitude 82° 45′ west. It was on this spot, after stupendous labor, that the Columbiad was cast with full success.

Things stood thus, when an incident took place which increased a hundredfold the interest attached to this great enterprise.

A Frenchman, an enthusiastic Parisian, as witty as he was bold, asked to be enclosed in the projectile, in order that he might reach the moon, and reconnoiter this terrestrial satellite. The name of this intrepid adventurer was Mi-

chel Ardan. He landed in America, was received with enthusiasm, held meetings, saw himself carried in triumph,
reconciled President Barbicane with his mortal enemy, Captain Nicholl, and, as a token of reconciliation, persuaded
them both to go with him in the projectile.

The proposition being accepted, the shape of the projectile was slightly altered. It was made of a cylindro-conical
form. This aerial coach was lined with strong springs and
partitions to lessen the shock of departure. It was provided
with food for a year, water for some months, and gas for
some days. An automatic apparatus supplied the three travelers with air to breathe. At the same time, on one of the
highest points of the Rocky Mountains, the Gun Club had
a gigantic telescope erected, in order that they might be
able to follow the course of the projectile through space.
All was then ready.

On the 30th of November, at the hour fixed upon, from
the midst of an extraordinary crowd of spectators, the departure took place, and for the first time, three human beings
left the terrestrial globe, and launched into interplanetary
space with almost a certainty of reaching their destination. These bold travelers, Michel Ardan, President Barbicane, and Captain Nicholl, were to make the passage in
ninety-seven hours, thirteen minutes, and twenty seconds.
Consequently, their arrival on the lunar disc could not take
place until the 5th of December at twelve at night, at the
exact moment when the moon should be full, and not on the
4th, as some misinformed newspapers had announced.

But an unforeseen circumstance, viz., the detonation produced by the Columbiad, had the immediate effect of trou-
bling the terrestrial atmosphere, by accumulating a large
quantity of vapor, a phenomenon which aroused universal

indignation, for the moon was hidden from the eyes of watchers for several nights.

The worthy J. T. Maston, the staunchest friend of the three travelers, started for the Rocky Mountains, accompanied by the Hon. J. Belfast, director of the Cambridge Observatory, and reached the station of Longs Peak, where the telescope was erected which brought the moon within an apparent distance of two leagues. The honorable secretary of the Gun Club wished himself to observe the vehicle of his daring friends.

The accumulation of the clouds in the atmosphere prevented all observations on the 5th, 6th, 7th, 8th, 9th, and 10th of December. Indeed it was thought that all observations would have to be put off to the 3rd of January in the following year; for the moon, entering its last quarter on the 11th, would then only present an ever-decreasing portion of her disc, insufficient to allow of their following the course of the projectile.

At length, to the general satisfaction, a heavy storm cleared the atmosphere on the night of the 11th to the 12th of December, and the moon, with half-illuminated disc, was plainly visible against the black sky.

That very night a telegram was sent from the station of Longs Peak by J. T. Maston and Belfast to the gentlemen of the Cambridge Observatory.

Now, what did this telegram say?

It announced that, on the 11th of December at 8h. 47m. P.M., the projectile launched by the Columbiad of Stone Hill had been detected by Messrs. Belfast and Maston—that it had deviated from its course from some unknown cause, and had not reached its destination; but that it had passed near enough to be retained by the lunar attraction; that its rectilinear movement had been changed to a circular one, and that, following an elliptical orbit round the star of night, it had become its satellite.

The telegram added that the elements of this new star had not been calculated; and indeed three observations made upon a star in three different positions are necessary to determine these elements. Then it showed that the distance separating the projectile from the lunar surface "might" be reckoned at about 2,833 miles.

It ended with this double hypothesis: either the attraction of the moon would draw it to herself, and the travelers thus attain their end; or the projectile, held in one immutable orbit, would gravitate around the lunar disc for all eternity.

With such alternatives, what would be the fate of the travelers? Certainly they had food for some time. But supposing they did succeed in their rash enterprise, how would they return? Could they ever return? Would they be able to send news of themselves? These questions, debated by the most learned pens of the day, strongly engrossed the public attention.

It is advisable here to make a remark which ought to be well considered by hasty observers. When a purely speculative discovery is announced to the public, it cannot be done with too much prudence. No one is obliged to discover either a planet, a comet, or a satellite; and whoever makes a mistake in such a case exposes himself justly to the derision of the masses. Far better is it to wait; and that is what the impatient J. T. Maston should have done before sending forth to the world this telegram which, according to his idea, told the whole result of the enterprise.

Indeed this telegram contained two sorts of errors, as was proved eventually. First, errors of observation, concerning the distance of the projectile from the surface of the moon, for on the 11th of December it was impossible to see it; and what J. T. Maston had seen, or thought he saw, could not have been the projectile of the Columbiad. Second, errors of theory on the fate in store for the said projectile; for, making it into a satellite of the moon was to run counter to all rational mechanical laws.

One single hypothesis of the observers of Longs Peak could ever be realized, that which foresaw the case of the travelers (if still alive) uniting their efforts with the lunar attraction to attain the surface of the disc.

Now these men, as clever as they were daring, had survived the terrible shock of their departure and it is their journey in the projectile car which is here related in its most dramatic as well as in its most singular details. This recital will destroy many illusions and surmises; but it will give a true idea of the strange adventures in store for such an enterprise; it will bring out the scientific instincts of Barbicane, the industrious resources of Nicholl, and the audacious humor of Michel Ardan.

Besides this, it will prove that their worthy friend J. T. Maston was wasting his time, as, leaning over the gigantic telescope, he watched the course of the moon through starry space.

CHAPTER 1

From 10:20 to 10:47 p.m.

As ten o'clock struck, Michel Ardan, Barbicane, and Nicholl took leave of the numerous friends they were leaving on the earth. The two dogs, destined to propagate the canine race on the lunar continents, were already shut up in the projectile. The three travelers approached the orifice of the enormous cast-iron tube, and a crane let them down to the conical top of the projectile.

There, an opening made for the purpose gave them access to the aluminum car. The tackle of the crane being hauled outside, the mouth of the Columbiad was instantly disencumbered of its last supports.

Nicholl, once introduced with his companions inside the projectile, began to close the opening by means of a strong plate, held in position by powerful screws. Other plates, closely fitted, covered the lenticular glasses, and the travelers, hermetically enclosed in their metal prison, were plunged into profound darkness.

"And now, my dear companions," said Michel Ardan, "let us make ourselves at home; I am a domesticated man and strong in housekeeping. We had better make the best of our new lodgings, and make ourselves comfortable. And first let us try and see a little. Gas was not invented for moles!"

So saying, the carefree fellow lit a match by striking it on the sole of his boot; and approached the burner fixed to the receptacle, in which the carbonized hydrogen, stored at high pressure, was to light and warm the projectile for a hundred and forty-four hours, or six days and six nights.

The gas caught fire, and thus lighted the projectile looked like a comfortable room with thickly padded walls, furnished with a circular divan, and a roof rounded in the shape of a dome.

The objects it contained, arms, instruments, and utensils, securely fastened against the rounds of wadding, could bear the shock of departure with impunity. Humanly speaking, every possible precaution had been taken to bring this rash experiment to a successful termination.

Michel Ardan examined everything, and declared himself satisfied with his installation.

"It is a prison," said he, "but a traveling prison; and, with the right of putting my nose to the window, I could well stand a lease of a hundred years. You smile, Barbicane. Have you any *arrière-pensée?* Do you say to yourself, 'This prison may be our tomb?' Tomb, perhaps; still I would not change it for Mahomet's, which floats in space, but never advances an inch!"

While Michel Ardan was speaking, Barbicane and Nicholl were making their last preparations.

Nicholl's chronometer stood at twenty minutes past ten P.M. when the three travelers were finally enclosed in their projectile. The chronometer was set within a tenth of a second on that of Murchison the engineer. Barbicane consulted it.

"My friends," said he, "it is twenty minutes past ten. At forty-seven minutes past ten Murchison will launch the electric spark on the wire which communicates with the charge of the Columbiad. At that precise moment we shall leave our spheroid. Thus we have still twenty-seven minutes to remain on the earth."

"Twenty-six minutes, thirteen seconds," replied the methodical Nicholl.

"Well!" exclaimed Michel Ardan, in a good-humored tone, "much may be done in twenty-six minutes. The gravest questions of morals and politics may be discussed, and even solved. Twenty-six minutes well employed are worth more than twenty-six years in which nothing is done. A few seconds of a Pascal or a Newton are more precious than the whole existence of a crowd of raw simpletons——"

"And you conclude, then, you everlasting talker?" asked Barbicane.

"I conclude that we have twenty-six minutes left," replied Ardan.

"Twenty-four only," said Nicholl.

"Well, twenty-four, if you like, my noble captain," said Ardan; "twenty-four minutes in which to investigate——"

"Michel," said Barbicane, "during the passage we shall have plenty of time to investigate the most difficult questions. For the present we must occupy ourselves with our departure."

"Are we not ready?"

"Doubtless; but there are still some precautions to be taken, to deaden as much as possible the first shock."

"Have we not the water-cushions placed between the partition-breaks, whose elasticity will sufficiently protect us?"

215

"I hope so, Michel," replied Barbicane gently, "but I am not sure."

"Ah, the joker!" exclaimed Michel Ardan. "He hopes!—He is not sure!—and he waits for the moment when we are encased to make this deplorable admission! I beg to be allowed to get out!"

"And how?" asked Barbicane.

"Humph!" said Michel Ardan, "it is not easy; we are aboard the train, and the conductor's whistle will blow in less than twenty-four minutes."

"Twenty," said Nicholl.

For some moments the three travelers looked at each other. Then they began to examine the objects imprisoned with them.

"Everything is in its place," said Barbicane. "We have now to decide how we can best place ourselves to resist the shock. Position cannot be an indifferent matter; and we must, as much as possible, prevent the rush of blood to the head."

"Just so," said Nicholl.

"Then," replied Michel Ardan, ready to suit the action to the word, "let us put our heads down and our feet in the air, like the clowns at the Great Circus."

"No," said Barbicane, "let us stretch ourselves on our sides; we shall resist the shock better that way. Remember that, when the projectile starts, it matters little whether we are in it or before it; it amounts to much the same thing."

"If it is only 'much the same thing,' I feel better," said Michel Ardan.

"Do you approve of my idea, Nicholl?" asked Barbicane.

"Entirely," replied the captain. "We've still thirteen minutes and a half."

"That Nicholl is not a man," exclaimed Michel; "he is a chronometer with seconds, an escapement, and eight holes."

But his companions were not listening; they were making their final arrangements with the most perfect coolness. They were like two methodical travelers in a car, seeking to place themselves as comfortably as possible. We might well ask ourselves of what materials are made the hearts of these Americans, to which the approach of the most frightful danger added no pulsation.

Three thick and solidly-made berths had been placed in the projectile. Nicholl and Barbicane arranged them in the center of the disc forming the floor. There the three travelers were to stretch themselves some moments before their departure.

During this time, Ardan, not being able to keep still, turned in his narrow prison like a wild beast in a cage, chatting with his friends, speaking to the dogs Diana and Satellite, to whom, as may be seen, he had given significant names.

"Ah, Diana! Ah, Satellite!" he exclaimed, teasing them; "so you are going to show the moon-dogs the good habits of the dogs of the earth! That will do honor to the canine race! If ever we do come down again, I want to bring back a crossbreed of moon-dogs, which will make a stir!"

"If there *are* dogs in the moon," said Barbicane.

"There are," said Michel Ardan, "just as there are horses, cows, donkeys, and chickens. I bet that we shall even find chickens."

"A hundred dollars we shall find none!" said Nicholl.

"Done, captain!" replied Ardan, clasping Nicholl's hand. "But, by the bye, you have already lost three bets with our president, as the necessary funds for the enterprise were

217

found, the operation of casting has been successful, and lastly, the Columbiad has been loaded without accident, six thousand dollars."

"Yes," replied Nicholl. "Thirty-seven minutes, six seconds past ten."

"It is understood, captain. Well, before another quarter of an hour you will have to count out nine thousand dollars more to the president; four thousand because the Columbiad will not burst, and five thousand because the projectile will rise more than six miles in the air."

"I have the dollars," replied Nicholl, slapping the pocket of his coat. "I only ask to be allowed to pay."

"Come, Nicholl, I see that you are an orderly man, something I could never be; but you have indeed made a series of bets of very little advantage to yourself, allow me to tell you."

"And why?" asked Nicholl.

"Because, if you win the first, the Columbiad will have burst, and the projectile with it; and Barbicane will no longer be there to reimburse your dollars."

"My stake is deposited at the bank in Baltimore," replied Barbicane simply; "and if Nicholl is not there, it will go to his heirs."

"Ah, you practical men, you positive minds," exclaimed Michel Ardan; "I admire you the more for not being able to understand you."

"Forty-two minutes past ten!" said Nicholl.

"Only five minutes more!" answered Barbicane.

"Yes, five little minutes!" replied Michel Ardan; "and we are enclosed in a projectile, at the bottom of a gun 900 feet long! And under this projectile are rammed 400,000 pounds of gun-cotton, which is equal to 1,600,000 pounds of ordinary powder! And friend Murchison, with his chronometer in hand, his eye fixed on the needle, his finger on the electric apparatus, is counting the seconds and getting ready to launch us into interplanetary space."

"Enough, Michel, enough!" said Barbicane, in a serious voice; "let us prepare. A mere few instants separate us from an eventful moment. One clasp of the hand, my friends."

"Yes," exclaimed Michel Ardan, more moved than he wished to appear.

And the three bold companions were united in a last embrace.

"God preserve us!" said the religious Barbicane.

Michel Ardan and Nicholl stretched themselves on the berths placed in the center of the disc.

"Forty-seven minutes past ten!" murmured the captain.

Twenty seconds more! Barbicane quickly put out the gas and lay down by his companions.

The profound silence was broken only by the ticking of the chronometer marking the seconds.

Suddenly a dreadful shock was felt, and the projectile, under the force of six billion liters of gas, developed by the combustion of pyroxylin, mounted into space.

CHAPTER 2

The First Half-hour

WHAT had happened? What effect had this frightful shock produced? Had the ingenuity of the constructors of the projectile obtained any happy result? Had the shock been deadened, thanks to the springs, the four plugs, the water-cushions, and the partition-breaks? Had they been able to subdue the frightful pressure of the initial speed of more than 12,000 yards, which was enough to traverse Paris or New York in a second? This was obviously the question suggested to the thousand spectators of this moving scene. They forgot the aim of the journey, and thought only of the travelers. And if one among them—J. T. Maston for example—could have cast one glimpse into the projectile, what would he have seen?

Nothing then. The darkness was profound. But its cylindro-conical partitions had resisted wonderfully. Not a rent or a dent anywhere! The wonderful projectile was not even heated under the intense deflagration of the powder, nor liquefied, as they seemed to fear, in a shower of aluminum.

The interior showed but little disorder; indeed, only a few objects had been violently thrown toward the roof; but the most important seemed not to have suffered from the shock at all; their fixtures were intact.

The First Half-hour

On the movable disc, sunk down to the bottom by the smashing of the partition-breaks and the escape of the water, three bodies lay apparently lifeless. Barbicane, Nicholl, and Michel Ardan—did they still breathe? or was the projectile nothing now but a metal coffin, bearing three corpses into space?

Some minutes after the departure of the projectile, one of the bodies moved, shook its arms, lifted its head, and finally succeeded in getting on its knees. It was Michel Ardan. He felt himself all over, gave a sonorous "Hem!" and then said:

"Michel Ardan is whole. How about the others?"

The courageous Frenchman tried to rise, but could not stand. His head swam, the rush of blood blinded him; he was like a drunken man.

"Bur-r!" said he. "This produces the same effect as two bottles of Corton, though it is perhaps less agreeable to swallow."

Then, passing his hand several times across his forehead and rubbing his temples, he called in a firm voice:

"Nicholl! Barbicane!"

He waited anxiously. No answer; not even a sigh to show that the hearts of his companions were still beating. He called again. The same silence.

"The devil!" he exclaimed. "They look as if they had fallen from a fifth story on their heads. Bah!" he added, with that imperturbable confidence which nothing could check, "if a Frenchman can get on his knees, two Americans ought to be able to get on their feet. But first let's get some light on the matter!"

Ardan felt the tide of life return by degrees. His blood became calm, and returned to its accustomed circulation.

221

Another effort restored his equilibrium. He succeeded in rising, drew a match from his pocket, and approaching the burner lighted it. The receptacle had not suffered at all. The gas had not escaped. Besides, the smell would have betrayed it; and in that case Michel Ardan could not have carried a lighted match with impunity through the space filled with hydrogen. The gas mixing with the air would have produced a detonating mixture, and the explosion would have finished what the shock had perhaps begun.

When the burner was lit, Ardan leaned over the bodies of his companions: they were lying one on the other, an inert mass, Nicholl above, Barbicane underneath.

Ardan lifted the captain, propped him up against a divan, and began to rub vigorously. This massage, used with judgment, restored Nicholl, who opened his eyes, and instantly recovering his presence of mind, seized Ardan's hand and looked around him.

"And Barbicane?" said he.

"Each in turn," replied Michel Ardan imperturbably. "I began with you, Nicholl, because you were on the top. Now let us look to Barbicane."

Saying which, Ardan and Nicholl raised the president of the Gun Club and laid him on the divan. He seemed to have suffered more than either of his companions; he had lost some blood, but Nicholl was reassured to find that the hemorrhage came from a slight wound on the shoulder, a mere graze, which he bound up carefully.

Still, Barbicane was a long time coming to, which frightened his friends, who did not hold back on the massage.

"He is breathing though," said Nicholl, putting his ear to the chest of the wounded man.

"Yes," replied Ardan, "he is breathing like a man who is

used to doing it every day. Rub, Nicholl; let us rub harder."

And the two improvised practitioners worked to such good effect that Barbicane recovered his senses. He opened his eyes, sat up, took his two friends by the hands, and his first words were:

"Nicholl, are we moving?"

Nicholl and Barbicane looked at each other; they had not yet concerned themselves about the projectile; their first thought had been for the traveler, not for the car.

"Well, are we really moving?" repeated Michel Ardan.

"Or quietly resting on the ground in Florida?" asked Nicholl.

"Or at the bottom of the Gulf of Mexico?" added Michel Ardan.

"What an idea!" exclaimed the president.

And this double hypothesis suggested by his companions had the effect of bringing him back to reality.

In any case they could not decide on the position of the projectile. Its apparent motionlessness, and the lack of communication with the outside, prevented them from solving the question. Perhaps the projectile was unwinding its course through space. Perhaps after a short rise it had fallen upon the earth, or even into the Gulf of Mexico—a fall which the narrowness of the peninsula of Florida made conceivable.

The case was serious, the problem interesting, and one that must be solved as soon as possible. Thus, highly excited, Barbicane's moral energy triumphed over physical weakness, and he rose to his feet. He listened. Outside was perfect silence; but the thick padding was enough to intercept all sounds coming from the earth. Yet one circumstance struck Barbicane, viz., that the temperature inside the projectile was singularly high. The president drew a thermometer from its case and consulted it. The instrument showed 113° Fahrenheit.

"Yes," he exclaimed, "yes, we are moving! This stifling heat, penetrating through the partitions of the projectile, is produced by its friction on the atmospheric strata. It will soon diminish, because we are already floating in space, and after having been nearly stifled, we shall suffer intense cold."

"What!" said Michel Ardan. "According to you, Barbicane, we are already beyond the limits of terrestrial atmosphere?"

"Without a doubt, Michel. Listen to me. It is fifty-five minutes past ten; we have been gone about eight minutes; and if our initial speed had not been reduced by the friction, six seconds would be enough for us to pass through the forty miles of atmosphere that surround the globe."

"Just so," replied Nicholl; "but in what proportion do you estimate the reduction of speed by friction?"

"In the proportion of one-third, Nicholl. This reduction is considerable, but according to my calculations it is nothing less. If, then, we had an initial speed of 12,000 yards, on leaving the atmosphere this speed would be reduced to 8,000 yards. In any case we have already passed through this interval, and——"

"And then," said Michel Ardan, "friend Nicholl has lost his two bets: four thousand dollars because the Columbiad did not burst; five thousand dollars because the projectile has risen more than six miles. Now, Nicholl, pay up."

"Let us prove it first," said the captain, "and we will pay afterward. It is quite possible that Barbicane's reasoning is correct, and that I have lost my nine thousand dollars. But a new hypothesis presents itself to my mind, that cancels the wager."

"What is that?" asked Barbicane quickly.

"The hypothesis that, for some reason or other, fire was never set to the powder, and we have not started at all."

"My goodness, captain," exclaimed Michel Ardan, "that hypothesis is worthy of my brain! It cannot be a serious one. For have we not been half annihilated by the shock? Did I not recall you to life? Is not the president's shoulder still bleeding from the blow it has received?"

"Granted," replied Nicholl; "but one question."

"Well, captain?"

"Did you hear the detonation, which certainly must have been loud?"

"No," replied Ardan, much surprised; "certainly I did not hear the detonation."

"And you, Barbicane?"

"Nor I, either."

"Very well," said Nicholl.

"Well, now," murmured the president, "why did we not hear the detonation?"

The three friends looked at each other with a disconcerted air. It was a quite inexplicable phenomenon. The projectile had started, and consequently there must have been a detonation.

"Let us first find out where we are," said Barbicane, "and let down the panel."

This very simple operation was soon accomplished. The nuts which held the bolts to the outer plates of the right-hand scuttle gave way under the pressure of the monkey-wrench. These bolts were pushed outside, and buffers covered with India-rubber stopped up the holes which let them through. Immediately the outer plate fell back upon its hinges like a porthole, and the lenticular glass which closed the scuttle

225

appeared. A similar one was let into the thick partition on the opposite side of the projectile, another in the top of the dome, and finally, a fourth in the middle of the base. They could, therefore, make observations in four different directions: the firmament by the side and most direct windows, the earth or the moon by the upper and lower openings in the projectile.

Barbicane and his two companions immediately rushed to the uncovered window. But it was lit by no ray of light. Profound darkness surrounded them, which, however, did not prevent the president from exclaiming:

"No, my friends, we have not fallen back upon the earth; no, nor are we submerged in the Gulf of Mexico. Yes! we are mounting into space. See those stars shining in the night, and that impenetrable darkness heaped up between the earth and us!"

"Hurrah! hurrah!" exclaimed Michel Ardan and Nicholl in one voice.

Indeed, this thick darkness proved that the projectile had left the earth, for the soil, brilliantly lit by the moonbeams, would have been visible to the travelers, if they had been lying on its surface. This darkness also showed that the projectile had passed the atmospheric strata, for the diffused light spread in the air would have been reflected on the metal walls, a reflection which was lacking. This light would have lit the window, and the window was dark. Doubt was no longer possible; the travelers had left the earth.

"I have lost," said Nicholl.

"I congratulate you," replied Ardan.

"Here are the nine thousand dollars," said the captain, drawing a roll of greenbacks from his pocket.

"Would you like a receipt for it?" asked Barbicane, taking the sum.

"If you do not mind," answered Nicholl; "it is more businesslike."

And coolly and seriously, as if he had been at his strongbox, the president drew forth his notebook, tore out a blank leaf, wrote a proper receipt in pencil, dated and signed it with the usual flourish, and gave it to the captain, who carefully placed it in his pocketbook.

Michel Ardan, taking off his hat, bowed to his two companions without speaking. So much formality under such circumstances left him speechless. He had never before seen anything so "American."

This affair settled, Barbicane and Nicholl had returned to the window, and were watching the constellations. The stars looked like bright points against the black sky. But from that side they could not see the orb of night, which, traveling from east to west, was rising by degrees toward the zenith. Its absence drew the following remark from Ardan:

"And the moon; will she perchance miss our rendezvous?"

"Do not alarm yourself," said Barbicane; "our future globe is at its post, but we cannot see her from this side; let us open the other."

As Barbicane was about to leave the window to open the opposite scuttle, his attention was attracted by the approach of a brilliant object. It was an enormous disc, whose colossal dimension could not be estimated. Its face which was turned to the earth was very bright. One might have thought it a small moon reflecting the light of the large one. It advanced with great speed, and seemed to describe an orbit round the earth, which would intersect the passage of the projectile. The body revolved upon its axis, and exhibited the phenomena of all celestial bodies abandoned in space.

"Ah!" exclaimed Michel Ardan. "What is that? Another projectile?"

Barbicane did not answer. The appearance of this enormous body surprised and troubled him. A collision was possible, and might be attended with deplorable results; either the projectile would deviate from its path, or a shock, breaking its impetus, might precipitate it to the earth; or, lastly, it might be irresistibly drawn away by the powerful asteroid.

The president caught at a glance the consequences of these three hypotheses, any one of which would, one way or the other, bring their experiment to an unsuccessful and fatal termination. His companions stood silently looking into space. The object grew fantastically as it approached them, and by an optical illusion the projectile seemed to be rushing at them.

"By Jove!" exclaimed Michel Ardan, "we shall run into one another!"

Instinctively the travelers drew back. Their dread was great, but it did not last many seconds. The asteroid passed several hundred yards from the projectile and disappeared, not so much from the rapidity of its course, as that its face being opposite the moon, it was suddenly merged into the perfect darkness of space.

"Bon voyage," exclaimed Michel Ardan, with a sigh of relief. "Surely the infinity of space is large enough for a poor little projectile to travel through without fear. Now, what was that portentous globe which nearly struck us?"

"I know," replied Barbicane.

"Oh, indeed! you know everything."

"It is," said Barbicane, "a simple meteorite, but an enormous one, which the attraction of the earth has retained as a satellite."

"Is it possible?" exclaimed Michel Ardan. "The earth then has two moons like Neptune?"

"Yes, my friend, two moons, though it generally passes for having only one; but this second moon is so small, and its speed so great, that the inhabitants of the earth cannot see it. It was by noticing disturbances that a French astronomer, M. Petit, was able to determine the existence of this second satellite and calculate its elements. According to his observations, this meteorite will accomplish its revolution around the earth in three hours and twenty minutes, which implies a fantastic rate of speed."

"Do all astronomers admit the existence of this satellite?" asked Nicholl.

"No," replied Barbicane; "but if, like us, they had met it, they could no longer doubt it. Indeed, I think that this meteorite, which, had it struck the projectile, would have caused us no little trouble, will give us the means of deciding what our position in space is."

"How?" said Ardan.

"Because its distance is known, and when we met it, we were exactly five thousand eighty-seven and a half miles from the surface of the terrestrial globe."

"More than two thousand French leagues," exclaimed Michel Ardan. "That beats all hollow the express trains of the pitiful globe called Earth."

"I should think so," replied Nicholl, consulting his chronometer; "it is eleven o'clock, and it is only thirteen minutes since we left the American continent."

"Only thirteen minutes?" said Barbicane.

"Yes," said Nicholl; "and if our initial speed of almost seven miles were kept up, we would cover about twenty-five thousand miles an hour."

"That is all very well, my friends," said the president, "but the insoluble question still remains. Why did we not hear the detonation of the Columbiad?"

For want of an answer the conversation dropped, and Barbicane began thoughtfully to let down the shutter of the second side. He succeeded; and through the uncovered glass the moon filled the projectile with a brilliant light. Nicholl, as an economical man, put out the gas, now useless, and whose brilliancy prevented any observation of interplanetary space.

The lunar disc shone with incomparable purity. Her rays, no longer filtered through the vapory atmosphere of the terrestrial globe, shone through the glass, filling the air in the interior of the projectile with silvery reflections. The black curtain of the firmament in reality heightened the moon's brilliancy, which in this void of ether unfavorable to diffusion did not eclipse the neighboring stars. The heavens, thus seen, presented quite a new aspect, and one which the human eye could never dream of.

One may conceive the interest with which these bold men watched the orb of night, the great aim of their journey. In its motion the earth's satellite was insensibly nearing the zenith, the mathematical point which it ought to attain about ninety-six hours later. Her mountains, her plains, every projection was as clearly discernible to their eyes as if they were observing it from some spot upon the earth; but its light was developed through space with incomparable intensity. The disc shone like a platinum mirror. Of the earth flying from under their feet, the travelers had already lost all recollection.

It was Captain Nicholl who first recalled their attention to the vanishing globe.

"Yes," said Michel Ardan, "do not let us be ungrateful to it. Since we are leaving our country, let our last looks be directed to it. I wish to see the earth once more before it is completely hidden from my eyes."

To satisfy his companions, Barbicane began to uncover the window at the bottom of the projectile, which would allow them to observe the earth direct. The disc, which the force of the projection had beaten down to the base, was removed, not without difficulty. Its fragments, placed carefully against the wall, might serve again upon occasion. Then a circular gap appeared, about twenty inches in diameter, hollowed out of the lower part of the projectile. A glass cover, six inches thick and strengthened with copper fastenings, closed it tightly. Beneath was fixed an aluminum plate, held in place by bolts. The screws being undone, and the bolts let go, the plate fell down, and visual communication was established between the interior and the exterior.

Michel Ardan knelt by the glass. It was cloudy, seemingly opaque.

"Well!" he exclaimed, "what about the earth?"

"The earth?" said Barbicane. "There it is."

"What! that little thread; that silver crescent?"

"Doubtless, Michel. In four days, when the moon is full, at the very time we reach it, the earth will be new, and will appear to us only as a slender crescent which will soon disappear, and for some days will then be enveloped in utter darkness."

"That the earth?" repeated Michel Ardan, looking as hard as he could at the thin slip of his native planet.

The explanation given by President Barbicane was correct. The earth, in relation to the projectile, was entering its last phase. It was in its octant, and showed a finely-traced crescent against the dark background of the sky. Its light, rendered bluish by the thick stratum of the atmosphere, was less intense than that of the crescent moon, but it was of considerable dimensions, and looked like an enormous arch stretched across the firmament. Some brilliantly lighted spots, especially on its concave part, showed the presence of high mountains, often disappearing behind thick splotches such as are never seen on the lunar disc. They were rings of clouds placed concentrically around the terrestrial globe.

However, as a result of a natural phenomenon, identical to that which occurs on the moon when it is in its octants, it was now possible to see all of the contour of the earth. Its entire disc appeared quite visibly through an effect of moonshine, though less significant than the earthshine of the moon. And it is easy to understand the reason for this lesser intensity. When this shine occurs upon the moon, it is the result of the rays of the sun which the earth reflects toward its satellite. Here, through an inverse process, it was due to the solar rays reflected by the moon toward the earth. Now, earthly light is approximately thirteen times stronger than that of the moon, because of the difference of size between the two bodies. Hence, the consequence that, in the phenomenon of this shine, the dark part of the earthly disc is less clearly defined than that of the lunar disc, since the intensity of the phenomenon is directly proportionate to the lighting power of the two planets. One must also add that the earthly crescent appeared to form a more elongated curve than that of the disc—a pure result of irradiation.

While the travelers were trying to pierce the profound darkness, a brilliant cluster of shooting stars burst upon their eyes. Hundreds of meteorites, ignited by the friction of the atmosphere, irradiated the shadow of the luminous train, and lined the cloudy parts of the disc with their fire. At this period the earth was in its perihelion, and the month of December is so propitious to these shooting stars that astronomers have counted as many as twenty-four thousand in an hour. But Michel Ardan, disdaining scientific reasonings, preferred thinking that the earth was thus saluting the departure of her three children with her most brilliant fireworks.

Indeed this was all they saw of the globe lost in shadow, a minor spheroid of the solar system rising and setting to the great planets like a simple morning or evening star! This globe, on which they had left all their affections, was nothing more than a fugitive crescent, scarcely perceptible in space!

Long did the three friends look without speaking, though united in heart, while the projectile sped onward with an evenly decreasing speed. Then an irresistible drowsiness crept over their brains. Was it weariness of both body and mind? No doubt; for, after the excitement of those last hours upon earth, reaction was inevitable.

"Well," said Nicholl, "since we must sleep, let us sleep."

And stretching themselves on their berths, they were all three soon in a profound slumber.

But they had not been asleep more than a quarter of an hour, when Barbicane sat up suddenly, and rousing his companions with a loud voice, exclaimed:

"I have found it!"

"What have you found?" asked Michel Ardan, jumping from his bed.

"The reason why we did not hear the detonation of the Columbiad."

"And it is—?" said Nicholl.

"Because our projectile was traveling faster than sound!"

CHAPTER 3

Settling In

THIS curious but certainly correct explanation once given, the three friends returned to their slumbers. Could they have found a calmer or more peaceful spot to sleep in? On earth, houses in towns and cottages in the country feel every shock given to the exterior of the globe. At sea, vessels rocked by the waves are nothing but shock and motion. In the air, the balloon oscillates incessantly on the fluid strata of varied densities. This projectile alone, floating in an absolute vacuum, in the midst of absolute silence, offered its guests absolute repose.

Thus the sleep of our adventurous travelers might have been indefinitely prolonged, if an unexpected noise had not awakened them at about seven o'clock in the morning of the 2nd of December, eight hours after their departure.

This noise was a very unmistakable dog's bark.

"The dogs! It is the dogs!" exclaimed Michel Ardan, rising at once.

"They are hungry," said Nicholl.

"By Jove!" replied Michel. "We have forgotten them."

"Where are they?" asked Barbicane.

The first meal in space

They looked and found one of the animals crouched under the divan. Terrified and shaken by the initial shock, it had remained in the corner till its voice returned with the pangs of hunger.

It was the amiable Diana, still very confused, who crept out of her retreat, though not without much persuasion, Michel Ardan encouraging her with his most gracious words.

"Come, Diana," said he; "come, my girl! Thou whose destiny will be noted in cynegetic annals; thou whom the pagans would have given as companion to the god Anubis, and Christians as friend to St. Roch; thou, worthy of being cast in bronze by the lord of the underworld, like the doggy that Jupiter gave to beauteous Europa as the prize for a kiss; thou, whose fame will surpass that of the canine heroes of Montargis Saint Bernard; thou who art rushing into interplanetary space and wilt perhaps be the Eve of all Selenite dogs; thou who up above wilt justify the words of Toussenel, 'In the beginning, God created man, and, seeing him so weak, gave him He a dog;' come, Diana, come here!"

Diana, flattered or not, advanced gradually, uttering plaintive cries.

"Good," said Barbicane; "I see Eve, but where is Adam?"

"Adam?" replied Michel; "Adam cannot be far off; he is there somewhere; we must call him. Satellite! here, Satellite!"

But Satellite did not appear. Diana would not leave off howling. They found, however, that she was not bruised, and they fed her, which silenced her complaints.

As to Satellite, he seemed quite lost. They had to hunt a long time before finding him in one of the upper compartments of the projectile, where some unaccountable shock must have violently hurled him. The poor beast, much hurt, was in pitiful shape.

"The devil!" said Michel. "There goes our acclimatization project!"

They brought the unfortunate dog down with great care. Its skull had been broken against the roof, and it seemed unlikely that he could recover from such a shock. Meanwhile, he was stretched comfortably on a cushion. Once there, he heaved a sigh.

"We will take care of you," said Michel; "we are responsible for your existence. I would rather lose an arm than a paw of my poor Satellite."

Saying which, he offered some water to the wounded dog, who swallowed it with avidity.

This attention paid, the travelers observed the earth and the moon attentively. The earth was now only discernible by a cloudy disc ending in a crescent, rather more contracted than that of the previous evening; but its expanse was still enormous, compared with that of the moon, which was approaching nearer and nearer to a perfect circle.

"By Jove!" said Michel Ardan, "I am really sorry that we did not start when the earth was full, that is to say, when our globe was in opposition to the sun."

"Why?" asked Nicholl.

"Because we should have seen our continents and seas in a new light—the latter resplendent under the solar rays, the former cloudy as represented on some maps of the world. I should like to have seen those poles of the earth on which the eye of man has never yet rested."

"I dare say," replied Barbicane; "but if the earth had been *full,* the moon would have been *new;* that is to say, invisible, because of the rays of the sun. It is better for us to see the destination we wish to reach, than the point of departure."

"You are right, Barbicane," replied Captain Nicholl;

"and, besides, when we have reached the moon, we shall have time during the long lunar nights to consider at our leisure the globe on which our fellow-creatures swarm."

"Fellow-creatures, indeed!" exclaimed Michel Ardan; "they are no more our fellows than the Selenites are! We inhabit a new world, peopled by ourselves alone--the projectile! I am Barbicane's fellow, and Barbicane is Nicholl's. Beyond us, around us, human nature is at an end, and we are the only population of this microcosm until we become pure Selenites."

"In about eighty-eight hours," replied the captain.

"Which means?" asked Michel Ardan.

"That it is half-past eight," replied Nicholl.

"Very well," retorted Michel; "then it is impossible for me to find even the shadow of a reason why we should not proceed immediately to breakfast."

Indeed the inhabitants of the new star could not live without eating, and their stomachs were suffering from the imperious laws of hunger. Michel Ardan, as a Frenchman, declared himself chief cook, an important function, which no one contested. The gas gave sufficient heat for the culinary operations, and the larder furnished the elements of this first feast.

The breakfast began with three cups of excellent soup, thanks to the liquefaction in hot water of those precious Liebig bouillon cubes, made from the best parts of the ruminants of the Pampas. The soup was followed by steaks, compressed by hydraulic press, as tender and succulent as if brought straight from the famous kitchens of the Café Anglais. Michel, who was imaginative, even maintained that they were "rare."

Preserved vegetables ("fresher than off the farm," said

the amiable Michel) succeeded the meat dish and were followed by some cups of tea with bread and butter in the American fashion. The beverage, which was declared exquisite, was brewed from some of the choicest leaves, of which the emperor of Russia had sent several chests for the benefit of the travelers.

And lastly, to crown the repast, Ardan brought out a fine bottle of Nuits, which was found "by chance" in the provision-box. The three friends drank to the union of the earth and her satellite.

And, as if it had not already done enough through the generous wine which it had distilled on the slopes of Burgundy, the sun decided to join in the festivities. At this very moment the projectile emerged from the conical shadow cast by the terrestrial globe, and the rays of the radiant orb struck the lower disc of the projectile directly, because of the angle which the moon's orbit makes with that of the earth.

"The sun!" exclaimed Michel Ardan.

"No doubt," replied Barbicane; "I expected it."

"But," said Michel, "the conical shadow which the earth leaves in space extends beyond the moon?"

"Far beyond it, if the atmospheric refraction is not taken into consideration," said Barbicane. "But when the moon is enveloped in this shadow, it is because the centers of the three stars, the sun, the earth, and the moon, are all in one and the same straight line. Then the *nodes* coincide with the *phases* of the moon, and there is an eclipse. If we had started when there was an eclipse of the moon, all our passage would have been in darkness, which would have been a pity."

"Why?"

"Because, though we are floating in space, our projectile,

bathed in the solar rays, will receive their light and heat. That economizes the gas, which is in every respect a good economy."

Indeed, under these rays which no atmosphere now tempered, either in heat or brilliancy, the projectile grew warm and bright, as if it had passed suddenly from winter to summer. The moon above, the sun beneath, were inundating it with their fires.

"It is pleasant here," said Nicholl.

"I should think so," said Michel Ardan. "With a little arable earth spread on our aluminum planet we should have green peas in twenty-four hours. I have but one fear, which is that the walls of the projectile might melt."

"Calm yourself, my worthy friend," replied Barbicane; "the projectile withstood a very much higher temperature than this as it slid through the strata of the atmosphere. I should not be surprised if it looked like a meteor on fire to the eyes of the spectators in Florida."

"But then J. T. Maston will think we are roasted!"

"What astonishes me," said Barbicane, "is that we have not been. That was a danger we had not provided for."

"I feared it," said Nicholl simply.

"And you never mentioned it, sublime captain," exclaimed Michel Ardan, clasping his friend's hand.

Barbicane now began to settle himself into the projectile as if he were never to leave it. One must remember that this aerial car at its base had a surface of fifty-four square feet. Its height to the roof was twelve feet. Carefully laid out in the inside, and little encumbered by instruments and traveling utensils, which each had their particular place, it left the three travelers a certain freedom of movement. The thick window inserted in the bottom could bear any amount of weight, and Barbicane and his companions walked upon it as if it were a solid floor; but the sun striking it directly with its rays lit the interior of the projectile from beneath, thus producing singular effects of light.

They began by investigating the state of their store of water and provisions, neither of which had suffered, thanks to the care taken to deaden the shock. Their provisions were abundant, and plentiful enough to last the three travelers for more than a year. Barbicane wished to be cautious, in case the projectile should land on a part of the moon which was utterly barren. As to water and the reserve of brandy, which consisted of fifty gallons, there was enough for only two months; but according to the last observations of astronomers, the moon had a low, dense, and thick atmosphere, at least in the deep valleys, and there springs and streams could not but exist. Thus, during their passage, and for the first year of their settlement on the lunar continent, these adventurous explorers would suffer neither hunger nor thirst.

Now about the air in the projectile. There, too, they were safe. Reiset and Regnault's apparatus, intended for the production of oxygen, was supplied with chlorate of potassium for two months. It necessarily consumed a certain quantity of gas, for it was obliged to keep the producing substance at a temperature of above 400°. But there again they were well stocked. Moreover, the apparatus required but little care. It worked automatically. At this high temperature, the chlorate of potassium turned into potassium chloride, releasing all the oxygen that it contained. Now how much did eighteen pounds of potassium chloride yield? The seven pounds of oxygen required for the travelers' daily consumption.

But it was not enough to renew the oxygen consumed; it was also necessary to absorb the carbon dioxide they exhaled. During the last twelve hours the atmosphere of the projectile had become charged with this deleterious gas. Nicholl discovered the state of the air by observing Diana panting painfully. The carbon dioxide, by a phenomenon similar to that produced in the famous Grotto del Cane, had collected at the bottom of the projectile owing to its weight. Poor Diana, with her head low, would suffer before her masters from the presence of this gas. But Captain Nicholl hastened to remedy this state of things, by placing on the floor several receptacles containing caustic potash, which he shook about for a time, and the substance, attracting the carbon dioxide, soon completely absorbed it, thus purifying the air.

An inventory of instruments was then begun. The thermometers and barometers had resisted, all but one minimum thermometer, the glass of which was broken. An excellent aneroid was drawn from the padded box which contained it and hung on the wall. Of course it was only affected by and indicated the pressure of the air inside the projectile, but it also showed the quantity of moisture which it contained. At that moment its needle oscillated between 29.84 and 29.64, indicating fair weather.

Barbicane had also brought several compasses, which he found intact. One must understand that under present conditions their needles were acting *wildly,* that is without any *constant* direction. Indeed, at the distance they were from the earth, the magnetic pole could have no perceptible action upon the apparatus; but the box placed on the lunar disc might perhaps exhibit some strange phenomena. In any case it would be interesting to see whether the earth's satellite was like herself subject to magnetic influence.

A hypsometer to measure the height of the lunar mountains, a sextant to take the height of the sun, a theodolite or alidade for measuring both horizontal and vertical angles, and field glasses which would be useful as they neared the moon, all these instruments were carefully looked over, and pronounced good in spite of the violent shock.

As to the pickaxes, shovels, and different tools which were Nicholl's especial choice; as to the sacks of different kinds of seed and shrubs which Michel Ardan hoped to transplant into Selenite ground, they were stowed away in the upper part of the projectile. There was a sort of granary there, loaded with things which the extravagant Frenchman had heaped up. What they were no one knew, and the good-tempered fellow did not explain. Now and then he climbed up by cramp-irons riveted to the walls, but kept the inspection to himself. He arranged and rearranged, he plunged his hand rapidly into certain mysterious boxes, singing in one of the falsest of voices an old French refrain to enliven the situation.

Barbicane observed with some interest that his rockets and other explosives had not been damaged. These were important, because, being heavily loaded, they were to help lessen the fall of the projectile, when drawn by lunar attraction (after having passed the point of neutral attraction) on to the moon's surface; a fall which ought to be six times less rapid than it would have been on the earth's surface, thanks to the difference of bulk of the two bodies.

The inspection ended in general satisfaction, and each returned to peer at space through the side windows and the lower glass coverlid.

There was the same view. The whole extent of the celestial sphere swarmed with stars and constellations of wonderful purity, enough to drive an astronomer out of his mind! On one side the sun, like the mouth of a lighted oven, a dazzling disc without a halo, standing out against the dark background of the sky! On the other, the moon returning its fire by reflection, and apparently motionless in the midst of the starry world. Then, a large spot that seemed to tear through the firmament, bordered by a silvery cord: it was the earth! Here and there nebulous masses like large flakes of starry snow; and from the zenith to the nadir, an immense ring formed by an impalpable dust of stars, the "Milky Way," in the midst of which the sun ranks only as a star of the fourth magnitude!

The observers could not take their eyes from this novel spectacle, of which no description could give an adequate idea. What reflections it suggested! What emotions hitherto unknown awoke in their souls! Barbicane wished to begin the relation of his journey while under its first impressions, and hour by hour made note of all the facts happening in the beginning of the enterprise. He wrote quietly, with his large square writing, in a somewhat businesslike style.

During this time Nicholl, the calculator, rechecked the formulae of their passage, and juggled figures with unparalleled dexterity. Michel Ardan chatted first with Barbicane, who did not answer him, and then with Nicholl, who did not hear him, with Diana, who understood none of his theories, and lastly with himself, questioning and answering, going and coming, busy with a thousand details, at one time bent over the lower glass, at another roosting in the heights of the projectile, and always singing. In this microcosm he represented French loquacity and excitability, and we beg you to believe that they were well represented.

The day, or rather (for the expression is not correct) the lapse of twelve hours, which forms a day upon earth, closed with a plentiful supper carefully prepared. No accident of any nature had yet happened to shake the travelers' confidence; so, full of hope, already sure of success, they fell asleep peacefully, while the projectile at a uniformly decreasing rate of speed crossed the highways of the sky.

CHAPTER 4

A Little Algebra

THE night went by without incident. The word "night," however, is scarcely applicable.

The position of the projectile with regard to the sun did not change. Astronomically, it was daylight on the lower part, and night on the upper; so when during this narrative these words are used, they represent the lapse of time between the rising and setting of the sun upon the earth.

The travelers' sleep was rendered more peaceful by the projectile's excessive speed, for it seemed absolutely motionless. Not a motion betrayed its onward course through space. The rate of progress, however rapid it might be, cannot produce any sensible effect on the human organism when it takes place in a vacuum, or when the mass of surrounding air travels along with the body which is carried within it. What inhabitant of the earth perceives its speed, which, however, is at the rate of 56,000 miles per hour? Motion under such conditions is "felt" no more than repose; and when a body is in repose it will remain so as long as no external force displaces it; if moving, it will not stop unless an obstacle comes in its way. This indifference to motion or repose is called inertia.

Barbicane and his companions might have believed

themselves perfectly stationary, being shut up in the projectile; indeed, the effect would have been the same if they had been on the outside of it. Had it not been for the moon, which was increasing above them, they might have sworn that they were floating in complete stagnation.

That morning, the 3rd of December, the travelers were awakened by a joyous but unexpected noise; it was the crowing of a cock which sounded through the car.

Michel Ardan, who was the first on his feet, climbed to the top of the projectile, and shutting a box, the lid of which was partly open, said in a low voice,

"Will you hold your tongue? That creature will spoil my design!"

But Nicholl and Barbicane were now awake.

"A cock!" said Nicholl.

"Why no, my friends," Michel answered quickly; "it was I who wished to awake you by this rural sound."

So saying, he gave vent to a splendid cock-a-doodledoo, which would have done honor to the proudest of roosters.

The two Americans could not help laughing.

"Fine talent that," said Nicholl, looking suspiciously at his companion.

"Yes," said Michel; "a typical joke of my country. It is very Gallic; we play at cocks that way in the best society."

Then turning the conversation:

"Barbicane, do you know what I have been thinking of all night?"

"No," answered the president.

"Of our Cambridge friends. You have already noticed that I am an ignoramus in mathematical subjects; and it is impossible for me to find out how the savants of the observatory were able to calculate what initial speed the projectile had to have on leaving the Columbiad in order to attain the moon."

"You mean to say," replied Barbicane, "to attain that neutral point where the terrestrial and lunar attractions are equal; for, from that point on, which is about nine-tenths of the distance, the projectile would simply fall upon the moon, on account of its weight."

"Granted," said Michel; "but, once more; how could they calculate the initial speed?"

"Nothing easier," replied Barbicane.

"And would you have known how to make that calculation?" asked Michel Ardan.

"Perfectly. Nicholl and I would have made it, if the observatory had not saved us the trouble."

"Very well, old Barbicane," replied Michel; "they might have cut off my head, beginning at my feet, before they could have gotten me to solve that problem."

"Because you do not know algebra," answered Barbicane quietly.

"Ah, there you are, you eaters of x; you think you have said it all when you have said 'algebra.'"

"Michel," said Barbicane, "can you forge metal without a hammer, or plow without a plowshare?"

"Hardly."

"Well, algebra is a tool, like the plow or the hammer, and a good tool to those who know how to use it."

"Seriously?"

"Quite seriously."

"And can you use that tool in my presence?"

"If it will interest you."

"And show me how they calculated the initial speed of our car?"

"Yes, my worthy friend; taking into consideration all the elements of the problem, the distance from the center of the earth to the center of the moon, of the radius of the earth, of its bulk, and of the bulk of the moon, I can tell exactly what ought to be the initial speed of the projectile, and that by one simple formula."

"Let us see."

"You shall see it; only I shall not give you the real course drawn by the projectile between the moon and the earth in considering their motion round the sun. No, I shall consider these two orbs as perfectly motionless, which will answer all our purpose."

"And why?"

"Because that would be trying to solve the problem called 'the problem of the three bodies,' for which the integral calculus is not yet far enough advanced."

"Then," said Michel Ardan, in his sly tone, "mathematics has not said its last word?"

"Certainly not," replied Barbicane.

"Well, perhaps the Selenites have carried the integral calculus farther than you have; and, by the bye, what is this 'integral calculus'?"

"It is a calculation the converse of the differential," replied Barbicane seriously.

"Much obliged."

"In other words, it is a calculus through which you can find finite quantities whose differential you already know."

"Well, that, at least, is clear," Michel answered in the most satisfied of tones.

"And now," continued Barbicane, "a slip of paper and a bit of pencil, and before a half-hour is over I expect to have found the required formula."

Thereupon, Barbicane plunged into his work, while Nicholl observed space, leaving his companion to lunch alone.

Half an hour had not elapsed before Barbicane, raising his head, showed Michel Ardan a page covered with algebraic signs, in the middle of which this general formula could be seen:

$$\tfrac{1}{2}\,(v_2 - v_0{}^2) = gr\left\{\frac{r}{x} - 1 + \frac{m'}{m}\left(\frac{r}{d-x} - \frac{r}{d-r}\right)\right\}$$

"Meaning which?" asked Michel.

"Meaning," answered Nicholl, "that one half of v-two minus v-zero squared is equal to *gr* times *r* over *x* minus one, plus *m* prime over *m* times *r* over *d* minus *x*, minus *r* over *d* minus *r* . . ."

"*X* over *y* on top of *z*, all riding on *p*," shouted Michel Ardan in a burst of laughter. "And you understand that, captain?"

"Nothing could be clearer."

"But, of course!" retorted Michel. "It is all self-evident, and I could not ask for more."

"All right, you everlasting joker!" answered Barbicane. "You asked for algebra, and now you'll get it till you're chin deep in it!"

"I'd rather be hanged!"

"I say," said Nicholl, who had been examining the formula with a knowing eye, "this looks very well worked out to me, Barbicane. It is the integral of the equation of the active forces, and I have no doubt it would give us the result we are seeking."

"But I want to understand it!" Michel cried. "I would give ten years of Nicholl's life to be able to understand it!"

"Well, then, listen," Barbicane went on. "One half of *v*-two minus *v*-zero squared is the formula that gives us the half-variation of the active force."

"Fine, and does Nicholl know what that means?"

"Of course, Michel," replied the captain. "All these signs, which seem cabalistic to you, form the plainest, the clearest, and the most logical language to those who know how to read it."

"And you claim, Nicholl," asked Michel, "that by means of these hieroglyphics, more incomprehensible than Egyptian ibises, you can find what initial speed it was necessary to give to the projectile?"

"Incontestably," replied Nicholl; "and even by the same formula I can always tell you its speed at any given point of its transit."

"On your word?"

"On my word."

"Then you are as clever as our president."

"No, Michel; the difficult part is what Barbicane has done; that is, to get an equation which shall satisfy all the conditions of the problem. The remainder is only a question of arithmetic, merely requiring knowledge of the four basic rules."

"That is something in itself!" replied Michel Ardan, who, for the life of him, had never been able to do addition right, and who defined its rule as follows: "Small Chinese puzzle allowing one to obtain infinitely variable results."

Meanwhile, Barbicane was insisting that Nicholl, had he thought about it, would certainly have been able to work out the formula.

"I am not sure," Nicholl said. "For the more I look at it, the more ingenious I think it is."

"Now, listen," said Barbicane to his ignorant companion, "and you will see that each of those letters means something."

"I am listening," said Michel, with resignation.

"*D*," said Barbicane, "is the distance from the center of the earth to the center of the moon, for one must always figure the power of attraction from the center."

"That, I can understand."

"*R* is the radius of the earth."

"*R* for radius, granted."

"*M* is the mass or bulk of the earth, *m* prime the mass of the moon. Indeed, we must take into account the bulk of both bodies, since their power of attraction is proportionate to their volume."

"That's understood."

"*G* is for gravity, the speed acquired at the end of a second by a body falling to the surface of the earth. Clear?"

"As spring water!" answered Michel.

"Now, I call *x* the variable distance separating the projectile from the center of the earth, and *v* the velocity or speed of the projectile at that distance."

"Good."

"The expression *v* zero, which you see in that equation, is, finally, the velocity or speed which the projectile will have on leaving the atmosphere."

"Just so," said Nicholl; "it is from that point that we must calculate the velocity, since we already know that the velocity at departure was exactly one and a half times more than on leaving the atmosphere."

"That's beyond me," said Michel.

"It is a very simple calculation," said Barbicane.

"Not as simple as I am," retorted Michel.

"That means, that when our projectile reached the limits

of the terrestrial atmosphere it had already lost one-third of its initial speed."

"As much as that?"

"Yes, my friend; merely by friction against the atmospheric strata. You understand that the faster it goes the more resistance it meets with from the air."

"That I admit," answered Michel; "and I understand it, although your v zeroes and v zero squareds are rattling around in my head like nails in a bag."

"First effects of algebra," replied Barbicane; "and now, to finish, we are going to prove the given number of these different expressions, that is, work out their value."

"Finish me!" replied Michel.

"Of these expressions," said Barbicane, "some are known, the others are to be worked out."

"I will handle the latter," said Nicholl.

"Let us take r," said Barbicane. "This is the radius of the earth which, at the latitude of Florida, from which we left, is equal to 3,950 miles. D, the distance from the center of the earth to the center of the moon, is fifty-six times the radius of the earth, or——"

Nicholl figured rapidly.

"Or," he said, "220,200 miles, when the moon is at its perigee, that is, closest to the earth."

"Good," said Barbicane. "Now, m prime over m, or the relationship of the mass of the moon to that of the earth, is one eighty-first."

"Right," said Michel.

"G, gravity, in Florida is ten and three-quarters yards. Which makes gr equal to——"

"24.1 square miles," answered Nicholl.

"And now?" asked Michel Ardan.

"Now that I have replaced these letters by figures," answered Barbicane, "I am going to find the velocity of *v* zero, that is, the speed the projectile must have on leaving the atmosphere so as to reach the point of equal attraction with no speed at all. Since at that moment, there will be no speed, I posit that it will be equal to zero, and that *x*, the distance at which this neutral point is located, will be represented by nine-tenths of *d*, that is, of the distance that separates the two centers."

"I have a vague feeling that that ought to be right," said Michel.

"I will then have: *x* equals nine-tenths of *d*, and *v* equals zero, so that my formula will become——"

Barbicane rapidly wrote on the paper:

$$v_0^2 = 2gr \left\{ 1 - \frac{10r}{9d} - \frac{1}{81} \left(\frac{10r}{d} - \frac{r}{d-r} \right) \right\}$$

Nicholl read it avidly.

"That's it! That's it!" he cried.

"Is it clear?" asked Barbicane.

"It is written in letters of fire!" answered Nicholl.

"What remarkable fellows!" Michel muttered.

"Have you finally understood it?" asked Barbicane.

"Have I understood it?" cried Michel Ardan. "Why, my head is splitting with it!"

"Well, then," Barbicane resumed, "*v* zero squared equals 2*gr* multiplied by one minus 10*r* over 9*d* minus one eighty-first, multiplied by 10*r* over *d* minus *r* over *d* minus *r*."

"And now," said Nicholl, "to find out the speed of the projectile when it left the atmosphere, we have only to calculate that."

The captain, as a practitioner accustomed to any and all difficulties, began to write with frightful rapidity. Divisions and multiplications grew under his fingers; the figures were like hail on the white page. Barbicane watched him, while Michel Ardan nursed a growing headache with both hands.

"Well?" asked Barbicane, after some minutes' silence.

"Well!" replied Nicholl; "every calculation made, v zero, that is to say, the speed necessary for the projectile on leaving the atmosphere, to enable it to reach the equal point of attraction, ought to have been——"

"Yes?" said Barbicane.

"Twelve thousand yards."

"What!" exclaimed Barbicane, starting; "you say——"

"Twelve thousand yards."

"The devil!" cried the president, making a gesture of despair.

"What is the matter?" asked Michel Ardan, much surprised.

"What is the matter? Why, if at this moment our speed had already diminished one-third by friction, the initial speed ought to have been——"

"Eighteen thousand yards."

"And the Cambridge Observatory stated that twelve thousand yards was enough at starting; and our projectile, which only started with that speed——"

"Well?" asked Nicholl.

"Well, it will not be enough."

"Fine!"

"We shall not be able to reach the neutral point."

"The deuce!"

"We shall not even get halfway."

"Holy jumping projectile!" exclaimed Michel Ardan, jumping as if it were already at the point of striking the terrestrial globe.

"And we shall fall back to earth!"

CHAPTER 5

In Cold, Cold Space

THIS revelation came like a thunderbolt. Who could have expected such an error in calculation? Barbicane would not believe it. Nicholl checked his figures: they were exact. As to the formula which had determined them, they could not question its correctness; obviously an initial velocity of eighteen thousand yards in the first second was necessary to enable them to reach the neutral point.

The three friends looked at each other silently. There was no longer any thought of lunch. Barbicane, with clenched teeth, knitted brows, and hands clasped convulsively, was watching through the window. Nicholl had crossed his arms, and was examining his calculations. Michel Ardan was muttering:

"That is just like those scientists: they never do anything else. I would give twenty pistoles if we could fall upon the Cambridge Observatory and crush it, along with the whole lot of figure foulers it contains."

Suddenly a thought struck the captain, which he at once communicated to Barbicane.

"Ah!" said he; "it is seven o'clock in the morning; we have already been gone thirty-two hours; more than half our passage is over, and we are not falling that I am aware of."

Barbicane did not answer, but, after a rapid glance at the captain, took a compass with which to measure the angular distance of the terrestrial globe; then from the lower window he took an exact reading, in view of the fact that the projectile was apparently stationary. Then rising and wiping his forehead, on which large drops of perspiration were standing, he put some figures on paper. Nicholl understood that the president was deducting from the terrestrial diameter the projectile's distance from the earth. He watched him anxiously.

"No," exclaimed Barbicane, after some moments, "no, we are not falling! no, we are already more than 125,000 miles from the earth. We have passed the point at which the projectile would have stopped if its speed had only been 12,000 yards at starting. We are still going up."

"That is evident," replied Nicholl; "and we must conclude that our initial speed, under the power of the 400,000 pounds of gun-cotton, must have exceeded the intended 12,000 yards. Now I can understand how, after thirteen minutes only, we met the second satellite, which gravitates round the earth at a distance of more than 5,000 miles."

"And this explanation is the more probable," added Barbicane, "because, in throwing off the water enclosed between its partition-breaks, the projectile found itself relieved of a considerable weight."

"Just so," said Nicholl.

"Ah, my good Nicholl, we are saved!"

"Very well, then," said Michel Ardan quietly; "since we are safe, let us eat."

Nicholl was not mistaken. The initial speed had been, very fortunately, much above that estimated by the Cambridge Observatory; but the Cambridge Observatory had nevertheless made a mistake.

The travelers, recovered from this false alarm, sat down and lunched merrily. If they ate a great deal, they talked even more. Their confidence was greater after than before "the incident of the algebra."

"Why should we not succeed?" said Michel Ardan; "why should we not arrive safely? We are launched; we have no obstacle before us, no stones in our way; the road is open, more so than that of a ship battling with the sea; more open than that of a balloon battling with the wind; and if a ship can reach its destination, a balloon go where it pleases, why cannot our projectile attain its end and aim?"

"It *will* attain it," said Barbicane.

"If only to do honor to the people of America," added Michel Ardan, "the only people who could bring such an enterprise to a happy termination, and the only one which could produce a President Barbicane. Ah, now we are no longer in trouble, it occurs to me: What will become of us? We shall get right royally bored."

Barbicane and Nicholl made a gesture of denial.

"But I have provided for the contingency, my friends," replied Michel; "you have only to speak, and I have chess, checkers, cards, and dominoes at your disposal; all that we lack is a billiard-table."

"What!" exclaimed Barbicane; "you brought along such nonsense?"

"Certainly," replied Michel, "and not only to distract ourselves, but also with the laudable intention of setting them up in moon clubs."

"My friend," said Barbicane, "if the moon is inhabited, its inhabitants must have appeared some thousands of years

258

Chess, cards, and dominoes for distractio

before those of the earth, for we cannot doubt that their star is much older than ours. If then these Selenites have existed there hundreds of thousands of years, and if their brain is of the same organization as the human brain, they have already invented all that we have invented, and even what we may invent in future ages. They have nothing to learn from *us,* and we have everything to learn from *them.*"

"What!" said Michel; "you believe that they have artists like Phidias, Michelangelo, or Raphael?"

"Yes."

"Poets like Homer, Virgil, Milton, Lamartine, Hugo?"

"I am sure of it."

"Philosophers like Plato, Aristotle, Descartes, Kant?"

"I have no doubt of it."

"Scientists like Archimedes, Euclid, Pascal, Newton?"

"I could swear it."

"Comedians like Arnal, and photographers like—like Nadar?"

"For certain."

"Then, friend Barbicane, if they are as strong as we are, and even stronger—these Selenites—why have they not tried to communicate with the earth? Why have they not launched a lunar projectile to our terrestrial regions?"

"Who told you that they have never done so?" said Barbicane seriously.

"Indeed," added Nicholl, "it would be easier for them than for us, for two reasons: first, because the attraction on the moon's surface is six times less than on that of the earth, which would allow a projectile to rise more easily; secondly, because it would be enough to send such a projectile only 20,000 miles, instead of 200,000, which would require ten times less force of projection."

259

"Then," continued Michel, "I repeat, why have they not done it?"

"And I repeat," said Barbicane; "who told you that they have not done it?"

"When?"

"Thousands of years before man appeared on earth."

"And the projectile—where is the projectile? I demand to see the projectile."

"My friend," replied Barbicane, "the sea covers five-sixths of our globe. From that we may draw five good reasons for supposing that the lunar projectile, if ever launched, is now at the bottom of the Atlantic or the Pacific, unless it sped into some crevasse at that period when the crust of the earth was not yet hardened."

"Old Barbicane," said Michel, "you have an answer for everything, and I bow before your wisdom. But there is one hypothesis that would please me better than all the others, which is, that the Selenites, being older than we, are wiser, and have not invented gunpowder."

At this moment Diana joined in the conversation by a sonorous barking. She was asking to be fed.

"Ah!" said Michel Ardan, "while we were arguing, we forgot about Diana and Satellite."

Immediately a good-sized meal was given to the dog, who devoured it hungrily.

"Do you see, Barbicane," said Michel, "we should have made a second Noah's ark of this projectile, and taken with us to the moon a couple of every kind of domestic animal."

"I dare say; but we would not have had the room for it."

"Oh!" said Michel, "we might have squeezed a little."

"The fact is," replied Nicholl, "that cows, bulls, oxen, and horses, and all ruminants, would have been very useful on the lunar continent, but unfortunately the car was not meant to be either a stable or a barn."

"Well, we might at least have brought a donkey, only a little donkey; that courageous beast which old Silenus loved to ride. I love those old donkeys; they are the least favored animals in creation; they are beaten not only while alive, but even after they are dead."

"How do you make that out?" asked Barbicane.

"Why," said Michel, "they make their skins into drums."

Barbicane and Nicholl could not help laughing at this ridiculous remark. But a cry from their merry companion stopped them. The latter was leaning over the spot where Satellite lay. He rose, saying:

"Well, Satellite is no longer ill."

"Ah!" said Nicholl.

"No," answered Michel, "he is dead! There," added he, in a pitiful tone, "that will be a problem. I much fear, my poor Diana, that you will leave no progeny in the lunar regions!"

Indeed the unfortunate Satellite had not survived his wound. He was quite dead. Michel Ardan looked at his friends with a rueful countenance.

"One question presents itself," said Barbicane. "We cannot keep the dead body of this dog with us for the next forty-eight hours."

"No! certainly not," replied Nicholl; "but our scuttles are fixed on hinges; they can be let down. We will open one, and throw the body out into space."

The president thought for some moments, and then said:

"Yes, we must do so, but at the same time taking very great precautions."

"Why?" asked Michel.

"For two reasons which you will understand," answered

Barbicane. "The first relates to the air shut up in the projectile, and of which we must lose as little as possible."

"But we manufacture our own air, don't we?"

"Only in part. We make only the oxygen, my worthy Michel; and with regard to that, we must watch that the apparatus does not furnish the oxygen in too great a quantity; for an excess would bring us very serious physiological troubles. But if we make the oxygen, we do not make the nitrogen, that medium which the lungs do not absorb, and which remains intact; and that nitrogen may escape rapidly through the open portholes."

"Oh! the time it takes to throw out poor Satellite?" said Michel.

"Agreed! but we must act quickly."

"And the second reason?" asked Michel.

"The second reason is that we must not let the outer cold, which is extreme, penetrate the projectile or we shall be frozen to death."

"But the sun?"

"The sun warms our projectile, which absorbs its rays; but it does not warm the vacuum in which we are floating at this moment. Where there is no air, there is no heat any more than there is diffused light; and just as it is dark so it is cold where the sun's rays do not strike direct. This temperature is only the temperature produced by the radiation of the stars; that is to say, what the terrestrial globe would experience if the sun were to disappear one day."

"Which is not to be feared," replied Nicholl.

"Who knows?" said Michel Ardan. "But, while admitting that the sun may not go out, might it not happen that the earth will move away from it?"

"There!" said Barbicane, "there is Michel with his ideas."

"Well," continued Michel, "do we not know that in 1861 the earth passed through the tail of a comet? So, if we suppose a comet whose power of attraction is greater than that of the sun, the terrestrial orbit will bend toward the wandering star, and the earth, becoming its satellite, will be drawn such a distance away that the rays of the sun will have no more effect on its surface."

"That *might* happen, indeed," replied Barbicane, "but the consequences of such a displacement need not be so awful as you suppose."

"And why not?"

"Because the heat and the cold would be equalized on our globe. It has been calculated that, had our earth been carried along in its course by the comet of 1861, it would have experienced, when farthest from the sun, a heat only sixteen times greater than that which the moon sends us, and which, when concentrated at the focus of the strongest lenses, produces no appreciable effect."

"So?" asked Michel.

"Just a minute," answered Barbicane. "It has also been calculated that, at its perihelion, that is, its nearest approach to the sun, earth would have undergone a heat 28,-000 times greater than that of summer. But this heat, which is sufficient to melt solids and evaporate waters, would have formed a thick ring of cloud, which would have modified that excessive temperature; hence the compensation between the cold of the aphelion and the heat of the perihelion, for a tolerable average."

"At how many degrees," asked Nicholl, "is the temperature of the planetary spaces estimated?"

"Formerly," Barbicane replied, "this temperature was imagined to be extremely low. Figuring its proportional decrease, results of millions of degrees below zero were attained. But now Fourier, one of Michel's fellow countrymen, an illustrious member of the French Academy of Sciences, has brought these figures back to more exact estimates. According to him, temperature in space is not supposed to go more than 76 degrees below zero Fahrenheit."

"Pooh!" said Michel, "a mere nothing!"

"That is approximately the same," answered Barbicane, "as the temperature recorded in the polar regions, at Melville Island or Fort Reliance, some 68 degrees below zero."

"It remains to be proved," said Nicholl, "that Fourier did not go astray in his calculations. If I am not wrong, another French scientist, M. Pouillet, estimates the temperature of space at 256 degrees below zero, which is something we shall be able to verify."

"Not at present," Barbicane replied, "because the solar rays, beating directly upon our thermometer, would give, on the contrary, a very high temperature. But, when we arrive on the moon, during its fifteen-day-long night at either face, we shall have leisure to make the experiment, for our satellite lies in a vacuum."

"What do you mean by vacuum?" asked Michel. "Is it an absolute vacuum?"

"It is absolutely devoid of air."

"And is the air replaced by nothing whatever?"

"By the ether only," replied Barbicane.

"And pray what is the ether?"

"The ether, my friend, is an agglomeration of imponderable atoms, which, relatively to their dimensions, according to books on molecular physics, are as far removed from each other as the celestial bodies are in space. Their distance from each other, however, is less than one four-hundred-millionth of an inch. It is these atoms which, by their vibratory motion, produce both light and heat in the universe, making in each second four hundred and thirty trillion oscillations, each of which is only one or two hundred-thousandths of an inch wide."

"Billions of billions!" Michel Ardan cried out. "Who ever counted those oscillations, anyway? Those, friend Barbicane, are the kind of scientists' figures that terrify the ear but mean nothing to the mind."

"Still, one has to figure—"

"No. It is better to compare. A trillion does not mean a thing. An object of comparative size expresses everything. For instance: when you have told me that Uranus is 76 times bigger than the earth, Saturn 900 times bigger, Jupiter 1,300 times bigger, and the sun 1,300,000 times bigger, I will know no more than before. So, I prefer—by far—those old farmer's-almanac types of comparisons, that tell you right out: the Sun is a pumpkin two feet across, Jupiter is an orange, Saturn a crab apple, Neptune a large heart-cherry, Uranus a cherry, Earth a pea, Venus, a small pea, Mars a large pinhead, Mercury a mustard seed, and Juno, Ceres, Vesta, and Pallas, mere grains of sand! That way at least you know where you're at!"

After this outburst by Michel Ardan against scientists and those trillions they reel off without wincing, they proceeded to the burial of Satellite. They had merely to drop him into space, in the same way that sailors drop a body into the sea.

But, as President Barbicane suggested, they must act quickly, so as to lose as little as possible of that air whose elasticity would rapidly have spread it into space. The bolts of the right scuttle, the opening of which measured about twelve inches across, were carefully drawn, while Michel, quite grieved, prepared to launch his dog into space. The glass, raised by a powerful lever, which enabled it to overcome the pressure of the inside air on the walls of the projectile, turned rapidly on its hinges, and Satellite was thrown out. Scarcely a particle of air could have escaped, and the operation was so successful that later on Barbicane did not fear to dispose in this way of the rubbish littering the car.

CHAPTER 6

Questions and Answers

O N the 4th of December, when the travelers awoke after fifty-four hours' journey, the chronometer marked five o'clock of the terrestrial morning. In time they were just five hours and forty minutes over half of what was assigned to their sojourn in the projectile; but they had already accomplished nearly seven-tenths of the way. This peculiarity was due to their regularly decreasing speed.

Now when they observed the earth through the lower window, it looked like nothing more than a dark spot, drowned in the solar rays. No more crescent, no more moonshine! The next day, at midnight, the earth would be *new,* at the very moment when the moon would be full. Above, the orb of night was coming ever nearer the line followed by the projectile, so as to meet it at the given hour. All around, the black vault was studded with brilliant points, which seemed to move slowly; but, at the great distance they were from them, their relative size did not seem to change. The sun and stars appeared exactly as they do to us upon earth. As to the moon, she was considerably larger; but the travelers' glasses, not very powerful, did not allow them as yet to make any useful observations upon her surface, or reconnoiter her topographically or geologically.

Thus the time passed in never-ending conversations all about the moon. Each one brought forward his own supply of special knowledge; Barbicane and Nicholl always serious, Michel Ardan always fanciful. The projectile, its situation, its direction, incidents which might happen, the precautions necessitated by their fall on to the moon, were inexhaustible matters of conjecture.

As they were breakfasting, a question of Michel's, relating to the projectile, provoked a rather curious answer from Barbicane, which is worth repeating.

Michel, supposing their vehicle to be suddenly stopped, while still under its formidable initial speed, wished to know what the consequences of the stoppage would have been.

"But," said Barbicane, "I do not see how it could have been stopped."

"But let us suppose it was," said Michel.

"It is an impossible supposition," said the practical Barbicane; "unless the impulsive force had failed; but even then its speed would diminish by degrees, and it would not have stopped suddenly."

"Suppose that it had struck a body in space."

"What body?"

"Why, that enormous meteor which we met."

"Then," said Nicholl, "the projectile would have been broken into a thousand pieces, and we with it."

"More than that," replied Barbicane; "we should have been burned to death."

"Burned?" exclaimed Michel, "by Jove! I am sorry it did not happen, 'just to see.' "

"And you would have seen," replied Barbicane. "It is

known now that heat is only a modification of motion. When water is warmed—that is to say, when heat is added to it—it means that its particles are set in motion."

"Well," said Michel, "that is an ingenious theory!"

"And a true one, my worthy friend; for it explains every phenomenon of caloric. Heat is but the motion of molecules, a simple oscillation of the particles of a body. When they apply the brake to a train, the train comes to a stop; but what becomes of the motion which it had previously possessed? It is transformed into heat, and the brake becomes hot. Why do they grease the axles of the wheels? To prevent their heating, because this heat would be generated by motion thus lost in the transformation. Do you understand?"

"Yes, I understand," replied Michel, "perfectly. For example, when I have run a long time, when I am overheated and perspiring in large drops, why am I obliged to stop? Simply because my motion has changed into heat."

Barbicane could not help smiling at Michel's reply; then, returning to his theory, said:

"Thus, in case of a shock, it would have been with our projectile as with a bullet which falls in a burning state after having struck the metal plate; it is its motion which has turned into heat. Consequently I affirm that, if our projectile had struck the meteor, its speed thus suddenly checked would have raised a heat great enough to turn it into vapor instantaneously."

"Then," asked Nicholl, "what would happen if the earth's motion were to stop suddenly?"

"Her temperature would be raised to such a pitch," said Barbicane, "that she would be at once reduced to vapor."

"Well," said Michel, "that is a way of ending the earth which will greatly simplify things."

"And if the earth fell upon the sun?" asked Nicholl.

"According to calculation," replied Barbicane, "the fall would develop a heat equal to that produced by 16,000 globes of coal, each equal in bulk to our terrestrial globe."

"Good additional heat for the sun," replied Michel Ardan, "of which the inhabitants of Uranus or Neptune would doubtless not complain; they must be perishing with cold on their planets."

"Thus, my friends," said Barbicane, "all motion suddenly stopped produces heat. And this theory allows us to infer that the heat of the solar disc is fed by a hail of meteors falling incessantly on its surface. They have even figured——"

"Oh, dear!" murmured Michel, "here come more figures, now!"

"They have even calculated," continued the imperturbable Barbicane, "that the shock of each meteor on the sun must produce a heat equal to that of 4,000 loads of coal of equal size."

"And what is the heat of the sun?" asked Michel.

"It is equal to that produced by the combustion of a layer of coal surrounding the sun to a depth of seventeen miles."

"And that heat——"

"Would be enough to boil something like thirty-nine trillion cubic yards of water per hour."

"And it does not roast us!" exclaimed Michel.

"No," replied Barbicane, "because the terrestrial atmosphere absorbs four-tenths of the solar heat; besides, the quantity of heat intercepted by the earth is but a two-billionth part of the entire radiation."

"I see that all is for the best," said Michel, "and that this atmosphere is a useful invention; for it not only allows us to breathe, but it prevents us from roasting."

"Yes!" said Nicholl, "unfortunately, it will not be the same in the moon."

"Bah!" said Michel, ever optimistic. "If there are inhabitants, they must breathe. If there are no longer any, they must have left enough oxygen for three people, if only at the bottom of ravines, where its own weight will have caused it to accumulate, and we will not climb the mountains; that is all."

And Michel, rising, went to look at the lunar disc, which shone with intolerable brilliancy.

"By Jove!" said he, "it must be hot up there!"

"Without considering," replied Nicholl, "that a day up there lasts 360 hours!"

"And to compensate for that," said Barbicane, "the nights are the same length; and, as heat is restored by radiation, their temperature can only be that of the planetary space."

"A fine country, that!" exclaimed Michel. "Never mind! I wish I were there already! Ah! my dear comrades, it will be rather curious to have the earth for our moon, to see it rise on the horizon, to recognize the shape of its continents, and to say to oneself, 'There is America, there is Europe'; then to follow it when it is about to lose itself in the sun's rays! By the bye, Barbicane, do the Selenites have eclipses?"

"Yes, eclipses of the sun," replied Barbicane, "when the centers of the three orbs are on a line, the earth being in the middle. But they are only partial, during which the earth, cast like a screen over the solar disc, allows the greater portion to be seen."

"And why," asked Nicholl, "is there no total eclipse? Does not the cone of the shadow cast by the earth extend beyond the moon?"

"Yes, if we do not take into consideration the refraction

produced by earth's atmosphere. No, if we take that refraction into consideration. Thus let *delta* prime be the horizontal parallax, and *p* the visible semidiameter——"

"Oh!" said Michel. "A half of *v* zero squared. Please speak plainly, you algebraic man!"

"Very well," replied Barbicane; "in popular language the mean distance from the moon to the earth being sixty terrestrial radii, the length of the cone of the shadow, on account of the refraction, is reduced to less than forty-two radii. The result is that when there are eclipses, the moon finds itself beyond the cone of pure shadow, and that the sun sends her its rays, not only from its edges, but also from its center."

"Then," said Michel, in a scoffing tone, "why are there eclipses, when there ought not to be any?"

"Simply because the solar rays are weakened by this refraction, and the atmosphere through which they pass extinguishes the greater part of them!"

"That reason satisfies me," replied Michel. "Besides we shall see when we get there. Now, tell me, Barbicane, do you believe that the moon is an old comet?"

"There's an idea!"

"Yes," replied Michel, with an amiable swagger, "I have a few ideas of that sort."

"But that idea does not spring from Michel," answered Nicholl.

"Well, then, I am a plagiarist."

"No doubt about it. According to the ancients, the Arcadians claim that their ancestors inhabited the earth before the moon became her satellite. Starting from this fact, some scientists have seen in the moon a comet whose orbit one day brought it so near to the earth that it was held there by the earth's attraction."

"Is there any truth in this hypothesis?" asked Michel.

"None whatever," said Barbicane, "and the proof is, that the moon has preserved no trace of the gaseous envelope which always accompanies comets."

"But," continued Nicholl, "before becoming the earth's satellite, could not the moon, when in her perihelion, have passed so near the sun as by evaporation to get rid of all those gaseous substances?"

"It is possible, friend Nicholl, but not probable."

"Why not?"

"Because—to tell the truth, I do not know."

"Ah!" exclaimed Michel, "what hundreds of volumes we might make of all that we do not know!"

"Ah! indeed. What time is it?" asked Barbicane.

"Three o'clock," answered Nicholl.

"How time goes by," said Michel, "in the conversation of scientists such as we! To be sure, I feel I am learning too much! I feel that I am becoming a well!"

Saying which, Michel hoisted himself to the roof of the projectile, "the better to observe the moon," as he put it. During this time his companions were watching through the lower window. Nothing new to note.

When Michel Ardan came down, he went to the side scuttle; and suddenly they heard an exclamation of surprise!

"What is it?" asked Barbicane.

The president approached the window, and saw a sort of flattened sack floating a few yards from the projectile. This object seemed as motionless as the projectile, and was consequently animated with the same ascending movement.

"What can that thing be?" continued Michel Ardan. "Is it one of the tiny space bodies which our projectile has kept within its field of attraction, and which will accompany it to the moon?"

273

"What astonishes me," said Nicholl, "is that the specific weight of the body, which is certainly less than that of the projectile, allows it to keep so perfectly on a level with it."

"Nicholl," replied Barbicane, after a moment's reflection, "I do not know what the object is, but I do know why it remains on our level."

"And why?"

"Because we are floating in space, my dear captain, and in space bodies fall or move (which is the same thing) with equal speed whatever their weight or shape; it is the air which, by its resistance, creates differences in weight. When you create a vacuum in a tube, all the objects you send through it, grains of dust or grains of lead, fall at the same rate. Here in space the same cause creates the same effect."

"Quite so," said Nicholl, "and everything we throw out of the projectile will accompany it until it reaches the moon."

"Ah! fools that we are!" exclaimed Michel.

"Why that expletive?" asked Barbicane.

"Because we should have filled the projectile with useful objects, books, instruments, tools, etc. We could have thrown them all out, and all would have followed in our train. But happy thought! Why cannot we walk outside like that meteor? Why cannot we launch ourselves into space through the scuttle? What enjoyment it would be to feel oneself thus suspended in ether, more favored than the birds who must use their wings to keep themselves up!"

"Granted," said Barbicane, "but how to breathe?"

"Hang the air, to be missing just when we need it!"

"But if it were not missing, Michel, your density being less than that of the projectile, you would soon be left behind."

"So, it is a vicious circle?"

"As vicious as can be."

"Then we must remain in our car?"

"We must."

"Ah!" exclaimed Michel, in a loud voice.

"What is the matter?" asked Nicholl.

"I know, I guess what that so-called meteor is! It is no asteroid which is accompanying us! It is not a piece of a planet."

"What is it then?" asked Barbicane.

"It is our unfortunate dog! It is Diana's husband!"

Indeed, this deformed, unrecognizable object, reduced to nothing, was the body of Satellite, flattened like a bagpipe without wind, and ever rising, rising!

CHAPTER 7

A Moment of Intoxication

THUS a phenomenon, curious but logical, unusual but explicable, was happening under these strange conditions. Every object thrown from the projectile would follow the same course and never stop until it did. That gave them a subject for conversation which the whole evening could not exhaust. Besides, the excitement of the three travelers increased as they drew near the end of their journey. They expected unforeseen incidents, and new phenomena; and nothing would have astonished them in the frame of mind they then were in. Their overexcited imagination went faster than the projectile, whose speed was notably diminishing, though they did not feel it themselves. But the moon grew larger to their eyes, and they fancied now that if they stretched out their hands they could seize it.

The next day, the 5th of December, at five in the morning, all three were on foot. That day was to be the last of their journey, if the calculations were right. That very night, at twelve o'clock, in eighteen hours, exactly at the full moon, they would reach its brilliant disc. The next midnight would see their journey ended, the most extraordinary of ancient or modern times. Thus from the first of the morning, through the scuttles silvered by its rays, they saluted the orb of night with a confident and joyous hurrah.

The moon was advancing majestically along the starry firmament. A few more degrees, and she would reach the exact point where her meeting with the projectile was to take place. According to his own observations, Barbicane reckoned that they would land on her northern hemisphere, where stretch immense plains, and where mountains are rare. A favorable circumstance if, as they thought, the lunar atmosphere was stored only in its depths.

"Besides," observed Michel Ardan, "a plain is easier to disembark upon than a mountain. A Selenite, deposited in Europe on the summit of Mont Blanc, or in Asia on the top of the Himalayas, would not be quite at his destination yet!"

"And," added Captain Nicholl, "on flat ground, the projectile will remain motionless when it has once touched; whereas on a declivity it would roll like an avalanche, and not being squirrels we should not come out safe and sound. So it is all for the best."

Indeed, the success of their daring enterprise no longer appeared doubtful. Yet Barbicane was preoccupied with one thought; but not wishing to make his companions uneasy, he kept silence on the subject.

The direction the projectile was taking toward the moon's northern hemisphere, showed that her course had been slightly altered. The shot, mathematically calculated, was to have carried the projectile to the very center of the lunar disc. If it did not land there, there must have been some deviation. What had caused it? Barbicane could neither imagine nor determine the scope of the deviation, for there was no frame of reference. He hoped, however, that it would have no other result than that of bringing them near the upper border of the moon, a region more suitable for landing.

Without imparting his uneasiness to his companions, Barbicane contented himself with constantly observing the moon, in order to see whether the course of the projectile would not be altered; for the situation would have been terrible if it failed in its aim, and being carried beyond the disc should be launched into interplanetary space.

At that moment, the moon, instead of appearing flat like a disc, showed its convexity. If the sun's rays had struck it obliquely, the shadow thrown would have brought out the high mountains, which would have been clearly detached. The eye might have gazed into the crater's gaping abysses, and followed the capricious fissures which wound through the immense plains. But all relief was as yet leveled in intense brilliancy. They could scarcely distinguish those large spots which give to the moon the appearance of a human face.

"Face, indeed!" said Michel Ardan; "but I am sorry for the amiable sister of Apollo. A very pitted face!"

But the travelers, now so near their goal, were incessantly observing this new world. They imagined themselves walking through its unknown countries, climbing its highest peaks, descending into its lowest depths. Here and there they fancied they saw vast seas, scarcely kept together under so rarefied an atmosphere, and watercourses emptying the mountain tributaries. Leaning over the abyss, they hoped to catch some sounds from that orb forever mute in the solitude of space.

That last day left them most exciting recollections, of which they took down the most trifling details. A vague uneasiness took possession of them as they neared the end.

This uneasiness would have been doubled had they felt how their speed had decreased. It would have seemed to them quite insufficient to carry them to their goal. For, at this point, the projectile "weighed" almost nothing. Its weight was ever decreasing, and would be entirely annihilated at the line where lunar and terrestrial attractions neutralize each other and create such strange effects.

But in spite of his preoccupation, Michel Ardan did not forget to prepare the morning meal with his accustomed punctuality. They ate with a good appetite. Nothing was so excellent as the soup liquefied by the heat of the gas; nothing better than the preserved meat. Some glasses of good French wine crowned the repast, causing Michel Ardan to remark that the lunar vines, warmed by that ardent sun, ought to distill even more generous wines; that is, if they existed. In any case, the far-seeing Frenchman had taken care not to forget in his collection some precious cuttings of the Médoc and Côte d'Or vine-stands, upon which he founded his hopes.

Reiset and Regnault's apparatus worked with great regularity. Their air remained perfectly pure. Not an atom of carbon dioxide resisted the potash; and as to the oxygen, Captain Nicholl said "it was certainly of the first quality." The little watery vapor enclosed in the projectile mixing with the air tempered the dryness; and many apartments in London, Paris, or New York, many theaters, are certainly not in such a hygienic condition.

But in order to act with regularity, the apparatus had to be kept in perfect shape; so each morning Michel checked the escape regulators, tried the taps, and regulated the heat of the gas by the pyrometer. Everything had gone well up to that time, and the travelers, imitating the worthy J. T. Mas-

279

ton, began to acquire a degree of embonpoint which would have rendered them unrecognizable if their imprisonment had been prolonged to some months. In a word, they behaved like chickens in a coop; they were getting fat.

In looking through the scuttle Barbicane saw the specter of the dog, and other divers objects which had been thrown from the projectile, obstinately following them. Diana howled lugubriously on seeing the remains of Satellite, which seemed as motionless as if they reposed on the solid earth.

"Do you know, my friends," said Michel Ardan, "that if one of us had succumbed to the shock consequent on departure, we should have had a great deal of trouble to bury him? What am I saying? To *etherize* him, as here ether takes the place of earth. You see the accusing body would have followed us into space like a remorse."

"That would have been sad," said Nicholl.

"Ah!" continued Michel, "what I regret is not being able to talk a walk outside. What voluptuousness to float amid this radiant ether, to bathe oneself in it, to wrap oneself in the sun's pure rays. If Barbicane had only thought of furnishing us with a diving apparatus and an air-pump, I could have ventured out and assumed fanciful attitudes of feigned monsters on the top of the projectile."

"Well, old Michel," replied Barbicane, "you would not have made a feigned monster long, for in spite of your diver's dress, swollen by the expansion of air within you, you would have burst like a shell, or rather like a balloon which has risen too high. So do not regret it, and do not forget this —as long as we float in space, all sentimental walks outside the projectile are forbidden."

Michel Ardan allowed himself to be convinced to a certain extent. He admitted that the thing was difficult but not "impossible," for that was a word which he never uttered.

The conversation passed from this subject to another, never lagging for an instant. It seemed to the three friends as though, under present conditions, ideas shot up in their brains as leaves shoot out at the first warmth of spring. They felt overgrown with them.

In the middle of the questions and answers which crossed each other, during that morning, Nicholl put one question which did not find an immediate solution.

"Ah, indeed!" said he; "it is all very well to go to the moon, but how do we get back again?"

His two interlocutors looked surprised. One would have thought that this possibility now occurred to them for the first time.

"What do you mean by that, Nicholl?" asked Barbicane gravely.

"To ask for means to leave a country," added Michel, "when we have not yet arrived there, seems to me rather inopportune."

"I do not say that, wishing to draw back," replied Nicholl; "but I repeat my question, and I ask, 'How shall we return?' "

"I have no idea," answered Barbicane.

"And I," said Michel, "if I had known how to return, I would never have started."

"There's an answer!" cried Nicholl.

"I quite approve of Michel's words," said Barbicane; "and add, that the question is of no interest at present. Later, when we think it proper to return, we will take counsel together. If the Columbiad is not there, the projectile will be."

"A fine thing! A bullet without a gun!"

"The gun," replied Barbicane, "can be manufactured. Powder can be made. Metals, saltpeter, and coal must all be present in the depths of the moon, and we need only go 20,000 miles in order to fall to the terrestrial globe by virtue of the mere laws of gravity."

"Enough," said Michel with animation. "Let us stop this talk of returning: we have already entertained the idea too long. As to communicating with our former earthly colleagues, that will not be difficult."

"And how?"

"By means of meteors launched by lunar volcanoes."

"Ingenious, Michel," said Barbicane in a convinced tone of voice. "Laplace has calculated that a force five times greater than that of our guns would suffice to send a meteor from the moon to the earth, and there is not one volcano which has not a greater power of propulsion than that."

"Hurrah!" exclaimed Michel; "these meteors will make handy postmen, and cost nothing. And how we shall be able to laugh at the post-office administration! But now I think of it——"

"What do you think of?"

"A capital idea. Why did we not fasten a wire to our projectile, and we could have exchanged telegrams with the earth?"

"The deuce!" answered Nicholl. "Do you consider as nothing the weight of a wire 220,000 miles long?"

"As nothing. They could have trebled the Columbiad's charge; they could have quadrupled or quintupled it!" exclaimed Michel, whose voice took on a more excited intonation each time.

"There is but one little objection to make to your proposi-

Dancers in spa

tion," replied Barbicane, "which is that, during the rotary motion of the globe, our thread would have wound itself round it like a chain on a capstan, and would inevitably have brought us back to the ground."

"By the thirty-nine stars of the Union!" said Michel, "I have nothing but impracticable ideas to-day; ideas worthy of J. T. Maston. But I have a notion that, if we do not return to earth, J. T. Maston will be able to come to us."

"Yes, he'll come," replied Barbicane; "he is a worthy and courageous comrade. Besides, what is easier? Is the Columbiad not still buried in the soil of Florida? Is there any lack of cotton and nitric acid for the manufacture of pyroxylin? Will not the moon again go through the zenith of Florida? In eighteen years' time will she not occupy exactly the same place as to-day?"

"Yes," continued Michel, "yes, Maston will come, and with him our friends Elphinstone, Blomsberry, all the members of the Gun Club, and they will be well received. And later on there will be trains of projectiles between the earth and the moon! Hurrah for J. T. Maston!"

It is probable that, if the Hon. J. T. Maston did not hear the hurrahs uttered in his honor, his ears at least tingled. What was he doing then? Doubtless, posted in the Rocky Mountains, at the station of Longs Peak, he was trying to find the invisible projectile gravitating into space. If he was thinking of his dear companions, we must recognize that they were not far behind, for under the influence of their strange excitement, they were devoting all of their best thoughts to him.

But whence this excitement, which was so visibly increasing among the tenants of the projectile? Their sobriety could not be doubted. Must this strange irritation of the brain be attributed to the peculiar circumstances under which they found themselves, to their proximity to the orb of night, from which only a few hours separated them, to some secret influence of the moon acting upon their nervous systems? Their faces were as rosy as if they had been exposed to the roaring flames of a furnace; their breaths were rapid, and their lungs worked like bellows; their eyes shone with extraordinary brilliance; their voices resounded in loud accents; their words escaped like a champagne cork driven out by carbonic acid; their gestures became dangerous, as they took so much room to perform them; and, strange to say, none of them noticed this great tension of their minds.

"Now," said Nicholl, in a short tone, "now that I do not know whether we shall ever return from the moon, I want to know what we are going to do there?"

"What we are going to do there?" replied Barbicane, stamping with his foot as if he were in a fencing saloon; "I have no idea."

"You have no idea!" exclaimed Michel, with a bellow which provoked a sonorous echo in the projectile.

"No, not the slightest inkling," retorted Barbicane, in the same loud tone.

"Well, I know," replied Michel.

"Speak, then," cried Nicholl, who could no longer contain the growling of his voice.

"I shall speak if it suits me," exclaimed Michel, seizing his companion's arm with violence.

"*It must* suit you," said Barbicane, with fire in his eye and a threatening hand. "You were the one who got us to take this fantastic journey, and we want to know what for!"

"Yes," said the captain, "now that I do not know *where* I am going, I do want to know *why* I am going."

"Why?" exclaimed Michel, jumping a yard high, "why? To take possession of the moon in the name of the United States; to add a fortieth State to the Union; to colonize the lunar regions; to cultivate them, to people them, to transport there all the prodigies of art, of science, and industry; to civilize the Selenites, unless they are more civilized than we are; and to constitute them as a republic, if they are not one already!"

"And what if there are no Selenites?" retorted Nicholl, who, under the influence of this unaccountable intoxication, was becoming extremely cantankerous.

"Who says that there are no Selenites?" exclaimed Michel in a threatening tone.

"I do," howled Nicholl.

"Captain," said Michel, "do not repeat that insolence, or I will knock your teeth down your throat!"

The two adversaries were going to fall upon each other, and the incoherent discussion threatened to degenerate into a fight, when Barbicane intervened with one bound.

"Stop, miserable men," said he, separating his two companions; "if there are no Selenites, we will do without them."

"Yes," exclaimed Michel, who was not too concerned one way or the other, "yes, we will do without them. Selenites? Down with the Selenites!"

"The empire of the moon belongs to us," said Nicholl.

"Let us three constitute the republic."

"I will be the congress," cried Michel.

"And I the senate," retorted Nicholl.

"And Barbicane, the president," howled Michel.

"Not a president elected by the nation," replied Barbicane.

"Very well, a president elected by the congress," cried

Michel; "and as I am the congress, you are unanimously elected!"

"Hurrah! hurrah! hurrah! for President Barbicane!" exclaimed Nicholl.

"Hip! hip! hip!" vociferated Michel Ardan.

Then the president and the senate struck up in a tremendous voice the popular song, *Yankee Doodle,* while from the congress resounded the manly tones of the *Marseillaise.*

Then they struck up a frantic dance, with maniacal gestures, idiotic stampings, and somersaults like those of the boneless clowns in the circus. Diana, joining in the dance, and howling in her turn, jumped to the top of the projectile. An unaccountable flapping of wings was then heard amid most fantastic cock-crows, while five or six hens fluttered like bats against the walls.

Then the three traveling companions, acted upon by some unaccountable influence above that of intoxication, inflamed by the air which had set their respiratory apparatus on fire, fell motionless to the bottom of the projectile.

CHAPTER 8

195,285 Miles Out

WHAT had happened? Whence the cause of this singular intoxication, the consequences of which might have been disastrous? A simple blunder of Michel's, which, fortunately, Nicholl was able to correct in time.

After being in a faint for several minutes, the captain, recovering first, soon collected his scattered senses.

Although he had breakfasted only two hours before, he felt a gnawing hunger, as if he had not eaten anything for several days. Everything about him, stomach and brain, was excited to the highest degree.

He got up and demanded that Michel give him some more to eat. Michel, utterly done up, did not answer. Nicholl then tried to prepare some tea destined to help the absorption of a dozen sandwiches. He first tried to get some fire, and struck a match sharply.

What was his surprise to see the sulphur shine with so extraordinary a brilliancy as to be almost unbearable to the eye. From the gas-burner which he lit rose a flame equal to a jet of electric light.

A revelation dawned on Nicholl's mind. That intensity of light, the physiological troubles which had arisen in him,

the excitement of all his moral and quarrelsome faculties—
he understood all.

"The oxygen!" he exclaimed.

And, leaning over the air apparatus, he saw that the tap
was allowing the scentless, tasteless, colorless gas to escape
freely, life-giving, but in its pure state producing the gravest
disorders in the system. Michel had thoughtlessly left the
tap of the apparatus wide open.

Nicholl hastened to stop the escape of oxygen with
which the atmosphere was saturated, which would have been
the death of the travelers, not by suffocation, but by combustion.

An hour later, the air less charged with it restored the
lungs to their normal condition. By degrees the three friends
recovered from their intoxication; but they were obliged to
sleep off their oxygen intoxication as a drunkard does his
wine.

When Michel learned his share of the responsibility of
this incident, he was not much disconcerted. This unexpected drunkenness broke the monotony of the journey.
Many foolish things had been said while under its influence,
but just as quickly forgotten.

"Besides," added the merry Frenchman, "I am not sorry
to have tasted a little of this heady gas. Do you know, my
friends, that a curious establishment might be founded with
oxygen rooms where people whose system is weakened
could for a few hours live a more active life. Just imagine
parties where the room was saturated with this heroic fluid,
theaters where it was kept in high dosage; what passion in
the souls of the actors and spectators! What fire, what enthusiasm! And if, instead of an assembly only, a whole people could be saturated, what activity in its functions, what a

supplement to life it would derive! From an exhausted nation they might make a great and strong one, and I know more than one state in old Europe which ought to put itself under the regime of oxygen for the sake of its health!"

Michel spoke with so much animation that one might have fancied that the tap was still too open. But a few words from Barbicane soon damped his enthusiasm.

"That is all very well, friend Michel," said he, "but will you inform us where the chickens came from that joined in our concert?"

"Chickens?"

"Yes."

Indeed, half a dozen chickens and a fine cock were walking about, flapping their wings and cackling.

"Ah, the awkward things!" exclaimed Michel. "The oxygen has made them revolt."

"But what do you expect to do with these chickens?" asked Barbicane.

"To acclimatize them on the moon, by Jove!"

"Then why did you hide them?"

"A joke, my worthy president, a simple joke, which has proved a miserable failure. I wanted to set them free on the lunar continent, without saying anything. Oh, what would have been your amazement on seeing these earthly-winged animals pecking in the lunar fields!"

"You rascal, you unmitigated rascal," replied Barbicane, "you do not need oxygen to make you cut up. You are always in the state we were in under the influence of the gas; you are always mad!"

"Ah, who says that we were not wise then?" replied Michel Ardan.

After this philosophical reflection, the three friends set

about restoring the order of the projectile. Chickens and cock were returned to their coop. But, while proceeding with this operation, Barbicane and his two companions had a most decided sense of a new phenomenon.

From the moment of leaving earth, their own weight, that of the projectile, and the objects it enclosed, had been subject to an increasing diminution. If they could not feel this loss by the projectile, a moment had to arrive when it would be appreciable insofar as they themselves and the utensils and instruments they used were concerned.

It is needless to say that a scale would not show this loss; for the weight destined to weigh the object would have lost exactly as much as the object itself; but a spring-balance, for example, the tension of which was independent of gravity, would have given a just estimate of this loss.

We know that the attraction, or the weight, is in proportion to the densities of bodies, and inversely to the squares of the distances. Hence this effect: If the earth had been alone in space, if the other celestial bodies had been suddenly annihilated, the projectile, according to Newton's laws, would weigh less as it got farther from the earth, but without ever losing its weight entirely, for the terrestrial attraction would always have made itself felt, at whatever distance.

But, in reality, a time must come when the projectile would no longer be subject to the laws of gravity, if we could dismiss all other celestial bodies whose effect could be held to be zero.

Actually, the projectile's course was being traced between the earth and the moon. As it grew more distant from the earth, the terrestrial attraction diminished in inverse ratio to the square of the distance; but the lunar attraction rose in proportion. There must then come a point where these two attractions would neutralize each other: the projectile would possess weight no longer. If the moon's and the earth's sizes had been equal, this point would have been at an equal distance between the two orbs. But, taking their different sizes into consideration, it was easy to reckon that this point would be situated at 47/52nds of the whole journey, *i.e.,* at 195,285 miles from the earth.

At this point, a body having no principle of speed or displacement in itself, would remain motionless forever, being attracted equally by both orbs, and not being drawn any more toward one than toward the other.

Now if the projectile's impulsive force had been correctly calculated, it would attain this point without speed, having lost all trace of weight, as would have all the objects within it.

What would happen then? Three hypotheses presented themselves.

1. Either it would retain a certain amount of motion, and pass the point of equal attraction, and fall upon the moon by virtue of the excess of the lunar attraction over the terrestrial.

2. Or, its speed failing, and unable to reach the point of equal attraction, it would fall back to earth by virtue of the excess of the terrestrial attraction over the lunar.

3. Or, lastly, animated with sufficient speed to enable it to reach the neutral point, but not sufficient to pass it, it would remain forever suspended in that spot like the alleged tomb of Mahomet, between the zenith and the nadir.

Such was their situation; and Barbicane clearly explained the consequences to his traveling companions, which greatly interested them. But how would they know when the projectile had reached this neutral point situated at that distance?

Specifically, when neither themselves nor the objects enclosed in the projectile would be any longer subject to the laws of weight.

Up to this time, the travelers, while feeling that this action was constantly decreasing, had not yet become aware of its total absence. But that day, about eleven o'clock in the morning, Nicholl having accidentally let a glass slip from his hand, the glass, instead of falling, remained suspended in the air.

"Ah!" exclaimed Michel Ardan, "that is a rather amusing example of physics!"

And immediately divers other objects, firearms and bottles, abandoned to themselves, held themselves up as by enchantment. Diana too, placed in space by Michel, reproduced without any trickery the wonderful suspension practiced by such as Caston and Robert-Houdin. Indeed the dog did not seem to know that she was floating in air.

The three adventurous companions were surprised and amazed, despite their scientific reasonings, for they felt themselves being carried into the domain of wonders and weight really missing from their bodies. If they stretched out their arms, they did not attempt to drop. Their heads were shaky on their shoulders. Their feet no longer clung to the floor of the projectile. They were like drunks who have no stability. Fiction has created men who had no reflection in mirrors, others without a shadow. But here reality, by the neutralization of attractive forces, produced men in whom nothing had any weight, and who weighed nothing themselves.

Suddenly Michel, taking a spring, left the floor and remained suspended in the air, like Murillo's monk in the *Angels' Kitchen.*

The two friends joined him instantly, and all three formed a miraculous "Ascension" in the center of the projectile.

"Is it to be believed? Is it probable? Is it possible?" exclaimed Michel. "And yet it is so. Ah! if Raphael had seen us thus, what an 'Assumption' he would have thrown upon canvas!"

"The 'Assumption' cannot last," replied Barbicane. "If the projectile passes the neutral point, the lunar attraction will draw us to the moon."

"Then our feet will be upon the roof," replied Michel.

"No," said Barbicane, "because the projectile's center of gravity is very low; it will gradually turn over."

"Then all our furnishings will turn upside down—literally!"

"Calm yourself, Michel," replied Nicholl; "no such upset is to be feared; not a thing will move, for the projectile's turnover will take place imperceptibly."

"Just so," continued Barbicane; "and when it has passed the point of equal attraction, its base, being the heavier, will draw it perpendicularly to the moon; but, in order for this phenomenon to take place, we must have passed the neutral line."

"Pass the neutral line, eh!" cried Michel. "Then let us do as the sailors do when they cross the equator. Let's drink to it!"

A slight side movement brought Michel back toward the padded side; thence he took a bottle and glasses, placed them "in space" before his companions, and, merrily clinking glasses, they toasted the line with a triple hurrah.

The influence of these attractions lasted scarcely an

hour; the travelers felt themselves insensibly drawn toward the floor, and Barbicane fancied that the conical end of the projectile was varying a little from its normal direction toward the moon. By an inverse motion the base was approaching first; the lunar attraction was prevailing over the terrestrial; the fall toward the moon was beginning, almost imperceptibly as yet, as it would be only about one-twentieth of an inch in the first second. But by degrees the attractive force would become stronger, the fall would be more decided, the projectile, drawn by its base, would turn its cone to the earth, and fall with ever-increasing speed on to the surface of the Selenite continent; their destination would then be attained. Now nothing could prevent the success of their enterprise, and Nicholl and Michel Ardan shared Barbicane's joy.

Then they chatted about all the phenomena which had astonished them one after the other, particularly the neutralization of the laws of weight. Michel Ardan, always enthusiastic, drew conclusions which were purely fanciful.

"Ah, my worthy friends," he exclaimed, "what progress we should make if on earth we could throw off some of that weight, some of that chain which binds us to her; it would be the prisoner set at liberty; no more fatigue of either arms or legs. And, if it is true that flying on the earth's surface, keeping oneself suspended in the air merely by the play of the muscles requires a strength a hundred and fifty times greater than that which we possess, a simple act of volition, a caprice would bear us into space, if attraction did not exist."

"Just so," said Nicholl, smiling; "if we could succeed in suppressing weight as they suppress pain by anæsthesia, that would change the face of modern society!"

"Yes," cried Michel, full of his subject, "let us destroy weight, and there will be no more burdens! Then, no more cranes, hoists, capstans, winches, or any other such useless things!"

"Well said," replied Barbicane; "but if nothing had any weight, nothing would keep in its place, not even your hat on your head, worthy Michel; nor your house, whose stones only adhere by weight; not a boat, whose stability on the water is caused only by weight; not even the ocean, whose waves would no longer be equalized by terrestrial attraction; and lastly, not even the atmosphere, whose molecules, being no longer held in their places, would disperse in space!"

"That would really be too bad," retorted Michel. "Nothing like these matter-of-fact people for bringing one brutally back to reality."

"But console yourself, Michel," continued Barbicane, "for if no orb exists from whence all laws of weight are banished, you are at least going to visit one where it is much less than on the earth."

"The moon?"

"Yes, the moon, on whose surface objects weigh six times less than on earth, a phenomenon that is easy to perceive."

"And we shall feel it?" asked Michel.

"Of course, since four hundred pounds will only weigh sixty on the surface of the moon."

"And our muscular strength will not diminish?"

"Not at all; instead of jumping one yard high, you will be able to jump eighteen feet."

"But we shall be regular Herculeses on the moon!" exclaimed Michel.

"The more so," replied Nicholl, "that, if the height of the

Selenites is in proportion to the size of their globe, they will be scarcely a foot high."

"Lilliputians!" ejaculated Michel. "I shall be cast as Gulliver. We are going to play out the fable of the giants. This is the advantage of leaving one's own planet and gallivanting through the solar world."

"One moment, Michel," answered Barbicane; "if you wish to play the part of Gulliver, only visit the inferior planets, such as Mercury, Venus, or Mars, whose size is a little less than that of the earth; but do not venture into the great planets, Jupiter, Saturn, Uranus, Neptune; for there the order would be the opposite, and you would become Lilliputian."

"And in the sun?"

"In the sun, if its density is four times less than that of the earth, its size is thirteen hundred and twenty-four thousand times greater, and the attraction is twenty-seven times greater than on the surface of our globe. Keeping everything in proportion, the inhabitants would have to be at least two hundred feet tall."

"By Jove!" exclaimed Michel; "I should be nothing more than a pigmy, a shrimp!"

"Gulliver among the giants," said Nicholl.

"Just so," replied Barbicane.

"And it would not be quite useless to carry along some pieces of artillery to defend oneself."

"Sure," replied Nicholl; "but your projectiles would have no effect on the sun; they would fall back to the ground after a few yards."

"That is pretty hard to believe!"

"But it is certain," replied Barbicane. "The attraction is so great on that enormous orb, that an object weighing 70 pounds on the earth would weigh 1,930 pounds on the surface of the sun. Your hat, twenty pounds; your cigar, half a pound! If you were to fall upon it you would weigh—let me see—about 5,000 pounds, a weight such that you would never be able to rise again."

"The devil!" said Michel; "one would want a portable crane. However, we will be satisfied with the moon for the present; there at least we shall cut a great figure. We will see later on about the sun, where you cannot even have a drink unless you have a capstan to raise the glass to your mouth!"

CHAPTER 9

The Consequences of a Deviation

B ARBICANE had now no fear of the issue of the journey, at least as far as the projectile's impulsive force was concerned; its own speed would carry it beyond the neutral line; it would certainly not return to the earth; it would certainly not remain motionless on the line of attraction. One single hypothesis remained to be realized, the arrival of the projectile at its destination by the action of lunar attraction.

It was in reality a fall of over 20,000 miles, to an orb, it is true, where weight could only be reckoned at one-sixth of terrestrial weight; a formidable fall, nevertheless, and one against which every precaution must be taken without delay.

These precautions were of two sorts, some to lessen the shock when the projectile should touch lunar soil, others to delay the fall, and consequently make it less violent.

To lessen the shock, it was a pity that Barbicane was no longer able to employ the means which had so effectively reduced the shock at departure, that is to say, water used as springs and the partition-breaks. The partitions still existed but water was lacking, for they could not use their reserve, which was precious, in case during the first days the liquid element should be absent from the lunar soil.

And indeed this reserve would have been quite insufficient to act as a spring. The layer of water stored in the projectile at the time of starting upon their journey occupied no less than three feet in depth, and spread over a surface of not less than fifty-four square feet. It had a volume of almost eight square yards, and weighed over 12,500 pounds. Besides, the cistern did not contain one-fifth part of that; they must therefore give up this efficient means of lessening the shock of arrival.

Happily, Barbicane, not content with employing water, had furnished the movable disc with strong spring plugs, destined to reduce the shock against the base after the breaking of the horizontal partitions. These plugs still existed; they had only to readjust them and replace the movable disc; every piece, easy to handle, as their weight was now scarcely felt, was quickly mounted.

The different pieces were fitted without trouble, it being only a matter of bolts and screws; tools were not wanting, and soon the reinstated disc sat on its steel plugs, like a table on its legs. One inconvenience resulted from the replacing of the disc. The lower window was blocked up; thus it was impossible for the travelers to observe the moon from that opening while they were being precipitated perpendicularly upon her; but they would have to do without that. Anyway, by the side openings they could still see vast lunar regions, as an aeronaut sees the earth from the car of his balloon.

This replacing of the disc was an hour's work. It was past twelve when all preparations were finished. Barbicane took fresh readings on the inclination of the projectile, but to his annoyance it had not turned over sufficiently for its fall; it seemed to follow a curve parallel to the lunar disc. The orb of night shone splendidly in space, while in the opposite direction, the orb of day blazed with fire.

Their situation was fraught with reasons for concern. "Will we get there?" asked Nicholl.

"Let us act as if we were going to," replied Barbicane.

"You are scaredy-cats," retorted Michel Ardan. "We will get there, and more rapidly than we might wish."

This answer brought Barbicane back to his preparations, and he set about placing the contrivances intended to break their descent.

We may remember the scene of the meeting held at Tampa Town, in Florida, when Captain Nicholl came forward as Barbicane's enemy and Michel Ardan's adversary. To Captain Nicholl's maintaining that the projectile would smash like glass, Michel replied that he would break its fall by means of rockets properly placed.

Thus, powerful fireworks, taking their starting point from the base and bursting outside, could, by producing a recoil, check to a certain degree the projectile's speed. These rockets were to burn in space, it is true; but oxygen would not fail them, for they could supply themselves with it, like the lunar volcanoes, the burning of which has never yet been stopped by the want of atmosphere round the moon.

Barbicane had accordingly supplied himself with these fireworks, enclosed in little steel guns, which could be screwed on to the base of the projectile. Inside, these guns were flush with the bottom; outside, they protruded about six inches. There were twenty of them. An opening left in the disc allowed for lighting the match with which each was provided. All the effect was felt outside. The burning mixture had been already rammed into each gun. They had, then, nothing to do but to raise the metallic buffers fixed in the base, and replace them by the guns, which fitted closely in their places.

This new work was finished about three o'clock, and after taking all these precautions there remained but to wait.

But meanwhile, the projectile was visibly nearing the moon, and obviously undergoing her influence to a certain degree; though its own velocity also drew it in an oblique direction. From these conflicting influences resulted a line which might become a tangent. But it was certain that the projectile would not fall directly on to the moon; else its lower part, by reason of its weight alone, should have been turned toward her.

Barbicane's uneasiness increased as he saw his projectile resist the influence of gravitation. The unknown was opening before him, the unknown in interplanetary space. The man of science thought he had foreseen the only three hypotheses possible—the return to the earth, the return to the moon, or stagnation on the neutral line; and now a fourth hypothesis, pregnant with all the terrors of the infinite, surged up unexpectedly. To face it without flinching, one had to be a resolute scientist like Barbicane, a phlegmatic being like Nicholl, or an audacious adventurer like Michel Ardan.

Conversation turned toward this subject. Other men would have considered the question from a practical point of view; they would have asked themselves whither their projectile-carriage was carrying them. Not so with these; they sought for the cause which had produced this effect.

"So we have become diverted from our route," said Michel; "but why?"

"I very much fear," answered Nicholl, "that, in spite of all the precautions taken, the Columbiad was not precisely pointed. An error, however small, would be enough to throw us out of the moon's attraction."

"Then they must have aimed badly?" asked Michel.

"I do not think so," replied Barbicane. "The perpendicularity of the gun was exact, its direction to the zenith of the spot incontestable; and the moon passing to the zenith of the spot, we were to have landed square on it. There is another reason, but it escapes me."

"Will we not be too late?" asked Nicholl.

"Too late?" said Barbicane.

"Yes," continued Nicholl. "The Cambridge Observatory's note says that the transit ought to be accomplished in ninety-seven hours, thirteen minutes and twenty seconds; which means that *sooner* the moon will *not* be at the point indicated, and that *later* it will have passed it."

"True," replied Barbicane. "But we started the 1st of December, at thirteen minutes and twenty-five seconds to eleven at night; and we ought to arrive on the 5th at midnight, at the exact moment when the moon would be full; and it is now the 5th of December. It is half-past three in the afternoon, eight and a half hours ought to see us at the end of our journey. Why are we not getting there?"

"Might it not be an excess of speed?" answered Nicholl; "for we know now that our initial velocity was greater than intended."

"No! a hundred times, no!" replied Barbicane. "An excess of speed, if the direction of the projectile had been right, would not have prevented us reaching the moon. No, there has been a deviation. We have been turned away from our course."

"By whom? by what?" asked Nicholl.

"I cannot say," replied Barbicane.

"Well, then, Barbicane," said Michel, "do you wish to

know my opinion on the subject of finding out about this deviation?"

"Speak."

"I would not give half a dollar to know it. That we have deviated is a fact. Where we are going to matters little; we shall soon see. Since we are being borne along in space we shall end by falling into some center of attraction or other."

Michel Ardan's indifference could not satisfy Barbicane. Not that he was uneasy about the future, but he wanted to know at any cost *why* his projectile had deviated.

But the projectile continued its course sideways to the moon, and with it the mass of things thrown out. Barbicane could even prove, by the elevations of landmarks upon the moon, which were less than five thousand miles away, that its speed was becoming uniform—fresh proof that there was no fall. Its impulsive force still prevailed over the lunar attraction, but the projectile's course was certainly bringing it nearer to the moon, and they might hope that at a nearer point the weight, predominating, would cause a decided fall.

The three friends, having nothing better to do, continued their observations; but they could not yet determine the topographical details of the satellite; too much relief was leveled by the reflection of the solar rays.

They watched thus through the side windows until eight o'clock at night. The moon had then grown so large in their eyes that it filled half of the firmament. The sun on one side, and the orb of night on the other, flooded the projectile with light.

At that moment Barbicane thought he could estimate the distance which separated them from their aim at no more than 1750 miles. The speed of the projectile seemed to him to be somewhat more than 200 yards a second, or about 450 miles an hour. Under centripetal force, the base of the projectile was tending toward the moon; but the centrifugal still prevailed; and it was probable that the straight line of its course would be changed to a curve of some sort, the nature of which they could not at present determine.

Barbicane was still seeking the solution of his insoluble problem.

Hours passed without any result. The projectile was visibly nearing the moon, but it was also evident that it would never reach her. As to the nearest distance at which it would pass her, that must be the result of the two forces, attraction and repulsion, affecting its motion.

"I ask but one thing," said Michel; "that we may pass near enough to penetrate her secrets."

"Cursed be the thing that has caused our projectile to deviate from its course," cried Nicholl.

And, as if a light had suddenly broken in upon his mind, Barbicane answered, "Then cursed be the meteor which crossed our path."

"What?" said Michel Ardan.

"What do you mean?" exclaimed Nicholl.

"I mean," said Barbicane in a decided tone, "I mean that our deviation is due solely to our meeting with that wandering body."

"But it did not even brush us as it passed," said Michel.

"What does that matter? Its mass, compared to that of our projectile, was enormous, and its attraction was enough to influence our course."

"So little!" cried Nicholl.

"Yes, Nicholl; but however little it might be," replied Barbicane, "in a distance of 210,000 miles it took no more to make us miss the moon."

304

CHAPTER 10

Observers of the Moon

BARBICANE had obviously hit upon the only plausible reason for this deviation. However slight it might have been, it had sufficed to modify the course of the projectile. It was a fatality. The bold attempt had miscarried by a fortuitous circumstance; and, except for some exceptional event, they could now never reach the moon's disc. Would they pass near enough to be able to solve certain physical and geological questions until then insoluble? This was the question, and the only one, which occupied the minds of these bold travelers. As to the fate in store for themselves, they did not even want to think about it. But what would become of them amid these infinite solitudes, where they would soon be without air? A few more days, and they would fall asphyxiated in this wandering projectile. But a few days to these intrepid fellows was a century; and they devoted all their time to observe that moon which they no longer hoped to reach.

The distance which then separated the projectile from the satellite was estimated at about 500 miles. Under these conditions, as regards the visibility of the details of the disc, the travelers were farther from the moon than are the inhabitants of earth with their powerful telescopes.

305

Indeed, we know that the instrument mounted by Lord Rosse at Parsonstown, which magnifies 6,500 times, brings the moon to within an apparent distance of forty miles. And, more than that, with the powerful one set up at Longs Peak, the orb of night, magnified 48,000 times, is brought to within less than five miles, and objects having a diameter of thirty feet are seen quite distinctly.

So that, at this distance, the topographical details of the moon, observed without glasses, could not be determined with precision. The eye caught the vast outline of those immense depressions inappropriately called "seas," but it could not recognize their nature. The prominence of the mountains disappeared under the splendid irradiation produced by the reflection of the solar rays. The eye, dazzled as if it was leaning over a bath of molten silver, turned from it involuntarily.

Yet the oblong form of the orb was quite clear already. It appeared like a gigantic egg, with the small end turned toward the earth. Indeed the moon, liquid or pliable in the first days of its formation, was originally a perfect sphere; but, being soon drawn within the attraction of the earth, it became elongated under the influence of gravitation. In becoming a satellite, it lost its native purity of form; its center of gravity moved up in front of the center of its figure; and from this fact some scientists drew the conclusion that the air and water had taken refuge on the opposite surface of the moon, which is never seen from the earth.

This alteration in the primitive form of the satellite was only perceptible for a few moments. The distance of the projectile from the moon diminished very rapidly under its speed, though that was much less than its initial velocity—but eight or nine times greater than that which propels our express trains. The oblique course of the projectile, from its very obliquity, gave Michel Ardan some hopes of striking the lunar disc at some point or other. He could not think that they would never reach it. No! he could not believe it; and this opinion he often repeated. But Barbicane, who was a better judge, always answered him with merciless logic.

"No, Michel, no! We can only reach the moon by a fall, and we are not falling. Centripetal force keeps us under the moon's influence, but centrifugal force draws us irresistibly away from it."

This was said in a tone which crushed Michel Ardan's last hope.

The portion of the moon which the projectile was nearing was the northern hemisphere, which selenographic maps place at the bottom; for these maps are generally drawn after the outline given by the telescopes, and we know that they reverse the objects. Such was the *Mappa Selenographica* of Beer and Maedler which Barbicane consulted. This northern hemisphere presented vast plains, checkered with isolated mountains.

At midnight the moon was full. At that precise moment the travelers should have alighted upon it, if the mischievous meteor had not diverted their course. The orb was exactly in the condition determined by the Cambridge Observatory. It was mathematically at its perigee, and at the zenith of the twenty-eighth parallel. An observer placed at the bottom of the enormous Columbiad, pointed perpendicularly to the horizon, would have framed the moon in the mouth of the gun. A straight line drawn through the axis of the piece would have passed through the center of the orb of night.

It is needless to say, that during the night of the 5th–6th of December, the travelers took not an instant's rest. Could they close their eyes when so near this new world? No! All their feelings were concentrated in one single thought:— To see! As representatives of the earth, of humanity, past and present all centered in them! It was through their eyes that the human race was looking at these lunar regions, and penetrating the secrets of its satellite! A strong emotion filled their hearts and they moved silently from one window to the other.

Their observations, reproduced by Barbicane, were rigidly determined. To take them, they had glasses; to check on them, maps.

The first observer of the moon was Galileo. His inadequate telescope magnified only thirty times. Nevertheless, he was the first to recognize mountains in the spots which dot the lunar disc, "as eyes dot the tail of the peacock," and he measured a few heights to which he exaggeratedly attributed an elevation equal to one-twentieth of the diameter of the disc, or some five and a half miles. Galileo made no map based on his observations.

A few years later, an astronomer of Danzig, Hevelius —by procedures which were accurate only twice a month, at the first and last quadratures—reduced Galileo's elevations to only one twenty-sixth of the lunar diameter, which was an exaggeration in the opposite direction. Yet he was the scientist to whom we owe the first map of the moon. The light round spots on it represent circular mountains, and the dark spots indicate huge seas which in reality are nothing but plains. To these mountains and stretches of water, he gave earthly names. Thus we find a Sinai rising in the middle of Arabia, and Etna in the middle of Sicily, Alps, Apennines, Carpathians, then the Mediterranean, Palus-Maeotis, Pontus-Euxinus, and the Caspian Sea. These names, incidentally, are poorly attributed, for neither the mountains nor the seas look anything like their counterparts on our globe. At most, in the large white splotch, attached at its southern end to larger continents and ending in a point, might one recognize an upside-down image of the Indian sub-continent, the Bay of Bengal and Cochin China. Consequently, these names were not retained. Another mapmaker, more familiar with the human heart, suggested a new nomenclature, which human vanity was quick to adopt.

This observer was Father Riccioli, a contemporary of Hevelius'. He made up a very rough map, full of bad mistakes. But he gave the lunar mountains the names of great men of antiquity and of scientists of his period, a custom which has been largely followed since then.

A third map of the moon was made up in the seventeenth century by Dominique Cassini; while better than Riccioli's as to execution, it is not correct on the score of measurements. Several reductions of it were published, but its copper-plate, long retained at the Royal Printing Office in Paris, was finally sold for weight as waste metal.

La Hire, the illustrious mathematician and draughtsman, made up a map of the moon that was thirteen feet high, but it was never engraved.

After him, a German astronomer, Tobias Mayer, toward the middle of the eighteenth century, started publication of a magnificent lunar map, based on measurements of the moon which he had scientifically checked out; but his death, in 1762, kept him from completing this fine work.

Then came Schroeter, of Lilienthal, who sketched numerous moon maps, and also one Lohrmann, of Dresden, who made up a plate divided into twenty-five sections, four of which were engraved.

It was in 1830 that Messrs. Beer and Maedler drafted their famous *Mappa Selenographica,* after an orthographic projection. This map accurately reproduces the lunar disc, as it appears to us; however, the shapes of mountains and plains are correct only in its central part; everywhere else, in the northern or southern, eastern or western parts, these shapes, being foreshortened, cannot be compared to those in the center. This topographical map, thirty-seven and a half inches high and divided into four parts, is the masterpiece of lunar cartography.

Beyond these scholars, one must still mention the lunar reliefs done by the German astronomer Julius Schmidt, the topographical work of Father Secchi, the magnificent photographic prints of the English amateur Waren de la Rue, and finally a map done on an orthographic projection by Messrs. Lecouturier and Chapuis, a very fine specimen made up in 1860, very sharp in its drawing and very clear in its presentation.

Such is a list of the various maps relating to the lunar world. Barbicane had two of them, those of Messrs. Beer and Maedler and Messrs. Chapuis and Lecouturier. They were greatly to facilitate his work as an observer.

As for the optical instruments at his disposal, he had excellent marine glasses, specially constructed for this journey, which magnified objects to one hundred times their size. They would thus have brought the moon to within an apparent distance of less than 2,500 miles from the earth. And, by the same token, at a distance which at three o'clock in the morning did not exceed seventy-five miles, and in a space which no atmosphere clouded, these instruments would bring the lunar surface to within well under 1,500 yards.

CHAPTER 11

Fancy and Reality

"Have you ever seen the moon?" a professor, ironically, asked one of his pupils.

"No, sir!" replied the pupil, still more ironically, "but I must say I have heard a lot about it."

In one sense, the pupil's witty answer might be given by a large majority of sublunary beings. How many people have heard about the moon, yet have never seen it—at least through a glass or a telescope! How many have never even examined the map of their satellite!

In looking at a selenographic map, one peculiarity strikes us.

Contrary to the arrangement on the earth and Mars, the continents occupy more particularly the southern hemisphere of the lunar globe. These continents do not show such decided, clear, and regular boundary lines as South America, Africa, and the Indian peninsula. Their angular, capricious, and deeply indented coasts are rich in gulfs and peninsulas. They remind one of the confusion in the Sunda Islands, where the land is excessively indented. If navigation ever existed on the surface of the moon, it must have been amazingly difficult and dangerous; and we may well pity the Selenite sailors and hydrographers; the former, when they came upon these perilous coasts, the latter when they took soundings of their stormy banks.

We may also notice that, on the lunar sphere, the south pole is much more continental than the north pole. On the latter, there is but one slight strip of land separated from the other continents by vast seas.* Toward the south, continents cover almost the whole of the hemisphere. It is therefore possible that the Selenites have already planted their flag on one of their poles, while all our Franklins, Rosses, Kanes, Dumont d'Urvilles, and Lamberts have never yet been able to attain that unknown point of the terrestrial globe.

As for islands, they are numerous on the surface of the moon. Nearly all oblong or circular, and as if traced with the compass, they seem to form one vast archipelago, comparable to that charming group lying between Greece and Asia Minor, which mythology in ancient times adorned with its most graceful legends. Involuntarily the names of Naxos, Tenedos, Milo, and Carpathos come to mind, and we almost expect to see Ulysses' vessel or the "clipper" of the Argonauts. So at least it was in Michel Ardan's eyes. To him it was a Grecian archipelago that he saw on the map. To the eyes of his matter-of-fact companions, the aspect of these coasts recalled rather the parceled-out land of New Brunswick and Nova Scotia, and where the Frenchman discovered traces of the heroes of fable, these Americans were marking the most favorable points for the establishment of stores in the interests of lunar commerce and industry.

To complete the description of the continental part of

---

* It is of course understood that by "seas" we mean those immense stretches, probably once covered by water, which are today only vast plains.

the moon, a few words about its orographic characteristics. One can very clearly see mountain ranges on it, as well as individual mountains, amphitheatres or circles, and declivities. All of lunar relief is included within that division. It is extraordinarily uneven. It is one huge Switzerland, an uninterrupted Norway, entirely due to plutonic action. Its surface, so roughly scarred, is the result of successive contractions of the crust at the time when the body of the star was in the process of formation. The lunar disc therefore lends itself well to the study of great geological phenomena. As has been pointed out by several astronomers, its surface, though older than that of the earth, has remained fresher. There are no waters there to impair the original relief and by their increasing action to bring about a kind of general leveling, no air to modify the profiles of the mountains through its decomposing influence. There, the work of plutonism, unaltered by neptunian forces, remains in all its original purity. It is the earth, as it was before tides and currents started covering it over with layers of sediment.

After wandering over these vast continents, the eye is attracted by the seas which are still greater. Not only their formation, but their situation and aspect remind one of the terrestrial oceans; but again, as on earth, these seas occupy the greater portion of the globe. Yet in point of fact, these are not liquid spaces, but plains, the nature of which the travelers hoped soon to determine.

Astronomers, we must allow, have graced these so-called seas with at least odd names, which science has respected up to the present time. Michel Ardan was right when he compared this map to a "Map of Love," such as might have been drawn up by a Mlle. de Scudéry or a Cyrano de Bergerac.

"Only," said he, "it is no longer the sentimental map of

the seventeenth century; it is the map of life, very neatly divided into two parts, one feminine, the other masculine; the right hemisphere for woman, the left for man."

In speaking thus, Michel made his prosaic companions shrug their shoulders. Barbicane and Nicholl looked upon the lunar map from a very different point of view than their imaginative friend. Nevertheless, their imaginative friend was just a little in the right. Judge for yourselves.

In the left hemisphere stretches the Sea of Clouds, where human reason is so often shipwrecked. Not far off lies the Sea of Showers, fed by all the fever of existence. Near this is the Ocean of Storms, where man is ever fighting against his passions, which too often gain the victory. Then, worn out by deceit, treasons, infidelity, and the whole body of terrestrial misery, what does he find at the end of his career? That vast Sea of Moisture, barely softened by some drops of the waters from the Gulf of Dew! Clouds, rain, storms, and humors—does the life of man contain aught but these? Is it not summed up in these four words?

The right hemisphere, "dedicated to the ladies," includes smaller seas, whose significant names contain every incident of a feminine existence. There is the Sea of Serenity, over which the young girl bends; the Lake of Dreams, reflecting her joyous future; the Sea of Nectar, with its waves of tenderness and breezes of love; the Sea of Fertility; the Sea of Crises, then the Sea of Vapors, whose dimensions are perhaps a little too restricted; and lastly, that vast Sea of Tranquility, in which every false passion, every useless dream, every unsatisfied desire is at length absorbed, and whose waves flow peacefully into the Lake of Death!

What a strange succession of names! What a singular division of the moon's two hemispheres, joined to one another like man and wife, and forming that sphere of life carried into space! And was not the imaginative Michel right in thus interpreting the fancies of the ancient astronomers?

But while his imagination thus roved over "the seas," his grave companions were considering things more geographically. They were learning this new world by heart. They were measuring angles and diameters.

To Barbicane and Nicholl, the Sea of Clouds was an immense depression in the terrain, spotted by a few circular mountains, and covering a large portion of the western side of the southern hemisphere; it had a surface of about 530,-000 square miles, and its center was at latitude 15° south and longitude 20° west. The Ocean of Storms, *Oceanus Procellarum,* the greatest plain of the lunar disc, covered a surface of some 2,052,000 square miles, with its center at latitude 10° north and longitude 45° east. From its bosom emerged the admirable radiating mountains of Kepler and Aristarchus.

Farther to the north and separated from the Sea of Clouds by high ranges, there was the Sea of Showers, *Mare Imbrium,* with its central point at latitude 35° north and longitude 20° east; it was approximately circular in shape and covered a surface of some 1,206,250 square miles. Not far from there, the Sea of Moisture, *Mare Humorum,* a small basin of only 276,250 square miles, was located at latitude 25° south and longitude 40° east. Finally, three inlets could also be seen along the coastline of this hemisphere: the Gulf of Heats, the Gulf of Dew, and the Bay of Rainbows, small plains lying between high mountain ranges.

The "feminine" hemisphere, naturally the more fanciful, was characterized by smaller and more numerous seas. These were, toward the north, the Sea of Cold, *Mare Fri-*

315

goris, at latitude 50° north and longitude 0°, covering 475,-
000 square miles, and bordering on the Lake of Death and
the Lake of Dreams; the Sea of Serenity, *Mare Serenitatis,*
at latitude 25° north and longitude 20° west, covering a
surface of 537,500 square miles; the Sea of Crises, *Mare
Crisium,* clearly defined, very round, engulfing, at latitude
17° north and longitude 55° west, a surface of 250,000
square miles, a veritable Caspian Sea enveloped in a belt of
mountains. Then, toward the equator, at latitude 5° north
and longitude 25° west, appeared the Sea of Tranquility,
Mare Tranquilitatis, occupying some 759,430 square miles;
this sea at the south led into the Sea of Nectar, *Mare Nec-
taris,* a stretch of 180,000 square miles at latitude 15° south
and longitude 35° west, and at the east into the Sea of Fertility, *Mare Fecunditatis,* the largest in this hemisphere, covering 1,360,625 square miles, at latitude 3° south and
longitude 50° west. Finally, at the extreme north and extreme
south, two other seas could be seen, Humboldt's Sea, *Mare
Humboldtianum,* covering 40,625 square miles, and the
Southern Sea, *Mare Australe,* over a surface of 162,500
square miles.

In the center of the lunar disc, straddling the equator
and meridian zero, there opened up the Central Bay, *Sinus
Medii,* a sort of hyphen between the two hemispheres.

This was a breakdown of the ever-visible surface of the
earth's satellite as it appeared to Nicholl's and Barbicane's
eyes. When they added up these various measurements,
they found that the surface of this hemisphere was 29,613,-
500 square miles, of which 20,735,000 for the volcanoes,
mountain ranges, amphitheatres, islands, or in a word all
that appeared to make up the solid part of the moon, and
8,815,000 for the seas, lakes, swamps, all appearing to make

up its liquid part. All of which nevertheless remained of absolutely no interest to the worthy Michel.

This hemisphere, as can be seen, was 13½ times smaller than the terrestrial hemisphere. Nevertheless, selenographers have already enumerated more than 50,000 craters upon it. So it is truly a puffy, furrowed surface, a veritable skimmer, justifying the unpoetical appellation the English have put upon it, of "green cheese."

Michel Ardan leapt up when Barbicane pronounced this unflattering name.

"Well," he cried out, "so that is how Anglo-Saxons, in the nineteenth century, call beautiful Diana, blonde Phoebe, adorable Isis, charming Astarte, the Queen of Night, the daughter of Latona and Jupiter, the younger sister of radiant Apollo!"

CHAPTER 12

Orographic Details

THE course taken by the projectile, as we have before remarked, was taking it toward the moon's northern hemisphere. The travelers were far from the central point which they would have struck, had their course not undergone an irremediable deviation.

It was half past midnight; and Barbicane then estimated the distance at 875 miles, which was a little greater than the length of the lunar radius, and which would diminish as it advanced nearer to the North Pole. The projectile was at this time not at the level of the equator, but at the tenth parallel, and from that latitude, carefully located on the map, to the pole Barbicane and his two companions were able to observe the moon under the best conditions.

Indeed, by means of glasses, the above-named distance of 875 miles was reduced to eight and three-quarters miles. The telescope of the Rocky Mountains brought the moon much nearer; but terrestrial atmosphere singularly lessened its power. Thus Barbicane, posted in his projectile, with the glasses to his eyes, could seize upon details which were imperceptible to earthly observers.

"My friends," said the president at that point, in a serious voice, "I do not know where we are going; I do not know whether we shall ever see the terrestrial globe again. Nevertheless, let us proceed as if our work would one day be useful to our fellow-men. Let us keep our minds free from every other consideration. We are astronomers; and this projectile is a room in the Cambridge Observatory, carried into space. Let us therefore observe!"

This said, work was begun with great exactness; and he faithfully set down the various aspects of the moon, at the different distances which the projectile reached.

At the time that the projectile was as high as the tenth parallel, north latitude, it seemed rigidly to follow the twentieth degree, east longitude.

We must here make one important remark with regard to the map by which they were taking observations. In the selenographical maps where, on account of the reversing of the objects by the glasses, the south is above and the north below, it would seem natural that, on account of that inversion, the east should be to the left hand, and the west to the right. But it is not so. If the map were turned upside down, showing the moon as we see her, the east would be to the left, and the west to the right, contrary to that which exists on terrestrial maps. The following is the reason of this anomaly. Observers in the northern hemisphere (say in Europe) see the moon to the south—in relation to them. When they take observations, they turn their backs to the north, the reverse position to that which they occupy when they study a terrestrial map. Since they do turn their backs to the north, the east is on their left, and the west on their right. To observers in the southern hemisphere (Patagonia for example), the moon's west would be quite to their left, and the east to their right, as the south is behind them.

Such is the reason of the apparent reversing of these two

cardinal points, and we must bear it in mind in order to be able to follow President Barbicane's observations.

With the help of Beer and Maedler's *Mappa Selenographica,* the travelers were able at once to recognize that portion of the disc enclosed within the field of their glasses.

"What are we looking at, at this moment?" asked Michel.

"At the northern part of the Sea of Clouds," answered Barbicane. "We are too far off to recognize its nature. Are these plains composed of arid sand, as the first astronomers maintained? Or are they nothing but immense forests, according to M. Waren de la Rue's opinion, who gives the moon an atmosphere, though a very low and a very dense one? That we shall know by and by. We must affirm nothing until we are in a position to do so."

This Sea of Clouds is rather doubtfully marked out upon the maps. It is supposed that these vast plains are strewn with blocks of lava thrown up by the neighboring volcanoes on its right, Ptolemy, Purbach, Arzachel. But the projectile was advancing, and sensibly nearing it. Soon there appeared the heights which bound this sea at this northern limit. Before them rose a mountain radiant with beauty, the top of which seemed lost in an eruption of solar rays.

"That is—?" asked Michel.

"Copernicus," replied Barbicane.

"Let us see Copernicus."

This mount, situated at 9° north latitude and 20° east longitude, rises to a height of 10,600 feet above the surface of the moon. It is quite visible from the earth; and astronomers can study it with ease, particularly during the phase between the last quarter and the new moon, because then the shadows are thrown lengthways from east to west, allowing them to measure the heights.

This Copernicus is the largest radiating system of the disc, next to Tycho, situated in the southern hemisphere. It rises isolated like a gigantic lighthouse on that portion of the Sea of Clouds which is bounded by the Ocean of Storms, thus lighting by its splendid rays two oceans at a time. They were a sight without equal, those long luminous swirls, so dazzling in the full moon, ranges which, passing the boundary on the north, extend to the Sea of Showers. At one o'clock of the terrestrial morning, the projectile, like a balloon borne into space, overlooked the top of this superb mountain.

Barbicane could perfectly recognize its chief features. Copernicus is comprised in the series of ringed mountains of the first order, in the division of great circles. Like Kepler and Aristarchus, which overlook the Ocean of Storms, sometimes it appears like a brilliant point through the cloudy light, and has been taken for a volcano in activity. But it is only an extinct one—like all those on that side of the moon. Its circumference showed a diameter of about fifty-five miles. The glasses discovered traces of stratification produced by successive eruptions, and the neighborhood was strewn with volcanic remains some of which were still inside the crater.

"There exist," said Barbicane, "several kinds of amphitheatres on the surface of the moon, and it is easy to see that Copernicus belongs to the radiating class. If we were nearer, we should see the cones bristling on the inside, which in former times were so many fiery mouths. A curious arrangement, without any exception on the lunar disc, is that the interior surface of these circles is appreciably lower than the exterior, contrary to such forms in terrestrial craters. It follows, then, that the general curve of the bottom of these circles gives a sphere of a smaller diameter than that of the moon."

"And why this peculiar disposition?" asked Nicholl.

"We do not know," replied Barbicane.

"What splendid radiation!" said Michel. "One could hardly see a finer spectacle, I think."

"What would you say, then," replied Barbicane, "if chance should bear us toward the southern hemisphere?"

"Well, I should say that it was still more beautiful," retorted Michel Ardan.

At this moment the projectile hung perpendicularly over the circle. The circumference of Copernicus formed almost a perfect circle, and its steep escarpments were clearly defined. They could even distinguish a second ringed enclosure. Around spread a grayish plain, of a wild aspect, on which every relief stood out in yellow. At the bottom of the circle, as if enclosed in a jewel case, sparkled for one instant two or three eruptive cones, like enormous dazzling gems. Toward the north the escarpments lowered down into a depression which would probably have given access to the interior of the crater.

In passing over the surrounding plains, Barbicane noticed a great number of less important mountains; and among others a little ringed one called Gay-Lussac, the breadth of which measured fourteen miles. Toward the south, the plain was very flat, without one elevation, without one projection. Toward the north, on the contrary, till where it was bounded by the Ocean of Storms, it resembled a liquid surface agitated by a storm, of which the hills and hollows formed a succession of waves suddenly congealed. Over the whole of this, and in all directions, lay the luminous lines, all converging to the summit of Copernicus. Some were up to twenty miles wide, over a length that could not be estimated.

The travelers discussed the origin of these strange rays; but they could not determine their nature any more than could terrestrial observers.

"But why," said Nicholl, "should not these rays be simply spurs of mountains which more vividly reflect the light of the sun?"

"No," replied Barbicane; "if it were so, under certain conditions of the moon, these ridges would cast shadows, and they do not cast any."

And indeed, these rays only appeared when the orb of day was in opposition to the moon, and disappeared as soon as its rays became oblique.

"But how have they endeavored to explain these lines of light?" asked Michel; "for I cannot believe that scientists would ever be caught short without an explanation."

"Yes," replied Barbicane; "Herschel has put forward an opinion, but he did not venture to affirm it."

"Never mind. What was the opinion?"

"He thought that these rays might be streams of cooled lava which shone when the sun beat straight upon them. It may be so; but nothing can be less certain. Besides, if we pass nearer to Tycho, we shall be in a better position to find out the cause of this radiation."

"Do you know, my friends, what that plain, seen from the height we are at, resembles?" said Michel.

"No," replied Nicholl.

"Well, with all those pieces of lava stretched out like spindles, it looks like an immense game of jackstraws thrown pellmell. All you need is the hook to pull them out one by one."

"Do be serious," said Barbicane.

"Well, let us be serious," replied Michel quietly; "and instead of jackstraws, let us say bones. This plain would then be nothing but an immense cemetery, on which would repose the mortal remains of a thousand extinct generations. Do you prefer that high-flown comparison?"

"One is as good as the other," retorted Barbicane.

"My word, you are difficult to please," answered Michel.

"My worthy friend," continued the matter-of-fact Barbicane, "it matters but little what it *resembles,* when we do not know what it *is.*"

"Well answered," exclaimed Michel. "That will teach me to reason with scientists."

Meanwhile, the projectile continued to advance with almost uniform speed around the lunar disc. The travelers, as may easily be imagined, did not dream of taking a moment's rest. Every minute changed the landscape which fled beneath their gaze. About half-past one o'clock in the morning, they caught a glimpse of the tops of another mountain. Barbicane, consulting his map, recognized Eratosthenes.

It was a ringed mountain fourteen thousand feet high, one of those circles so numerous on this satellite. With regard to this, Barbicane related Kepler's singular opinion on the formation of circles. According to that celebrated mathematician, these crater-like cavities had been dug by the hand of man.

"For what purpose?" asked Nicholl.

"For a very natural one," replied Barbicane. "The Selenites might have undertaken these immense works and dug these enormous holes for a refuge and shield from the solar rays which beat upon them during fifteen consecutive days."

"The Selenites are not fools," said Michel.

"A singular idea," replied Nicholl; "but it is probable that Kepler did not know the true dimensions of these circles, for the digging of them would have been a work for giants, quite beyond the Selenites."

"Why? If weight on the moon's surface is six times less than on the earth?" said Michel.

"But if the Selenites are six times smaller?" retorted Nicholl.

"And if there are *no* Selenites?" added Barbicane. Which put an end to the discussion.

Soon Eratosthenes disappeared under the horizon without the projectile being sufficiently near to allow close observation. This mountain separated the Apennines from the Carpathians.

In the lunar orography there have been discerned some chains of mountains, which are chiefly distributed over the northern hemisphere. Some, however, occupy certain portions of the southern hemisphere also.

Here is a table of these various ranges, listed from south to north, with their latitudes and the elevations of their highest peaks:

Doerfel	84°	South	24,930 ft.
Leibnitz	65°	"	24,920 ft.
Rook	20-30°	"	5,250 ft.
Altai	17-28°	"	13,265 ft.
Cordilleras	10-20°	"	12,785 ft.
Pyrenees	8-18°	"	11,910 ft.
Urals	5-13°	"	2,650 ft.
D'Alembert	4-10°	"	19,175 ft.
Haemus	5-21°	North	6,430 ft.
Carpathians	15-19°	"	6,360 ft.
Apennines	14-27°	"	18,050 ft.

Taurus	21-28°	„	9,000 ft.
Riphaeans	25-33°	„	13,680 ft.
Hercynians	17-33°	„	3,850 ft.
Caucasus	32-41°	„	18,260 ft.
Alps	42-49°	„	11,865 ft.

Of these various ranges, the most extensive is the Apennines, which runs over 375 miles, a distance, however, which is considerably under that of the great mountain ranges on earth. The Apennines run along the eastern shore of the Sea of Showers, and are continued to the north by the Carpathians, which cover about 250 miles.

The travelers could get only a glimpse of the summit of these Apennines, which run from a longitude of 10° west to 16° east; but the Carpathian range spread before their eyes from the eighteenth to the thirtieth degree of longitude east, and they were able to make note of its details.

One hypothesis appeared highly justified to them. Seeing the Carpathian range here and there displaying circular shapes and dominated by peaks, they concluded that at some time in the past it must have had impressive amphitheatres. These mountainous rings had probably in part been shattered by the huge downpours which formed the Sea of Showers. These Carpathians then were, in appearance, what the circles of Purbach, Arzachel, and Ptolemaeus would be if some cataclysm knocked down their left ramparts and transformed them into a continuous range. They have an average elevation of about 10,600 feet, which is comparable to the altitude of some earthly passes in the Pyrenees. Their southern slopes fall off sharply toward the huge Sea of Showers.

About two o'clock in the morning, Barbicane found that

they were at the level of the twentieth lunar parallel, not far from that little 5,115-foot mountain named Pytheas. The distance of the projectile from the moon was now no more than 750 miles, reduced to seven and a half by the strength of the glasses.

The *Mare Imbrium* stretched before the eyes of the travelers, like an immense depression the details of which were as yet not quite clear. Near them, on the left, stood Mount Lambert, the height of which is estimated at over 5,900 feet, and farther on, at the edge of the Ocean of Storms, at latitude 23° north and longitude 29° east, shone the radiant mountain of Euler. This peak, only 5,950 feet above the lunar surface, had been the object of an interesting study by the astronomer Schroeter. This scientist, seeking to find out the origin of the mountains of the moon, had wondered whether the volume of the crater always proved to be virtually the same as the volume of the ramparts forming it. It turned out that such a relationship did exist, and Schroeter therefore concluded that a single eruption of volcanic matter had been enough to form these ramparts, since successive eruptions would have altered the relationship. Mount Euler alone contradicted this general law, and it had required several successive eruptions to shape it, since the volume of its cavity was twice that of its enclosure.

All of these hypotheses might be acceptable to terrestrial observers, whose instruments served them only incompletely. But Barbicane was no longer satisfied to be content with them, and seeing that his projectile was now coming continuously closer to the lunar disc, he did not give up hope, if not of reaching it, at least of discovering the secrets of its formation.

327

CHAPTER 13

Lunar Landscapes

A T half-past two in the morning, the projectile was over the thirtieth lunar parallel and at the effective distance of 625 miles, reduced by the glasses to six and a quarter. It still seemed impossible, however, that it could ever touch any part of the disc. Its rotational speed, comparatively moderate, was inexplicable to President Barbicane. At that distance from the moon it ought to have been quite considerable, in order to enable it to bear up against her attraction. Here then was a phenomenon the cause of which still escaped them. Besides, there was no time for them to investigate its cause. All lunar relief was passing before the eyes of the travelers, and they did not wish to miss a single detail of it.

Under the glasses the disc appeared at the distance of six and a quarter miles. What would an aeronaut, borne to this distance from the earth, distinguish on its surface? We cannot say, since the greatest ascension has not been much over 25,000 feet.

This, however, is an exact description of what Barbicane and his companions saw at this height.

Large patches of different colors appeared on the disc.

Selenographers are not agreed upon the nature of these colors. There are several, and rather vividly marked. Julius Schmidt maintains that, if the terrestrial oceans were dried up, a Selenite observer could not distinguish on the globe as great a diversity of shades between the oceans and the continental plains as those on the moon present to a terrestrial observer. According to him, the color common to the vast plains known by the name of "seas" is a dark gray mixed with green and brown. Some of the large craters present the same appearance.

Barbicane knew this opinion of the German selenographer, an opinion shared by Beer and Maedler. Observation proved to him that right was on their side, and not on that of some astronomers who admit the existence of only gray on the moon's surface. In some parts the green color was very distinct, as when, according to Julius Schmidt, it came from the Seas of Serenity and Moisture. Barbicane also noticed large craters, without interior cones, which shed a bluish tint similar to the reflection of a sheet of steel freshly polished. These colors really did belong to the lunar disc, and did not result, as some astronomers claimed, either from imperfections in the lenses of the glasses or from the interposition of terrestrial atmosphere. Not a doubt existed in Barbicane's mind with regard to it, as he observed it through space, and so could not commit any optical error. He considered this fact as now scientifically proven. But, were these shades of green the result of some tropical vegetation, kept up by a low dense atmosphere? He could not yet say.

Farther on, he noticed a reddish tint, quite defined. The same shade had before been observed at the bottom of an isolated enclosure, known by the name of Lichtenberg's circle, which is situated near the Hercynian mountains, at the edge of the moon; but he could not tell the nature of it.

He was no more fortunate with regard to another peculiarity of the disc, for he could not decide upon the cause of it. This is what it was.

Michel Ardan was watching near the president, when he noticed long white lines, vividly lighted up by the direct rays of the sun. They were a succession of luminous furrows, very different from the radiation of Copernicus not long before; they ran parallel with each other.

Michel, with his usual self-assurance, hastened to exclaim:

"Look! Cultivated fields!"

"Cultivated fields!" replied Nicholl, shrugging his shoulders.

"Plowed, at any rate," retorted Michel Ardan. "But what plowmen those Selenites must be, and what giant oxen they must harness to their plows to cut such furrows!"

"Those are not furrows," replied Barbicane; "they are *rills.*"

"Rills?" replied Michel mildly. "What do they mean by 'rills' in the scientific world?"

Barbicane immediately enlightened his companion as to what he knew about lunar rills. He knew that they were a kind of furrow found on every part of the disc which was not mountainous; that these furrows, generally isolated, measured from 1,000 to 1,250 miles in length; that their breadth varied from 1,000 to 1,500 yards, and that their borders were strictly parallel; but he knew nothing more either of their formation or their nature.

Barbicane, through his glasses, observed these rills with great attention. He noticed that their edges fell off in steep

330

The earthmen study the moon's sur

declivities; they were long parallel ramparts, and with some small amount of imagination one might have admitted the existence of long lines of fortifications, raised by Selenite engineers.

Of these different rills some were perfectly straight, as if cut by a line; others were slightly curved, though still keeping their edges parallel; some crossed each other, some cut through craters; here they wound through ordinary cavities, such as Posidonius or Petavius; there they wound through the *maria,* such as the Sea of Serenity.

These natural irregularities naturally excited the imaginations of terrestrial astronomers. The first observations had not discovered these rills. Neither Hevelius, Cassini, La Hire, nor Herschel seemed to have seen them. It was Schroeter who in 1789 first drew attention to them. Others followed who studied them, such as Pastorff, Gruithuysen, Beer, and Maedler. At this time their number amounts to seventy; but, if they have been counted, their nature has not yet been determined; they are certainly *not* fortifications, any more than they are the ancient beds of dried-up rivers; for, on one side, the waters, so slight on the moon's surface, could never have worn such drains for themselves; and, on the other, they often cross craters of great elevation.

We must, however, allow that Michel Ardan had an idea, and that, without knowing it, he coincided in that respect with Julius Schmidt.

"Why," said he, "should not these unaccountable appearances be simply phenomena of vegetation?"

"What do you mean?" asked Barbicane quickly.

"Do not excite yourself, my worthy president," replied Michel; "might it not be possible that the dark lines forming that bastion were rows of trees regularly placed?"

"You stick to your vegetation, then?" said Barbicane.

"I like," retorted Michel Ardan, "to explain what you scientists cannot explain; at least my hypothesis has the advantage of indicating why these rills disappear, or seem to disappear, at certain seasons."

"And for what reason?"

"For the reason that the trees become invisible when they lose their leaves, and visible when they regain them."

"Your explanation is ingenious, my dear companion," replied Barbicane, "but inadmissible."

"Why?"

"Because, so to speak, there are no seasons on the moon's surface, and that, consequently, the phenomena of vegetation of which you speak cannot occur."

Indeed, the slight obliquity of the lunar axis keeps the sun at an almost equal height in every latitude. Above the equatorial regions the radiant orb almost invariably occupies the zenith, and it scarcely passes the limits of the horizon in the polar regions; thus, according to each region, there reigns a perpetual winter, spring, summer, or autumn, as in the planet Jupiter, whose axis also is but little inclined upon its orbit.

What origin can one attribute to these rills? That is a question difficult to solve. They certainly came later than the formation of craters and circles, for several have impinged upon them by breaking through their circular ramparts. Thus it may be that, contemporary with the final geological epochs, they are due to nothing more than the expansion of natural forces.

Meanwhile, the projectile had attained the fortieth degree of lunar latitude, at a distance of not more than 500 miles. Through the glasses objects appeared to be only five miles distant. At this point, under their feet, rose Mount Helicon, 1,550 feet high, and round about the left rose moderate elevations, enclosing a small portion of the Sea of Showers, under the name of the Bay of Irises.

The terrestrial atmosphere would have to be one hundred and seventy times more transparent than it is, to allow astronomers to make perfect observations on the moon's surface; but in the void in which the projectile floated no fluid interposed itself between the eye of the observer and the object observed. What is more, Barbicane found himself at a closer distance than the most powerful telescopes had ever afforded before, either that of Lord Rosse or that of the Rocky Mountains. He was, therefore, under extremely favorable conditions for solving that great question of the habitability of the moon; but the solution still escaped him; he could distinguish nothing but the desert beds of immense plains and, toward the north, arid mountains. Not a work betrayed the hand of man; not a ruin marked his course; not a group of animals was to be seen indicating life, even in an inferior degree. In no part was there movement, in no part was there an appearance of vegetation. Of the three kingdoms which share the terrestrial globe between them, one alone was represented on the lunar sphere, and that the mineral.

"Ah, indeed!" said Michel Ardan, a little out of countenance; "then you see no one?"

"No," answered Nicholl; "up to this time not a man, not an animal, not a tree! After all, if the atmosphere has taken refuge at the bottom of cavities, in the midst of the circles, or even on the opposite face of the moon, we draw no hasty conclusions!"

"Besides," added Barbicane, "even to the most piercing

eye a man cannot be distinguished farther than four and a half miles off; so that, if there are any Selenites, they can see our projectile, but we cannot see them."

Toward four in the morning, at the height of the fiftieth parallel, the distance was reduced to 375 miles. To the left ran a line of mountains capriciously shaped, lying in the full light. To the right, on the contrary, lay a black hollow resembling a deep well, unfathomable and gloomy, drilled into the lunar soil.

This hole was the Black Lake; it was Plato, a deep circle which can be conveniently studied from the earth, between the last quarter and the new moon, when the shadows fall from west to east.

This black color is rarely met with on the surface of the satellite. As yet it has been recognized only in the depths of the circle of Endymion, to the east of the Sea of Cold, in the northern hemisphere, and at the bottom of Grimaldi's circle, on the equator, toward the eastern border of the orb.

Plato is an annular mountain, situated at latitude 51° north, and longitude 9° east. Its amphitheatre is fifty-one miles long and thirty-eight miles wide. Barbicane regretted that they were not passing directly above this vast opening. There was an abyss to fathom, perhaps some mysterious phenomenon to surprise; but the projectile's course could not be altered. They must rigidly accept it. One cannot guide a balloon, much less a projectile, when enclosed within its walls.

Toward five in the morning the northern limits of the Sea of Showers was at length passed. The mounts of Condamine and Fontenelle remained—one on the left, the other on the right. That part of the disc, beginning with 60°, was becoming quite mountainous. The glasses brought them to within two and a half miles, less than that separating the summit of Mont Blanc from the level of the sea. The whole region was bristling with spikes and circles. Toward 60°, Philolaus stood predominant at a height of 11,500 feet with its elliptical crater, forty miles long and ten miles wide.

Seen from this distance, the disc had a very weird appearance. Landscapes were presented to the eye under very different conditions from those on the earth, and also very inferior to them.

The moon having no atmosphere, the consequences arising from the absence of this gaseous envelope have already been shown. No twilight on her surface; night following day and day following night with the suddenness of a lamp which is extinguished or lighted amid profound darkness—no transition from cold to heat, the temperature falling in an instant from boiling point to the cold of space.

Another consequence of this want of air is that absolute darkness reigns where the sun's rays do not penetrate. What on earth is called diffused light, the luminous matter which the air holds in suspension, which creates twilight and dawning, which produces shadows, half-shadows, and all the magic of *chiaroscuro,* does not exist on the moon. Hence the harshness of contrasts, which admits of only two colors, black and white. If a Selenite were to shade his eyes from the sun's rays, the sky would seem absolutely black, and the stars would shine to him as on the darkest night.

Judge of the impression produced on Barbicane and his two friends by this strange scene! Their eyes were confused. They could no longer grasp the respective distances of different planes. A lunar landscape without the softening

335

of the phenomena of *chiaroscuro* could not be rendered by an earthly landscape painter: it would be spots of ink on a white page—nothing more.

This aspect was not altered even when the projectile, at the level of 80°, was only separated from the moon by a distance of sixty-two and a half miles; nor even when, at five in the morning, it passed within less than thirty miles of the mountain of Gioja, a distance reduced by the glasses to three-tenths of a mile. It seemed as if the moon might be touched by the hand! It seemed impossible that, before long, the projectile would not strike her, if only at the north pole, the brilliant arch of which was so distinctly visible on the black sky. Michel Ardan wanted to open one of the scuttles and throw himself on to the moon's surface! A drop of thirty miles, but he did not care. Yet, anyway, a very useless attempt; for if the projectile could not attain any point whatever of the satellite, Michel, carried along by its motion, could not attain it either.

At that moment, at six o'clock, the lunar pole appeared. The disc presented to the travelers' gaze only one half brilliantly lit up, while the other disappeared in the darkness. Suddenly the projectile passed the line of demarcation between intense light and absolute darkness, and was plunged into profound night!

CHAPTER 14

The 354¹⁄₂-Hour Night

A T the moment when this phenomenon took place so rapidly, the projectile was skirting the moon's north pole at barely thirty miles distance. A few seconds had sufficed to plunge it into the absolute darkness of space. The transition was so sudden, without shade, without gradation of light, without attenuation of the luminous waves, that the orb seemed to have been extinguished by a powerful blow.

"The moon has melted, disappeared!" Michel Ardan exclaimed, aghast.

Indeed, there was neither reflection nor shadow. Nothing more was to be seen of that disc, formerly so dazzling. The darkness was complete, and rendered even more so by the rays from the stars. It was "that darkness" which engulfs the lunar nights that last three hundred and fifty-four and a half hours at each point of the disc, a long night resulting from the equality of the moon's movements of revolution and rotation, its revolving upon itself and around the earth. The projectile, immerged in the conical shadow of the satellite, experienced the action of the solar rays no more than any of its invisible points.

In the interior the obscurity was therefore complete. They could not see each other. Hence the necessity of dispelling the darkness. However desirous Barbicane might be to husband the gas, the reserve of which was small, he was obliged to use it for artificial light, an expensive brilliancy which the sun at the moment refused.

"Devil take the radiant orb!" exclaimed Michel Ardan, "which forces us to expend gas, instead of giving us its rays gratuitously."

"Do not let us accuse the sun," said Nicholl, "it is not to blame. Actually, the moon has come and placed itself like a screen between us and it."

"It is the sun!" continued Michel.

"It is the moon!" retorted Nicholl.

An idle dispute, which Barbicane put an end to by saying: "My friends, it is the fault neither of the sun nor of the moon; it is the fault of the *projectile,* which, instead of rigidly following its course, has awkwardly missed it. To be more just, it is the fault of that unfortunate meteor which so deplorably altered our original direction."

"Well," replied Michel Ardan, "since that matter is settled, let us have breakfast. After a whole night of watching it is fair to build ourselves up a little."

This proposal meeting with no contradiction, Michel prepared the meal in a few minutes. But they ate for eating's sake, they drank without toasts, without hurrahs. The bold travelers being borne away into gloomy space, without their accustomed retinue of rays, felt a vague uneasiness at their hearts. The "wild" shadow, so dear to Victor Hugo's pen, engulfed them on all sides.

However, they did talk about the interminable night of three hundred and fifty-four and a half hours, nearly fifteen days, which the law of physics imposed on the inhabitants of the moon. Barbicane gave his friends some explanation of the causes and consequences of this curious phenomenon.

"Curious, indeed," said he, "for, if each hemisphere of the moon is deprived of solar light for fifteen days, that above which we now float does not even enjoy during its long night any view of the earth so beautifully lit up. In a word it has a moon (applying that designation to our globe) on only one side of its disc. Now if this were the case with the earth—if, for example, Europe never saw the moon, and she was only visible at the antipodes, imagine to yourself the astonishment of a European on arriving in Australia."

"People would make the voyage for no other reason than to see the moon!" replied Michel.

"Well!" continued Barbicane, "that astonishment is the lot of the Selenites who inhabit the face of the moon opposite to the earth, a face which is ever invisible to our countrymen of the terrestrial globe."

"And which we should have seen," added Nicholl, "if we had arrived here when the moon was new, that is to say two weeks later."

"I will add, on the other hand," continued Barbicane, "that the inhabitants of the visible face are singularly favored by nature, to the detriment of their brethren on the invisible face. The latter, as you see, has dark nights of 354 hours, without one single ray to break the darkness. The other, on the contrary, when the sun which has given its light for fifteen days sinks below the horizon, sees a splendid orb rise on the opposite horizon. It is the earth, which is thirteen times greater than that diminutive moon that we know—the earth which develops on a diameter of two degrees, and bathes it in a light thirteen times greater, undiluted by atmospheric strata—the earth which disappears only at the moment when the sun reappears in its turn!"

"Nice words!" said Michel. "But slightly academic, perhaps."

"It follows, then," continued Barbicane, without flinching, "that the visible face of the disc must be very agreeable to inhabit, since it always looks on either the sun when the moon is full, or the earth when the moon is new."

"But," said Nicholl, "that advantage must be well balanced by the intolerable heat which the light brings with it."

"The inconvenience, in that respect, is the same for the two faces, for the earth's light is obviously without any heat. But the invisible face is even more scorched by the heat than the visible face. I say that for *you,* Nicholl, because Michel will probably not understand."

"Thank you," said Michel.

"Indeed," continued Barbicane, "when the invisible face receives at the same time light and heat from the sun, it is because the moon is new; that is to say, she is situated between the sun and the earth. It follows, then, considering the position which she occupies in opposition when full, that she is nearer to the sun by twice her distance from the earth; and that distance may be estimated at the two-hundredth part of that which separates the sun from the earth, or in round numbers 500,000 miles. So that invisible face is 500,000 miles nearer to the sun when it receives its rays."

"Quite right," replied Nicholl.

"On the other hand—" continued Barbicane.

"One moment," said Michel, interrupting his grave companion.

"What do you want?"

"I ask to be allowed to continue the explanation."

"And why?"

"To prove that I understand."

"Go ahead," said Barbicane, smiling.

"On the other hand," said Michel, imitating the tone and gestures of the president, "on the other hand, when the visible face of the moon is lit by the sun, it is because the moon is full, that is to say, in the opposite direction from the sun in relation to the earth. The distance separating it from the radiant orb is then increased in round numbers by 500,000 miles, and the heat which she receives must be a little less."

"Very well said!" exclaimed Barbicane. "Do you know, Michel, that, for an artist, you are intelligent?"

"Yes," replied Michel coolly, "that is how we all are on the Boulevard des Italiens."

Barbicane gravely clasped the hand of his amiable companion, and continued to enumerate the advantages afforded the inhabitants of the visible face.

Among others, he mentioned eclipses of the sun, which take place only on that side of the lunar disc; since, in order that they may take place, it is necessary for the moon to be *in opposition*. These eclipses, caused by the interposition of the earth between the moon and the sun, can last *two hours;* during which time, by reason of the rays refracted by its atmosphere, the terrestrial globe probably appears as nothing but a black point upon the sun.

"So," said Nicholl, "there is a hemisphere, that invisible hemisphere which is very ill supplied, very ill treated, by nature."

"Yes," Barbicane replied, "but not in its entirety. Indeed, by a movement known as libration, a balancing around its center, the moon presents to the earth a bit more than half of its disc. It is like a pendulum whose center of gravity leans toward the terrestrial globe and which regularly oscillates. Now, where does this oscillation come from? From the fact that its rotational movement around its own axis is endowed with a uniform rate of speed, whereas its movement of revolution follows an elliptical orbit around the earth and is not uniform. At its perigee, the speed of revolution is greater, and the moon shows us a certain portion of its western edge. At its apogee, the rotational speed is conversely greater, and a piece of the eastern edge appears. So it is a sort of bobbin of about eight degrees that becomes visible to us, at times in the west, at others in the east. The result is that we are able to see five hundred and sixty-nine one-thousandths of the moon's surface."

"Never mind," replied Michel; "if we ever become Selenites, we will inhabit the visible face. I like light."

"Unless, by some chance," answered Nicholl, "the atmosphere has condensed on the other side, as certain astronomers contend."

"That would be a consideration," said Michel simply.

Breakfast over, the observers returned to their posts. They tried to see through the darkened scuttles by extinguishing all light in the projectile; but not one luminous atom made its way through the darkness.

One inexplicable fact bothered Barbicane. Why, having passed within such a short distance of the moon—barely over thirty miles—why had the projectile not fallen to it? If its speed had been enormous, he could have understood that the fall would not have taken place; but, with a relatively moderate speed, that resistance to the moon's attraction could not be explained. Was the projectile under some foreign influence? Did some kind of body retain it in the ether? It was quite evident henceforth that it could never reach any point of the moon. Where was it going? Was it going farther from or nearer to the disc? Was it being borne in that profound darkness through the infinity of space? How could they learn, how calculate, in the midst of this night? All these questions made Barbicane uneasy, but he could not solve them.

Certainly, the invisible orb was *there,* perhaps only some few miles off; but neither he nor his companions could see it. If there was any noise on its surface, they could not hear it. There was no air, that medium of sound, to transmit the groanings of that moon which the Arabic legends call "a man already half granite, and still breathing."

That was enough to aggravate the most patient observers, to be sure. It was that very hemisphere which was hidden from their sight. That face which fifteen days sooner, or fifteen days later, had been, or would be, splendidly illuminated by the solar rays, was now lost in utter darkness. In fifteen days where would the projectile be? Who could say? Where would the conflicting attractions by chance have drawn it to?

It is generally admitted, on the basis of selenographic observations, that, in its constitution, the invisible hemisphere of the moon is absolutely similar to its visible hemisphere. About one-seventh of it, of course, can be seen through that movement of libration which Barbicane had mentioned. And, on these glimpsed bobbins, there were only plains and mountains, circles and craters, analogous to those already charted on maps. One could therefore conclude that it was of the same nature, the same kind of world, arid and dead. And yet, what if the atmosphere had taken refuge on that face? What if, along with air, water had brought life to those regenerated continents? What if vegetation still persisted there? If there were animals on those continents and in those seas? If man, under habitable conditions, were still living there? How many questions it would have been of interest to solve! How many such solutions could be drawn from the contemplation of that hemisphere! What a delight to be able to look upon that world which the human eye had never seen!

The disappointment experienced by the travelers, in the depths of this dark night, can be imagined. All observation of the lunar disc was impossible. The constellations alone claimed all their attention; and it must be admitted that no astronomers, not Faye, not Chaconac, nor Secchi, ever found themselves in circumstances so favorable to observe them.

Indeed, nothing could equal the splendor of this starry world, bathed in limpid ether. Its diamonds set in the heavenly vault sparkled magnificently. The eye took in the firmament from the Southern Cross to the North Star, those two constellations which in 12,000 years, by reason of the precession of the equinoxes, will resign their positions as polar stars, the one to Canopus in the southern hemisphere, the other to Vega in the northern. Imagination loses itself in this sublime Infinity, amid which the projectile was gravitating, like a new star created by the hand of man. From a natural cause, these constellations shone with a soft luster; they did not twinkle, for there was no atmosphere which, by the intervention of its layers unequally dense and of different degrees of humidity, produces this scintillation. These stars were soft eyes, looking out into the dark night, amid the silence of absolute space.

Long did the travelers thus stand mute, watching the constellated firmament, upon which the moon, like a vast screen, made an enormous black hole. But at length a painful sensation drew them from their watchings. This was intense cold, which soon covered the inside of the glass of the scuttles with a thick coating of ice. The sun was no longer warming the projectile with its direct rays, and thus it was gradually losing the heat stored up within its walls. This heat had rapidly evaporated into space by radiation, and a considerably lower temperature was the result. The humidity of the interior was changed into ice upon contact with the glass, preventing all observation.

Nicholl consulted the thermometer, and saw that it had fallen to one degree above zero. So that, in spite of the many reasons for economizing, Barbicane, after having used the gas for light, was now obliged also to use it for heat. The projectile's low temperature was no longer endurable. Its tenants would have been frozen to death.

"Well!" observed Michel, "we can no longer reasonably complain of the monotony of our journey! What variety we have had, at least in temperature. First we are blinded with light and saturated with heat, like the Indians of the Pampas! Then plunged into profound darkness, amid the cold, like the Eskimos of the North Pole. No, indeed! We have no right to complain; nature has really done itself proud in our honor."

"But," asked Nicholl, "what is the temperature outside?"

"Exactly that of planetary space," replied Barbicane.

"Then," continued Michel Ardan, "would not this be the time to make the experiment which we were not able to attempt when we were drowned in the sun's rays?"

"It is now or never," replied Barbicane, "for we are in a good position to verify the temperature of space, and see whether Fourier's or Pouillet's calculations are exact."

"In any case it is cold," said Michel. "See! The steam of the interior is condensing on the glasses of the scuttles. If it

345

gets any colder, the vapor of our breath will fall in snow around us."

"Let us prepare a thermometer," said Barbicane.

We may imagine that an ordinary thermometer would have afforded no result under the circumstances in which this instrument was to be exposed. The mercury would have been frozen in its ball, since below thirty-eight degrees below zero it is no longer liquid. But Barbicane had equipped himself with a spirit thermometer on Wolferdin's system, which has a range of excessively low temperatures.

Before beginning the experiment, this instrument was compared with an ordinary one, and then Barbicane prepared to use it.

"How shall we set about it?" asked Nicholl.

"Nothing is easier," replied Michel Ardan, who was never at a loss. "We open the scuttle rapidly; throw out the instrument; it follows the projectile with exemplary docility; and a quarter of an hour after, draw it in."

"By hand?" asked Barbicane.

"By hand," replied Michel.

"Well, then, my friend, do not expose yourself," answered Barbicane, "for the hand that you drew in again would be nothing but a stump frozen and deformed by the frightful cold."

"Really!"

"You would feel as if you had had a terrible burn, like that of iron at a white heat; for whether the heat leaves our bodies suddenly or enters suddenly, it is exactly the same thing. Besides, I am not at all certain that the objects we have thrown out are still following us."

"Why not?" asked Nicholl.

"Because, if we are passing through an atmosphere of the

Into the lunar nig

slightest density, these objects will be retarded. Again, the darkness prevents our seeing whether they are still floating around us. So, in order not to expose ourselves to the loss of our thermometer, we will fasten it, and we will then more easily be able to pull it back in again."

Barbicane's advice was followed. Through the scuttle rapidly opened, Nicholl threw out the instrument, which was held by a short cord, so that it might be more easily drawn back in. The scuttle had not been opened more than a second, yet that second had sufficed to let in a most intense cold.

"The devil!" exclaimed Michel Ardan. "It is cold enough to freeze a polar bear."

Barbicane waited until half an hour had elapsed, which was more than time enough to allow the instrument to fall to the level of the surrounding temperature. Then, it was rapidly pulled in.

Barbicane calculated the quantity of spirits-of-wine that had overflowed into the little vial soldered to the lower part of the instrument, and said:

"Two hundred and twenty degrees below zero!"

M. Pouillet was right and Fourier wrong. That was the formidable temperature of the starry space. Such, perhaps, is that of the lunar continents, when the orb of night has lost by radiation all the heat which fifteen days of sun have poured into it.

347

CHAPTER 15

Hyperbola or Parabola

O<small>NE</small> may, perhaps, be astonished to find Barbicane and his companions so little concerned with the future reserved for them in their metal prison which was bearing them through the infinity of space. Instead of wondering where they were going, they spent their time making experiments, as if they had been quietly installed in their own study.

One might answer that men so strong-minded were above such anxieties—that they did not trouble themselves about such trifles—and that they had something else to do than to occupy their minds with their future fate.

The truth was that they were not masters of their projectile; they could neither check its course, nor alter its direction. A sailor can change the head of his ship as he pleases; an aeronaut can give vertical motion to his balloon. They, on the contrary, had no power over their vehicle. Any maneuver was impossible. Hence the inclination to let things alone, or, as the sailors say, "let her run."

Where were they at this moment, at eight o'clock in the morning of the day called upon the earth the 6th of December? Very certainly in the neighborhood of the moon, and even near enough for it to look to them like an enormous black screen against the firmament. As to the distance which separated them, it was impossible to estimate. The projectile, held by some unaccountable force, had come within some thirty miles of grazing the satellite's north pole. But since entering the cone of shadow two hours before, had the distance increased or diminished? There was not the slightest reference point by which to estimate the direction or the speed of the projectile. Perhaps it was rapidly leaving the disc, so that it would soon quit the pure shadow. Perhaps, again, on the other hand, it might be nearing it so much that in a short time it might strike some high peak on the invisible hemisphere, which would doubtlessly have ended the journey much to the detriment of the travelers.

A discussion arose on this subject, and Michel Ardan, always ready with an explanation, gave it as his opinion that the projectile, held by the lunar attraction, would end by falling on the surface of the terrestrial globe like a meteorite.

"First of all, my friend," answered Barbicane, "every meteorite does not fall to the earth; it is only a small proportion which do so; and if we had become a meteorite, it does not necessarily follow that we should ever reach the surface of the moon."

"But how if we get near enough?" replied Michel.

"Pure mistake," replied Barbicane. "Have you not seen shooting stars rush through the sky by thousands at certain seasons?"

"Yes."

"Well, these stars, or rather corpuscles, only shine when they are heated by gliding over the atmospheric layers. Now, if they enter the atmosphere, they pass within at least forty miles of the earth, but they seldom fall upon it. The same

349

with our projectile. It may approach very near to the moon, and yet not fall upon it."

"But then," asked Michel, "I should be curious to know how our wandering vehicle will act in space?"

"I see but two hypotheses," replied Barbicane, after some moments' reflection.

"What are they?"

"The projectile has the choice between two mathematical curves, and it will follow one or the other according to the speed with which it is animated, and which at this moment I cannot estimate."

"Yes," said Nicholl, "it will follow either a parabola or a hyperbola."

"Just so," replied Barbicane. "With a certain speed it will assume the parabola, and with a greater the hyperbola."

"I like those grand words," exclaimed Michel Ardan; "one knows directly what they mean. And pray what is your parabola, if you please?"

"My friend," answered the captain, "the parabola is a curve of the second order, the result of the section of a cone intersected by a plane parallel to one of its sides."

"Ah! ah!" said Michel, in a satisfied tone.

"It is very nearly," continued Nicholl, "the course described by a bomb launched from a mortar."

"Perfect! And the hyperbola?"

"The hyperbola, Michel, is a curve of the second order, produced by the intersection of a conic surface and a plane parallel to its axis, and constitutes two branches separated one from the other, and extending indefinitely in both directions."

"Is it possible!" exclaimed Michel Ardan in a most concerned tone, as if they had told him of some serious event.

Hyperbola or Parabola

"What I particularly like in your definition of the hyperbola (I almost said hyperbulla) is that it is even more obscure than the word you set out to define."

Nicholl and Barbicane paid little attention to Michel Ardan's jokes. They were deep in a scientific discussion. What curve would the projectile follow? This was what they wanted to know. One maintained it would be a hyperbola, the other a parabola. They gave each other reasons bristling with x's. Their arguments were couched in language which made Michel jump. The discussion was hot, and neither would give in to his adversary on his chosen curve.

This scientific dispute lasted so long that it made Michel very impatient.

"Come, gentlemen of the cosines, will you stop throwing parabolas and hyperbolas at each other's heads? I want to understand the only interesting question in the whole affair. We shall follow one or the other of these curves? Good. But where will they lead us to?"

"Nowhere," replied Nicholl.

"How, nowhere?"

"That is obvious," said Barbicane. "They are open curves, which go on indefinitely."

"Ah, scientists dear to my heart," cried Michel, "what are one or the other to us from the moment we know that they equally lead us into infinite space?"

Barbicane and Nicholl could not keep from smiling. They had just been indulging in "art for art's sake." Never had so idle a question been raised at such an inopportune moment. The sinister truth remained that, whether hyperbolically or parabolically borne away, the projectile would never again meet either the earth or the moon.

What would become of these bold travelers in the immediate future? If they did not die of hunger, if they did not die of thirst, in a few days, when the gas failed, they would die from want of air, unless the cold had killed them first.

Still, important as it was to economize the gas, the excessive lowness of the surrounding temperature obliged them to consume a certain quantity. Strictly speaking, they could do without its *light,* but not without its *heat.* Fortunately the caloric generated by the Reiset and Regnault apparatus raised the temperature of the interior of the projectile a little, and, without much expenditure, they were able to keep it bearable.

But observations had now become very difficult through the scuttles. The dampness inside the projectile condensed on the windows and froze immediately. This obstruction had to be reduced by continual rubbing. In any case they were able to discover some phenomena of the highest interest.

Indeed, if this invisible disc had had an atmosphere, would one not have seen shooting stars streak it with their trajectories? If the projectile itself were going through such fluid strata, would one not have overheard some noise resounding through the lunar echoes, for example, the roaring of a storm, the crash of an avalanche, or the explosions of an active volcano? And if some fire-spitting mountain were decorated with flaming plumes would they not see their intense flashings? Such events, carefully observed, might singularly have shed new light on the dark question of how the moon was constituted. And Barbicane and Nicholl, peering out of their portholes like astronomers, kept up their observation with scrupulous patience.

But up to this point the disc had remained silent and dark. It did not answer the multiplicity of questions put to it by these ardent minds.

Which drew from Michel this reflection, rather correct as it seemed:

"If ever we undertake this journey over again, we shall do well to choose the time when the moon is new."

"Certainly," said Nicholl, "that circumstance would be more favorable. I agree that the moon, immersed in the sun's rays, would not be visible during the transit, but instead we should see the earth, which would be full. And what is more, if we were drawn round the moon, as at this moment, we should at least have the advantage of seeing the invisible part of her disc magnificently lit."

"Well said, Nicholl," replied Michel Ardan. "What do you think, Barbicane?"

"I think this," answered the grave president: "If ever we undertake this journey again, we shall start at the same time and under the same conditions. Suppose we had attained our goal, would it not have been better to have found continents in broad daylight than a country plunged in utter darkness? Would not our first installation have been made under better circumstances? Yes, obviously. As to the invisible side, we could have visited it in our exploring expeditions on the lunar globe. So that the time of the full moon was well chosen. But we should have arrived at our goal; and in order to do so, we should not have deviated from our path."

"I have nothing to say to that," said Michel Ardan. "We have, however, missed one fine chance of observing the other side of the moon! Who knows whether the inhabitants of other planets are not further advanced than earth's scientists on the subject of their satellites?"

To this remark of Michel Ardan's, it would have been easy to give the following reply: Yes, other satellites, because they are so much closer, have made their study that much easier. The inhabitants of Saturn, Jupiter, and Uranus, if they exist, may have established much simpler communications with their moons. The four satellites of Jupiter gravitate at respective distances from it of 270,650 miles, 430,500 miles, 686,750 miles, and 1,200,325 miles. But these distances are calculated from the center of the planet, and when one subtracts the length of the radius, which is 42,000 to 45,000 miles, one sees that the first satellite is less distant from the surface of Jupiter than the moon from the surface of our globe. Out of the eight moons of Saturn, four also are closer: Dione is 211,500 miles away; Tethys, 157,250 miles; Enceladus, 120,475 miles; and Mimas, finally, at an average distance of only 86,250 miles. Of Uranus' eight satellites, the first, Ariel, is only 129,000 miles from the planet.

Therefore, at the surface of those three planets, an experiment similar to President Barbicane's would have offered lesser difficulties. And if their inhabitants did undertake the venture, they were perhaps able to reconnoiter the make-up of the half of the disc which their satellite kept perpetually hidden from their eyes.* But if they never left their own planets, they are no further advanced than the astronomers on earth.

In the meantime, the projectile was describing in darkness an incalculable course which no reference point allowed them to ascertain. Had its direction been altered, either by the influence of the lunar attraction, or by the action of some unknown star? Barbicane could not say. But a change had

---

* Herschel has, indeed, established that for satellites the movement of rotation on their own axis is always equal to their movement of revolution around the planet. Consequently, they always present the same face to it. Alone, Uranus' system provides a rather striking difference: the movements of its moons take place in a direction almost perpendicular to the plane of the orbit, and the direction of the movements is retrogressive, which is to say that its satellites move in a direction opposite to that of the other bodies in the solar system.

taken place in the relative position of the vehicle; and Barbicane verified it about four in the morning.

The change consisted in this, that the base of the projectile had turned toward the moon's surface, and now so remained on a perpendicular passing through its axis. The attraction, that is to say the weight, had brought about this alteration. The heaviest part of the projectile inclined toward the invisible disc exactly as if it were falling toward it.

Was it falling? Were the travelers attaining that much desired goal? No. And the observation of a reference point, quite inexplicable in itself, showed Barbicane that his projectile was not nearing the moon, and that it was now moving along an almost concentric curve.

This reference point was a luminous brightness, which Nicholl sighted suddenly, on the limit of the horizon formed by the black disc. This point could not be mistaken for a star. It was a reddish incandescence which increased slowly, a decided proof that the projectile was moving toward it and not falling normally to the surface of the moon.

"A volcano! It is an active volcano!" cried Nicholl. "The interior fires of the moon are spewing forth! That world is not quite extinguished yet!"

"Yes, an eruption," replied Barbicane, who was carefully studying the phenomenon through his night glass. "What could it possibly be, if not a volcano?"

"But, then," said Michel Ardan, "in order to maintain that combustion, there must be air. So the atmosphere does surround that part of the moon."

"Perhaps so," replied Barbicane, "but not necessarily. The volcano, by the decomposition of certain substances, can provide its own oxygen, and thus throw flames into space. It even seems to me that the deflagration, by the intense brilliancy of the substances in combustion, must be produced in pure oxygen. We must not be in a hurry to proclaim the existence of a lunar atmosphere."

The fiery mountain must have been situated at about 45° south latitude on the invisible part of the disc; but, to Barbicane's great displeasure, the curve which the projectile was describing was taking it far from the point indicated by the eruption. Thus he could not determine its nature more exactly. Half an hour after being sighted, this luminous point had disappeared behind the dark horizon; but the verification of this phenomenon was of considerable consequence in their selenographic studies. It proved that all heat had not yet disappeared from the bowels of this globe; and where heat exists, who can affirm that the vegetable kingdom, nay, even the animal kingdom itself, has not up to this time resisted all destructive influences? The existence of this volcano in eruption, unmistakably recognized by these earthly scientists, would doubtless give rise to many theories favorable to the grave question of the habitability of the moon.

Barbicane allowed himself to be carried away by these reflections. He forgot himself in a silent reverie in which the mysterious destiny of the lunar world was uppermost. He was seeking to combine together the facts observed up to that time, when a new incident recalled him briskly to reality.

This incident was more than a cosmic phenomenon; it was a threatening danger, the consequences of which might be disastrous in the extreme.

Suddenly, in the midst of the ether, in the profound darkness, an enormous mass had appeared. It was like a moon, but an incandescent moon whose brilliancy was all the more intolerable as it cut sharply on the frightful darkness of space. This mass, circular in shape, cast a light which filled the projectile. The faces of Barbicane, Nicholl, and Michel Ardan, bathed in its white sheets, assumed that livid spectral appearance which physicians produce with the fictitious light of alcohol impregnated with salt.

"By Jove!" cried Michel Ardan, "we are hideous. What is that misbegotten moon?"

"A meteorite," replied Barbicane.

"A meteorite burning in space?"

"Yes."

This globe of fire was, indeed, a meteorite or fireball. Barbicane was not mistaken. But if such meteors of the cosmos, observed from earth, usually display only a light slightly less bright than that of the moon, here, in this dark ether, they were resplendent. These wandering bodies carry within themselves the basis of their incandescence. Surrounding air is not required for their deflagration. And while it is true that some of these fireballs go through the atmospheric strata only six or seven miles from earth, others, on the contrary, describe their trajectories at a distance to which earth's atmosphere cannot extend. Such were the fireballs which were seen, one on October 27, 1844, at a height of 320 miles, the other on August 18, 1841, disappearing at a distance of 455 miles. Some of these meteorites may be two to two-and-a-half miles wide and attain a speed that can reach above forty-five miles a second* in a direction opposite to that of the earth.

This shooting globe, suddenly appearing in the darkness, at a distance of at least 250 miles, seemed, according to Barbicane, to have a diameter of over 2,000 yards. It advanced at a speed of a mile and a quarter a second, or seventy-five

---

* The average speed of the movement of the earth, along the ecliptic, is only 18¾ miles per second.

miles a minute. It was crossing the projectile's path and should reach it within a few minutes. As it came closer, it grew to enormous proportions.

Imagine, if possible, the situation of the travelers. It is impossible to describe it. In spite of their courage, their *sang-froid,* their carelessness of danger, they were silent, motionless with stiffened limbs, a prey to frightful terror. Their projectile, the course of which they could not alter, was rushing straight toward this ignited mass, more intense than the open mouth of a furnace. It seemed to be rushing toward an abyss of fire.

Barbicane had seized the hands of his two companions, and all three looked through their half-open eyelids upon that white-hot asteroid. If thought was not destroyed within them, if their brains still worked amid all this awe, they must have given themselves up for lost.

Two minutes after the sudden appearance of the meteor (to them two centuries of anguish), the projectile seemed almost about to strike it, when the globe of fire burst like a bomb, but without making any noise in that void where sound, which is but the agitation of layers of air, could not be generated.

Nicholl uttered a cry, and he and his companions rushed to the scuttle. What a sight! What pen can describe it? What palette is rich enough in colors to reproduce so magnificent a spectacle?

It was like the opening of a crater, like the scattering of an immense conflagration. Thousands of luminous fragments lit up and irradiated space with their fires. Every size, every color, was there intermingled. There were rays of yellow and pale yellow, red, green, gray—a crown of fireworks of all colors. Of the enormous and much-dreaded globe there remained nothing but these fragments scattering in all directions, now become asteroids in their turn, some glinting like a sword, some surrounded by a whitish cloud, and others leaving behind them trains of shimmering cosmic dust.

These incandescent blocks crossed and struck each other, creating still smaller fragments, some of which struck the projectile. Its left scuttle was even cracked by a violent shock. It seemed to be floating amid a hail of howitzer shells, the smallest of which might destroy it instantly.

The light which saturated the ether was wonderfully intense, for the asteroids spread it in all directions. At one point, it was so bright that Michel, drawing Barbicane and Nicholl to his window, exclaimed, "The invisible moon, visible at last!"

And through a luminous emanation, which lasted several seconds, all three caught a glimpse of that mysterious disc which the eye of man now saw for the first time.

What could they distinguish at this distance which they could not estimate? Some stripes spread along the disc, real clouds formed in the midst of a very confined atmosphere, from which emerged not only all the mountains, but also projections of less importance; its circles, its yawning craters, as capriciously placed as on the visible surface. Then immense spaces, no longer arid plains, but real seas, oceans, widely distributed, reflecting on their liquid surface all the dazzling magic of the fires of space; and, lastly, on the surface of the continents, large dark masses, looking like immense forests under the rapid illumination of a lightning bolt.

Was it a delusion, an error of their eyes, an optical illusion? Could they give scientific confirmation to an observation so superficially obtained? Dared they pronounce an opinion about its habitability after so slight a glimpse of the invisible disc?

Meantime, the flashes in space subsided gradually; their accidental brilliancy died away; the asteroids dispersed in different directions and were extinguished in the distance. The ether returned to its accustomed darkness; the stars, eclipsed for a moment, again twinkled in the firmament, and the disc, so hastily discerned, was once again buried in impenetrable night.

CHAPTER 16

The Southern Hemisphere

THE projectile had just escaped a terrible danger, and a very unforeseen one. Who would have thought of such a rencounter with meteorites? These wandering bodies might create serious perils for the travelers. They were to them so many sandbanks upon that sea of ether which, less fortunate than sailors, they could not escape. But did these adventurers complain of space? No, since nature had given them the splendid sight of a cosmic meteor bursting from expansion, since this inimitable firework, which no Ruggieri could imitate, had lit up for a few seconds the invisible nimbus of the moon. In that flash, continents, seas, and forests had become visible to them. Did an atmosphere, then, bring to this unknown face its life-giving molecules? Questions still insoluble, yet forever nagging at human curiosity!

It was then half-past three in the afternoon. The projectile was following its curvilinear direction round the moon. Had its course been again altered by the meteor? It was to be feared so. But the projectile had to describe a curve unalterably determined by the laws of mechanics. Barbicane was inclined to believe that this curve would be a parabola rather than a hyperbola. But, admitting the parabola, the projectile ought quickly to have passed through the cone of shadow projected into the space away from the sun. This cone, indeed, is very narrow, the angular diameter of the moon being so little when compared with the diameter of the orb of day; and up to this time the projectile had been floating in this deep darkness. Whatever its speed (and it could not have been insignificant), its period of occultation continued. That was evident, but perhaps that should not have been the case in a supposed rigidly parabolical trajectory—a new problem which tormented Barbicane's brain, veritably imprisoned as it was in a circle of unknowns which it could not unravel.

None of the travelers thought of taking an instant's rest. Each one watched for an unexpected fact, which might throw some new light on their uranographic studies. About five o'clock, Michel Ardan distributed, under the name of dinner, some pieces of bread and cold meat, which were quickly swallowed without any of them abandoning his scuttle, the glasses of which were incessantly encrusted by the condensation of vapor.

About forty-five minutes past five in the evening, Nicholl, armed with his glass, sighted, toward the southern border of the moon and in the direction followed by the projectile, some bright points cut out against the dark shield of the sky. They looked like a succession of sharp peaklets stretching out in a tremulous line. They were very bright, as is the terminal line of the moon when in one of her octants.

They could not be mistaken. This was no longer a simple meteor, for this luminous ridge had neither its color nor its motion. Nor was it a volcano in eruption. And Barbicane did not hesitate to identify it.

"The sun!" he exclaimed.

362

The projectile is precipitated straigh
toward the meteo

"What! the sun?" answered Nicholl and Michel Ardan.

"Yes, my friends, it is the radiant orb itself lighting up the summit of those mountains situated on the southern edges of the moon. We are evidently nearing the south pole."

"After having passed the north pole," replied Michel. "We have made the circuit of our satellite, then?"

"Yes, my good Michel."

"Then, no more hyperbolas, no more parabolas, no more open curves to fear?"

"No, but a closed curve."

"Which is called——"

"An ellipse. Instead of wandering off in interplanetary space, it is probable that our projectile will describe an elliptical orbit around the moon."

"Indeed!"

"And that it will become *her* satellite."

"A moon of the moon!" cried Michel Ardan.

"Only, I would have you observe, my worthy friend," replied Barbicane, "that we are none the less lost for that."

"Yes, but in another manner, and much more pleasantly," answered the carefree Frenchman with his most amiable smile.

President Barbicane was right. Within this elliptical orbit, the projectile would doubtless go on gravitating eternally around the moon, like a sub-satellite. It was a new body added to the solar system, a microcosm inhabited by three people—who would soon die for want of air. Barbicane could therefore draw no satisfaction from this final solution, imposed upon their vehicle by the double influence of centripetal and centrifugal forces. His companions and he would once again see the lighted face of the lunar disc. Perhaps their existence might even last long enough for them to catch sight once more of the full earth superbly lighted by the rays of the sun! Perhaps they might have a chance to wave a last goodbye to that globe which they were destined never to return to! Then, their projectile would be nothing more than a burned-out mass, dead and similar to the inert asteroids that circulate within the ether. There was only one consolation for them: they would be leaving this impenetrable darkness, coming back to light, returning to the zones bathed in solar rays!

Meanwhile, the mountains that Barbicane had identified were becoming more and more clearly detached from the dark mass. They were Mounts Doerfel and Leibnitz, which arise in the region around the south pole of the moon.

All the mountains of the visible hemisphere have been measured with perfect exactness. One may be surprised at this perfection, and yet, these hypsometric methods are rigorously dependable. One can even assert that the altitudes of mountains on the moon are no less precisely determined than those of the mountains on earth.

The method most generally used is that which consists of measuring the shadow cast by the mountains, by taking into account the position of the sun at the time of the reading. Such a measurement can be easily made by means of a telescope provided with a reticule having two parallel lines, once it is admitted that the true diameter of the lunar disc is correctly known. This method also allows the measurement of the depth of the craters and cavities on the moon. Galileo used it, and since then, Messrs. Beer and Maedler put it to use with the greatest of success.

Another method, called that of tangent rays, may also be used to measure lunar heights. It can be applied at the moment when the mountains form luminous points distinct from the line of separation between dark and light, shining against the dark part of the disc. These luminous points are produced by the rays of the sun that are above those that determine the limit of the phase. Therefore, the measurement of the dark space between the luminous point and the nearest luminous part of the phase gives the exact elevation of that point. But, as can be understood, this method can apply only to those mountains which are close to the line of separation between dark and light.

A third method would consist of measuring the profile of the lunar mountains as it stands out against the background, by use of a micrometer; but this is applicable only to those heights which are close to the edge of the disc.

In any case, it will be noted that this measuring of shadows, spaces, or profiles, can be carried out only when the rays of the sun strike the moon obliquely in relation to the observer. When they hit it directly, or in a word when it is full, all shadows are firmly banished from it and no readings are then possible.

Galileo was the first, after having recognized the existence of mountains on the moon, to use the method of shadows cast for measuring their altitudes. He attributed to them, as already noted, an average height of 27,000 feet. Hevelius sharply reduced these figures, whereas Riccioli on the contrary doubled them. These measurements were excessive in one direction and the other. Herschel, equipped with more perfected instruments, came much closer to hypsometric accuracy. But that, in the final analysis, must be sought in the reports of modern observers.

Messrs. Beer and Maedler, the best selenographers in the whole world, measured 1,095 lunar mountains. From their calculations, we know that six of these mountains rise above

19,000 feet, and 22 above 15,750 feet. The highest peak on the moon is 24,950 feet; it is therefore not as high as those on earth, some of which rise as much as 3,000 to 3,600 feet higher. But one thing should be pointed out. If we compare the respective volumes of the two globes, the lunar mountains are relatively much higher than those on earth. The former rise as high as 1/470th of the diameter of the moon, and the latter only 1/1,440th of the diameter of earth. For a mountain on earth to have the same proportionate elevation as one on the moon, its perpendicular altitude would have to reach sixteen and a quarter miles, whereas the highest one actually is barely five miles high.

To follow this up by way of comparison, the Himalayas have three peaks that are higher than the ones on the moon: Mount Everest, 29,028 feet high; Kanchenjunga, 28,208 feet; and Dhaulagiri, 26,810, while Mounts Doerfel and Leibnitz, on the moon, have an altitude only equal to 24,950 feet. Newton, Casatus, Curtius, Short, Tycho, Clavius, Blanchini, Endymion, the highest mountains of the lunar Caucasus and Apennines, are higher than Mont Blanc, which is 15,776 feet. As high as Mont Blanc, are Moret, Theophilus, and Catharina; as high as Monte Rosa, or 15,203 feet, are Piccolomini, Werner, and Harpalus; as high as the Matterhorn (14,690 ft.), Macrobius, Eratosthenes, Albategnius, and Delambre; as high as Mount Teide, in the Canary Islands (12,198 ft.), Bacon, Cysatus, Phitolaus, and the peaks of the lunar Alps; as high as Mount Perdido in the Pyrenees (11,007 ft.), Roemer and Boguslawski; as high as Mount Etna (10,741 ft.), Hercules, Atlas, and Furnerius.*

---

* The modern reader will note that many of these "mountains" enumerated by the author are today identified as craters (depressions, or circles) rather than elevations.—ED.

Such are the points of comparison which allow us to appreciate the heights of the lunar mountains. And the trajectory being followed by the projectile was carrying it precisely toward this mountainous region of the southern hemisphere, where the finest examples of lunar orography rise up.

CHAPTER 17

Tycho

At six in the evening the projectile passed within thirty-seven and a half miles of the south pole, the same distance it had been from the north pole. The elliptical curve was being rigidly followed.

At this moment the travelers once more entered the salutary range of the rays of the sun. They saw once more the stars, moving slowly from east to west. The radiant orb was saluted by a triple hurrah. With its light it also sent heat, which soon was felt through the metal walls. The windows resumed their accustomed appearance. The layers of ice melted as if by enchantment; and immediately, for economy's sake, the gas was put out, the air apparatus alone still consuming its usual quantity.

"Ah!" said Nicholl, "these rays of heat are good. With what impatience the Selenites must await the reappearance of the orb of day!"

"Yes," replied Michel Ardan, imbibing as it were the brilliant ether, light, and heat, "they are the whole of life!"

At this moment the bottom of the projectile deviated somewhat from the lunar surface, in order to follow the slightly lengthened elliptical orbit. From this point, had the earth been at the full, Barbicane and his companions could have seen it, but immersed in the sun's radiation she was quite invisible. Another spectacle attracted their attention, that of the southern part of the moon, brought by the glasses to within 500 yards. They now could not leave the scuttles, and they noted every detail of this fantastic continent.

Mounts Doerfel and Leibnitz form two separate groups very near the south pole. The first group extends from the pole to the eighty-fourth parallel, on the eastern part of the orb; the second, along the eastern edge, extends from 65° of latitude to the pole.

On their capriciously formed ridge appeared dazzling sheets, as mentioned by Father Secchi. With more certainty than the illustrious Roman astronomer, Barbicane was enabled to recognize their nature.

"They are snow," he exclaimed.

"Snow?" repeated Nicholl.

"Yes, Nicholl, snow; the surface of which is deeply frozen. See how it reflects the luminous rays. Cooled lava would never give out such intense reflection. There must then be water, there must be air on the moon. As little as you please, but the fact can no longer be contested."

No, it could not be! And if ever Barbicane should see the earth again, his notes will bear witness to this great fact in selenographic observation.

These Mounts Doerfel and Leibnitz rose in the midst of plains of a medium extent, which were bounded by an indefinite succession of circles and annular ramparts. These two chains are the only ones met with in this region of circles. Comparatively but slightly marked, they throw up here and there some sharp points, the highest summit of which attains an altitude of 24,900 feet.

But the projectile was high above all this landscape, and

the projections disappeared in the intense brilliancy of the disc. To the eyes of the travelers there reappeared that archaic aspect of the lunar landscapes, raw in tone, without gradation of colors, and without degrees of shadow, harshly black and white, for want of diffusion of light. But the sight of this desolate world did not fail to captivate them by its very strangeness. They were moving over this region as if they had been borne on the breath of some storm, watching heights go by under their feet, piercing the cavities with their eyes, going down into the rills, climbing the ramparts, sounding these mysterious holes, and leveling all cracks. But no trace of vegetation, no appearance of cities; nothing but stratification, beds of lava, overflowings polished like immense mirrors, reflecting the sun's rays with overpowering brilliancy. Nothing belonging to a *living* world—everything to a dead world, where avalanches, rolling from the summits of the mountains, would hurtle noiselessly to the bottom of the abyss. They still had the motion, but the sound was lacking.

Barbicane noted through repeated observations that the prominences on the edges of the disc, although having been subjected to different forces than those in the central region, displayed a uniform structure. The same circular aggregation, the same rises in the ground. Yet, one might imagine that their characters were not necessarily similar. For, at the center, the still-malleable crust of the moon was subjected to the double attractions of moon and earth, pulling in opposite directions along one line that stretched from one to the other. At the edges, on the contrary, lunar gravity was, so to speak, perpendicular to the pull of the earth. It would seem therefore that irregularities in the surface produced under these two separate sets of conditions should assume different forms. Yet, that was not the case. Therefore, the moon must have found within itself alone the principle of its formation and its constitution. It was in no way beholden to outside influences. Which justified the remarkable proposition put forth by Arago: "No action external to the moon contributed in any way to the production of its topography."

However that might be, now in its present state, this world was the image of death, without its being possible to say that life had ever existed there.

Michel Ardan, however, thought he recognized a heap of ruins, to which he drew Barbicane's attention. It was about the 80th parallel, in 30° longitude. This heap of stones, rather regularly placed, represented a vast fortress, overlooking one of those long rills which in former days had served as a bed to the rivers of prehistorical times. Not far from it, rose to a height of 18,400 feet the annular mountain of Short, as high as the Asiatic Caucasus. Michel Ardan, with his accustomed ardor, held out for "the evidence" of his fortress. Beneath it he discerned the dismantled ramparts of a town; here the still intact arch of a portico, there two or three columns lying under their base; farther on, a succession of arches which must have supported the conduit of an aqueduct; in another part the collapsed pillars of a gigantic bridge, sunk in the thickest parts of the rill. He distinguished all this, but with so much imagination in his glance, and through glasses of such fantasy, that we must mistrust his observation. Yet, who could affirm, who would dare to say, that the amiable fellow did not really see that which his two companions refused to see?

Moments were too precious to be sacrificed in idle discussion. The Selenite city, whether imaginary or not, had already disappeared afar off. The distance of the projectile from the lunar disc was on the increase, and the details at ground level were being lost in a confused jumble. The prominences, the circles, the craters, and the plains alone remained, still showing their boundary lines distinctly.

At this moment, to the left, lay extended one of the finest circles of lunar orography, one of the curiosities of this continent. It was Newton, which Barbicane recognized without trouble, by referring to the *Mappa Selenographica.*

Newton is situated at exactly latitude 77° south, and longitude 16° east. It forms an annular crater, the ramparts of which, rising to a height of 23,700 feet, seemed to be impassable.

Barbicane pointed out to his companions that the height of this mountain above the surrounding plain was far from equaling the depth of its crater. This enormous hole was beyond all measurement, and formed a gloomy abyss, the bottom of which the sun's rays could never reach. There, according to Humboldt, reigns utter darkness, which the light of the sun and the earth cannot break. Mythologists would quite justifiably have made it into the mouth of their hell.

"Newton," said Barbicane, "is the most perfect type of these annular mountains, of which the earth possesses no sample. They prove that the moon's formation, by means of cooling, was due to violent causes; for, while, under the pressure of internal fires, the prominences rise to considerable height, the depths withdraw far below the lunar level."

"I do not dispute the fact," replied Michel Ardan.

Some minutes after passing Newton, the projectile directly overlooked the annular mountain of Moret. It skirted at some distance the summits of Blanchini, and at about half-past seven in the evening reached the circle of Clavius.

This circle, one of the most remarkable of the disc, is

situated at latitude 58° south, and longitude 15° east. Its height is estimated at 23,200 feet. The travelers, at a distance of 250 miles (reduced to two and a half by their glasses), could admire this vast crater in its entirety.

"Terrestrial volcanoes," said Barbicane, "are but molehills compared with those of the moon. Measuring the old craters formed by the early eruptions of Vesuvius and Etna, we find them little more than three miles in breadth. In France the crater of Cantal measures six miles across; in Ceylon the so-called crater, 42½ miles across, is considered the largest on the globe. What are these diameters against that of Clavius, which we overlook at this moment?"

"What is its breadth?" asked Nicholl.

"It is 142 miles," replied Barbicane. "This circle is certainly the largest on the moon, but many others measure 125, 100, or 75 miles."

"Ah! my friends," exclaimed Michel, "can you picture to yourselves what this peaceful orb of night must have been when its craters, filled with thunderings, spewed forth all in unison their torrents of lava, hails of stones, clouds of smoke, and tongues of flame! What a wonderful spectacle then, and now what decay! This moon is nothing more than a thin carcass of fireworks, whose crackers, rockets, serpents, and suns, after a superb brilliancy, have become nothing but shattered cardboard. Who can say the cause, the reason, the motive force of these cataclysms?"

Barbicane was not listening to Michel Ardan; he was contemplating these ramparts of Clavius, formed by broad mountains spread over several miles. At the bottom of the immense cavity burrowed hundreds of small extinguished craters, riddling the soil like a colander, and overlooked by a peak 15,000 feet high.

373

Around it, the plain appeared desolate. Nothing so arid as these prominences, nothing so sad as these ruins of mountains, and (if we may so express ourselves) these fragments of peaks and mountains which strewed the soil. The satellite seemed to have burst open at this spot.

The projectile was still advancing, and this chaos did not change. Circles, craters, and uprooted mountains succeeded each other incessantly. No more plains; no more seas. A never-ending Switzerland and Norway. And lastly, in the center of this deeply etched region, at its high point, the most splendid mountain on the lunar disc, the dazzling Tycho, which posterity will forever continue to call by the name of the illustrious Danish astronomer.

In observing the full moon in a cloudless sky no one has failed to remark this brilliant point of the southern hemisphere. Michel Ardan used every metaphor that his imagination could supply to designate it by. To him this Tycho was a focus of light, a center of radiation, a crater erupting with rays. It was the axle of a brilliant wheel, a starfish enclosing the disc with its silver tentacles, an enormous eye filled with flames, a glory carved for Pluto's head, a star launched by the Creator's hand, which had crashed against the face of the moon!

Tycho forms such a concentration of light that the inhabitants of the earth can see it without glasses, though they are 250,000 miles away! Imagine, then, its intensity to the eye of observers placed at a distance of only 350 miles! Seen through this pure ether, its brilliancy was so intolerable that Barbicane and his friends were obliged to blacken their glasses with the gas smoke so as to be able to bear the brightness. Then silent, scarcely uttering an interjection of admiration, they gazed, they contemplated. All of their feelings, all of their impressions were now concentrated in that look, as under any violent emotion all of life concentrates at the heart.

Tycho belongs to the system of radiating mountains, like Aristarchus and Copernicus; but, of all of them, it is the most complete and decided, unquestionably showing the effects of the frightful volcanic action to which the formation of the moon is due.

Tycho is situated in latitude 43° south, and longitude 12° east. Its center is occupied by a crater fifty-four miles broad. It assumes a slightly elliptical form, and is surrounded by an enclosure of annular ramparts, which on the east and west overlook the outer plain from a height of 15,000 feet. It is a group of Mont Blancs, placed round one common center and crowned by radiating beams.

What this incomparable mountain really is, with all the projections converging toward it, and the interior excrescences of its crater, photography itself has never been able to represent. Indeed, it is during the full moon that Tycho is seen in all its splendor. But, at that time, all shadows disappear, the foreshortening of perspective is gone, and all prints come out blank—a disagreeable fact; for this strange region would have been marvelous if reproduced with photographic exactness. It is but a group of hollows, craters, circles, a breathtaking jumble of crests; then, as far as the eye can see, a whole volcanic network cast upon this pimply ground. One can then understand that the bubbles of this central eruption have kept their original form. Crystallized by cooling, they have stereotyped that aspect which the moon formerly presented when under the Plutonian forces.

The distance which separated the travelers from the annular summits of Tycho was not so great but that they could catch the principal details. Even on the causeway forming the fortifications of Tycho, the mountains hanging on to the interior and exterior sloping flanks rose in tiers like gigantic terraces. They appeared to be higher by 300 or 400 feet to the west than to the east. No system of terrestrial encampment could equal these natural fortifications. A town built at the bottom of this circular cavity would have been utterly inaccessible.

Inaccessible and wonderfully extended over this soil covered with picturesque projections! Indeed, nature had not left the bottom of this crater flat and empty. It possessed its own peculiar orography, a mountainous system, making it a world in itself. The travelers could clearly distinguish cones, central hills, remarkable positions of the soil, naturally placed to receive the masterworks of Selenite architecture. There was marked out the place for a temple, here the ground of a forum, on this spot the plan of a palace, in another the plateau for a citadel; the whole overlooked by a central mountain of 1,500 feet. A vast circle, in which ancient Rome in its entirety would have fitted ten times over.

"Ah!" exclaimed Michel Ardan, enthusiastic at the sight, "what a magnificent city might be constructed within that ring of mountains! What a quiet place, what a peaceful refuge, beyond the range of all human woes! What a place it would be, calm and isolated, for all misanthropes to live, all people-haters, all those who are disgusted with social life!"

"All of them! It would be much too small to hold them all," Barbicane replied simply.

CHAPTER 18

Grave Questions

THE projectile had now passed the enclosure of Tycho, and Barbicane and his two companions watched with scrupulous attention the brilliant rays which the celebrated mountain shed so curiously all over the horizon.

What was this radiant glory? What geological phenomenon had designed these ardent beams? This question justifiably engrossed Barbicane's mind.

Under his eyes ran in all directions luminous furrows, raised at the edges and concave in the center, some over twelve miles, others over thirty miles broad. These brilliant streaks extended in some places as far as 750 miles from Tycho, and seemed to cover, particularly toward the east, the northeast and the north, half of the southern hemisphere. One of these jets extended as far as the circle of Neander, situated on the 40th meridian. Another, by a slight curve, furrowed the Sea of Nectar and broke against the chain of Pyrenees, after a circuit of 1,000 miles. Others, toward the west, covered the Sea of Clouds and the Sea of Moisture with a luminous network.

What was the origin of these sparkling rays, which shone on the plains as well as the elevations, however high they

377

might be? They all started from a common center, the crater of Tycho. They sprang from it. Herschel attributed their brilliancy to ancient lava flows congealed by the cold; an opinion, however, which has not been generally adopted. Other astronomers have seen in these inexplicable rays a kind of moraines, rows of erratic blocks, which had been thrown up at the period of Tycho's formation.

"And why not?" asked Nicholl of Barbicane, who was relating and rejecting these different opinions.

"Because the regularity of these luminous lines, and the violence necessary to carry volcanic matter to such distances, are inexplicable."

"Eh! by Jove!" replied Michel Ardan, "it seems easy enough to me to explain the origin of these rays."

"Indeed?" said Barbicane.

"Indeed," continued Michel. "It is enough to say that it is a vast star-shaped crack, such as is produced when a ball or a stone strikes against a pane of glass!"

"Well!" replied Barbicane, smiling. "And what hand would be powerful enough to throw the stone that produced such a shock?"

"The hand is not necessary," answered Michel, not at all confounded; "and as to the stone, let us suppose it to be a comet."

"Ah! those much-abused comets!" exclaimed Barbicane. "My good Michel, your explanation is not bad; but your comet is useless. The shock which produced that rent may have come from the inside of the star. A violent contraction of the lunar crust, while cooling, might have been enough to create that gigantic crack."

"A contraction! Something like a lunar stomach-ache," said Michel Ardan.

378

"Besides," added Barbicane, "that is the opinion of the English scientist, Nasmyth, and it seems to me to sufficiently explain the radiation of these mountains."

"That Nasmyth is no fool!" replied Michel.

For a long time the travelers, whom such a sight could never weary, continued to admire the splendors of Tycho. Their projectile, saturated with luminous gleams in the double irradiation of sun and moon, must have appeared like an incandescent globe. They had therefore passed suddenly from excessive cold to intense heat. Nature was thus preparing them to become Selenites.

Become Selenites! That idea once more brought up the question of the habitability of the moon. After what they had seen, could the travelers solve it? Could they decide for or against it? Michel Ardan incited his two friends to express their opinions, and asked them straight out whether they thought that men and animals were represented in the lunar world.

"I think that we can answer," said Barbicane, "but I do not believe that the question ought to be put in that form. I ask that it be put differently."

"Put it your own way," replied Michel.

"Here it is," continued Barbicane. "The problem is a double one, and requires a double solution. Is the moon habitable? Has the moon ever been inhabited?"

"Good!" replied Nicholl. "First let us see whether the moon is habitable."

"To tell the truth, I have no idea," answered Michel.

"And I answer in the negative," continued Barbicane. "In her present state, with her surrounding atmosphere certainly very much reduced, her seas for the most part dried up, her insufficient supply of water, restricted vegetation, sudden alternations of cold and heat, her days and nights of 354 hours—the moon does not seem habitable to me, nor does she seem suited to animal development, nor sufficient to supply the needs of existence as we understand it."

"Agreed," replied Nicholl. "But is not the moon habitable for creatures organized differently from ourselves?"

"That question is more difficult to answer, but I will try; and I ask Nicholl if *motion* appears to him to be a necessary result of *life,* whatever be its organization?"

"Without a doubt!" answered Nicholl.

"Then, my worthy companion, I would answer that we have observed the lunar continent at a distance of 500 yards at most, and that nothing seemed to us to move on the moon's surface. The presence of any kind of human life would have been betrayed by its appropriations such as various kinds of buildings, and even by ruins. Yet, what have we seen? Everywhere and always the geological works of nature, never the work of man. If, then, there exist representatives of the animal kingdom on the moon, they must be buried in those unfathomable cavities which the eye cannot reach; which I cannot admit, for they would have left traces of their passage on those plains which the atmosphere must cover, however thin it may be. Such traces are nowhere visible. There remains but one hypothesis, that of a living race to which motion, which is life, is foreign."

"One might as well say, living creatures who do not live," replied Michel.

"Just so," said Barbicane, "which for us has no meaning."

"Then we may form our opinion?" said Michel.

"Yes," replied Nicholl.

"Very well," continued Michel Ardan, "the Scientific Commission assembled in the projectile of the Gun Club, after having founded their argument on facts recently observed, decide unanimously upon the question of the habitability of the moon—'*No!* the moon is not habitable.' "

This decision was duly inscribed by President Barbicane in his notebook, where the minutes of the meeting of the 6th of December are to be found.

"Now," said Nicholl, "let us turn to the second question, an indispensable complement of the first. I ask the honorable commission, if the moon is not habitable, has she ever been inhabited?"

"Citizen Barbicane has the floor," said Michel Ardan.

"My friends," replied Barbicane, "I did not await this journey before forming an opinion on the past habitability of our satellite; but I will add that our personal observations only confirm my opinion. I believe, indeed I affirm, that the moon was once inhabited by a human race organized like our own; that she produced animals anatomically formed like the terrestrial animals: but I add that these races, human or animal, have had their day, and are now forever extinct!"

"Then," asked Michel, "the moon must be older than the earth?"

"No!" said Barbicane decidedly. "But it has grown old quicker, and its formation and deformation have been more rapid. Relatively, the organizing forces of matter were much more violent inside the moon than inside the terrestrial globe. The present state of this cracked, twisted, and burst disc abundantly proves this. The moon and the earth were nothing but gaseous masses originally. These gases passed into a liquid state under different influences, and the solid masses were formed later. But most certainly our sphere was still gaseous or liquid when the moon was solidified by cooling and had become habitable."

381

"I believe it," said Nicholl.

"Then," continued Barbicane, "an atmosphere surrounded it. The waters contained within this gaseous envelope could not evaporate. Under the influence of air, water, light, solar heat, and central heat, vegetation took possession of the continents prepared to receive it, and certainly life showed itself about this period, for nature does not expend herself in vain; and a world so wonderfully formed for habitation must necessarily have been inhabited."

"But," said Nicholl, "many phenomena inherent in the movements of our satellite must have interfered with the expansion of the animal and vegetable kingdoms. For example, its days and nights of 354 hours?"

"At the terrestrial poles they last six months," said Michel.

"An argument of little value, since the poles are not inhabited."

"Let us observe, my friends," continued Barbicane, "that if in the present state of the moon its long nights and long days create differences of temperature intolerable to living organisms, it was not so at the historical period of time. The atmosphere enveloped the disc with a fluid mantle; vapor deposited itself in the shape of clouds; this natural screen tempered the ardor of the solar rays, and retained the nocturnal radiation. Light, like heat, can diffuse itself in the air; hence an equality between the influences which no longer exists, now that that atmosphere has almost entirely disappeared. And now I am going to astonish you."

"Do astonish us!" said Michel Ardan.

"I firmly believe that at the period when the moon was inhabited, the nights and days did not last 354 hours!"

"And why?" asked Nicholl quickly.

"Because most probably then the rotary motion of the

moon upon her axis was not equal to her revolution, an equality which presents each part of her disc during fifteen days to the action of the solar rays."

"Granted," replied Nicholl, "but why should not these two motions have been equal, since they are now?"

"Because that equality has only been determined by terrestrial attraction. And who can say that this attraction was powerful enough to alter the motion of the moon at the period when the earth was still fluid?"

"And, incidentally," replied Nicholl, "who can say that the moon has always been a satellite of the earth?"

"And who can say," exclaimed Michel Ardan, "that the moon did not exist before the earth?"

Their imaginations carried them away into the infinite field of hypotheses. Barbicane sought to restrain them.

"Those speculations are too high," said he, "problems utterly insoluble. Do not let us enter upon them. Let us only admit the insufficiency of the primordial attraction; and then by the inequality of the two motions of rotation and revolution, the days and nights could have succeeded each other on the moon as they succeed each other on the earth. Besides, even without these conditions, life was possible."

"And so," asked Michel Ardan, "humanity has disappeared from the moon?"

"Yes," replied Barbicane, "after having doubtless remained for thousands of centuries; but gradually, the atmosphere becoming rarefied, the disc became uninhabitable, as the terrestrial globe will one day become by cooling."

"By cooling?"

"Certainly," replied Barbicane; "as the internal fires became extinguished, and the incandescent matter concentrated itself, the lunar crust cooled. The consequences of these phenomena gradually showed themselves in the disappearance of organized beings and the disappearance of vegetation. Soon the atmosphere became rarefied, probably stolen away by terrestrial attraction; then no more breathable air, and disappearance of water by means of evaporation. At this period the moon, becoming uninhabitable, was no longer inhabited. It was a dead world, such as we see it to-day."

"And you say that the same fate is in store for the earth?"

"Most probably."

"But when?"

"When the cooling of its crust shall have made it uninhabitable."

"And have they calculated the time which our unfortunate sphere will take to cool?"

"Certainly."

"And you know these calculations?"

"Perfectly."

"Well, then, speak out, my silent scholar," exclaimed Michel Ardan, "for you make me boil with impatience!"

"Very well, my good Michel," replied Barbicane quietly. "We know what diminution of temperature the earth undergoes in the period of a century. And, according to certain calculations, this mean temperature will, after a period of 400,000 years, be brought down to zero!"

"Four hundred thousand years!" exclaimed Michel. "Ah! I breathe again. Really I was frightened! To hear you, I had imagined that we did not have more than 50,000 years to live."

Barbicane and Nicholl could not help laughing at these worries of their companion. Then Nicholl, who wished to end the discussion, again put the second question, which had just been considered.

"Has the moon been inhabited?" he asked.

The answer was unanimously in the affirmative.

But during this discussion, fruitful in quite daring theories even though it did sum up the general ideas that science had accepted on this point, the projectile had run rapidly on toward the lunar equator, at the same time getting regularly farther from the disc. It had gone by Wilhelm's circle and the fortieth parallel at a distance of five hundred miles. Then, leaving at its right Pitatus on the thirtieth degree, it went along the southern end of the Sea of Clouds, which it had already approached at the north. Various circles appeared confusedly in the brilliant whiteness of the full moon: Bulliadus, Purbach, almost square in shape with the crater at its center, then Arzachel, whose internal mountain shines with an indefinable brilliance.

Finally, the projectile growing ever farther away, the outlines faded away beneath the travelers' eyes, the mountains were lost in the distance, and of all this wonderful, queer, and strange spectacle of the earth's satellite, soon all they had left was imperishable remembrance.

CHAPTER 19

The Struggle Against the Impossible

For a rather long time Barbicane and his companions looked silently and sadly upon that world which they had seen only from a distance, as Moses saw the land of Canaan, and which they were leaving without a possibility of ever returning to it. The projectile's position with regard to the moon had altered, and the base was now turned to the earth.

This change, when Barbicane noted it, did not fail to surprise him. If the projectile was to gravitate round the satellite in an elliptical orbit, why was not its heaviest part turned toward it, as the moon turns hers to the earth? That was a puzzling point.

In watching the course of the projectile they could see that on leaving the moon it followed a curve analogous to that traced in approaching her. It was describing a very long ellipse, which would most likely extend to the point of equal attraction, where the influences of the earth and its satellite neutralize each other.

Such was the conclusion which Barbicane very justly drew from facts already observed, a conviction which his two friends shared with him. At once the questions poured out.

"And once we arrive at this dead point, what will become of us?" asked Michel Ardan.

"We don't know," replied Barbicane.

"But one can draw some hypotheses, I suppose?"

"Two," answered Barbicane. "Either the projectile's speed will be insufficient, and it will remain forever immobilized on this line of double attraction——"

"I prefer the other hypothesis, whatever it may be," interrupted Michel.

"Or," continued Barbicane, "its speed will be sufficient, and it will continue its elliptical course, to gravitate forever around the orb of night."

"A revolution that is not at all consoling," said Michel, "reducing us to the state of humble servants of a moon we are accustomed to look upon as our own handmaid. Is that the fate in store for us?"

Neither Barbicane nor Nicholl answered.

"You remain silent," continued Michel impatiently.

"There is nothing to answer," said Nicholl.

"Is there nothing to try?"

"No," answered Barbicane. "Do you think we can fight against the impossible?"

"Why not? Would a Frenchman and two Americans shrink from such a word?"

"But what would you do?"

"Get control of this motion which is carrying us away."

"Get control of it?"

"Yes," continued Michel, getting animated, "or else reduce or alter it, and employ it to the accomplishment of our own ends."

"And how?"

"That is your affair. If artillerymen cannot control their

projectiles, they are not artillerymen. If the projectile is to command the gunner, we had better ram the gunner into the gun. My faith! fine scientists you are, who do not know what is to become of us after inducing me——"

"Inducing you!" cried Barbicane and Nicholl. "Inducing you! What do you mean by that?"

"No recrimination," said Michel. "I am not complaining. The trip has pleased me, the projectile agrees with me; but let us do all that is humanly possible to do to fall somewhere, even if it is not on the moon."

"We would like nothing better, my worthy Michel," replied Barbicane, "but how can we do it?"

"We cannot alter the motion of the projectle?"

"No."

"Nor diminish its speed?"

"No."

"Not even by lightening it, as they lighten an overloaded vessel?"

"What would you throw out?" said Nicholl. "We have no ballast on board; and indeed it seems to me that if lightened it would go much quicker."

"Slower."

"Quicker."

"Neither slower nor quicker," said Barbicane, trying to satisfy both his friends, "for we float in space, where we are no longer affected by specific weight."

"Well," cried Michel Ardan in a decided voice, "then there remains but one thing to do."

"What is it?" said Nicholl.

"To have lunch," answered the cool, audacious Frenchman, who always brought up this solution at the most difficult juncture.

In any case, if this operation had no influence on the projectile's course, it could at least be tried without inconvenience, and even with success from the stomach's point of view. Certainly Michel had none but good ideas.

So they ate at two in the morning; the hour mattered little. Michel served his usual repast, crowned by a glorious bottle drawn from his private cellar. If ideas did not crowd in on their brains, it was the fault of the Chambertin 1863.

The repast finished, observations began again.

Around the projectile, at an invariable distance, were the objects which had been thrown out. Evidently, in its rotational movement around the moon, it had not passed through any atmosphere, for the specific weight of these different objects would have checked their relative speed.

On the side of the terrestrial sphere nothing was to be seen. The earth was but a day old, having been new the night before at twelve; and two days must elapse before its crescent, moving beyond the solar rays, would serve as a clock to the Selenites, as in its rotational movement each of its points every twenty-four hours goes by the same lunar meridian.

On the moon's side the sight was different; the orb shone in all her splendor amid innumerable constellations, whose purity could not be troubled by her rays. On the disc, the plains were already returning to the dark tint which is seen from the earth. The other part of the nimbus remained brilliant, and in the midst of this general brilliance Tycho still shone prominently like a sun.

Barbicane had no means of estimating the projectile's speed, but reasoning showed that it must uniformly decrease, according to the laws of mechanics.

Having admitted that the projectile was describing an

orbit round the moon, this orbit must necessarily be elliptical; science proves that it must be so. No mobile body circulating round an attracting body defies this law. Every orbit described in space is elliptical, those of the satellites around the planets, those of the planets around the sun, that of the sun around whatever unknown body is its pivot. And why should the projectile of the Gun Club escape this natural arrangement?

In elliptical orbits, the attracting body always occupies one of the foci; so that at one moment the satellite is nearer, and at another farther from the orb around which it gravitates. When the earth is nearest the sun she is in her perihelion; and in her aphelion at the farthest point. Speaking of the moon, she is nearest to the earth in her perigee, and farthest from it in her apogee. To use analogous expressions which will be added to the astronomers' language, if the projectile remains as a satellite of the moon, we must say that it is in its "aposelene" at its farthest point, and in its "periselene" at its nearest.

In the latter case, the projectile would attain its maximum of speed; and in the former its minimum. It was evidently moving toward its aposelenitical point; and Barbicane. was right to think that its speed would decrease up to this point, and then increase little by little as it neared the moon. This speed would even become nil if this point were the same as that of equal attraction.

Barbicane studied the consequences of these different situations, and was thinking what inference he could draw from them, when he was roughly disturbed by a cry from Michel Ardan.

"By Jove!" he exclaimed, "I must admit we are downright simpletons!"

"I do not say we are not," replied Barbicane; "but why?"

"Because we have a very simple means of reducing the speed at which we are getting farther from the moon, and we do not use it!"

"And what is the means?"

"To utilize the great recoil power that is contained in our rockets."

"Right!" said Nicholl.

"We have not used that power yet," said Barbicane, "it is true, but we will use it."

"When?" asked Michel.

"When the time comes. Observe, my friends, that in the position occupied by the projectile, still an oblique position in relation to the lunar disc, our rockets, in altering its direction, might turn it from the moon instead of moving it nearer. And we do want to reach the moon, don't we?"

"Oh, yes," replied Michel.

"Let us wait, then. By some inexplicable influence, the projectile is turning its base toward the earth. It is probable that at the point of equal attraction, its conical cap will be directed straight at the moon; at that moment we may hope that its speed will be nil; then will be the moment to act, and with the influence of our rockets we may perhaps provoke a fall directly on the surface of the lunar disc."

"Bravo!" said Michel.

"And that was what we did not do, what we could not do on our first passage at the dead point, because the projectile was then endowed with too great a speed."

"Very well reasoned," said Nicholl.

"Let us wait patiently," continued Barbicane. "With every chance on our side, now after having so despaired, I may say I again think that we shall reach our goal."

This conclusion was a signal for Michel Ardan's hips and hurrahs. And none of the audacious fools remembered the question that they themselves had solved in the negative: No! the moon is not inhabited! No! the moon is probably not habitable! And nevertheless they were going to try everything to reach her.

One single question remained to be solved. At what precise moment would the projectile reach the point of equal attraction, at which the travelers had to play their trump card?

In order to calculate this to within a few seconds, Barbicane had only to refer to his notes, and to reckon the different heights taken on the lunar parallels. Thus the time necessary to travel the distance between the dead point and the south pole would be equal to the distance separating the north pole from the dead point. The hours representing the time traveled had been carefully noted, and the calculation was easy.

Barbicane found that this point would be reached at one in the morning on the 8th of December. And it was now three A.M. of the 7th. So that, if nothing interfered with its course, it would reach the given point in twenty-two hours.

The rockets had originally been placed to check the fall of the projectile upon the moon, and now they were going to employ them for a directly contrary purpose. In any case they were ready, and they had only to wait for the moment to set fire to them.

"Since there is nothing else to be done," said Nicholl, "I make a proposition."

"What is it?" asked Barbicane.

"I propose we go to sleep."

"What a notion!" exclaimed Michel Ardan.

"It is forty hours since we closed our eyes," said Nicholl. "A few hours of sleep will restore our strength."

"Never," interrupted Michel.

"Well," continued Nicholl, "every one to his taste; I shall go to sleep."

And stretching himself on the divan, he was soon snoring like a forty-eight-pound shot.

"That Nicholl has a good deal of sense," said Barbicane; "presently I shall follow his example."

Some moments later, his sustained bass was underlining the captain's baritone.

"Certainly," said Michel Ardan, finding himself alone, "these practical people sometimes have very good ideas."

And with his long legs stretched out, and his great arms folded under his head, Michel fell asleep in his turn.

But this sleep could be neither peaceful nor lasting, the minds of these three men were too much occupied, and a few hours later, about seven in the morning, all three were on foot at the same instant.

The projectile was still moving away from the moon, and turning its conical part more and more toward her, by some inexplicable phenomenon, but one which happily served Barbicane's ends.

Seventeen hours more, and the moment for action would have arrived.

The day seemed long. However bold the travelers might be, they were greatly impressed by the approach of that moment which would decide all—either precipitate their fall on to the moon, or forever chain them in an immutable orbit. They counted the hours which passed too slowly to suit them. Barbicane and Nicholl were obstinately plunged in their calculations, Michel going and coming between the narrow

393

walls, and watching that impassive moon with a longing eye.

At times recollections of the earth crossed their minds. They saw once more their friends of the Gun Club, and the dearest of all, J. T. Maston. At that moment, the honorable secretary was doubtless at his post on the Rocky Mountains. If he could see the projectile through the glass of his gigantic telescope, what would he think? After seeing it disappear behind the moon's south pole, he would see it reappear at the north pole! It must then be a satellite of a satellite! Had J. T. Maston given this unexpected news to the world? Was this the denouement of this great enterprise?

But the day passed without incident. The terrestrial midnight arrived. The 8th of December was beginning. One hour more, and the point of equal attraction would be reached. What speed were they now traveling at? They could not estimate it. But no error could vitiate Barbicane's calculations. At one in the morning this speed had to be and would be nil.

Anyway, another phenomenon would mark the projectile's stopping-point on the neutral line. At that spot the two attractions, lunar and terrestrial, would cancel each other out. Objects would no longer have any "weight." This singular fact, which had surprised Barbicane and his companions so much in going, would be repeated on their return under the very same conditions. That would be the precise moment when they must act.

Already the projectile's conical top was appreciably turned toward the lunar disc, presented in such a way as to utilize the whole of the recoil produced by the pressure of the rocket apparatus. The chances were in favor of the travelers. If its speed was utterly annulled on this dead point, a decided movement toward the moon would suffice, however slight, to determine its fall.

"Five minutes to one," said Nicholl.

"Everything is ready," replied Michel Ardan, directing a readied wick toward the flame of the gas.

"Wait!" said Barbicane, holding his chronometer in his hand.

At that moment gravity no longer had any effect. The travelers could feel within themselves its total disappearance. They were very near the neutral point, if not right upon it.

"One o'clock," said Barbicane.

Michel Ardan applied the lighted wick to a fuse leading to the rockets. No detonation was heard inside, for there was no air. But, through the scuttles, Barbicane saw a prolonged smoke, the flames of which were immediately extinguished.

The projectile sustained a certain shock, which was quite appreciably felt in the interior.

The three friends looked and listened without speaking, scarcely breathing. One might have heard the beating of their hearts amid this perfect silence.

"Are we falling?" asked Michel Ardan, at length.

"No," said Nicholl, "since the bottom of the projectile is not turning to the lunar disc!"

At this moment, Barbicane, leaving the scuttle, turned to his two companions. He was frightfully pale, his forehead wrinkled, and his lips contracted.

"We are falling!" said he.

"Ah!" cried Michel Ardan, "on to the moon?"

"On to the earth!"

"The devil!" exclaimed Michel Ardan, adding philosophically: "Well, when we came into this projectile we knew it would not be easy to get out of it!"

And now this fearful fall had begun. The speed retained had borne the projectile beyond the dead point. The explosion of the rockets could not reduce it. This speed in going had carried it over the neutral line, and in returning had done the same thing. The laws of physics condemned it *to pass through every point which it had already gone through.*

It was a terrible fall, from a height of 195,000 miles, and no springs to break it. According to the laws of gunnery, the projectile would strike the earth with a speed equal to that with which it left the mouth of the Columbiad, a speed of over 17,000 yards in the last second.

But, to give some figures of comparison, it has been reckoned that an object thrown from the top of the towers of Notre Dame, the height of which is only 200 feet, will arrive on the pavement at a speed of 300 miles per hour. Here the projectile must strike the earth with a speed of 144,000 miles per hour.

"We are lost!" said Nicholl, icily.

"Well, if we die," answered Barbicane, with a sort of religious enthusiasm, "the outcome of our journey will be magnificently broadened. It is His own secret that God will tell us! In the other life the soul will need nothing to help it to knowledge, neither machines nor engines! It will merge into eternal wisdom!"

"In fact," interrupted Michel Ardan, "the whole of the other world may well console us for the loss of that inferior orb called the moon!"

Barbicane crossed his arms on his breast, with a motion of sublime resignation, saying at the same time:

"The will of heaven be done!"

396

CHAPTER 20

The Soundings of the *Susquehanna*

"WELL, lieutenant, what of our soundings?"

"I think, sir, that the operation is nearing its completion," replied Lieutenant Bronsfield. "But who would have thought of finding such a depth so near in to shore, only 250 miles from the American coast?"

"Certainly, Bronsfield, there is a great depression," said Captain Blomsberry. "In this spot there is a submarine valley worn by the Peruvian Current, which skirts the coast of America as far as the Straits of Magellan."

"These great depths," continued the lieutenant, "are not favorable for laying telegraphic cables. A level bottom, like that supporting the American cable between Valentia and Newfoundland, is much better."

"I agree with you, Bronsfield. With your permission, lieutenant, how far have we gotten?"

"Sir, at this moment we have 3,500 fathoms of line out, and the weight that leads the sound has not yet touched bottom; for if it had, the sound would have come up of itself."

"Brook's apparatus is very ingenious," said Captain Blomsberry. "It gives us very exact soundings."

"Touch!" at this moment cried one of the forward men, who was superintending the operation.

The captain and the lieutenant went up to the forecastle.

"What does it read?" asked the captain.

"Three thousand six hundred and twenty-seven fathoms," replied the lieutenant, entering it in his notebook.

"Well, Bronsfield," said the captain, "I will enter that on my chart. Now haul in the sounding line. That will take several hours. In that time the engineer can fire up the boilers, and we shall be ready to start as soon as you have finished. It is ten o'clock, and with your permission, lieutenant, I will turn in."

"Do so, sir; do so!" replied the lieutenant obligingly.

The captain of the *Susquehanna,* a good man if ever there was one, and the humble servant of his officers, returned to his cabin, took a brandy-grog, which earned the steward no end of praise, and turned in, not without having complimented his servant on the way he made beds, and slept a peaceful sleep.

It was then ten o'clock. The eleventh day of the month of December was about to draw to a close in a magnificent night.

The *Susquehanna,* a corvette of 500 horse-power, of the United States Navy, was occupied in taking soundings in the Pacific Ocean about 250 miles off the American coast, following that long peninsula which stretches down along the coast of Mexico.

The wind had gradually subsided. There was no disturbance in the air. The pennant hung motionless from the main-top-gallant-mast truck.

Captain Jonathan Blomsberry (a first cousin of Colonel Blomsberry, one of the most ardent supporters of the Gun

Club, who had married a Horschbidden, an aunt of the captain and daughter of an honorable Kentucky merchant)—
Captain Blomsberry could not have wished for finer weather
in which to bring to a close his delicate operations of sounding. His corvette had not even felt the great storm which, by
sweeping away the groups of clouds on the Rocky Mountains, had permitted observation of the course of the famous
projectile. Everything had gone well, and with all his Presby-
terian fervor, he did not forget to thank heaven for it.

The series of soundings taken by the *Susquehanna* had
for its aim the finding of a favorable spot for the laying of a
submarine cable to connect the Hawaiian Islands with the
coast of America.

It was a great undertaking, due to the instigation of a
powerful company. Its managing director, the intelligent
Cyrus Field, even proposed covering all the islands of
Oceania with a vast electrical network, an immense enterprise, and one worthy of American genius.

The corvette *Susquehanna* had been entrusted with the
first operations of sounding. During the night of the 11th–
12th of December, she was at exactly latitude 27° 7′ north
and longitude 119° 55′ west.

The moon, then in her last quarter, was beginning to rise
above the horizon.

After Captain Blomsberry left, the lieutenant and officers
were standing together on the poop. At the appearance of
the moon, their thoughts turned to that orb which the eyes
of a whole hemisphere were contemplating. The best naval
glasses could not have discovered the projectile wandering
around its hemisphere, and yet all of them were pointed toward that brilliant disc which millions of eyes were looking
at at the same moment.

399

"They have been gone ten days," said Lieutenant Bronsfield at last. "What has become of them?"

"They have arrived, lieutenant," exclaimed a young midshipman, "and they are doing what all travelers do when they arrive in a new country, taking a walk!"

"Oh! I am sure of that, if you tell me so, my young friend," said Lieutenant Bronsfield, smiling.

"But," continued another officer, "their arrival cannot be doubted. The projectile was to reach the moon when it was full on the 5th at midnight. It is now the 11th of December, which makes six days. And in six times twenty-four hours, without darkness, one would have time to settle comfortably. I fancy I see our brave countrymen encamped at the bottom of some valley, on the banks of a Selenite stream, near their projectile half-buried by its fall amid volcanic rubbish, Captain Nicholl beginning his leveling operations, President Barbicane writing out his notes, and Michel Ardan filling the lunar solitudes with the aroma of his cigars."

"Yes! it must be so, it is so!" exclaimed the young midshipman, worked up to a pitch of enthusiasm by this ideal description of his superior officer.

"I should like to believe it," replied the lieutenant, who was quite unmoved. "Unfortunately we will never get direct news from the lunar world."

"Beg pardon, lieutenant," said the midshipman, "but cannot President Barbicane write?"

A burst of laughter greeted this answer.

"Not letters!" continued the young man quickly. "Of course, the post office does not operate there."

"Then, how about a telegram?" asked one of the officers ironically.

"Not that, either," replied the midshipman, not at all confused. "But it is very easy to set up graphic communication with the earth."

"How?"

"By means of the telescope at Longs Peak. You know it brings the moon to within five miles of the Rocky Mountains, and that it allows us to see objects on its surface only nine feet in diameter. Well, let our industrious friends construct a gigantic alphabet! Let them write words a hundred fathoms long, and sentences three miles long, and that way they can send us news of themselves!"

The young midshipman, who indeed had a certain amount of imagination, was loudly applauded; Lieutenant Bronsfield even allowed that the idea might be feasible. He added that, by the transmission of luminous rays gathered into clusters by parabolic mirrors, it would also be possible to establish direct communication; such rays, indeed, would be as visible on the surface of Venus or Mars as Neptune is from earth. He ended by saying that certain shiny spots previously observed on the nearest planets might well be deliberate signals that had been made toward earth. But he pointed out that, while through such means they could receive news from the lunar world, they would not be able to send any from earth unless the Selenites had at their disposal instruments for taking distant observations.

"Obviously," said one of the officers; "but what has become of the travelers? What they have done, what they have seen, that above all is what must interest us. Besides, if the experiment has succeeded (which I do not doubt), it will be tried again. The Columbiad is still sunk in the soil of Florida. It is now only a question of powder and shot; and every time the moon is at the zenith a cargo of visitors may be sent up."

"It is clear," replied Lieutenant Bronsfield, "that J. T. Maston will one day soon join his friends."

"If he will have me," cried the midshipman, "I am ready to go along!"

"Oh! volunteers will not be wanting," answered Bronsfield; "and, if permitted, half the earth's inhabitants will soon emigrate to the moon!"

This conversation among the officers of the *Susquehanna* was kept up until nearly one in the morning. It is impossible to describe what fantastic systems, what breathtaking theories were advanced by these daring minds. Since the start of Barbicane's adventure, nothing seemed impossible to Americans any longer. They were already planning to send, not just scientists, but a whole colony toward the Selenite shores, and a complete army, including infantry, artillery, and cavalry, to conquer the lunar world.

At one in the morning, the hauling-in of the sounding-line was not yet completed; 1,670 fathoms were still out, which would still entail several hours' work. According to the commander's orders, the fires had been lighted, and steam was being got up. The *Susquehanna* could have gotten under way that very instant.

At that moment (it was seventeen minutes past one in the morning) Lieutenant Bronsfield was preparing to leave the watch and return to his cabin, when his attention was attracted by a distant, hissing, and quite unexpected noise.

His comrades and he first thought that this hissing was caused by the letting-off of steam; but, lifting their heads, they found that the noise was coming from the very highest reaches of the air.

They had no time to question each other before the hissing became frightfully intense, and suddenly there appeared to their dazzled eyes an enormous meteor, ignited by the rapidity of its course and its friction through the atmospheric strata.

This fiery mass grew larger to their eyes, and fell, with the noise of thunder, upon the bowsprit of the corvette, which it sheered off close to the stem, and buried itself in the waves with a deafening roar!

A few feet nearer, and the *Susquehanna* would have been sunk with all on board!

At this instant Captain Blomsberry appeared, half-dressed, and, rushing on to the forecastle-deck, toward which all the officers had converged, he exclaimed,

"With your permission, gentlemen, what has happened?"

And the midshipman, making himself as it were the spokesman for all of them, cried,

"Commander, it is 'they' who have come back again!"

CHAPTER 21

J. T. Maston Recalled

THERE was great excitement aboard the *Susque-hanna*. Officers and men forgot the terrible danger they had just been in, the possibility that they might have been crushed and sunk to the ocean's bottom. All they could think of was the catastrophe that marked the end of the adventurous voyage. Thus, the most daring undertaking of ancient and modern times was costing the lives of the hardy pioneers who had attempted it.

"It is 'they' who have come back again!" the young midshipman had said, and every one had understood him. No one doubted but that that meteor was the projectile of the Gun Club. As to the travelers which it carried, opinions were divided regarding their fate.

"They are dead!" said one.

"They are alive!" said another. "The water is deep, and the shock was cushioned."

"But they had no air," continued a third speaker; "they must have died of suffocation."

"Burned!" replied a fourth. "The projectile was nothing but an incandescent mass as it crossed the atmosphere."

"What does it matter!" they exclaimed unanimously. "Living or dead, we must get them out!"

Meanwhile, Captain Blomsberry had assembled his officers, and "with their permission," was holding a council. They must immediately come to a decision. The most urgent task was to fish up the projectile. A difficult operation, though not impossible. But the corvette had no proper machinery, which had to be both specific and powerful; so it was resolved that they should put in at the nearest port, and advise the Gun Club of the projectile's fall.

This determination was unanimous. The choice of the port had to be discussed. The neighboring coast had no anchorage at 27° latitude. Considerably above the peninsula of Monterey, stands the important town from which it takes its name; but, on the edge of a total desert, it was not connected with the interior by a network of telegraphic wires, and electricity alone could spread such important news fast enough.

Some degrees above there was San Francisco Bay. Through the capital of the gold country communication would be easy with the heart of the Union. And in less than two days the *Susquehanna,* by going full steam ahead, could arrive in that port. She must therefore start at once.

The fires were made up; they could be under way immediately. Two thousand fathoms of line were still out, which Captain Blomsberry, not wishing to lose precious time in hauling in, resolved to cut off.

"We will fasten the end to a buoy," said he, "and that buoy will show us the exact spot where the projectile fell."

"Besides," replied Lieutenant Bronsfield, "we know our exact position: latitude 27° 7′ north and longitude 119° 55′ west."

405

"Well, Mr. Bronsfield," replied the captain, "now, with your permission, we will have the line cut."

A strong buoy, strengthened by a couple of spars, was thrown into the ocean. The end of the rope was carefully lashed to it; and, left solely to the rise and fall of the billows, the buoy would likely not appreciably deviate from the spot.

At this moment the engineer sent to inform the captain that steam was up and they could start, for which agreeable communication the captain thanked him. The course was then given north-northeast, and the corvette swung about to head at full steam direct for San Francisco. It was three in the morning.

Five hundred and fifty miles to cross was no great task for a good vessel like the *Susquehanna*. In thirty-six hours she had covered that distance; and on the 14th of December, at twenty-seven minutes past one in the afternoon, she entered San Francisco Bay.

Seeing a U. S. Navy ship arriving at full speed, her bowsprit broken, her mizzen mast shored up, public curiosity was greatly aroused. A dense crowd soon assembled on the dock, waiting for the crew to land.

After casting anchor, Captain Blomsberry and Lieutenant Bronsfield entered an eight-oared cutter, which soon brought them to land.

They jumped on to the dock.

"The telegraph?" they asked, ignoring the thousand questions addressed to them.

The officer of the port himself led them to the telegraph office through a huge collection of spectators.

Blomsberry and Bronsfield went in, while the crowd crushed at the door.

A few minutes later a fourfold telegram was sent out—the first copy to the Secretary of the Navy, Washington; the

406

second to the vice-president of the Gun Club, Baltimore; the third to the Hon. J. T. Maston, Longs Peak, Rocky Mountains; the fourth to the sub-director of the Cambridge Observatory, Massachusetts.

It was worded as follows:

In latitude 27° 7′ north, and longitude 119° 55′ west, on the 12th of December, at seventeen minutes past one in the morning, the projectile of the Columbiad fell into the Pacific. Send instructions.
—BLOMSBERRY, Commander *Susquehanna*.

Five minutes later, the whole town of San Francisco learned the news. Before six in the evening the different States of the Union had heard of the great catastrophe; and after midnight, by the cable, the whole of Europe knew the result of the great American experiment.

We will not attempt to picture the effect produced on the entire world by that unexpected denouement.

On receipt of the telegram the Secretary of the Navy telegraphed to the *Susquehanna* to wait in San Francisco Bay without banking her fires. Day and night she must be ready to put to sea.

The Cambridge Observatory called a special meeting; and, with that composure which distinguishes learned bodies in general, peacefully discussed the scientific significance of the question.

At the Gun Club, there was an explosion. All the gunners were assembled. Vice-President the Hon. Wilcome was in the act of reading the premature dispatch, in which J. T. Maston and Belfast announced that the projectile had just been seen in the gigantic reflector of Longs Peak, and also that it was held by lunar attraction, and was playing the part of sub-satellite to the lunar world.

We now know the truth on that point.

But on the arrival of Blomsberry's dispatch, so decidedly contradicting J. T. Maston's telegram, two parties were formed in the bosom of the Gun Club. On one side were those who admitted the fall of the projectile, and consequently the return of the travelers; on the other, those who, believing in the observations of Longs Peak, concluded that the commander of the *Susquehanna* had made a mistake. To the latter the alleged projectile was merely a meteor, nothing but a meteor, a shooting globe, which in its fall had smashed the bow of the corvette. It was difficult to answer this argument, for its speed must have made observation of the object very difficult. The commander of the *Susquehanna* and her officers might have made a mistake in all good faith; one argument, however, was in their favor, namely, that if the projectile had fallen to earth, its place of meeting with the terrestrial globe could take place only at $27°$ north latitude, and (taking into consideration the time that had elapsed, and the rotary motion of the earth) between $119°$ and $120°$ of west longitude.

In any case, it was unanimously decided in the Gun Club that Blomsberry's brother, Bilsby, and Major Elphinstone should go forthwith to San Francisco, and consult as to the means of raising the projectile from the depths of the ocean.

These devoted men set off at once; and the railroad, which will soon cross the whole middle of America, took them as far as St. Louis, where the swift mail-coaches awaited them.

Almost at the same moment in which the Secretary of the Navy, the vice-president of the Gun Club, and the sub-director of the Observatory received the dispatch from San Francisco, the Honorable J. T. Maston was undergoing the greatest excitement he had ever experienced in his life, an excitement which even the bursting of his pet gun had not caused him, when, once more, it was nearly costing him his life.

We may remember that the secretary of the Gun Club had started soon after the projectile (and almost as quickly) for the station on Longs Peak, in the Rocky Mountains, the erudite J. Belfast, director of the Cambridge Observatory, accompanying him. Once there, the two friends had moved in without delay, and now never for a second left the summit of their enormous telescope.

We know that this gigantic instrument had been set up according to the reflecting system, called by the English "front view." This arrangement subjected all objects to but one reflection, making the view consequently much clearer; the result was that, when they were taking observations, J. T. Maston and Belfast were placed in the *upper* part of the instrument and not in the lower. They climbed up by a circular staircase, a masterpiece of lightness, while below them opened a metal well terminated by the metallic mirror, which measured two hundred and eighty feet in depth.

It was on a narrow platform placed above the telescope that the two savants passed their existence, cursing the daylight, which hid the moon from their eyes, and the clouds which obstinately veiled it during the night.

What, then, was their delight when, after some days of waiting, on the night of the 5th of December, they caught a glimpse of the vehicle which was bearing their friends into space! This delight was followed by a great disappointment, when, trusting to a cursory observation, they launched their first telegram to the world, erroneously affirming that the projectile had become a satellite of the moon, gravitating in an immutable orbit.

From that moment it had never again shown itself to

their eyes—a disappearance all the more easily explained, since it was then passing behind the moon's invisible disc; but when it was time for it to reappear on the visible disc, one may imagine the impatience of the fuming J. T. Maston and his not less impatient companion. Each minute of the night they thought they saw the projectile once more, and yet they did not see it. Hence constant discussions and violent disputes between them, Belfast affirming that the projectile could not be seen, J. T. Maston maintaining that "it was as plain as the nose on your face."

"There is the projectile!" repeated J. T. Maston.

"No," answered Belfast; "that is an avalanche detached from a lunar mountain."

"Well, we shall see it to-morrow."

"No, we shall not see it any more. It has been carried away into space."

"Yes, we will!"

"No!"

And at these moments, when such ejaculations rained like hail, the well-known irritability of the secretary of the Gun Club constituted a permanent danger for the Honorable Belfast.

This double harness would soon have become impossible; but an unforeseen event cut short their everlasting discussions.

During the night of the 14th to the 15th of December, the two irreconcilable friends were busy observing the lunar disc, J. T. Maston as usual abusing the learned Belfast, who was also losing his temper. The secretary of the Gun Club was maintaining for the thousandth time that he had just seen the projectile, and adding that he could see Michel Ardan's face looking through one of the scuttles, at the same

The space travelers make a splashdown

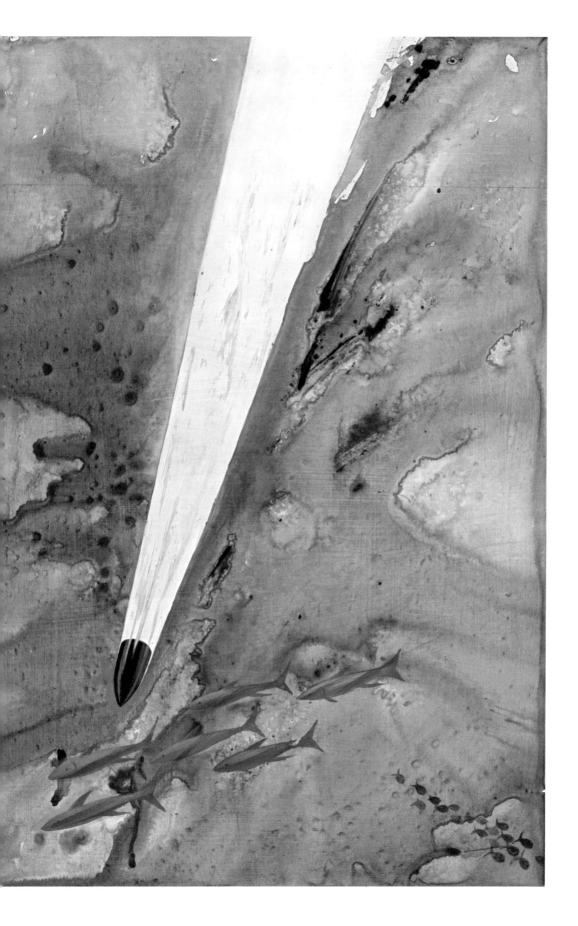

time underlining his argument by a series of gestures which his formidable hook rendered very unpleasant.

At this moment Belfast's servant appeared on the platform (it was ten at night) and gave him a telegram. It was the wire from the commander of the *Susquehanna*.

Belfast tore open the envelope, read, and uttered a cry.

"What?" said J. T. Maston.

"The projectile!"

"Well?"

"It has fallen to earth!"

Another cry, this time a perfect howl, answered him.

He turned toward J. T. Maston. The unfortunate man, imprudently leaning over the metal tube, had disappeared into the immense telescope. A fall of two hundred and eighty feet! Belfast, dismayed, rushed to the orifice of the reflector.

He breathed a sigh of relief. J. T. Maston, caught by his metal hook, was holding on by one of the props which maintained the width of the telescope, uttering fearful cries.

Belfast called. Help was brought, tackle was let down, and they hoisted up, not without some trouble, the imprudent secretary of the Gun Club.

He reappeared at the upper orifice without further mishap.

"Ah!" said he, "if I had broken the mirror?"

"You would have paid for it," replied Belfast severely.

"And that cursed projectile has fallen?" asked J. T. Maston.

"Into the Pacific!"

"Let us go!"

A quarter of an hour later, the two savants were descending the declivity of the Rocky Mountains; and two days later, at the same time as their friends from the Gun Club, they arrived at San Francisco, having worn out five horses on the way.

Elphinstone, Blomsberry's brother, and Bilsby rushed toward them on their arrival.

"What shall we do?" they exclaimed.

"Fish up the projectile," replied J. T. Maston, "and the sooner the better."

CHAPTER 22

The Salvage

THE spot where the projectile had sunk under the waves was precisely known; but machinery to grasp it and bring it to the surface of the ocean was still wanting. It must first be invented, then made. American engineers were not dismayed by such trifles. The grappling-irons once fixed, with steam to operate them, they were sure to raise it in spite of its weight, which was lessened by the density of the liquid in which it was plunged.

But fishing up the projectile was not the only thing that counted. They had to act promptly in the interest of the travelers. No one doubted that they were still living.

"Yes," incessantly repeated J. T. Maston, whose confidence infected everybody, "our friends are clever people, and they cannot have fallen like simpletons. They are alive, quite alive: but we must make haste if we wish to find them so. Food and water do not trouble me; they have enough for a long while. But air, air, that is what they will soon lack— so quick, quick!"

And they did go quick. They fitted up the *Susquehanna* for her new destination. Her powerful machinery was

413

brought to bear upon the hauling-chains. The aluminum projectile only weighed 19,250 pounds, a weight very inferior to that of the transatlantic cable which had been drawn up under similar conditions. The only difficulty was in fishing up a cylindro-conical projectile, the walls of which were so smooth as to offer no purchase for the hooks.

On that account Engineer Murchison hastened to San Francisco, and had some enormous grappling-irons fixed on an automatic system, which would never let the projectile go if it once succeeded in seizing it in its powerful claws. Diving-suits were also prepared, which, being waterproof and highly resistant, allowed for reconnoitering the bottom of the sea. He also had put on board very cleverly designed apparatuses of compressed air. They were regular chambers, complete with scuttles, which, with water let into certain compartments, could be let down into great depths. These apparatuses were in existence at San Francisco, where they had been used in the construction of a submarine break-water; and very fortunately it was so, for there was no time to construct any.

But in spite of the perfection of the machinery, in spite of the ingenuity of the scientists entrusted with the use of them, the success of the operation was far from being certain. How great were the chances against them, the projectile being under 20,000 feet of water! And if even it were brought to the surface, how would the travelers have borne the terrible shock which 20,000 feet of water had perhaps not sufficiently broken?

At any rate they must act quickly. J. T. Maston hurried the workmen day and night. He was ready to don the diving-suit himself, or try the air apparatus, in order to reconnoiter the situation of his courageous friends.

The Salvage

But, in spite of all the diligence displayed in preparing the different machines, in spite of the considerable sums placed at the disposal of the Gun Club by the Government of the Union, five long days (five centuries!) elapsed before the preparations were complete. During this time public opinion was excited to the highest pitch. Telegrams were exchanged incessantly throughout the entire world by means of electric wires and cables. The saving of Barbicane, Nicholl, and Michel Ardan was an international affair. Every people who had subscribed to the Gun Club fund was directly interested in the welfare of the travelers.

At length the hauling-chains, the air-chambers, and the automatic grappling-irons were put on board. J. T. Maston, Engineer Murchison, and the delegates of the Gun Club were already in their cabins. They had only to start.

The 21st of December, at eight o'clock at night, the corvette set out on a fine sea, with a northeasterly wind, and rather sharp cold. The whole population of San Francisco was gathered on the docks, greatly excited but silent, reserving their hurrahs for the return.

Steam was fully up, and the screw of the *Susquehanna* carried them briskly out of the bay.

It is needless to relate the conversation on board among the officers, sailors, and passengers. All these men had but one thought. All these hearts beat with the same emotion. While they were hastening to help them, what were Barbicane and his companions doing? What had become of them? Were they able to attempt any bold maneuver to regain their liberty? None could say. The truth is that any attempt by them was doomed to fail! Immersed nearly five miles beneath the ocean, this metal prison defied every effort of its prisoners.

415

On the 23d, at eight in the morning, after a rapid passage, the *Susquehanna* was apparently at the spot. They had to wait till twelve to take the reckoning exactly. The buoy to which the sounding line had been lashed had not yet been found.

At twelve, Captain Blomsberry, assisted by his officers who superintended the observations, took the reckoning in the presence of the delegates of the Gun Club. Then there was a moment of great concern. Her position determined, the *Susquehanna* was found to be several minutes westward of the spot where the projectile had disappeared beneath the waves. The ship's course was then changed so as to reach this exact point.

At forty-seven minutes past twelve they reached the buoy; it was in perfect condition, and must have shifted but little.

"At last!" exclaimed J. T. Maston.

"Shall we begin?" asked Captain Blomsberry.

"Without losing a second," Maston replied.

Every precaution was taken to keep the corvette completely motionless.

Before trying to seize the projectile, Engineer Murchison wanted to reconnoiter its exact position at the bottom of the ocean. The submarine apparatus destined for this expedition was supplied with air. The working of these machines was not without danger, for at 20,000 feet below the surface of the water, and under such great pressure, they were exposed to fracture, the consequences of which would be dreadful.

J. T. Maston, Blomsberry's brother, and Engineer Murchison, without heeding these dangers, took their places in the air-chamber. The commander, posted on his bridge, superintended the operation, ready to stop or reel in the chains on the slightest signal. The screw had been shipped, and the full power of the engines, centered on the capstan, could have quickly drawn the apparatus back up.

The descent began at twenty-five minutes past one in the afternoon, and the chamber, drawn under by its reservoirs full of water, disappeared from the surface of the ocean.

The concern of the officers and sailors on board was now split between the prisoners in the projectile and the prisoners in the submarine apparatus. As to the latter, they forgot themselves, and, glued to the windows of the scuttles, attentively watched the liquid mass through which they were passing.

The descent was rapid. At seventeen minutes past two, J. T. Maston and his companions had reached the bottom of the Pacific; but they saw nothing but an arid desert, no longer animated by either fauna or flora. By the light of their lamps, equipped with powerful reflectors, they could see the dark layers of water for a considerable extent of view, but the projectile was nowhere to be seen.

The impatience of these bold divers cannot be described, and having an electrical communication with the corvette, they made a signal already agreed upon, and for the space of a mile the *Susquehanna* moved their chamber along, a few yards above the bottom.

Thus they explored the whole submarine plain, deceived at every turn by optical illusions which almost broke their hearts. Here a rock, there a projection from the ground, seemed to be the much-sought-for projectile; but their mistake was soon discovered, and then they were in despair.

"But where are they? Where are they?" cried J. T. Maston.

And the poor man called loudly to Nicholl, Barbicane,

and Michel Ardan, as if his unfortunate friends could either hear or answer him through such an impenetrable medium!

The search continued under these conditions until the vitiated air in their chamber compelled the divers to ascend.

The hauling-in began about six in the evening, and was not ended before midnight.

"Tomorrow," said J. T. Maston, as he set foot on the bridge of the corvette.

"Yes," answered Captain Blomsberry.

"And on another spot?"

"Yes."

J. T. Maston did not doubt of their final success, but his companions, no longer upheld by the excitement of the first hours, understood all the difficulty of the enterprise. What had seemed easy at San Francisco, seemed here in the wide ocean almost impossible. The chances of success diminished in great proportion; and it was from chance alone that the meeting with the projectile might be expected.

The next day, the 24th, in spite of the fatigue of the previous day, the operation was renewed. The corvette advanced some minutes to westward, and the apparatus, provided with air, took the same explorers back to the depths of the ocean.

The whole day passed in fruitless research; the bed of the sea was deserted. The 25th brought no other result, nor did the 26th.

It was disheartening. They thought of those unfortunates shut up in the projectile for twenty-six days. Perhaps at that moment they were experiencing the first approach of suffocation; that is, if they had escaped the dangers of their fall. The air was wearing thin, and doubtless with the air all their courage and morale.

A quiet game of dominoe

"The air, possibly," answered J. T. Maston resolutely, "but their morale never!"

On the 28th, after two more days of search, all hope was gone. This projectile was but an atom in the immensity of the ocean. They must give up all idea of finding it.

But J. T. Maston would not hear of going away. He did not want to leave the place without at least identifying the tomb of his friends. But Commander Blomsberry could no longer hold out, and in spite of the insistence of the worthy secretary was obliged to give the order to sail.

On the 29th of December, at nine A.M., the *Susquehanna,* heading northeast, resumed her course toward San Francisco Bay.

It was ten in the morning; the corvette was under half-steam, as if regretting to leave the spot where the catastrophe had taken place, when a sailor, perched on the maintop-gallant crosstrees, watching the sea, cried suddenly:

"A buoy on the lee bow!"

The officers looked in the direction indicated, and with the help of their glasses saw that the object in question indeed had the appearance of one of those buoys which are used to mark the passages of bays or rivers. But, singular to say, a flag floating on the wind surmounted its cone, which emerged five or six feet out of water. This buoy shone under the rays of the sun as if its sides had been made of plates of silver.

Commander Blomsberry, J. T. Maston, and the delegates of the Gun Club had gone up to the bridge, and were examining this object straying at random on the waves.

All looked with feverish anxiety, but in silence. None dared give expression to the thoughts which came to the minds of all.

The corvette approached to within two cables' lengths of the object.

A shudder ran through the whole crew.

That flag was the American flag!

At this moment an absolute roar was heard; it was good old J. T. Maston, who had just fallen all in a heap. Forgetting on the one hand that his right arm had been replaced by an iron hook, and on the other that a simple India-rubber cap covered his brain-box, he had just struck himself a formidable blow.

They hurried toward him, picked him up, restored him to life. And what were his first words?

"Ah! triple brutes! quadruple idiots! quintuple boobies that we are!"

"What is wrong?" exclaimed everyone around him.

"What is wrong?"

"Come, speak!"

"What is wrong, simpletons," howled the terrible secretary, "is that the projectile weighs only 19,250 pounds!"

"Well?"

"And that it displaces twenty-eight tons, or in other words 56,000 pounds, so that consequently *it floats!*"

Ah! what stress the worthy man laid on the verb "float!" And it was true! All, yes! all these savants had forgotten this fundamental law, namely, that on account of its specific lightness, the projectile, after having been driven in its fall to the greatest depths of the ocean, must naturally return to the surface. And now it was floating quietly at the mercy of the waves.

The boats were put to sea. J. T. Maston and his friends rushed into them! Excitement was at its peak! Every heart beat loudly as the boats moved toward the projectile. What did it contain? Live men or dead? Live, yes! live at least unless death had struck Barbicane and his two friends since they had hoisted the flag.

Profound silence reigned on the boats. All were breathless. Eyes no longer saw. One of the scuttles of the projectile was open. Some pieces of glass remained in the frame, showing that it had been broken. This scuttle was now riding five feet above the water.

A boat came alongside, that of J. T. Maston, and J. T. Maston rushed to the broken window.

At that moment they heard a clear and merry voice, the voice of Michel Ardan, exclaiming in an accent of triumph:

"Blanks everywhere, Barbicane, blanks everywhere!"

Barbicane, Michel Ardan, and Nicholl were playing dominoes!

CHAPTER 23

The End

WE may remember the intense sympathy which had accompanied the travelers on their departure. If at the beginning of the enterprise they had excited such emotion both in the old and new world, with what enthusiasm would they be received on their return! Millions of spectators had beset the peninsula of Florida; would they not now rush to meet these sublime adventurers? Would those legions of strangers, hurrying from all parts of the globe toward the American shores, leave the Union without having seen Barbicane, Nicholl, and Michel Ardan? No! The ardent passion of the public would rise to a pitch in keeping with the greatness of the enterprise. Human creatures who had left the terrestrial sphere, and returned after this strange voyage into celestial space, could not fail to be received as the prophet Elijah will be when he comes back to earth. To see them first, then to hear them, that was the universal longing.

That desire was to be very promptly fulfilled by almost all the inhabitants of the Union.

Barbicane, Michel Ardan, Nicholl, and the delegates of the Gun Club, returning without delay to Baltimore, were received with indescribable enthusiasm. The notes of President Barbicane's voyage were ready to be given to the public.

The End

The New York Herald bought the manuscript at a price not yet known, but which must have been very high. Indeed, during the publication of *A Journey to the Moon,* the circulation of this paper rose to five millions of copies. Three days after the return of the travelers to earth, the slightest detail of their expedition was known. There remained nothing more but to see the heroes of this superhuman enterprise.

The expedition of Barbicane and his friends around the moon had enabled them to check out the various theories concerning the earth's satellite. These savants had observed *de visu,* and under very special circumstances. They could now tell what systems should be rejected, what retained, with regard to the formation of that orb, its origin, its habitability. Its past, present, and future had even given up their final secrets. Who could advance objections against conscientious observers, who at less than twenty-five miles distance had contemplated that curious mountain of Tycho, the strangest system of lunar orography? How answer those savants whose sight had penetrated the abyss of Plato's circle? How contradict those bold ones whom the chance of their enterprise had carried around to that invisible face of the disc, which no human eyes until then had ever seen? It was now their turn to impose some limit on that selenographic science, which had reconstructed the lunar world as Cuvier did the skeleton of a fossil, and say, "The moon *was* this, a habitable world, inhabited before the earth! The moon *is* that, a world uninhabitable, and now uninhabited."

To celebrate the return of its most illustrious member and his two companions, the Gun Club decided to give a banquet, but a banquet worthy of the conquerors, worthy of the American people, and under such conditions that all the inhabitants of the Union could directly take part in it.

All the main terminals of the railroads in the United

423

States were linked by flying rails; and on all the platforms, lined with the same flags, and decorated with the same ornaments, were tables laid and all served alike. At certain hours, successively calculated, marked by electric clocks which beat the seconds at the same time, the population were invited to take their places at the banquet tables.

For four days, from the 5th to the 9th of January, all trains were stopped, as they are on Sundays on the railways of the United States, and every road was open.

Only one high-speed locomotive, drawing a triumphal carriage, was allowed to travel for those four days on the railroads of the United States.

The engine was manned by a driver and a stoker, and bore, by special favor, the Hon. J. T. Maston, secretary of the Gun Club.

The carriage was reserved for President Barbicane, Captain Nicholl, and Michel Ardan.

At the whistle of the driver, amid the hurrahs, and all the admiring vociferations of the American language, the train left the platform of Baltimore. It traveled at a speed of two hundred miles an hour. But what was this speed compared with that which had carried the three heroes from the mouth of the Columbiad?

Thus they sped from one town to the other, where whole populations were at table on their arrival, saluting them with the same acclamations, lavishing the same bravos on them! They traveled in this way through the east of the Union, Pennsylvania, Connecticut, Massachusetts, Vermont, Maine, and New Hampshire; the north and the west through New York, Ohio, Michigan, and Wisconsin; returning to the south through Illinois, Missouri, Arkansas, Texas, and Louisiana; they went to the southeast by Alabama and Florida, up through Georgia and the Carolinas, visiting the center through Tennessee, Kentucky, Virginia, and Indiana, and, after a stop at the Washington station, re-entered Baltimore —and for four days they must have felt that the United States of America were seated at one immense banquet, saluting them simultaneously with the same hurrahs!

The apotheosis was worthy of these three heroes whom fable would have placed in the ranks of demigods.

And now will this attempt, unprecedented in the annals of travel, lead to any practical result? Will direct communication with the moon ever be established? Will there ever be a travel service through space, linking the solar system? Will men go from one planet to another, from Jupiter to Mercury, and after awhile from one star to another, from the North Star to Sirius? Will this means of locomotion allow us to visit the suns which swarm in the firmament?

To such questions no answer can be given. But, knowing the bold ingenuity of the Anglo-Saxon race, no one will be astonished that the Americans sought to make some use of President Barbicane's attempt.

Thus, a short time after the return of the travelers, the public received with marked favor the announcement of a limited-stock company, capitalized at a hundred million dollars, divided into a hundred thousand shares of a thousand dollars each, under the name of the "National Interstellar Communication Company," its president, Barbicane; vice-president, Captain Nicholl; secretary, J. T. Maston; director of operations, Michel Ardan.

And since Americans like to foresee everything in business, even bankruptcy, the Honorable Harry Trolloppe, as referee, and Francis Dayton, receiver, were appointed right from the start!